DEADLY BETRAYAL

THE CBS MURDERS

Donald Scott Richards

This is a work of fiction based on a true story. The core story upon which the novel is based took place in the locations and the cities that are cited. The true names of the characters have been changed. Conversations cited in this work, as well as certain events are fictitious and are the product of the author's imagination.

ISBN: 1-4107-5235-6 (e-book)
ISBN: 1-4107-5236-4 (Paperback)

This book is printed on acid free paper.

1st Books - rev. 07/14/03

This book is dedicated to the five who died including the three CBS employees.

It is also dedicated to those men and women of the law enforcement agencies who assisted. Their unselfish and tireless efforts brought about resolution to these terrible crimes. With particular recognition to:

The Federal Bureau of Investigation
The New York City Police Department
The Teaneck, New Jersey Police Department
The Ocean Township Police Department
The Kentucky State Police

Acknowledgments

There are so many people who were helpful to this novel being published, and I am grateful to each and every one. First, the love of my life, Jude FitzGibbon for her belief in me, her encouragement, and her critical editorial assistance. Kate, who encouraged in the early days. My friends Larry and Paula Kaufman who kindly read, edited, and suggested; Houston Stebbins and Dena Steele who were always supportive; and to the Tuxedo Park Writers' Group and Dr. Stuart Young who first suggested I write and who critiqued various drafts.

Richard Chartrand and Bob Paquette who took the time to re-live it with me. And the others who gave their time, added their memories and expertise, Bob Adomilli, Richard Bohan, Rich Brevard, Pat Colgan, Gene Burke, Dan Gibney, Robert Hazen, Frank Heaney, Don Koschlep, Ron Moretti, Reese Roussell, Augie Sanchez, Bob Sibert, Vern Swain, Charles Toal, Ken Walton, and Dolly.

For the fantastic photo work, Jeff Adise and Pat Racciopi.

I thank you all

dsr

Credits

Book cover design and creation
Jeff Adise and Pat Racciopi, Digital Colour Group

Cover photos
Pat Racciopi, Digital Colour Group

Photo of Author
Jeff Adise, Digital Colour Group

Cover photo of the Manhattan skyline
Peter Bennett, Ambient Images, Inc.

Photo backdrops
Scenic Design

One

2:45 AM
December 27th
Manhattan, New York

From the flashing lights of police cars, it wasn't hard to spot the site of the carnage. NYPD blue and whites sat blocking traffic at both ends of Baxter Street in Chinatown. A half dozen uniformed officers and barricades were holding back onlookers and the media. In the middle of the intersection, Dan stopped the car and stared down the block.

"Come on buddy, keep it moving," an NYPD uniformed officer said as he rapped his nightstick on Dan's car window. "Move it!"

Dan pulled over to the curb in front of a hydrant and sat in the car looking down the block. What was he doing here? He placed the red light and FBI placard on the dashboard, and walked toward the restaurant.

At the roadblock, Dan flashed his credentials to a uniformed policeman wearing sergeant stripes. "Sarge, who's in charge?"

"Detective LeBeau."

"I need to talk to him." Dan started to walk past the sergeant.

"Hold on a minute fella." The sergeant extended a muscled arm and blocked his path. "This is a homicide. I don't know why the FBI needs to be here. Why do you need to see LeBeau?"

"That's between me and LeBeau." Dan glared at the sergeant. The sergeant held and returned the intense gaze. Then without breaking eye contact, he called to a uniformed officer. "Hey Murphy. Come here a minute."

"What, sergeant?" said a uniformed officer as he trotted towards the pair.

"For some reason FBI Agent," the sergeant glanced at Dan's identification, "Robertson, thinks he needs to speak with LeBeau. Escort him, find LeBeau, and as soon as this guy's finished, bring him back so he doesn't contaminate our crime scene."

"Thanks sergeant," Dan said, keeping his anger in check. He slipped his badge onto his coat pocket, ignored the sergeant's stare, and followed Murphy.

Baxter Street was narrow and difficult to navigate on the best of days, but tonight it was a total impasse. Up and down the entire block, Radio Motor Patrol cars, or RMPs, their lights flashing and radios crackling, were parked half on the sidewalk, half on the street. Eight black minivans from the Coroner's Office lined the middle of the street, their drivers waiting for the release of the remains. Murphy silently led Dan around and between cars. At the restaurant, they ducked under the yellow "Crime Scene—Do Not Enter" tape, walked up the stairs, and stepped into the foyer.

Dan took in the crime scene. Tables and chairs were overturned and riddled with bullet holes. Tablecloths were stained with spilled food, pieces of bone, body, brains, hair, and lots of blood. The mirrors on the walls had bullet holes in them, all of which had been marked with a wax pencil. On the floor near the door, small numbered pieces of paper had been placed near each spent cartridge.

Several detectives were directing the collection of evidence. While Dan looked over the scene, Murphy walked over to a detective wearing a fedora and spoke in hushed tones.

The ME was examining one of the eight blood-soaked bodies that lay where it had fallen. One victim was an old man—missing the lower part of one arm and half of his neck. Two were young women, one with the left side of her face gone, and the other with most of her chest blown away. The other five victims were young men. Dan's eyes quickly darted among them. One of the men had been cut in half at the waist, another had a diagonal row of bullet holes across his chest. The third had no face left on his skull. It might be easy to misidentify someone. Maybe there'd been a mistake and Sammy hadn't been killed. The head of the last young man was turned slightly away, as if he tried to avoid facing his death. Dan stepped to his left to get a better look.

"What do think you're doing?" It was the detective with the fedora, stepping over the bodies and around the furniture towards him. "You've got no business being here! Who the hell do you think you are?"

Dan ignored the detective's shouts, and stepped over the body so he could see. Dan's shoulders sagged. The back of the young man's skull was missing, but he could see the face. It was Sammy. No mistake. He wanted to reach down and touch Sammy's face, wipe the blood from the two bullet holes in his cheek, but that was impossible.

The detective finally reached him. "I'm LeBeau. What the hell do you want?"

"My name's Robertson. I'm an FBI Agent." He showed his identification, and tried to think of something to tell LeBeau that wouldn't sound asinine. "I got a call that there'd been some people killed."

"Yeah?"

"I thought I might know one of them."

"What was their name—this person you might just happen to know?"

"They're not here." As he said it, Dan felt in not acknowledging Sammy, he had betrayed him. But if he told this detective the whole story . . . No, the operation was need-to-know, and there was no need for this detective to know.

"Who called you?" LeBeau asked.

"Never mind. Obviously somebody made a mistake. Sorry I bothered you." Dan turned and walked to the door.

"You mean that on a whim, in the middle of the night, you go look at some dead Chinese on the off chance you might know one of them?" LeBeau shouted. "Fella, if that's how you get your jollies, you're a real sick fuck. Murphy, make sure this guy leaves and never comes back."

After Murphy led him back to his car, Dan drove to his meeting with Jimmy Lee. He could get some more coffee there. It was going to be a long night and a longer day to follow.

As he drove out of Chinatown, all Dan could think about was Sammy. He thought about the killer, and how he could even the score. It had to be the Chinese gang—the Tong. He pulled up in front of the coffee shop, went inside and spotted Lee sitting on a stool at the counter, the only patron in the place.

From his outward appearance, no one would have guessed Jimmy Lee was a NYPD Detective. He dressed modestly in the same way his father and most other Chinese men did, and his mannerisms and way of speaking still bore the strong stamp of his cultural upbringing. Lee raised his eyes from his coffee cup and looked at Dan.

As he touched Lee lightly on the shoulder, Dan quietly said, "Thanks for calling me." He slipped onto the next red naugahyde-covered stool, looked up at the bored waiter and asked for coffee.

"I still can't believe it," Lee said, staring into his coffee cup, as if it contained the explanation of why it had happened. His complexion looked gray.

Dan took the cup of coffee from the waiter, mumbling, "Thanks." He didn't want to tell Lee he'd been to the crime scene, so he asked, "What was it like?"

"I've seen quite a few messy crime scenes in my twenty-two years as a cop, but this one was a massacre."

Dan nodded, sipped his coffee, and listened.

"You know, I keep kicking myself over this whole idea of putting an undercover agent in the middle of the Tongs. Could I have done more to protect Sammy?"

"I've had the same thoughts. He was a good kid." Dan's eyes filled with tears, and he didn't care if Lee noticed. The hurt was deep. The two of them sat in silence for a few more minutes, each in their own thoughts. "The NYPD's Jade Squad has done some undercover work in the past haven't they? A lot of those cops were really young, right out of the academy. Ever run into any problems in those operations?"

"No, never like this. Once the Tongs identified our guys as cops, they refused to have anything to do with them. The problem was, most of our group had grown up in the same community they were trying to infiltrate. Who knows, maybe they pushed a little too hard."

"That's where I thought we had the edge with Sammy," Dan said. "He grew up in Seattle. No one in New York knew him. I thought that would go a long way towards keeping him safe. Besides, you and I both kept telling him to be patient and not to hurry things along."

"Dan, I don't know about you, but more and more when things like this happen, it gets to me. Maybe I'm just getting too old for this. There are times I wonder if I shouldn't just go ahead and retire," Lee said, as he tightened his lips and slowly shook his head.

"Jimmy, what happened tonight was terrible, but so far, nothing else has worked," Dan said. "We've both seen the extortion, prostitution, narcotics, and murder-for-hire that comes out of Chinatown. The Tongs control all of it. Remember that ship carrying illegal Chinese immigrants that ran aground? They were behind that. I still think our idea of a joint investigation into the Tongs was a good one."

"I know. What do you need to know about what happened tonight?"

"Well, to start with, why don't you tell me who's heading up the investigation?" Dan began, as he took some notes and pretended not to know the answers to his questions.

"It's LeBeau. Richie LeBeau. He works out of Midtown North Precinct."

"This happened in Chinatown. That's the 5th Precinct. Isn't that a little outside his territory?"

"The top brass wanted this headed up by the best Homicide Detective on the force. I guess they figured they had to show a strong response for public relations reasons," said Jimmy as he rolled his eyes back into his head in disgust. "So LeBeau caught the case."

Dan nodded. "Take me through what you've learned, Jimmy. I may not need all of it, but just the same, I better know it."

The two men talked for the better part of an hour before Dan told Lee he needed to head over to his office and prepare to face the fireworks once he notified the FBI brass.

Dan left the coffee shop and drove across the street to the New York City office of the FBI. The endless cups of coffee were a godsend and allowed him to regain his mental sharpness. Dan rubbed his eyes still ringed in red.

He sat in the darkened office, his desk lamp the only illumination in a sea of gray metal desks. First he wrote up his notes into a memorandum he knew they'd want. Then he made telephone calls to the FBI brass and told them Sammy Ho had been killed. He was told to wait at the office. Everyone would come there and decide what kind of spin they would give to it when they broke the story to the brass at FBI Headquarters in Washington, D.C.

Enormous waves of fatigue swept over Dan as his body begged for sleep. The caffeine kicked in, jacked him up and refocused him. Each time his mind cleared, images of Sammy returned.

Two

6:30 AM
December 27th
Manhattan, New York

Dan's intercom buzzed, piercing the quiet of the deserted office. He punched the lighted button. "Robertson."

"Dan this is Nick. We're ready for you."

He heard the strain in Nick Thomas' voice and could feel the tension. "On my way." He sighed deeply, gathered a few papers and his coffee cup. Thomas was the Assistant Director in Charge of the New York Office. His office was on the same floor as Dan's, one of four floors occupied by the FBI in the forty-two-story Jacob Javitz Federal Building on Foley Square.

Dan took the shortcut through the men's room and glanced at himself in the mirror. Today he thought he looked a lot older than forty-two. His blue eyes were bloodshot, and his eyelids drooped. He gave a quick comb to his brown hair, generously sprinkled with silvery gray at the temples.

When he came out of the men's room, he saw the hallways were still dark—employees wouldn't start arriving for another two hours—but Thomas' outer office was bathed in golden light coming through the window as the sun made its appearance over the Atlantic.

Dan paused in the doorway when he saw Thomas on the phone. Although Sammy's death had dragged him out of bed too, Thomas was impeccably dressed in a French-cuffed shirt and silk tie. His blond blow-dried hair offset his tanned face.

Thomas waved him in, and motioned for Dan to take a seat in one of the four burgundy leather tufted Queen Anne chairs that formed a half-circle in front of the AD's enormous mahogany desk, once used exclusively by J. Edgar Hoover whenever he was in New York. Dan's superior, Ike Blackman, the Organized Crime Coordinating Supervisor, occupied another chair. He acknowledged Dan with a barely perceptible nod, but Dan sensed something more directed towards him from Blackman. Whatever it was, it wasn't good.

Thomas hung up. "Thanks for coming in early. It's a sad day." His eyes shifted to Dan. "Tell us what happened."

Dan struggled to control the emotion in his voice. "Late last night, Sammy Ho was having dinner at a restaurant in Chinatown. At approximately 1:30 AM, four people, believed to be men, wearing dark ski masks, came into the restaurant and fired automatic weapons at everybody in the place. According to survivors, the shooting lasted about fifteen seconds.

The gunmen ran out, jumped into a waiting silver van, and sped off. Sammy was killed, along with seven others. Ten others were wounded, taken to the hospital, but are expected to live."

"I didn't realize that others were killed, too," said Blackman.

"Any idea what was behind the shooting, Dan?" Thomas asked.

"It appears to be gang-related. The NYPD's working to identify the dead and wounded, comparing them with known Tong members."

"We can't allow anybody to kill an FBI Agent and get away with it," Blackman said, his face red. "We've got to pull out all the stops and show those young turks who they're up against. How many agents do you want to throw at it, Nick?"

Dan held up a hand. "Hold on a minute."

The room became quiet and both men looked at Dan.

"What haven't you told us?" Thomas asked.

"We can't go public that one of the victims was FBI. It might get somebody else killed."

"Why's that?"

"Because Sammy Ho was undercover tonight, posing as Sammy Wu. A detective on the Jade Squad called and told me about it."

"You mean to tell me that you told somebody in the NYPD about an FBI Undercover Operation?" Blackman shouted. "When the hell did you get approval for a UCO in Chinatown?"

"The NYPD's Jade Squad knew about it, because it was a joint operation. An NYPD informant introduced Sammy to some of the players in Chinatown where that Tong runs things. And since you signed off on it, Ike, you know very well . . ."

"This was nothing more than an ill-conceived cowboy operation that . . ." Blackman said.

"Stop right there." Thomas said. He gave a stern look to Blackman. "Hear Dan out."

Dan nodded. "As supervisor of this squad, I was directed to investigate Non-Traditional organized crime. We had a cultural deficit until a Chinese-American was assigned to my squad. I needed Sammy to help us understand the culture and the language. Sammy grew up in Seattle and spoke both Cantonese and Mandarin. The problem was he hadn't experienced the criminal activities of the Tongs. My counterpart at the NYPD is Detective Jimmy Lee, who heads up their Jade Squad. His unit is tasked to address criminal problems in the Chinese community. They haven't been able to put a case together against the Tongs, since no one ever wants to testify."

Blackman started to say something, but a withering look from Thomas made him change his mind.

"I met with Lee and we came to the same conclusion. If we could get an undercover man into the Tong's operations, it would go a long way towards developing a prosecutable case. The NYPD had informants who could make the introductions, and the FBI would come up with a Chinese agent—someone unknown in New York's Chinatown—who could go undercover."

Blackman was having difficulty remaining silent.

"Lee and I worked out the details of a Memorandum of Understanding for the joint investigation, and Gary Wright signed off on it."

"When we were ready to put someone undercover, I sent a memo to you requesting approval. Ike, I received your authorization to—"

"I never got any such request," Blackman snarled. "If I had, I'd definitely have remembered it. I never gave my approval to this fiasco."

Dan stared at Blackman. He'd encountered office politics before, but had never had a superior tell such a bold-faced lie. Blackman was trying to distance himself from the murder of an agent. 'Plausible deniability,' but this time, it wasn't very plausible. Dan knew Blackman had signed off on the memo, and a copy was in the file.

"Let's come back to that," said Thomas cautiously. "Continue, Dan."

"The Ghost Shadows Tong used the Golden Dragon Restaurant as a base of operations for their gambling, extortion, prostitution, narcotics, and murder-for-hire. Lee and I sent Sammy to the restaurant to try and spot Tong members and gradually work his way in."

"When was that, Dan?" Thomas asked.

"About three weeks ago. Sammy had been in the restaurant about a half a dozen times."

"Cut to the chase!" Blackman interrupted.

Dan was increasingly annoyed with Blackman, but continued, "Lee and I briefed Ho about last night's visit."

"What back up did you have in place for Sammy?" Blackman interrupted again.

Dan's head snapped towards Blackman. "At this stage of the UCO, since no direct contact with Tong members had yet been made, we deemed the danger to Sammy as minimal."

"By *we* do you mean you and Lee?" asked Blackman.

"Yes."

"And that *we* doesn't include Nick or me, does it?"

"No."

"You didn't provide Sammy Ho with backup. As a result, he's dead."

"You think I haven't been going over everything I've done, asking myself the same questions?" Dan realized he was shouting. "For god's sake, I feel responsible."

"I agree on that point," Blackman said.

"Ike, that's enough," Thomas said. "Dan, have you written up a memo on this whole matter?"

"Right here." Dan handed Thomas the memo.

"Good. I want you to bring me the UCO authorization memo and anything else that might be relevant—no, better yet, bring me the whole file. Give me Jimmy Lee's phone number. I'll make contact with the NYPD Police Commissioner. I'll decide who from the FBI should review this unfortunate incident. In the mean time, I don't want any of you discussing this. There will not be a press release. Am I clear?"

They nodded.

"That's all for now. Later today we'll talk about this. Dan, stay a minute?"

Blackman gave Dan one last hateful look.

"Close the door on your way out, Ike," Thomas said.

Thomas came around and leaned back against the front edge of his desk. The two men studied each other for a moment, and then he spoke. "I know this is hard on you."

"It was . . . in the time it takes to snap your fingers. No warning, no nothing. He was gone."

"But you can't become immobilized, there's a lot to be done," Thomas said.

"I know that Nick, and I want to direct the investigation into Sammy's murder."

"That probably isn't a good idea," Thomas said in a quiet voice. "You're hurting, Dan. You're too close to it. Your objectivity would be questioned. There are things I need you to take care of. Running the investigation isn't one of them."

"Why not? Ike's determined to lay Sammy's death on me. Don't I get the chance to find out who did it?"

"We've known each other a long time, Dan. You're just going to have to trust me on this."

Dan was too tired and overwrought to think clearly. "Maybe."

"What I need you to do," Thomas said, "is to go with me to inform Sammy's wife of his death."

"I'm not sure how much good I'd be. I've never done that."

"This is the fourth time for me. It's never easy."

* * *

The meeting with Sue Ho had gone badly. She knew what had happened from the moment Dan and Nick introduced themselves. She was hysterical and her six-month-old son was crying, and at times Dan felt he would lose it as well. Dan offered what comfort he could, telling her how much he and everyone on the squad would miss Sammy. Every word was true, but he didn't expect it would make a difference.

Three

3:15 PM
December 27th
Manhattan, New York

"You asked for the Ghost Shadows investigative file," Dan said, sitting once again in Thomas' office. "I have it here."

"Fine, leave it with me."

"We need to talk about it. I went through the file. The UCO authorization memo is missing."

Thomas sat perfectly still for a moment. "That's . . . a problem."

"Nick, it was in the file. I'd never proceed with a UCO without approval."

"What do you think happened to it?"

"No idea. I looked for it. My file clerk looked for it. It was there. Now it's gone."

"Dan, I want to believe you. If it were up to me, maybe we could run it down. But there's too much at stake here. We have a dead agent operating in an undercover role without backup. You tell me you'd received the proper authorization from Blackman. He says you didn't. Now you can't find a memo, which would corroborate what you told me. Dan, this doesn't leave us too many options."

"What do you mean?"

"We're not going to be the ones to call the shots. The FBI guidelines are clear. We have to hand it over to Headquarters."

"But the Memorandum of Understanding would show that—"

"It would show that you had approval to conduct a joint investigation with the NYPD. That memorandum doesn't give you authorization to put an agent undercover."

Dan sighed. "So what can I expect?"

"Here's what will happen. I'll make a telephone call to the Deputy Assistant Director who heads up the Office of Professional Responsibility. I'll tell them I've got to kick the UCO authorization issue to them, and they'll tell me they want to handle Sammy's murder investigation as well. Because of its sensitivity and the NYPD's involvement, I'll say the New York office should handle it. I'll make those points as strongly as possible." Thomas sighed. "But I'll lose the argument. When they come to New York, I'll turn over this file and the investigation into Sammy's murder to them. This will take on a life of its own."

Dan finally met Thomas' gaze. "So what do you suggest I do while I wait for the Washington Gestapo to kick my butt?"

"When the OPR agents show up, don't let them see that crappy attitude. Stop talking to anyone about the UCO or Sammy's murder. I mean anyone!"

"You mean I'm off the Ghost Shadows Tong investigation?"

"I mean that whole case is on hold until we can get this mess straightened out. After that, it'll still be yours."

"And in the meantime?"

"Throw yourself into your work. By the way, I'm transferring Casey Brody to your squad. She's an excellent financial investigator who's been working a multi-million dollar fraud case. She's bringing a case with her, which I originally got from Jim Westerfield at Manhattan Bank & Trust. He told me they had a big problem."

"What about?"

"They'd been providing business financing for a diamond merchant, who now owes them millions of bucks. Westerfield wasn't sure what was going on, but told me the whole thing smelled. I told him the case would be assigned to an agent who knows what they're doing. Brody has been working it, and we don't have anybody else who can quickly get up to speed on the case. Bottom line is, you get both Brody and the case. I told her Supervisor, and he broke the news to her. I need you to keep me up to date in case Westerfield calls."

"Brody is a good agent, and I'm glad to get her. But this is a financial fraud case. I have an Organized Crime squad. I don't get it."

"You need an accountant on your squad." Thomas answered flatly with finality in his voice. "Get involved with her investigation. Get out on the street with your agents, and re-experience what it's like to investigate."

"It sounds real exciting," Dan said with no enthusiasm.

"Would it be such a bad thing? A nice low-key case with no lives at stake? Consider it a break until we can get the Ghost Shadows investigation back on track."

"If we ever do. Okay Nick, I'll spend some time on Casey's fraud case. Getting out on the street may be a good idea."

"Good," Thomas said. "We'll talk later."

Dan accessed the FBI's computerized files and located the case that Casey was bringing with her. While the computer files were only a summary of the investigation, they provided enough information to allow him to get the gist. Dan called her. "Got a minute?"

A few minutes later Casey was sitting in his office. The enthusiastic look on her face told him she loved the work. She had bright green eyes and a nice smile. A breath of fresh air, so eager, ready and positive. Working with her might be better than he imagined.

"I'm not really sure what to make of this case. I read the summary on the computer, but I'm still not clear on what's happening."

"Actually, neither am I," Casey said. "That's part of the problem. But here's the story. A few months ago, Thomas got a call from Mike Westerfield at MBT Factors, a subsidiary of Manhattan Bank & Trust. What these guys do is called 'factoring.' They take a merchant's sales invoices and immediately loan him eighty-five percent of face value of the invoice. The merchant then tells his customer to send their invoice payments to a post office box they call a lock box, controlled by MBT Factors. MBT takes the customer's check, matches it against the outstanding invoice, and applies the payment, less their fifteen percent fee."

"Fifteen percent?"

"Oh it's pricey, but if the merchant doesn't have a lot of working capital, he needs these guys. Anyway, MBT Factors had been doing a lot of business in the Garment District, but with the volatility of that business, they'd really been taking a beating. So about a year ago, they thought doing business in the Diamond District would be a smart move, so they put out the word they were looking to expand."

"So they found Bernie Schwartz."

"Right. Bernie and his wife Sarah own and run Fontaine Diamonds on West Forty-seventh Street. Fontaine was marginally profitable with annual sales of around twenty-three and a half mil', but Schwartz wanted his business to go big time. Problem was, he didn't have enough capital to pull it off, and the quality of the jewelry he was putting out wasn't all that great. His home's in New Rochelle—but he tells everybody he lives in Larchmont, where the big bucks are—but his place was only worth eight hundred thou', and it was mortgaged to the roof."

"Okay, that wasn't in the file. So why'd MBT take on such a bad risk?"

Casey shrugged. "They listened to their checkbook instead of their brains. They were after an *in* in the Diamond District. At first, everything went fine. Schwartz faxed sales invoices to MBT, a day or two later MBT put eighty-five percent of the invoice amount into Fontaine's bank account—which, by the way, just happened to be at MBT. They like to keep an eye on their money. Then, some time over the next ninety days, a check showed up in the lock box from the customer, payable to MBT Factors for the full amount. Everything was fine."

"How long before the wheels came off?"

"Maybe three or four months. First, MBT got a check in their lockbox that'd been written on a Fontaine account. MBT called Schwartz. He told them how sorry he was, his client had sent him a check payable to Fontaine, he wanted to do the right thing, et cetera. Instead of endorsing the client's check over to MBT, he deposited the client's check then wrote a check on Fontaine's account and sent it to them. MBT was suspicious, but they figured they got their money, so they let Schwartz off with a slap on the wrist."

"A lot of those things happened. Each time, the people at MBT were annoyed, but when they looked into it, Schwartz had some bullshit but plausible explanation. One time it was the customer; another time it was Fontaine's bookkeeper, and so on. MBT even tried surprise audits to try and catch Schwartz playing with the numbers. He would put them off for a couple of days, and when they finally saw Fontaine's books, everything was A-okay."

"Finally they stumbled on to something by just pure dumb luck. Last summer Westerfield was at a cocktail party at the Union Club here in Manhattan. One of the guys he ran into was Matthew Hirsh, who owns the Blair Jewelry Stores chain. Westerfield made a passing remark to Hirsh, something like, 'I'm pleased we've finally had a chance to do business together.' Hirsh looked at him like he was from the moon. So Westerfield explained about MBT Factors and Fontaine, and mentioned that Blair Jewelry had been purchasing wholesale jewelry from Fontaine."

"And Hirsh had never heard about it," Dan said.

"Not only that, Hirsh volunteered to look into it, and a week later told Westerfield that Blair hadn't purchased anything from Fontaine for the last three years. Over that time, no Blair checks had been written, payable to MBT Factors. But MBT Factors' records showed Blair payments to the tune of 1.7 million dollars. That's when Westerfield called Thomas."

"Interesting. What have you come up with so far?"

Casey dug through the stack of papers on her lap and came up with a list. "I got a printout of all the Fontaine customers whose invoices were used as collateral for the line of credit—all in all, about one hundred and eighty of them. MBT was worried about us directly contacting these clients, since gossip in the Diamond business apparently moves as fast as it does in the Bureau. So they let me use the bank's audit division as my alter ego. MBT wrote letters to all of those businesses, and told them they were doing a routine audit and needed to confirm purchases made from Fontaine Diamonds."

"Help me with something here," Dan said. "MBT Factors has been getting all their invoices paid, including their 15% fee?"

"Yeah. It's not quite as curious as it sounds, they allow a 30-day float."

"Whatever. But . . . where's the crime, Casey?"

"As I said, I'm not sure. I've got some theories, but I'd like to look more closely at the numbers before I commit to one. Westerfield just feels—and I agree— that Schwartz isn't faking invoices for nothing. They should start getting responses from the customers in a day or two. Then I may have a better idea of what's going on."

"Could you let me know as soon as you hear?"

"Um, why?" Casey asked, wondering where Dan was going with it. "Do you see a problem?"

"No, not really," Dan said. "It's just that Thomas asked me to keep him up to speed on this case since Westerfield contacted him directly. There's always the possibility that Westerfield will call Thomas, and I want to make sure he's totally up to snuff."

"That makes sense." Casey was reassured, and grinned.

For the first time in awhile Dan felt good, more relaxed, and maybe even a little happy. He smiled. "Keep me posted."

Four

9:10 AM
December 28th
Manhattan, New York

Casey stood in the doorway of Dan's office and said, "Westerfield just called. His audit department finished the breakdown of the Fontaine Diamond customers. Want it now or later?"

"Now is good. What'd you learn?"

Casey sat down. "Except for a few minor discrepancies due to things like consignment pieces and returns, all the responses agree to the penny with the Fontaine invoices."

"What do we do now? Start going door to door? Find out who's real and who's not?"

"I'd love to but . . . things are different in the Diamond District. Say we check on Wynkoop Jewelers,

23

who did half a million in business with Fontaine last year, and find its some hole in the wall. It could be a bogus company, and the hole in the wall is just a mail drop. Or, Wynkoop may be a legit wholesaler who operates out of a real hole in the wall. That's not uncommon in the Diamond District."

"So get a subpoena and look over Wynkoop's books."

Casey shook her head. "Westerfield doesn't want rumors to start flying. He's afraid we'd blow MBT's reputation."

"Did you check Fontaine's customers with the tax people?"

"Yeah. They're all registered corporations. But that only means that someone—maybe Schwartz—paid to have an outfit incorporated."

Dan rubbed his eyes and looked at the ceiling. "Some of those companies have got to be phony fronts. Look at Blair."

"Right. But some are real. At this point we can't tell which is which without trashing Fontaine's reputation. That would trash MBT's reputation, which would kill their business in the Diamond District. I say we try for an *in* at Fontaine. Somebody who can tell us what's what. I'm seeing Westerfield today, and I'm going to ask him to get a list of Fontaine's employees."

Dan leaned back in his chair, his hands behind his head, and thought about what Casey had said. He'd had to fight himself to keep from calling Jimmy Lee last night. He wanted to know if there was any progress in finding Sammy's killers. He wanted to know so bad he could taste it. But Thomas was right. If he began poking around in the Tong murders, it could get him hung out to dry. He needed a distraction. Like maybe a nice, laid-back accounting case. Dan leaned forward, and was propelled back into an upright sitting position, staring at Casey.

"Mind if I come along to see Westerfield?"

"No, not at all, but—"

"Don't worry. I'll let you run your investigation. I just need to get back out on the street."

"Okay. Let's go."

They drove uptown to Forty-seventh Street and Park Avenue to the offices of Manhattan Bank & Trust, which also housed MBT Factors, in the building once owned by Manufacturers Hanover Trust. On the eighteenth floor, a receptionist told Westerfield they had arrived.

"What's Westerfield like?" Dan asked.

"He needs our help, but isn't the kind of guy who feels he has to kiss your ass to get it."

"Sounds like a combination we can work with," Dan said as a tall, fortyish man with a pleasant smile and a bow tie walked towards them.

"Hello Casey. Nice to see you again. Hope you haven't been waiting long," Westerfield turned to Dan. "And you must be Mr. Robertson. Pleased to meet you."

"How do you do, Mr. Westerfield? Please call me Dan."

"Then call me Mike. Why don't you come back to my office?" Not waiting for a response, Westerfield turned and walked through a door and down the hall.

"Of course," Dan said to the air as he quickly walked to catch up. They turned a corner and came to the doorway to Westerfield's office. The rich mahogany furniture was offset by original oil paintings hung against rice papered walls, all upstaged by a fabulous view overlooking Park Avenue. It was the private sector at its most tempting.

"Mr.   Westerfield—Mike—Beautiful   office. Fantastic view!"

"Thanks. Tell the truth, most of the time I'm too busy to notice." Westerfield motioned to a sofa and chairs situated around a large, low table. "Won't you have a seat? Can I get you something to drink? Coffee?"

"Coffee would be great," Dan said.

"The same," Casey added.

Westerfield made a call and ordered coffee.

"Thanks for taking the time to meet with us," Dan said. "Casey told me how helpful you've been to the investigation."

"On the contrary. The FBI's been helping MBT Factors. My thanks to you."

There was a knock on the door, and Westerfield opened it for a plainly dressed woman carrying a silver tray laden with a silver coffee service and china.

"Thank you, Maria," Westerfield said.

The woman gave a slight nod and silently slipped out the door.

"So what's your take on Fontaine Diamonds, Mike?" Dan asked as he stirred his coffee.

"Their sales figures are impressive. That was the main reason we took them on as a client." Westerfield took a sip of coffee. "But this Blair Jewelry business is disturbing."

"What do you think about Fontaine's owner?" Dan asked. "This guy . . ."

"Bernie Schwartz," Casey said.

"That's tough," Westerfield said. "He's slick, but you have to be to stay in business in the Diamond District. It's cutthroat competition. But Schwartz strikes me as a little too smug. Cocky. The kind of guy who would refuse to play by the rules. Did you get the results from our Audit Division?"

"Yes. They're . . . intriguing," Casey said.

"Or, in other words, where's the crime?" Dan said.

"I'm hoping you can tell me," Westerfield said.

"I see a few possibilities," Casey said. "Money laundering. The mob might pay 15% for the chance for clean money. Or . . . has Fontaine been experiencing a lot of growth lately?"

"Yes. About forty percent growth in each of the last two years. That's an immensely high rate, but Schwartz told us he needed our financial backing in order to expand."

"He could be operating a Ponzi scheme where essentially he's paying you back with your own money. In order to make it work, and get the 15% you take off the top, he has to keep raising the stakes. Say he sends you invoices worth . . . round numbers, a million dollars in January. You advance him eight hundred fifty grand, and he has to pay back a million by the end of February. In February, he submits invoices for one point two million, for which he gets . . ."

"One million and twenty thousand," Westerfield said.

"Thanks. So by the first of March he pays you your million and pockets the twenty grand—plus a couple of months' interest on a million or more."

"But . . . he's just digging himself a deeper and deeper hole, isn't he?"

"Eventually the whole thing will crash and burn. But before it does, I'd bet that Schwartz takes whatever's outstanding in his account and heads for Switzerland."

"My God." Westerfield said.

"How much loss exposure from Fontaine does MBT have?" Dan asked.

Westerfield stopped and drew a breath. "Based on current outstanding receivables, we calculate that it's just over seventeen million dollars."

"But . . ." Casey said, "he may be legit and experiencing a growth spurt. The Blair Jewelry thing might have been a fluke. Our best shot is to find a cooperating witness, but in order to do that we need a list of Fontaine's employees. Can you get one for us?"

"Of course."

As they drove back down the FDR, Casey was quiet, but Dan noticed her glancing at him.

"Don't worry, you did fine," Dan said. "It just bothers me that the only hard evidence we have to go on is that Blair isn't really a Fontaine customer."

"I agree. But if Blair isn't a customer, who's being billed and paying MBT back the money that's been advanced to Fontaine?"

Dan smiled. "That is what we, the ace investigators, are going to find out."

Five

2:05 PM
December 29th
Manhattan, New York

After Sammy's funeral, Dan drove back to Manhattan, lost in thoughts. He recalled the flower arrangements on spindly metal stands, Sammy's closed casket, Sue Ho with her arms encircling her two small children, the eulogy by Sammy's brother, a final prayer, and a few last words to Sue. Dan felt a deep sadness he knew would never go away. Hardly aware of what he was doing, he parked his car in the basement of the Federal building and rode the elevator to his office.

Dan had barely taken off his coat when a stranger walked in. The man, dressed in a cheap, wrinkled suit, stuck out his hand. "Hi, I'm Bert Wallace from Washington. Are you Dan Robertson?"

Dan didn't shake his hand. "Why do you want to know?"

With an insincere smile Wallace said, "I need to interview you about your unauthorized undercover operation and that Chinese agent getting killed."

"You're from OPR."

"Yeah I am. Didn't I say that? Must've forgotten." Wallace set his brief case on Dan's desk, opened it, and dug out a file. "Look, can we hurry up and get this done? I want to catch a flight back to D.C. tonight. Last one's at 7:30."

Dan slammed the man's briefcase shut and leaned across it. "Who the hell do you think you are?" he yelled. "I just got back from 'that Chinese agent's' funeral! He had a name, Sammy Ho, in case you didn't bother to find out! You come in here like you own the goddamned place, you don't say who the hell you are, or why you're here, and you've clearly already made up your mind about this 'unauthorized undercover operation.' Then you tell me you have to hurry back to Washington."

"Hey, I only—"

"Well, you know I'm real sorry that you have to go through the motions on this one, but if you're going to do this, you'll do it by the book. Spend some time reviewing the file that Thomas is holding for you. Interview the others—Thomas, Wright, Blackman, anyone else who had anything to do with this case. Sleep on it. Then come back in the morning and interview me, armed with information—not conclusions!"

The noise from the bullpen had stopped. Everyone within a hundred feet of Dan's office stopped to listen. For the most part, he was a quiet man, so to hear him explode like that—especially at an OPR agent from headquarters—was a shock for them.

It was a shock for Wallace too. He stood staring wide-eyed at Dan, his jaw clenched. Still, he gave himself time to cool down before he responded.

"I'll see you at nine o'clock tomorrow morning," he said as he opened his briefcase, threw in the file, and slammed it shut. When he dragged it off the desk, he knocked Dan's nameplate onto the floor. He glanced at it, then turned his back and stormed out.

Dan picked it up. "Don't bother. I'll get it." Then he dropped into his chair, and with his elbows on his desk, put his face in his hands. How could someone so incompetent and insensitive wind up in such a position of power? He knew there were a lot of Wallaces in the FBI, but every time he met one, he had the same reaction.

"What was that all about?" Casey said softly, standing in his doorway.

He looked up at her, "Just another asshole from headquarters, trying to make a name for himself. Look, I really can't talk about it. Did you get that list of Fontaine employees from Westerfield?"

"Yeah, take a look at this," she said as she set the list on the corner of his desk. "You'll notice that nepotism is king in the Diamond District." Casey pointed to the sheet. "Bernie Schwartz lists himself as President of Fontaine, and his wife Sarah as Vice President."

"I think we can forget about either of them talking to us. What about this Golda Hillberg?"

"She's the telephone operator and Sarah Schwartz's sister."

"Who's this next guy, Abe Moses?"

"Married to Sarah's other sister."

"And Aaron Benjamin? What does he do?"

"Not sure. The guy's married to Bernie's sister."

"And I thought only the Mafia was a family business. Is there anyone here who isn't related?"

Casey pointed to the next name. "Christina Marino. She's an accountant and bookkeeper."

"She would definitely know what was going on."

"That leaves Mary Lee Wen. Don't tell me she's related."

"No. She's a clerical employee. An assistant to the bookkeeper, Marino."

"And that's it. Only two possibilities, Marino and Wen."

"Yeah, slim pickings," Casey said. "I plan to do a work-up on both of them—marital status, age, address, car info, past employers, how long they've worked for Fontaine. See if they pop up in our files or the NYPD's."

"In other words, do they have a history of this, or any kind of fraud, or . . ."

". . . do they have anything to lose?"

"Right, "Dan said. "How long do you think it'll take you?"

"I'm not sure. I was going to get the Investigative Analysts on it."

"The IA's are pretty fast. They can probably knock it out in a day or two."

"Don't see why not. Of course if you were to tell them it was a priority matter, I'm sure they would turn it around immediately." Casey raised her eyebrows.

"All right, I'll make the call, "Dan said. "Let me know as soon as anything comes back. If you don't mind, I'd like to tag along on the interviews. See if we can talk these women into helping."

"Fine with me," Casey said. "Thought I'd ask the IA's to do some checking on Bernie Schwartz. He may have been involved in something in the past. I also know a guy at the Business Insurance Clearinghouse office. If Schwartz made insurance claims for business losses, I'd like to know about it. I'll tell Assistant U.S. Attorney Len Weinstein we're trying to get two women who work for Fontaine to cooperate."

"Sounds good. In the meantime, I'll brief Thomas." Dan called the IA's and made the request for expediency. Then he called to see if he could speak to Thomas.

A few minutes later Dan stepped into Thomas' office, anxious to tell him Casey's plan. But before he could speak, Thomas said, "Close the door! Come in and sit down." There was an edge in his voice.

As soon as Dan's seat hit the chair, Thomas yelled, "What the hell were you thinking?"

"About what?"

"I just had a visit from the OPR man, Bert Wallace. What did you do to piss him off like that?"

"Me? Piss him off? Nick, he told me he wanted to interview me about my 'unauthorized undercover operation' that happened to get 'that Chinese agent' killed. He didn't even know Sammy's name. And then he had the gall to tell me he wanted to wrap it up fast so he could catch a flight back to Washington."

"That wasn't the version I got from him. He said you had no intention of being interviewed and told him to go fuck himself. Did you say that?"

"I wasn't that eloquent."

Thomas barely suppressed a laugh, and then became serious. "Do you have any recollection of how I told you to handle the OPR probe?"

"Look, "Dan said. "I respectfully suggested he spend today reviewing the file, talk to everyone else, then come back and interview me in the morning."

"Respectfully?"

"I wasn't trying to be difficult, but this guy caught me right after Sammy's funeral."

Thomas stared at Dan and shook his head.

"Changing the subject, I wanted to give you an update on where we are with the Fontaine Diamonds investigation." Dan briefed Thomas on the Westerfield interview, the employee's list, and what he and Casey planned to do.

"Sounds fine. Do what you need to in order to solve it quickly, or close it. We've got plenty of organized crime cases that need your time far more than that white-collar case. And watch your step with the OPR guy."

Six

10:15 AM
December 30th
Manhattan, New York

"How soon after the investigation began did you see the need for an Under Cover Operation?" Bert Wallace asked.

"The Ghost Shadows investigation began in July. The joint investigation with the NYPD Jade Squad got off the ground in October. Probably early December."

The interview had been going for an hour. The tension was still there, but Dan was making an effort to be civil. Wallace had softened his confrontational stance.

"What steps did you take to initiate that particular UCO?"

"I asked Sammy Ho to go undercover. He said he would. We filled out the paperwork and asked headquarters for approval for a Level I UCO."

Wallace pulled a document out of his file and handed it to Dan. "Would you look at this, and tell me if this is a copy of the request for a Level I UCO?"

Dan sighed and made an effort to keep his voice even. "Look, Bert, this is taking a lot more time than it should. You're treating me like an imbecile and taking up my whole day as a payback for me lacing into you. We don't like each other. We never will. Let's accept it, cut the crap, and wrap this up."

From the expression on Wallace's face, Dan could tell he had hit the truth and embarrassed the man. "Of course that is what I sent to the Undercover Unit at Headquarters. How many authorization requests do you get from New York asking approval for an undercover investigation into the Ghost Shadows Tong?"

Wallace's face reddened and his jaw clenched. He barely controlled himself. "I think we can dispense with further questions about the UCO authorization. Let's get down to the nitty gritty. The central issue is the question of authorization, or lack of authorization, for the use of Sammy Ho in an undercover role in a Level One UCO. Tell me what you did to seek approval for that."

"I prepared an authorization memo, sent it to Blackman. He signed it, and sent a copy back to me. I put it into the case file. He was supposed to send the original to headquarters."

A smirk appeared on Wallace's face. "It was never received at headquarters. And when I reviewed the case file yesterday, I didn't see any such memo. When I spoke to Ike Blackman, he told me he had neither seen, nor signed such a memo. Why would he say that?"

"Either Mr. Blackman experienced a memory meltdown, or he's lying."

"Are you calling your superior a liar?"

"Someone is lying. I know it isn't me. Is there anything else you need to ask me?"

"Just one more question." Wallace flipped back a page on his lined tablet. "Is there anything that would corroborate your version of the authorization memo?"

"Only this." Dan handed a document to Wallace. "It's a copy of the Sammy Ho approval memo from my computer. Of course it's unsigned, and won't show who's lying."

Wallace began to read the memo.

Dan gathered his things and stood. "With all respect, Bert. I suspect this little farce we just went through really doesn't matter." Dan walked out of the room, not waiting for a response.

Throughout the afternoon, Dan handled paperwork from other investigations. He had let his work languish while he dealt with Sammy Ho's murder and the OPR inquiry, and realized he had practically lost touch with other cases. Little by little, the noise level of the office faded as agents and support people left for homes, families, and personal lives. Dan finally found the bottom of his incoming mail tray, and rubbed his tired eyes.

He was aware he was no longer alone, looked up, and was surprised to see Casey standing in the doorway of his office, smiling and holding a brown paper bag in her hand. "Your three favorite food groups," she said with an infectious laugh. "Coffee, non-fat milk, and artificial sweetener."

She stepped into the office and sat down. As she crossed her legs, her skirt rode up and exposed a shapely thigh. She pulled the hem back down to a modest position, just above her knee, but not before

Dan noticed. She handed him a Styrofoam cup from the bag and took the second one for herself.

"Thanks for stopping by," Dan said. "My week has been rotten. I thought I needed to be alone. But I think I need some company."

"Want to talk?"

Dan hesitated. He wanted to talk, but this could become awkward for both of them. For the first time, he had a chance to take a long look at her, her olive complexion set off by her sparkling eyes, and full lips.

He returned a smile. "Like to join me for a drink?"

Her eyes became even more alive, and she burst into a wide smile. "I'd love to. I'll grab my purse."

The two FBI sedans headed up the east side of Manhattan, over to Second Avenue at Nineteenth Street, found parking places within a block of the restaurant.

As they walked through the door, the tuxedoed maître d' sized them up. "Table for two?"

The restaurant was about three-quarters full, a mixture of neighborhood residents, the after-work crowd, and those who appreciated the restaurant as much as he did. They were seated, gave their drink orders.

Their waiter appeared with their drinks.

"I'm curious," Dan said when he was gone. "Where does the name Casey come from? Everybody calls you that, but that's not the name on your personnel file."

She smiled. "My dad really wanted a fifth son. When I arrived, I guess there must have been some negotiation between my mom and dad, because they ended up naming me for both of them. Kathleen for my mom, and Carter for my dad. I didn't see myself as a Kathleen, or a Carter, so I started using the first initial of each name, and KC became Casey."

"It makes perfect sense," Dan said with a laugh.

"What I loved most about growing up with my brothers was the chance to really enjoy fierce competition. It didn't matter whether it was football, tennis, or skiing."

"Then that would explain it," he said.

"What's that?"

"I've heard that since you've come to New York, no matter what squad you were on, you've been challenging the other agents. In fact, you've established a new work ethic, and chalked up more arrests and convictions. You're the best thing that's happened to my squad in a long time."

She blushed. "Thank you."

Dan grew quiet and appeared deep in his thought. He stared at his glass. Casey reached out and touched his arm. "How are you doing? I know it's been terrible for you. Sammy and everything else."

"A terrible week."

Casey waited for him to continue.

"My undercover agent is killed. I can't prove the undercover operation was authorized. I'm prevented from investigating his murder. Then OPR comes into town and wants to nail me."

"That's a lot to be hit with all at once."

"The worst part of it? I've been told not to do anything. Not even talk to anyone about it. It's like having your head in a guillotine, waiting for the blade to drop."

Casey listened intently.

"But that's only part of the story. Sammy's murder dredged up some bad memories." Dan paused and looked down. "It began eight years ago. I chose to work late one night. When I got home around midnight, I found my wife Ellen murdered. The police said it was an intruder who raped and murdered her. They never caught the guy. For the last eight years I've had the same dream of coming home, seeing Ellen, but not being able to do anything."

"How horrible for you! I'm so sorry. I can't even imagine your pain."

"That's why I throw myself so completely into the cases I work. I couldn't find who murdered her. Maybe by solving every case I handle, I can make up for my not being there to keep her alive."

"Now I understand a little better how this must have hit you. Being told you can't investigate Sammy's death was like being prevented from solving your wife's murder." She reached out, took his hand as her eyes filled with tears.

"Casey, I shouldn't have brought it up. It's been a long day. Why don't we call it a night?"

"You're right. We both need some rest."

Dan walked Casey to her car, and stood with her on the sidewalk. Casey reached out and took his hand.

"Thanks, Casey."

"Thanks for sharing something difficult to talk about. I'll see you tomorrow. Safe home." She kissed him on the cheek, got into her car and drove off.

Dan watched her drive down the street and around the corner. He touched the spot where her lips had kissed his cheek. Slowly he turned, walked to his car, and headed home.

Seven

8:45 AM
December 31st
Manhattan, New York

Christmas and Hanukkah decorations had been replaced with those for New Years' Eve. Manhattan stores featured gowns, tuxedo rentals, and overpriced bottles of champagne for shoppers who had put it off until the last moment.

The small maroon Pontiac station wagon pulled to a stop in the open parking lot on West Forty-sixth Street between Avenue of the Americas and Seventh Avenue. A young Asian woman got out of the car and began walking down Forty-sixth Street, east toward the Avenue of the Americas.

Dan turned to Casey. "Ready?"

"Let's go."

The two of them set off behind her and soon caught up, one on each side. The woman was startled when she realized they were there.

"Mrs. Wen," Casey said quickly. "We're FBI Agents. I'm Casey Brody. The man on your right is Dan Robertson." Both agents showed FBI identification. "We need to talk to you about Fontaine Diamonds."

She responded in Chinese.

"Don't play games, Mrs. Wen," Dan said. "Spare us the foreign language routine."

"Leave me alone," she said in perfectly clear English. "I don't know anything about Fontaine Diamonds."

"Yes you do, Mrs. Wen," Casey said. "Would you prefer we talk to you at Fontaine?"

They reached Sixth Avenue and waited for the light to change.

"Think very carefully before you refuse to talk to us," Dan said. "You could be arrested, prosecuted and imprisoned for the fraud against MBT Factors. Think about your husband and two children in Teaneck."

Mary Lee Wen started to walk faster.

"Think about the shame you would bring on your family," Dan said. "Talk to us, help us, you'll have a chance to avoid all of that."

They crossed Sixth Avenue and turned toward Forty-seventh Street. Mary Lee Wen's eyes darted about rapidly. Dan and Casey kept up with her quickened pace.

"How do you know about me and my family?" Tears welled up in her eyes.

"We know everything," Casey said. "We know about the fraud problem at Dante's Designs when you worked there. We know about the phony invoices at Fontaine."

At Forty-seventh Street they turned east toward Fifth Avenue.

Mary Lee Wen stopped in the middle of the sidewalk. They stopped too. Pedestrians maneuvered around them. She averted eye contact with the agents and said, "If you know all that, you don't need me to tell you anything. There's nothing to tell. Please, don't walk any further with me. I can't be seen with you. I can't help you. Please!"

Casey squared her shoulders and stared at her. "If you care about your loved ones you'll call me. Here's my card."

Without raising her eyes to look at them, she took the card.

"Do the smart thing and call," Dan said.

Casey and Dan stepped aside, and watched her walk away. She glanced over her shoulder every few steps to see if they had followed.

"What do you think?" Casey asked.

"She's scared. Question is, will she come around? So what was that about Dante's Designs?"

"The Investigative Analysts learned she used to work at Dante's in the Garment District. Dante's had some financial problems and tried to rip off a bank in order to solve them. They got caught, and the two top men took a fall. Would you believe Mary Lee Wen and Christina Marino both worked there? Neither of them was charged, but their names were recorded. Now they both work at Fontaine."

Both agents jumped out of the way as a New York City street sweeper came towards them, spinning brushes spraying water and the garbage across the sidewalk. They stood and watched it pass and nail some less nimble pedestrians.

Dan refocused on their conversation. "Interesting. So this pair was together before, and aren't strangers to fraud. Can we play one off the other?"

"Don't know. We need to get a feel for Marino before we can answer that."

"Why don't we take a shot at her today?"

"I can't. Got a meeting with an Assistant U.S. Attorney on an old case of mine. After five months, it's going to trial. Why don't you try to see if you can spot her today? If you don't, we can try her at home tonight."

"Sure," Dan said. "Leave me your notes and the photo you got from her driver's license. I'll give it a go."

Casey said goodbye and left. Dan looked at the photo of Christina Marino, a dark-haired woman. Her driver's license said she was thirty-five and lived in Queens. Not bad looking from her picture. If you allowed for the usual DMV photo uglification.

The shops and businesses on West Forty-seventh Street, between Fifth Avenue and the Avenue of the Americas, known as the "Diamond District," were beginning to open up. Steel grates were being rolled up, lights were coming on, trays and trays of glittering diamond jewelry were being set out in window displays. Dan found 52 West Forty-seventh Street and walked into the storefront of Fontaine Diamonds. He strolled around, playing customer, looking at tray after tray of gold and diamond jewelry in glass cases. Westerfield had said their merchandise was second-rate, but to Dan, it looked impressive.

"May I help you?" A salesman flashed a plastic smile.

"Thanks. I'm still browsing." Dan leaned over the display cases; his eye was on the images in the mirror behind the counter. No sign of Christina Marino. He took his time and looked over the items on display. He heard movement and saw a partial reflection of a female employee. Trying to be nonchalant, he looked around, turned slightly to catch the stairs in one of the mirrors, and saw Mary Lee Wen. She raised her eyes, saw Dan, and stiffened.

He returned her stare through the mirror's reflection, but gave no indication of recognition.

She concluded her business with the man, turned, looked over her shoulder, and hurried up the stairs.

Dan thanked the salesman and left.

He found a spot across the street from Fontaine, in a seldom-used doorway leading to a second floor of a building. From there Dan could see the pedestrian traffic on both sides of the street, as well as the hawkers trying to steer customers into stores. Hasidic men conducted their business on the sidewalk, exchanging wads of money for diamonds in folded tissue paper.

Suddenly a young man in jeans and a sweatshirt bolted out of a shop and ran down the street, weaving in and out around traffic. Another man ran out of the same shop shouting, "Thief! Stop him!"

Dan witnessed something he'd never seen before. From shops on both sides of the street, merchants poured out onto the sidewalks. By the time the young man was halfway down the block, he was being pursued by a mob at least one hundred strong. NYPD officers left their kiosk and joined the chase, shouting into their hand-held radios as they ran.

"He'll be lucky if he reaches the corner," a man near Dan said.

"Why's that?" Dan asked.

"If he makes the corner, the cops will get him. If he doesn't, the mob'll probably kill him."

"Not a good idea to rob someone in the Diamond District."

"A very bad idea," the man said. "Other than a couple of streets in Little Italy protected by the Mafia, this block of Forty-seventh Street is probably one of the most crime-free places in Manhattan."

The race was over, and the man was being pulled in one direction by the policemen and in another direction by the mob. Dan shifted his eyes back to Fontaine, watching for Marino.

An hour and a half later Marino walked out of Fontaine. She wasn't great looking, but had a body to die for. Wearing a tight, black sweater, a short red leather skirt and red spike heels, her shoulder-length black hair blew in the wind. As people swarmed past her, she purposefully strutted along the sidewalk up Forty-seventh Street toward Fifth Avenue. Her head held high, looking straight ahead, Marino was wearing the expressionless "New York Face."

She didn't notice as he walked behind her, quickly catching up.

As she neared Fifth Avenue, she pulled open the door of Arby's restaurant and took her place at the end of the line. Dan stood in the same line, two people between them.

Dan watched her take her roast beef sandwich and black coffee and begin looking for a vacant table. Two men appeared to have finished eating, so she walked over and waited next to their table. They smiled at her, and then stood to leave. She ignored them and sat down.

Dan took the seat opposite her. "Hello. Miss Marino."

"Who's asking?"

"Robertson, FBI." He showed her his identification, and watched her as she studied it. She was better looking up close.

"Whatta you want?"

"To ask you some questions about Fontaine."

"Forget it. I got no reason to talk to you."

"Sure you do. You got lucky at Dante's Designs. You could've been prosecuted. This time, you're out of luck. You're helping with the fraud. You're going to take a fall."

"That a fact? I suppose you're gonna make me a better offer?"

"I could. If you help us."

"Get outta here. I got nothing to say to you." She started to stand.

"Sit down, Miss Marino. Even if you don't talk, you better listen."

Marino sat back down.

"Look, do you think Schwartz gives a damn about you? When we arrest him for fraud, he'll do anything to get himself off. Who do you think he'll pin it on? You're the one who keeps the books."

She was listening but refused to look at him.

"You think he hasn't thought about that? The most difficult thing to defend yourself against is a lie. Do you think he wouldn't lie about you to save himself?"

"I can take care of myself. I got nothin' to say to you."

Dan laid his card on the table. "You're smart. Cooperate with us—stay out of jail."

His eyes locked on hers as he slid the card across the table. Dan stood and said, "Give it some serious thought."

Eight

1:25 PM
December 31st
Manhattan, New York

"Interesting conversation you had with Christina Marino," Casey said. "What's our next move?"

"It's your case, but I suggest we take a shot at both Marino and Wen at home. I don't think we should phone them. It's too easy for them to hang up."

"Sounds good, but let's give them a day or so. A false sense of security usually works to our advantage."

"Okay. Did you talk to your guy at the Business Insurance Clearinghouse about Fontaine and Schwartz?"

"Yeah. Seems Schwartz hasn't always had a lucrative diamond business. About three or four years ago the cops responded to a late night burglar alarm at

The Gold Bug—the name of Schwartz's business in those days. Didn't see anybody inside. No forced entry. They called Schwartz to come open up, and everybody walked through the place. The safe was open, not torched. Looked like someone had forgotten to close it. Schwartz took a quick look and started hollering that a hundred loose diamonds were missing. An insurance investigator told Schwartz he could go ahead and make a claim, but there'd be a pretty good chance they would counter with criminal and civil fraud charges. Schwartz decided not to pursue it. Within a month, The Gold Bug filed for bankruptcy."

"Anything else?" Dan asked.

"A couple of claims for jewelry lost in the mail. None involved any big numbers."

"So how soon after The Gold Bug went bankrupt did Schwartz start Fontaine Diamonds?"

"Six months," Casey said. "Amazing! You're down to rock bottom, and bingo, within months you've got enough money to start a new business. Is this a great country, or what?"

"Does your insurance guy say Schwartz is a real scumbag, or is this kind of thing typical in the Diamond District?"

"Most of the scams he sees involve dealers ripping each other off or duping the man off the street—cubic zirconium for diamonds, gold plate for solid gold. He said receivable financing fraud would be a new one on him."

"Thanks. Hate to cut this short, but I've got to get on to some other things."

Casey left, and Dan made a call.

"Fifth Precinct, Sergeant Malloy."

"Sarge, I need to talk to Jimmy Lee."

"Detective Lee."

"Jimmy, this is Dan Robertson."

"Hey, Dan! How's it going?"

"I'm okay, Jimmy. How about you?"

"Hanging in there," Lee said. "You know I was thinking about Sammy Ho. How's his family?"

"Not great. They decided there was nothing to keep them here, so his wife and kids moved back to Seattle to be near both families."

"I feel for them. What can I do for you?"

"Have you come up with anything on the shootings?"

"Based on the cartridge casings and the fragmented slugs, ballistics says both a .22 caliber and a couple of 9 mm guns were used. The .22 was probably a High Standard handgun, and the 9 mm came from two different Heckler and Kochs."

"I can see the High Standard, but a Heckler and Koch—that's heavy firepower. Any of them have a history?"

"The lab hasn't finished with the comparisons, but so far these weapons are new to the NYPD."

"Anything on the van?"

"Nothing matches that was recently stolen. Hasn't been spotted by the Patrol Division. We don't have any license plate to work with, and everyone on the street at the time has developed amnesia."

"What about your snitches in the Tongs?"

"They tell me they're trying, but if you ask me, I think they're too scared to ask questions. That shooting sent an impressive message. Has the FBI come up with anything?"

"I'm the wrong person to ask, Jimmy."

"Why's that?"

"The memo authorizing our use of Sammy in the UCO has disappeared," Dan said. "Our Internal Affairs—OPR has me in their gun sights. I've been ordered not to have anything more to do with the Tong investigation, or the inquiry into the shooting. I'm not even supposed to be calling you."

"Didn't hear a word. Anything I can do?"

"Just take my calls, and let me know if you come up with anything."

"You got it. Gotta run. Good talking to you."

Dan looked up to see Thomas standing in the doorway with his arms across his chest.

"I had a telephone conversation with the OPR Deputy Assistant Director," Thomas said after he walked into the office and closed the door.

"And?"

"They're mulling over the UCO thing. There seems to be two camps of thought. One camp thinks you really screwed up and want to hang you out to dry, maybe busted back to the bricks, transferred to a non-preference office."

"And the other?"

"They seem to be looking at the bigger picture. They're concerned if the FBI comes down hard on you, Sammy's family will interpret it as a sign that the Bureau admits you did something wrong. The family might be encouraged to file a lawsuit against you and the FBI, since we've got deep pockets. But if that's the direction they go, OPR isn't sure what to do."

"I see."

"But don't worry. I think the cover-your-ass school is winning. You'll probably get a reprimand but not much more."

"Did you help them see the pitfalls of nailing me and suggest an alternative?"

"Moi?" Thomas said with a smile.

Nine

7:55 PM
January 2nd
Teaneck, New Jersey

Dan and Casey parked in front of the quaint white Cape Cod home with black shutters and trim.

"118 Winsome Road." Casey read the computer printout. "Mary Lee Wen, her husband, David, and two kids."

They were buffeted by a gust of frigid wind when they got out of the car.

"Brrr," Casey said. "After the nice weather the last two days, I thought we were in for a mild winter."

Dan rang the bell. Through the glass sidelights on either side of the door, the agents saw a man approach, turn on the porch light, and look out at them.

"Who is it?" he shouted.

"FBI." Both agents held their credentials up to the glass.

"What do you want?"

"We need to talk to you," Dan yelled. "Unless you want the whole neighborhood to know your business, open the door."

The door opened a crack and the man closely examined their credentials, but made no effort to invite them in.

"Are you David Wen?" Casey asked.

"Yes." His tone was defiant, but Dan noticed his hand was trembling.

"We need to talk with Mary Lee Wen," Casey said.

"Why?"

Dan saw a woman's head peek around the doorway from the kitchen, then quickly disappear. "Mrs. Wen?" he shouted in her direction.

David Wen glanced towards the kitchen door. He let the agents in, said something in Chinese, and Mary Lee Wen slowly emerged from the kitchen, her head lowered.

David Wen stood his ground. "Ask my wife your questions."

"Mrs. Wen," Casey said, "remember we talked to you in Manhattan a couple of days ago?"

David Wen turned to stare at his wife. She obviously hadn't told him.

In a quiet voice, spoken from a bowed head, she said, "Yes."

"We told you we'd be back."

David Wen's face contorted in rage, and he screamed something in Chinese to his wife. Her whole body jumped, but her head remained bowed.

"Mrs. Wen," Casey said, trying to regain control of the situation, "we believe you work for a man who is stealing from a bank. We want your cooperation to prove it. Would you prefer to talk with us, rather than go to jail?"

Mary Lee Wen remained silent, but Dan saw tears rolling down her cheeks.

"I . . . I don't know anything about that," she finally said.

"Yes you do," Casey said. "This is your last chance before we start arresting people. You and Marino were lucky when they made the arrests at Dante's Designs. Your luck has run out."

David Wen reacted like he had been hit again and shouted at his wife. She quietly answered him in Chinese. It didn't appear David Wen knew about the arrests at Dante's.

Dan felt bad for Mary Lee Wen. She was caught between two terrors. "Mrs. Wen, are you going to help us?"

She didn't respond, but her small body shook as she sobbed.

"You should go now," David Wen said.

Casey handed David Wen a business card. "Have a heart-to-heart talk with your wife. Afterwards, call me."

The agents let themselves out. Behind them, Dan heard the sound of the door being locked, then David Wen shouting.

"She's ready to crack," Dan said. "One more time should bring her around. Question is how will her husband react to this? Did you catch the look on his face when we mentioned talking to her?"

"Yeah. When I brought up the arrests at Dante's Designs he seemed ready to kill her," Casey said. "I've got this feeling neither of them are going to get much sleep tonight. Want to try Marino again tomorrow night?"

"We could, but Wen might talk to her and tell her about our visit. It'd be better to take a run at her tonight. We could make it to Queens before nine."

"Yeah, but . . . I promised my nephew I'd come see his basketball game tonight. There'll be other games."

"No, go to the game. You promised. Drop me at the office to get my car, then you hightail it to the game. You can probably catch the second half. I'll make a run over to Queens. Hey, with my luck she probably won't be home."

"Thanks," Casey said, a grateful smile on her face. "It'll mean a lot to him."

After a quick ride back into Manhattan, the agents parted, and Dan headed to Queens. His dark blue Chevy wove its way through traffic as it emerged from the Midtown Tunnel onto the Long Island Expressway, the lights of Manhattan behind and those in Queens ahead. Twenty minutes later he pulled into a space. He was about to buzz when someone came out. Dan slipped in the door, went to her apartment and rang the bell.

He heard footsteps approach the door, and saw the peephole darken. "Who is it?"

"Dan Robertson, FBI."

"What the hell do you want?"

"To talk to you."

"About what?"

"You know." No answer came from the other side of the door. "Look, do you really want to keep shouting through the door? You can let me in and have a little privacy. Your choice." Dan waited for her decision. He heard the door chain being unhooked, and then the door opened. "Thank you, Miss Marino."

Dan looked around the apartment. It was a studio apartment, with a combination living room/bedroom. Through a doorway he saw a small kitchen, and another door, probably the bathroom. While there wasn't much space, all of it appeared to be used well. The walls were covered from floor to ceiling with framed reprints of famous paintings, stained glass, and photographs. There were reproductions of Italian Baroque furniture upholstered with satin brocade. But there were contradictions. An expensive, perfectly aligned chess set on the coffee table next to a disorderly stack of books and magazines. A crucifix on the wall over the bed, and fashion magazines piled on the floor beside it. The top of the desk was neatly arranged, but papers were sticking out of the drawers.

Marino was wearing tight-fitting jeans and a sweatshirt. She plopped cross-legged on the sofa, and Dan sat in a chair. Marino took a swig from a beer bottle and stared at him.

He tried to find a way to soften the situation. "Pretty eclectic," he said, motioning to the objects in the room. "All sorts of tastes."

"Yeah, that's me. Eclectic."

"I understand you went to school at night, and earned a degree in accounting."

"What's it to you?"

"I worked my way through college, too."

"Well, let's hear it for our college man," she said as she raised the beer bottle in a mock toast.

"Life hasn't given you many breaks, has it?"

"You can fuckin' say that again."

"Look Miss Marino—"

"Christy. I go by Christy," she said, softening just a bit.

"Okay, Christy. You don't have much use for cops do you?"

"All they think about is how much they can screw you, the goddamned pigs."

"I'm trying to give you a chance to avoid that."

"By becoming a snitch?"

"By saving yourself. You know what's going on at Fontaine, and you're involved. Knowing Schwartz, I doubt you're getting much out of it. Somebody's going to take a fall. Why you?"

"Why the fuck do you care what happens to me?"

"Quite frankly, I don't. I just want to put Schwartz away. Doesn't mean it can't be a good deal for you."

She silently considered his words as she took another swig of beer.

"You skated at Dante's Designs when it came down. I can tell you for a fact that if you don't cut a deal this time, you're going to take a fall, but you don't have a lot of time left to decide."

He could tell by her silence that he'd stirred her thoughts. That was a good place to leave it. She looked up at him as he stood.

"Think about it." He placed another business card on the coffee table and let himself out.

There wasn't much traffic on the way back to Manhattan, which gave him a chance to think. Why had he taken such a hard line with Mary Lee Wen, and a softer one with Christy Marino? Even though she was street tough, Christy Marino was far more vulnerable. According to the IA report, she finished high school and worked the usual crappy jobs for a while, then got a BA and CPA certification. She'd moved up to respectability from wherever she'd been. But she didn't seem entirely comfortable with it. She was also alone. Mary Lee Wen had a husband and children around, but Christy Marino had no one.

Dan found her attractive in spite of her coarse, hard manner. But something else appealed to him. Christy Marino had touched something in him. She had strength of character—that reminded him of Ellen. The self-made woman who believed in herself enough to take on the world, fists up, ready to fight. But Christy was like a wild animal caught in a trap, knowing it was doomed, yet fiercely attacking anyone who tried to free it. That was it. That's what had gotten to him. She had a spirit like Ellen's. Now he understood where the attraction came from. His interest in the Fontaine Diamonds investigation ratcheted up a notch.

Ten

8:45 AM
January 3rd
Manhattan, New York

Dan was catching up on paperwork when Casey walked in. He laid down his pen and leaned back. "Morning, Casey. How you doing?"

"Not bad." She settled into one of the chairs. "And you?"

"A little sluggish. Didn't get home until ten thirty."

"How'd it go?"

"Struck out."

"So you weren't able to charm Marino into cooperating," Casey said with a smile. "What was she like?"

"A real street-tough kid. She thinks she can defend herself against anything."

59

"Does she live alone?"

"Yeah, why . . .?"

"I was thinking about this after I left you last night. I'm . . . a little worried. For your sake."

"My sake?"

"Dan, I know you're under the magnifying glass over the UCO, and what happened to Sammy. If for nothing more than appearance's sake, it probably isn't a good idea for you to interview a potential witness without someone else present. Especially if that witness is female. At night. In her apartment."

Dan was teetering on the edge of exploding. How dare she question him? It bordered on insubordination. At the same time he was beginning to see Casey as something more than a subordinate, and that was worrisome. He didn't think she wished him ill, and realized she might be right.

"Point well taken, Casey."

"Enough said. Think she'll come around?"

"For her sake, I hope so."

Later that morning Dan briefed Thomas on the Fontaine investigation.

Dan made an early evening of it, and got out of the office by six, only to compete with the evening rush traffic. It was 6:45 when he turned the key, pushed open the door, and turned on the lights. From the living room, he heard the sound of the television.

"Squawk!" came a voice from the living room. "Cocktail time!"

Dan smiled as he turned off the television. "Hello, Nevermore. How are you?"

"Squawk! Open the door!"

"Okay, Nevermore. I'm coming."

Dan finished taking off his coat, and opened the African Gray's cage. Dan took a whiff, looked into the bottom, and said, "Nevermore, what have you been eating? I've got to clean your cage, you dirty bird."

The parrot cocked his head, then said, "Dirty Bird."

"That's right, Nevermore."

"Nevermore!"

"Yeah. Promise you will nevermore do this."

"Squawk! Nevermore!"

Dan pulled out the tray and replaced the newspaper in the bottom of the cage.

"Cocktail time!"

"Okay, you talked me into it, you silver-tongued devil."

Dan poured himself a scotch, turned on the stereo, picked a CD, and a cigar. As he sat back and watched the cigar smoke waft toward the ceiling, his thoughts drifted to Christy Marino. She was a complex person. Driven to better herself and at the same time participating in a self-destructive fraud.

He walked into the kitchen and got another scotch. As he did, Nevermore flew into the kitchen and landed on his shoulder. Dan felt like a cross between a pirate and Inspector Clouseau.

"It's a good thing the guys on the squad don't see us together like this. They might begin to wonder about me."

Nevermore rode his shoulder as Dan walked back into the living room and sat down. The bird worked his way down Dan's arm, waddled across the table, then turned and looked back at Dan.

Dan spotted the bird dropping Nevermore left on his shoulder.

"Nevermore, you dirty bird!"

"Dirty bird," the parrot repeated.

He took his handkerchief and began to clean the spot. "Nevermore, this isn't funny."

The bird bobbed his head up and down, and Dan thought for sure he saw a smile on its face.

* * *

The shadowy figure crossed the foyer and stood at the stair that led to the bedrooms. Tall, broad shoulders, powerful arms—a man. From the doorway of the living room, Dan watched him glance back over his shoulder. Dan wanted to reach out and stop him, but found his feet were rooted to the spot in which he stood. Silently the man climbed the carpeted stairs, one gloved hand on the banister, the other gripping a pistol.

At the top of the stairs the man again stopped, cocked his head, and listened and heard nothing. Dan looked over the man's shoulder as both peered into the master bedroom. Alone in their bed, Ellen was asleep, her auburn hair splayed across the pillow. Through the bedroom window, soft moonlight gently caressed her face.

Dan sat up in bed and shook the images out of his head. A distant siren wailed. A garbage truck growled and banged. New York sounds. He wasn't in his house in California. This was his apartment in Manhattan.

He reached across the bed and felt only cold emptiness. Ellen wasn't there. It had been a dream. The same dream.

Eleven

8:45 AM
January 4th
Manhattan, New York

"What's up?" Dan asked, as he returned to his desk to find Casey waiting for him.

"Took another run at Mary Lee Wen this morning," Casey said, speaking quickly. "Waited across from where she parks. Finally gave up at 10:30. She never showed. Phoned her at home—got her answering machine. Called her at Fontaine—they said she hadn't come in or called. You remember her angry husband. Maybe she's at home with instructions not to leave or answer the phone."

"Could be," Dan said slowly.

"Are you thinking something else?"

"David Wen lost face because his wife's actions brought the FBI to his home. What do you think?"

"Possible," Casey said. "Want to try Marino again tonight and pressure her to tell us where Mary Lee Wen is?"

"Sure. Let's eat while the traffic clears out, then run over to Queens."

* * *

At 7:00 PM, they drove over to Queens in two cars. They slipped through the apartment inner door, found their way to her apartment, and pressed the bell.

"Who is it?" Christy shouted.

"Dan Robertson, Miss Marino."

"Go away! I don't want to talk to you."

"You certainly have a way with women," Casey said.

Dan shouted, "We need to talk to you about Mary Lee Wen."

The words were barely out of his mouth when the door was yanked open by a wide-eyed Christy Marino. "What about Mary Lee?"

"Can we come in?" Dan asked.

"Yeah, sure," she said, her eyes darting back and forth between Dan and Casey as they stepped inside. "Where is she?" Christy was pacing.

"I was hoping you could tell us," he said.

She shook her head, still pacing. "I haven't seen her since yesterday. Have you been trying to talk to her, too?"

"Yeah," Dan said. "We talked to her in Manhattan and in Teaneck, but her husband wanted none of it."

Christy stopped dead. "David was there when you tried to talk to her?"

"Yeah," Casey said. "Why?"

Christy sighed and appeared to collect her thoughts. "Mary Lee is terrified of David. He intimidates her, and has a violent temper." She avoided eye contact. "She didn't show at work today. I tried all day to call her at home. All I get is that fuckin' machine."

"Could she be at home, with instructions not to answer the phone or the door?" Casey asked.

"Maybe. I don't know. I'm afraid for her. That asshole's been pissed at her, but it never involved the cops."

"Tell you what we're going to do," Dan said. "Tomorrow Casey will take a ride over to Teaneck and see if she can spot her car."

"Yeah?" Christy said in a low voice. The tough exterior was gone.

"We'll ask the neighbors if they've seen her or her car. We'll visit David Wen tomorrow night and try to force him to tell us where his wife is. I'm sure there's a logical explanation." Dan put his hand on Christy's arm. "Don't worry, we'll find her and let you know. Anything we can do for you?"

"Yeah. Leave me alone."

When they got to the door, Casey turned back. "Have you thought any more about telling us what's going on at Fontaine?"

"Casey—" Dan said.

"How the fuck can you ask me that at a time like this?" Christy screamed. "I'm frantic about Mary Lee, and the only damn thing you want is to turn me into a fuckin' stool pigeon!" Christy literally shoved them into the hall with the door as she pushed it closed.

"Can you believe that bitch?" Casey railed. "If it isn't something she wants to talk about—"

"Take it easy," Dan said. "Didn't you see how upset she was?"

"Take it easy?" Casey answered in disbelief. "Since when did the FBI become a locating service to help find friends of witnesses?"

"What do you mean by that?"

"You've got me spending a day or more trying to find that damn Chinese woman and committed me to another late night trying to talk to her husband. You know he's going to tell us to take a hike. All of that just so we can give some answers to this bimbo in Queens because she's upset. Have you totally lost your perspective?"

"Sounds like you've lost your perspective," Dan said. "I don't see you cultivating any other witnesses in this case. Correction, your case. If we can't get either of these women to cooperate, you're going to have to shut this case down. We've got one shot at getting someone to cooperate—Christy Marino."

"Dan—"

"Let me tell you something else. Be tough any time you want, if that's what makes you feel good. But try it with her and you're gonna walk away with nothing. She's street tough and not easy to crack. You ought to be able to see that. I'm going home."

Dan strode down the hall leaving Casey standing, her mouth open.

Dan lowered the car window as he drove back into Manhattan. The cold air felt wonderful and cooled his anger. As it did, he began to wonder if he really was losing his perspective. The sight of Christy Marino's tear-filled eyes came to mind. She only had one friend—Mary Lee Wen. Obviously their friendship had developed a long time before. Mary Lee Wen needed a friend as much as Christy Marino. One woman alone, the other, trapped in an abusive marriage, but in each other they found someone whom they could lean on and trust.

No, he had the right perspective. When it came down to it, Dan knew Christy couldn't be coerced. She had to be won over. If he could earn her trust, she could deliver the case against Fontaine. And if that trust could be earned by tracking down Mary Lee Wen, it was a small price to pay.

* * *

12:40 PM
January 5th
Manhattan, New York

"I struck out. Neighbors have seen her husband and the kids, but nobody's seen Mary Lee," Casey said on her cell phone.

Dan thought he heard a trace of resentment in Casey's voice, a holdover from their spat. "Do one more thing before you head back? Swing by the Teaneck PD, and see if they have any info about the Wens?"

"Sure, Dan."

He hung up the phone. Had he come down too hard on Casey? He didn't think so. Maybe she was a good white-collar investigator, but she seemed to lack a healthy dose of the street smarts you develop when you investigate organized crime. Or was that just him being elitist? Then again, she was only 30 and hadn't been doing it as long as him.

During lunch with other supervisors, his cell phone rang. He excused himself and found a place where he could have a conversation.

"Dan?" Casey said. "I'm here at the Teaneck Police Department. Christy Marino tried to file a missing persons report, but they refused to take a report by phone from someone who wasn't family."

"What happened? Did David Wen file a report?"

67

"An officer went to Wen's house last night. He wasn't home, so they left a message to call. Wen hasn't gotten back to them. Without him confirming she's really missing, no report has been filed."

"No report and no Mary Lee Wen. Come on back."

Twelve

3:55 PM
January 5th
Manhattan, New York

It seemed that lately the smallest thing anybody said or did was enough to set Dan off. Why was he getting into arguments with other people at the FBI? With the exception of Bert Wallace from OPR, he really liked most of the people he worked with. He'd gotten along fine with Blackman before the UCO memo flap. It was so unlike him to feel superior to others and to fly into emotional tirades at the least provocation. Was there a correlation between Christy and Dan's short-temper? Maybe. His mind kept drifting back to Christy Marino. She was so like Ellen. He hadn't been able to save Ellen. He had to save Christy. It was becoming an obsession.

He called Fontaine and asked for Mary Lee Wen. She wasn't there. He remembered David Wen's rage. His wife was missing. So why wouldn't he notify the police? If they left him a phone message, why didn't he call back? Wen had to be hiding something.

Maybe Mary Lee Wen had finally gotten fed up and left. David Wen wouldn't report it because he couldn't stand to lose face. But if Mary Lee had run, why hadn't she told Christy? Why do that to your friend? Unless Christy was acting. If so, she was one hell of an actress.

Darkness descended on Manhattan. Dan and Casey agreed to wait until after eight to try and talk with David Wen.

Dan had some supper at a nearby deli, then drove to New Jersey. The commute traffic had cleared out, and he found himself in Teaneck a lot sooner than he planned. He pulled to the curb, up the block from the Wen house, and waited for Casey. With the engine running and the heater keeping him warm, he leaned his head back, closed his eyes, and waited.

"NY 6-5 to NY 6-1," the FBI radio cracked with Casey's voice.

Dan sat up in the seat and keyed the mike. "This is NY 6-1. Go ahead, NY 6-5."

"Where are you?"

"About five houses up the block from the target. Where are you?"

"Just turning the corner. Flash your lights."

Dan turned the headlights on and off. A pair of headlights in the rear view mirror flashed in reply. He followed Casey to the Wen house. Casey rang the bell. They waited, not knowing if anyone was home.

Dan saw Wen coming towards the door. "Get ready. Here he comes."

The porch light came on, and David Wen looked out the door's sidelight. He stared at them, said nothing, and didn't open the door.

"FBI, Mr. Wen," Dan said.

"We need to talk to you, Mr. Wen," Casey said. "Please open the door."

Wen opened the door the width the safety chain would allow. Out of habit, Dan planted his foot along the bottom of the door. He glanced over and saw that Casey was leaning against the door, then shifted his eyes back to Wen.

"What do you want?" Wen asked.

"We want to talk to you about your wife," Dan said.

Silence, then Wen finally opened the door but made no effort the invite them further than the foyer.

"Mr. Wen, where is your wife?" Dan's eyes bored holes into David Wen.

"Not here."

"Where is she?" Casey asked.

David Wen's eyes darted from one agent to the other, then looked at nothing. "I don't know."

"How long has she been gone?" Dan asked.

"A day or two."

"Have you filed a missing persons report with the police?" Casey asked.

"No."

"The Teaneck Police left you a phone message," Dan said. "Have you talked to them?"

"No."

"Mr. Wen," Casey said. "Your wife is missing. You're not sure how long she's been gone or where she is?"

"Has this happened before?" Dan said quietly.

David Wen turned his angry gaze on Dan. "Yes."

They waited, but he added nothing.

"Would you care to elaborate?" Casey asked after a moment.

"No. Now, unless there's something more, I want you to leave," Wen said as he opened the door.

The two agents gave him a hard look, then walked out. They'd gotten all they were going to get.

When they were almost to the street, Dan said, "Why don't you join me in my car and we'll talk about this for a minute?"

Casey walked over to his car and got in. Dan started the car and turned the heat on high, then sat back and took a deep breath. "What do you think that was all about?"

"I think he's lying through his teeth. I think he knows where she is, but has no intention of telling us or the cops."

"Did you catch his answer when we asked him if it had happened before? After he said yes he looked like he wanted to kick himself."

"Maybe he sends her away whenever she pisses him off," Casey said. "It looked to me like he was barely keeping his temper in check while we were talking. Think it's more than just losing face?"

"I'm not sure," Dan said, and realized he was having a conversation with Casey without any of the rancor of the previous night. He was happy about that.

"I'm not sure she took off on her own. With David Wen it's more than just embarrassment. He's furious."

"I had the same thought. Capable of violence, you think?"

Casey took a moment to consider. "I could see that. But at this point, we'd be hard pressed to come up with enough to accuse him of wife-beating."

"Yeah. Until Mary Lee Wen shows up battered and bruised, or worse, there's nothing we can do."

"Christy Marino's our only hope of finding out what's really going on at Fontaine," Casey said as he stared straight ahead, focusing on nothing. "We should treat her pretty gently, huh?"

"It's been suggested. Goodnight, Casey."

"Good night, Dan."

Half an hour later, Dan parked the FBI car in the basement of his building and rode the elevator to his apartment. He opened the door, turned off the television, let Nevermore loose, took off his jacket, poured himself a scotch, and sank into the familiar comfort of his leather easy chair.

Weariness permeated every inch of his body. The days were long, and he wasn't sleeping. Part of it was his concern over what OPR had in mind for him. He had done everything by the book when he set up the UCO, and now he was going to be labeled a cowboy because Blackman was covering his ass. But he was too tired to get mad about it tonight.

He sipped his scotch. There was more than fatigue here, or even the OPR thing. One of his agents had been killed. Sammy. Young, family man, his whole life ahead. Gone. Sammy was dead and it still hurt.

He used to talk out this sort of thing with Ellen. God, he missed her. When the agents on his squad went home to their families, Dan came home to Nevermore. Not that Nevermore was bad company. But there were limits.

Dan took another sip of scotch. As he set the glass back down on the table, he noticed the flashing red light on his answering machine. He toyed with the idea of ignoring the message. He didn't really feel like talking to anyone, and resented the intrusion. But curiosity got the better of him.

"The following new message was received at seven fifteen p.m." Nothing but background noise since the caller hung up without saying a word.

Dan took another sip of scotch. Probably just as well. He'd have been a lousy conversationalist. He shook his head and admitted tonight the gods wanted him to be alone.

Suddenly he reached into his briefcase, and fished around for a particular sheet of paper. Although it was a little late to be calling, he picked up the phone.

The phone hadn't rung one complete time when it was answered. "Hello?"

"Christy?"

"Yeah?"

"Dan Robertson. I hope it's not too late—"

"No, it's okay. Did you find out anything about Mary Lee?"

"We talked to the Teaneck PD, and they told us you tried to file a missing persons report, and why they couldn't take—"

"Damn it! Do you know where she is?"

"No, I'm sorry, I don't."

"Did you talk to David?"

"Yeah. He admits she isn't around, but denies knowing where she is."

"Did he finally file the damn missing persons report with the cops in Teaneck?"

"Not yet. I'm not sure he's going to."

"That fuckin' asshole! He's lying. I'm sure of it."

"That's what we thought. He didn't want to talk to us. Barely civil. All we got from him were one word answers."

"Bastard!"

"There was one thing he said that I wanted to ask you about."

"What's that?"

"We asked him if his wife had ever been missing before. He said 'yes.' Has she been?"

Silence at the other end. Finally he asked, "Christy?"

"I'm not sure about that," Christy said. "I don't think so, but hell, I could be wrong."

He'd hit a nerve. "Sounds like you know something," he said gently.

"What the fuck are you talking about? You think you've got me all figured out, don't you? Truth is, you don't know shit about me!"

"Hey, I'm not your enemy! I'm trying to help find your friend. If you know something that might help, tell me!"

"Are you finished?"

"Yeah," Dan said. "Have you got anything to tell me?"

She said nothing but Dan thought he heard her quietly sobbing.

"No," she said in words that seemed hard for her to get out. "But let me know if you learn anything. Okay?"

"I will. Are you going to be all right?"

"Yeah. I can take care of myself," she said, and then hung up.

Dan placed the receiver back on the hook.

"I hope you're right."

Thirteen

10:04 AM
January 6th
Manhattan, New York

David Wen's attitude, and the barely-veiled desperation of Christy Marino were still on Dan's mind. Something was going on that just didn't add up.

Jimmy Lee would understand the dynamics of a Chinese man's relationship with his wife, so Dan called him. "Hey Jimmy, we're working on a case where a Chinese woman may be involved in a fraud. When we tried to talk to her at home, her husband was visibly enraged and unloaded on her after we left. Now his wife has disappeared. What's going on, culturally, I mean?"

"Well, it's perfectly all right for a Chinese man to withhold information from his wife, but she can't do the same to him. So just keeping secrets would be part of the problem. And secrets about criminal activity, with loss of face to the family—he'd go nuclear."

"Any chance he might beat her, or worse?"

"Depends. Hard to say. In this country—"

"Would he send her away?"

"Maybe, but more likely he would want to keep an eye on her, and remind her what an embarrassment she was to his reputation."

"Thanks, Jimmy. That helps. Anything on the murders in the restaurant?"

"Not yet. I'll call you if there is anything."

"Thanks." Dan hung up. Could David Wen actually have killed his wife? Maybe. Christy said he had a violent temper. But if he did, where's her body? Dan would send Casey on a tour of the morgue. But in the meantime—

He phoned the Investigative Analysts. "Larry, Dan Robertson on the C-6 desk. How's the world treating you?"

"Same ol', same ol'. Find anything good in those rush workups we did for you on the Fontaine case?"

"I'd been meaning to give you a call," Dan said. "They were very useful."

"Good. Rumor has it that OPR is after you. You gonna be okay?"

Dan bristled. It was bad enough being under the microscope without having everyone know. Nothing he could do about it. As an organization, the FBI was terrific about keeping secrets, but internal information leaked like a sieve into the office scuttlebutt.

"Yes, OPR is after me, and yes, I'll be okay."

"Glad to hear that. It always seems like the jerks skate free and the good guys get nailed. What can I do for you?"

"Remember Mary Lee Wen, works for Fontaine?"

"Yeah. Lives in Jersey, right?"

"That's the one," Dan said. "She's missing. A woman who works with her is really concerned, and wanted to file a missing persons report. Teaneck PD won't take a report from anyone but family. Don't know if she tried to file one with the NYPD, but it wouldn't surprise me."

"What are you getting at?"

"Is it going to set off any alarm bells at the PD if you look for Mary Lee Wen in NYPD Central Records?"

"Not if I do it right. What do you need to know?"

"Has a missing persons report been filed on her?"

"Shouldn't be a problem to find out."

"Also, if one was filed, can we amend it so I get a call if anything shows up?"

"It can be done. It'll depend on the detective in the particular precinct. If he decides not to tell you, there's nothing we can do. Which precincts are involved?"

"Well, Fontaine is on Forty-seventh Street."

"Midtown North. We're probably okay there. Where else?"

"The friend lives in the Sunnyside section of Queens."

"Okay, that's the 104th. Could be a crapshoot. Some of the guys over there are all right, but not all of them," Fletcher said. "But the report goes into the computer in Central Records. We might get a cop who actually likes the FBI."

"Are there any?"

"A few," Fletcher said. "Anything else?"

"Can you check to see if anything has come up on her car?"

"Sure. Think something's happened to her?"

"I don't know. She just vanished. I don't know what to believe."

"I'll try to have something for you soon."

"Thanks."

Dan began to feel like he was finally doing something to find Mary Lee Wen.

Larry Fletcher got back to him that afternoon. Mary Lee Wen's car had been found on West Thirty-sixth Street, abandoned and vandalized. A forensic team found hair on the rain guard over the door, blood on the seat, and a .22 cartridge casing on the floor.

* * *

8:05 PM
January 6th
Queens, New York

Dan pulled to the curb in front of Christy Marino's apartment building, a bottle of cognac beside him. Why had he come? And why had he come without Casey? Good question. He'd been asking himself that since he'd left Manhattan. He'd promised Christy he'd share any news he had about Mary Lee Wen. Maybe that would win her trust and develop her as a witness. If the truth be known, Dan was beginning to care about Christy. He wasn't sure how he was going to deal with that.

He took the cognac and made his way to her apartment.

"Dan Robertson," he said on the intercom.

She buzzed him in. When he stepped off the elevator, she was standing in the hallway, and Dan followed her back into the apartment.

"Christy," he said, holding both her hands. "I don't know what it means, but Mary Lee's car was found on the west side of Manhattan."

"No! It can't be!" She sobbed, burying her face in his shoulder.

"They didn't find her," he said softly, "But the police found blood and part of a bullet in her car."

Christy cried and Dan poured the cognac. "Here, you need this."

"Thanks." She took a sip. "Who did this?"

"I didn't say she was killed. She's missing. Don't give up hope."

"Who the hell do you think you're talking to? She disappears. Her car turns up nowhere near where she works or lives. Blood and part of a bullet in it. Can you honestly tell me that you think she's alive?"

Dan stared into his glass of cognac. "No, I can't."

Christy covered her face with her hands and sobbed.

"Are you going to be okay?"

She raised her head. "It doesn't matter."

"What do you mean?"

"What the hell are you anyway, some kind of a Boy Scout? Still trying to make things right? Can't you get it straight? Nothing matters!"

Dan sat quietly for a moment not really knowing what to say. "Do you think David Wen might have killed her?"

"I don't know, how the hell am I supposed to know? What I know is that she didn't deserve to die. She was a sweet, loving woman."

Dan struggled to find the right words. He cared about her, but still had a job to do.

"I don't want to leave it like this," he said. "I'm worried about leaving you alone. We'll find out who killed Mary Lee. I'll share with you anything we learn about what happened. I'll tell you everything. But in return, I want something."

"What?"

"Tell me everything you know about what's happening at Fontaine. You knew Mary Lee would never cooperate, and you knew your testimony might have landed her in prison. So you refused to help us in order to protect her. I admire you for that. But you can't help her anymore. The only one you can help is yourself. If you don't, nobody will be there for you. I'll help you, but only if you'll help me."

Christy was silent for a long time, staring into her drink with red-rimmed eyes. "You worthless bastard," she said at last. "You came here with news about Mary Lee, but instead of being a man about it and just telling me, you tried to use it to manipulate me into becoming a snitch!"

"I told you, I'm willing to help you—"

"You lousy shit! Get the hell out of my apartment."

Dan set down his glass and walked out the door. He heard Christy sobbing as the door closed.

As Dan drove back into Manhattan, he thought about their exchange. Why, after he had insinuated himself into her grief, did he try to turn her into an informant? He felt bad for her. Yet, if she refused to cooperate, she might go to prison. That's a laugh. If she refused to cooperate, the case would die, and nobody would go to prison. She was smart enough to have figured that out. Well, it was a good shot. If it worked out, all the better. If not, it simplified his feelings towards her.

The last of the Friday night commute traffic was leaving the city—maybe to a weekend place or a ski trip to Vermont. He remembered how he used to look forward to weekends. He and Ellen would fill every minute with fun, laughter, and love. Now he dreaded weekends. The time away from work confronted him with the loneliness he tried to avoid all week. The high points of his weekend were to do laundry, watch football, rent videotapes, and talk to Nevermore. He needed to get a life.

Fourteen

10:30 AM
January 8th
Queens, New York

Christy parked her BMW at the curb, opened the trunk, and gathered two shopping bags of presents, wrapped in Christmas paper. Beautifully dressed, hair and makeup done perfectly, draped in her mink coat, she walked up the sidewalk of the familiar working-class house in Queens. She rang the doorbell and waited, rocking slightly from foot to foot. The living room curtains parted slightly. Finally the door opened, and a woman in her sixties, dressed in black, gray hair, slightly bent by osteoporosis, stood in the doorway.

"Hi, Mamma," Christy said with a forced smile.

"So now I'm your Mamma? Last time it was 'mind your own business.'"

"I know it's a little late, but Merry Christmas, Mamma! I have some presents . . . for . . . you."

But her mother had turned and walked away from the door.

Christy followed her into the house and set the bags of presents on the living room floor. She draped her coat over the sofa, and followed her mother into the kitchen. Maria Marino stood at the stove, her back to her daughter.

Christy walked over and peered over her shoulder. "Mmmm. Smells great! What are you cooking, Mamma?"

"What you should be cooking, if you had a family of your own."

Christy turned and walked to the kitchen table where, for the first twenty years of her life, she had eaten meals with her mother and father. She sat down and gently touched the tabletop with her fingers, remembering.

Louis Marino appeared in the doorway. "Who was at the door?" Then he saw Christy and disgustedly said, "Oh, it's you."

Christy forced a smile, sprang to her feet and walked across the room to her father. "Merry Christmas, Papa!"

She tried to throw her arms around him and give him a kiss.

"What do you want?" he said as he pushed her away.

She glanced back and forth from her mother to her father. "I just thought, maybe . . . maybe today we could be a family again." Christy started to cry. "Please, Mamma . . . Papa . . . I . . . I need you."

"So now you want to have a family? So now you need us? Well, maybe we don't need you. Really . . .

Merry Christmas, Mamma!" Maria turned her back on Christy, faced the stove and resumed stirring the pot.

Christy burst into a flood of tears and ran from the kitchen, her father following behind her. She grabbed her coat and purse, and headed for the front door.

"Christy?" her father called to her at the last minute.

She turned to him, hopeful.

"I think it's better if you don't come again."

She gathered herself up. "Sure, Papa. It doesn't matter any more."

She turned and ran out the front door, determined not to let her father see her pain.

Fifteen

10:30 AM
January 8th
Queens, New York

Dan sat in Arby's restaurant with Detectives Lou Stevenson and Sam Boston of the Teaneck PD.

"It took us an hour and a half to get here," Boston said, shaking his head. "I don't understand why anybody would commute into Manhattan."

"Because they need the job," Dan said. "I avoid it by living here, but it's expensive. What was Wen's reaction to his wife's car being located?"

"What struck me the most," Stevenson said, "was his complete lack of emotional response when we told him his wife might have been killed."

"He calmly told us her blood type, and let us take hair samples from her brush," Boston said. "When we left, he simply thanked us for telling him, and said that whenever the NYPD released her car, he'd make arrangements to have it towed back to New Jersey."

"Do you consider him a suspect?" Dan asked.

"We don't have anything to go on at this point, but we've got a bad feeling he might have done it," Stevenson said. "Would you find out everything the FBI knows about him?"

"Sure. I'll check on it later today."

"And just so you're not blind-sided, we're asking the detectives in the Tenth Precinct to give us whatever the NYPD has on him."

"That's fine," Dan said. "Is there anything in particular that makes him a good suspect?"

"He just doesn't act like a bereaved husband," Boston said.

"So how does Mary Lee Wen figure into your fraud investigation?" Boston asked.

Dan explained factoring accounts receivable, and how Mike Westerfield thought Schwartz might be ripping off MBT Factors. He told the detectives how he and Casey had tried to talk both Mary Lee Wen and Christy Marino into cooperating, but that without their help the case would probably have to be closed down.

"It sounds like there's barely a crime there," Stevenson said.

"I know he's pulling something," Dan said. "I'm just not sure what. That's why we need Marino. If she doesn't come around, we're going to have to let this case die."

"Okay, so help us out on our case. We're here to talk to Mary Lee Wen's employer. What can you tell us about this guy who owns Fontaine Diamonds?" Stevenson asked.

"Name's Bernie Schwartz. He and his wife Sarah own Fontaine." Dan sipped his coffee. "We don't know a whole lot about him. A couple of insurance scams, and the usual customer complaints. Nothing out of the ordinary for a diamond merchant. With the exceptions of Marino and Wen, he has a bunch of relatives working for him."

Stevenson looked at his wristwatch. "Let's get it done."

As they headed to Fontaine they noticed the pedestrian traffic had picked up on Forty-seventh Street. They maneuvered around people and passed men standing on the sidewalk making diamond sales.

"Did you see that?" Boston twisted his head around to watch.

"See it every day," Dan said. "A risky way of doing business, but it sure cuts down on the overhead."

Dan deftly wove among other pedestrians, sidestepping, speeding up, and slowing down. Boston and Stevenson tried to walk in a straight line, but found themselves having to stop in front of people as each decided which way to zig or zag. Dan remembered how long it took him to get his Manhattan legs. "This is it," Dan said as they stopped in front of Fontaine. "Offices are on the second floor, showroom on the first. You guys take the lead, I'll just hang back and listen."

"Fine by me," Stevenson pulled open the door and walked in.

Two men and a woman, standing in the showroom, looked up. "May I help you?" one of the men said.

Stevenson pulled out his badge. "Teaneck Police Department. Need to talk to Mr. Schwartz."

The employees looked at each other. One of them said, "He's not here. Won't you come back another time?"

Both Boston and Stevenson knew he was lying. Before they could respond, they saw a man reach the bottom of the stairs and heard someone above him yell,

"Hey Bernie! Wait a minute." A second man descended the stairs and the two talked.

"Looks like Mr. Schwartz has returned," Stevenson said.

"Must have been mistaken," the man said.

Schwartz looked at the Detectives, finished his conversation, then walked across the showroom, sizing up the strangers. His clothes were rumpled and too tight, and he hadn't shaved.

"You Bernie Schwartz?" Boston asked.

"Who the fuck wants to know?" Schwartz said defiantly.

Boston flipped open his badge. "Teaneck PD."

Schwartz looked at each of the three men, taking their measure. "I was just leaving for a meeting. Come back tomorrow."

"We're busy tomorrow," Stevenson said. "Why don't you give us five minutes, and show up a little late for your meeting?"

"Or, if that doesn't work for you, we'll call some NYPD Detectives to join us. I'm sure they'd be delighted for you to join them in a little ride to the Precinct Station House."

Schwartz stared at the detectives and Dan standing their ground and effectively blocking his path to the door.

"Shit!" Schwartz mopped his forehead with his handkerchief. "What the fuck do you want?"

"We want to ask you a few questions about Mary Lee Wen," Boston said. "Let's go back upstairs to your office."

Schwartz turned around and saw his employees watching the exchange. Dan spotted Christy. Neither gave any hint of recognition.

"Get back to work you assholes!" Schwartz glared at them, then turned to the investigators. "Five minutes. No more!"

Dan and the detectives gave each other sly, barely perceptible smiles as they followed Schwartz upstairs. His office at the end of the hall had a large window that looked out on Forty-seventh Street. The window was grimy, and a Venetian blind was hanging from one strap. The top of Schwartz's desk was cluttered with invoices, computer printouts, telephone messages and letters. His ashtray overflowed with cigarette butts. Files were stacked on chairs, coats tossed on the floor, along with remains of the last month's take-out meals.

Schwartz sat behind the desk and made no effort to find chairs for anyone else. He wiped his sweaty palms and face with his handkerchief. There were already dark stains around his armpits, and his pungent body odor permeated the whole office.

"Does Mary Lee Wen work for you?" Stevenson asked.

"Yeah."

"Is she here today?" Boston said.

"Nah."

"When's the last time you saw her?" Stevenson asked.

"I fuckin' can't remember. I ain't seen the Chink for a few days, and when you talk to her, tell her I'm gettin' real fuckin' pissed off about it," Schwartz said nonchalantly as he examined his fingernail and the ear wax lodged under it.

"Are you aware she's missing?"

"No shit? Maybe that's why she ain't fuckin' here."

"Can you think of any reason someone might want to harm her?"

"Does not showing up for work count?" Schwartz looked at his wristwatch. "Two more minutes and I'm fuckin' outta here."

"Are you aware of any personal problems Mrs. Wen might have had?" Boston asked.

"Nah. Anything else?" Schwartz stood up and began to walk to the door.

"Mr. Schwartz, the five minutes aren't up," Stevenson said.

"It'll be up by the time we get to the fuckin' door," Schwartz said as he walked past the investigators into the hall.

"Is there anything in particular that Mrs. Wen was working on that might bear on her disappearance?" Dan asked. He immediately got looks from Boston and Stevenson, but only shrugged his shoulders in response.

Schwartz hesitated in his stride for just a second, then continued walking down the hallway. "Nah. I can't think of anything." Schwartz reached the top of the stairs.

"Would you call us if you hear anything about her?" Boston asked as they descended the stairs.

"Whatever. Leave your card." Schwartz headed for the door.

"Did you know Mrs. Wen's car was found on the west side of Manhattan near the Hudson River?" Stevenson asked.

"No shit?" Schwartz had his hand on the door. "Why the fuck she was parking over there?" Schwartz shrugged, walked out the door, and wiped the perspiration from his face as he walked down the street.

Boston wrote Stevenson's name on his business card and handed it to one of the employees. The detectives and Dan walked out and stood watching Schwartz look over his shoulder at them as he walked away.

"If he didn't smell so bad, I could be coaxed into strangling him." Boston said.

"You'd be doing the world a favor, Sam," Stevenson said.

"If you looked up the word 'asshole' in the dictionary, you'd find a picture of Schwartz," Boston said. "What a piece of work!"

"I don't care how you do it, Robertson," Stevenson said. "But find a way to nail that guy."

The men walked to the parking garage to retrieve their cars. While they were waiting, Dan asked, "Think he knows anything?"

Boston was poking a penny on the ground with the toe of his shoe. "Maybe. I've seen murderers as calm as can be, and others who were nervous as a cat. This guy pretends he could care less."

Are you saying you think Schwartz could have murdered her?"

"I don't know. I guess I look at everybody as a suspect."

"And you think he pretends to care less?"

"Yeah, could be," Stevenson said. "There are people who could care less about what happens to others, but Schwartz's pretense is a cover-up—it's a ploy."

"What makes you say that?" Dan asked.

"Gut feeling," Stevenson said. "What do you think, Sam?"

"I think he knows something, but being apathetic is one way to reassure himself."

The first attendant arrived with the detectives' car, followed immediately by another in Dan's. As the men started to get in to drive away, Dan turned to Boston. "Thanks for letting me tag along. I'll call you later with whatever the FBI's got on Wen."

Dan reviewed his impressions of Schwartz as he drove back to the FBI office. He didn't like Schwartz, but being unlikable didn't make him a killer. Wen's indifference was a lot harder to explain away. He could easily see Schwartz doing the fraud, but David Wen had the feel of a killer.

Sixteen

1:00 PM
January 8th
Manhattan, New York

Dan returned to the office, called Larry Fletcher, and asked the Investigative Analyst to check FBI files for David Wen. Fletcher called back and said there was nothing. Dan relayed that to Sam Boston, and spent the rest of the afternoon returning phone calls and handling the mountain of mail that had accumulated over the course of the day. He was still lost in it when he heard a voice from his doorway.

"Miss Caradine said you had an update on the Fontaine case," Thomas said. "What's happened?"

"Nothing much." Dan told Thomas about the repeated attempts to gain Christy Marino's cooperation, the disappearance of Mary Lee Wen, the discovery of her car, the Teaneck PD suspicions that David Wen might have killed her, and the interview of Bernie Schwartz.

"Sounds like you've remembered how to investigate," Thomas said. "Don't waste anymore time on it. The case is going nowhere. Shut it down and call Westerfield."

"It's too bad. I enjoyed working the case, even if it didn't go anywhere. Heard anymore from OPR?"

"Nothing. I'm not sure which way it'll go. These things usually take a couple of months before everybody can agree. Even then, you have to wait until the Director signs off on it." Thomas stood, and paused in the doorway. "Don't forget to call Westerfield."

"Got it covered." After Thomas left, Dan looked at the telephone and tried to decide whether to go ahead and get it out of the way, or wait until morning. He glanced at his watch. 6:30 P.M. Westerfield had probably already left, so he decided to hold off. Dan was almost out the door when his phone rang.

He vacillated a moment, then walked back into his office. "Robertson."

At first the caller said nothing. Dan waited.

"It's me," came a woman's voice, so low in volume, he had to strain to hear. "Dan?"

"Christy?" He sat back down. "Are you all right?"

"I'm scared."

"Of what?"

"Of the same thing happening to me that happened to Mary Lee."

"What do you think happened to her? Do you know?"

"I don't know anything for sure."

"Who do you think might have hurt her?" Dan asked.

"Maybe David, or . . ."

"That's what the Teaneck PD thinks too. Maybe they'll put enough together for an arrest." Dan tried to sound reassuring but wasn't sure he was succeeding.

She hesitated. "I'm ready to tell you what's going on at Fontaine, but you have to promise to help me."

His mind raced. This dead case was coming back to life. It gave him a rush that he hadn't felt in years. He needed to concentrate on what she was saying. "How can I help you?"

"Don't let anything happen to me," she said. "I never wanted to fuckin' rely on anybody my whole life, but something tells me I can trust you. It's the only damn thing I want."

"Don't worry, nobody's going to hurt you. I'll keep you safe, I promise. If you're going to help us, we'd better have an attorney cut a deal for you. I'm not sure how safe you'd be in jail."

"I won't go to jail. Please Dan, help me." She began to cry.

Dan wasn't sure what to say. He wanted to drive to Queens and reassure her in person, but thought better of it. He could make his reassurances over the phone, but that struck him as detached and impersonal. Besides, he was afraid he'd promised more than he could realistically guarantee. Keeping a witness alive was an inexact science at best. There was the witness protection plan, but you couldn't offer that until the witness had testified in grand jury or open court. But . . . as far as he knew, Wen didn't have any reason to kill her. And neither did Schwartz, as long as he didn't know she was talking to the FBI. Still, should he take the chance—?

"I think you'd be safer in a hotel."

"I don't want to go to no hotel." A trace of her bravado returned.

That told Dan what he needed to know. She didn't feel so threatened that she needed to hide out. "Okay, continue to go to work as usual, but let's meet and talk tomorrow. Okay?"

"Yeah, but only if you're there."

"There's going to be other people there too. Casey Brody, and the Assistant U. S. Attorney, and we need your lawyer."

"Okay. But you've got to be there." It sounded like she realized what she was committing to.

"I'll be there."

"Call me tomorrow after work. I'll set up everything, and tell you where to come." Dan sensed she was reluctant to hang up. "I'll be waiting for your call. If you need to talk, call me. And Christy?"

"Yeah."

"You made the right decision."

"I hope so."

"I know so. I'll talk to you tomorrow."

He sat at his desk for a moment and tried to imagine how much courage it took for her to call. He wouldn't let her down.

* * *

"Got a call from Christy Marino last night. She's ready to cooperate," Dan said as Casey arrived the next morning.

Casey punched a fist into the air and gave a whoop, the last thing that Dan expected to see from an accountant. "What do you think turned her around?"

"Probably the disappearance of Mary Lee Wen. Christy fears she's dead, and that the same thing might happen to her. Who would have the motive?"

"Bernie Schwartz . . ."

"Schwartz doesn't know either one talked to us," Dan said.

"Both Marino and Wen worked for Dante's Designs. Could it be something that dates back to then?"

"If so, it's been a long time coming. Still, would you see if anyone connected to that case was just released from prison?"

"Sure. They're friends, and twice involved in shady dealings. If Christy was leading Wen into a life of crime, could David Wen be angry enough to kill Marino too?"

"It's possible. But at this point neither woman has been charged with a crime. Seems a little premature for him to do something like that."

"Not if he knew more about their criminal involvement than we do," Casey said. "Somehow I can't see Mary Lee Wen withholding information from her husband."

"But she did, didn't she? And Jimmy Lee says the anger we saw was as much about keeping secrets as about losing face. Christy hasn't been keeping secrets from anyone."

"Okay, I'll buy that. I'm dying to hear what she has to say," Casey said. "I consider myself a pretty good white-collar crime investigator, but this one has given me fits."

"This is what we need to do. Get an Assistant U.S. Attorney assigned to this case. Ask their opinion on getting a public defender for her. If the answer is yes, set that up. Reserve the small conference room for this afternoon. I hope we're not setting ourselves up for embarrassment."

"How?"

"If she gets cold feet and doesn't show up, I'd hate to be left turning slowly in the wind."

"I see." Casey headed for the door.

"I'll brief Thomas," Dan said. "Let's hold off calling Westerfield until we know we have something. I don't want to get him all excited, only to tell him later that it didn't pan out. Another day shouldn't make any difference."

Dan wondered how Christy was dealing with her decision. He had heard what it was like to work for a boss you were going to testify against. You knew the boss had no idea of what you were doing, but at the same time, everything you said or did made you think that your secret was out. But Christy was tough. She'd be all right. For the most part, white-collar criminals didn't resort to violence. For their frauds, they preferred using a pen rather than a gun. But Dan hadn't convinced himself that there was nothing to worry about.

Seventeen

6:00 PM
January 9th
Manhattan, New York

Again Dan glanced at his wristwatch. It was almost 6:00 P.M. "She should be here."

"We know."

He looked around the small conference room and saw the others were making use of their time while they waited. AUSA Leonard Weinstein was reviewing a grand jury transcript. In the corner, Public Defender's Office attorney Elizabeth McMillan was on the telephone in a hushed conversation. Dan knew Casey was downstairs at the garage entrance where she would ensure Christy Marino's admission to the basement parking area and accompany her to the twenty-eighth floor.

He answered his cell phone.

"Dan, the package is here."

"The audience awaits."

A few minutes later, the door to the conference room opened and in walked Christy Marino. When she saw Dan, she allowed herself to exhale. Her gaze shifted tentatively to Weinstein then to McMillan.

"Hello, Miss Marino. It's nice to meet you. I'm Len Weinstein from the U.S. Attorney's Office." He gave her a dead fish handshake.

"Hi," Christy said to the woman.

"I'm Beth McMillan from the Public Defender's Office. Thanks for coming." She shook Christy's hand with both of hers. "Don't worry. Everything's going to work out just fine."

"I hope so."

"Ms. Marino, why don't you take a seat at the end of the table," Weinstein motioned to a chair, "and Beth and I will sit on either side of you."

"No. I'll sit on the side of the table with Dan beside me," Marino said. "If Beth wants to sit on the other side, its okay."

Weinstein shot a look at Dan, but had once again smiled by the time his gaze shifted back to Christy. "Of course. The most important thing is that you're comfortable with the others."

"I trust Dan. I don't know either of you."

Dan suppressed a smile as he helped her out of her coat. Her usual attire of a short skirt, tight sweater and spike heels didn't escape the notice of anyone in the room, and it seemed to annoy Casey.

Weinstein kept smiling. "If I may, just so we're all clear about the reason you are meeting with us today, according to Agent Brody, you've decided to assist the government in their prosecution of individuals in the employ of Fontaine Diamonds for the bank fraud they are committing against MBT Factors, a wholly-owned subsidiary of Manhattan Bank & Trust. Is that correct, Miss Marino?"

"If I may," McMillan said, flashing Weinstein a plastic smile. "You must appreciate that I'll need to meet with Miss Marino in private before I'm able to place a proffer before you which outlines what my client is prepared—"

"Stop it!" Marino said. "You're fighting over me like two dogs over a scrap of meat. I told Dan I'd tell you what I know, but I ain't going to no damn jail. And you can't let anything happen to me. If you won't do that, then I'm fuckin' outta here."

The room got quiet. Dan patted Christy's forearm.

Weinstein spoke first. "I think we all understand why you're here today, Miss Marino. If I offended you, please accept my apologies. The government would never consider exploiting the information you have in your possession without providing you with some manner of legal benefit for imparting it. That goes without saying."

"I'd feel better if you said it."

McMillan, Dan and Casey tried to stifle their laughter.

"Len, I'd like to make a suggestion," McMillan said.

Christy leaned over to whisper in Dan's ear. "Listen. I can't work with these fuckin' creeps. That Weinstein already wants to jail me for not being a good little girl. So let them work out the details—"

"Excuse me, Miss Marino," McMillan said. "I would rather you wouldn't talk to the FBI without me present."

"Yeah, sure," Christy said, then kept whispering. "I just want to deal with you and maybe Casey. Okay, Dan?"

"Okay." Dan turned to the lawyers. "What Christy—Miss Marino wants you to know is that she's prepared to tell us what she knows about Fontaine. What she wants in return is the government's stipulation that she doesn't go to jail. She says the AUSA and Ms. McMillan can work out the details in an agreement, but that she wants me and Casey to be the ones to whom she tells everything." Dan turned back to Christy. "Is what I just said to these people what you wanted me to say?"

"Close enough."

"I'm not comfortable with that," McMillan said.

"Well, get comfortable with it," Christy said, "'cause that's how it's gonna be."

Weinstein removed his glasses, lowered his head, and rubbed his eyes with the thumb and forefinger. "May I make a suggestion?"

The others looked at him.

"Beth, take fifteen minutes alone with Ms Marino. Get the gist of what she can provide. Tell the rest of us the general outline. If it sounds adequate to everyone, let's put together a one-page agreement, which outlines what each of us will do. We can write it out by hand and sign it. Beginning tomorrow, Miss Marino can be debriefed in detail about the fraud at Fontaine. By whomever she wants. What do you say?"

"Sounds reasonable."

Dan led McMillan and Christy to the conference room, then rejoined Weinstein and Casey.

As he walked back into the first conference room, Dan saw Weinstein glaring at him. "Is something wrong, Len?"

"What the hell do you think you're doing?"

"What do you mean?"

"Casey told me this case finally broke, and you show up with a cooperating witness who doesn't want to talk to anybody but you. Are you grandstanding to make yourself look good, or just sleeping with her?"

"Knock it off!" Dan shouted back, his face flushed in anger. "You're wrong on both counts. She phoned me and said she wanted to cooperate just when I was ready to pull the plug on the case. I had no idea she was going to make these demands."

Dan took a deep breath. It was stupid to do battle with a prosecutor over how a case was worked, and given everything else he had hanging over him at the moment, he didn't need extra aggravation. He paused until he could control his voice. "Doesn't it make sense to have Casey and me do the interview? After all, we do know everything about the case."

Dan glanced at Casey who remained silent. He then looked back at Weinstein. Quiet hung in the room while Dan waited out Weinstein's move in this stupid game of chicken.

"Okay, you and Casey find out what she has to offer," Weinstein said, "But if she can't provide something substantial right away, I'm going to immediately decline prosecution and close this case. Agreed?"

Dan bristled at an AUSA telling him how to investigate. But he remembered he was trying to end the disagreement, not prolong it, so he gave a slight nod. "Agreed."

Christy and McMillan returned and took a seat. Christy didn't make eye contact with anyone. She stared at the table in front of her.

"Miss Marino is in a position to provide the government with an overview and details of the fraud by individuals at Fontaine Diamonds against MBT Factors," McMillan said. "She can provide information about the use of the fraudulently obtained funds, who is responsible, how it was accomplished, why it was so difficult to uncover, and how the government can prove it."

Dan glanced at Weinstein and Casey. It was better than they'd hoped for.

"In return for her testimony before a federal grand jury and in trial," McMillan said, "Miss Marino will be given immunity from prosecution in this matter and enters the witness protection program."

"Provided Miss Marino does, in fact, furnish what has been proffered," Weinstein said, "as well as testify before both bodies, the government would certainly entertain providing her with use immunity and place her in the program."

Christy exhaled and closed her eyes in relief.

"However," Weinstein said, "should Miss Marino fail to provide full and complete information concerning the fraud by individuals at Fontaine and/or fail to provide truthful and complete testimony before a grand jury or in open court, the immunity and protection will be withdrawn, and she will become a target of prosecution in this matter." Weinstein looked directly at Christy. "Is that understood and agreed to?"

McMillan looked over at Christy who nodded.

"Yes, Len," McMillan said. "Understood, and agreed to."

While Weinstein and McMillan wrote out the agreement, Dan turned to Christy. "Is there anything we can get for you?"

"Yeah. Black coffee."

Dan started to stand, but Casey put a hand on his shoulder. "That's okay, Dan. I'll get it."

Marino reached for her purse and pulled out a pack of cigarettes and a lighter. Dan started to tell her the federal office building was non-smoking but thought better of it. He saw her hands shaking as she tried to light the cigarette, so he wrapped his hands around hers to steady them. She looked at him in surprise as he let his hands stay around hers a moment longer than necessary. He pulled his hands away, embarrassed she had noticed.

Casey returned with the coffee and Christy sipped it between drags on her cigarette.

The short agreement was finished, signed, and witnessed. Dan and Casey would begin debriefing Christy on the afternoon of the following day. Weinstein, McMillan and Casey left for home, and Dan accompanied Christy down the elevator to the parking garage.

"Where'd you park?" he asked.

"Over there," pointing across the cavernous space.

Dan saw the usual collection of nondescript FBI sedans, painted in somber colors. Nothing matched Christy's style. "Which one?"

"On the other side of that white Taurus."

As they rounded the front of the Ford, he saw the navy blue BMW coupe. "Nice set of wheels."

"Thanks," Marino said as she fished for her keys in her purse. She unlocked the door, tossed her purse on the front passenger seat, then turned towards Dan. "I'm still frightened. Is everything going to be okay?"

Dan leaned his elbow on the top of the door and raised her chin up to the point where they looked each other in the eye. "It's all going to work out. I won't let anything happen to you."

She searched his face for any trace of doubt, and found none. Then she turned and pulled a large envelope out of the car and handed it to him.

"What's this?"

"Everything I know about what's going on at Fontaine, and copies of some of the records and bank accounts. In case anything happens to me . . . I'd feel better knowing you have them." Tears welled up in her eyes as she stood on her tiptoes and kissed his cheek.

Dan watched her car pull away and wondered what prompted her to do that. He decided to call it a day, returned for his briefcase and coat, and went home. Any hope for an early spring would have to wait because snow had begun to fall on New York.

* * *

After his usual ritual with Nevermore, he sat in front of the television and ate a microwaved dinner while Nevermore had some grapes. He realized how tired he was when he noticed that Leno was on and Nevermore had taken himself back to his cage. Dan turned off the television, peeled off his clothes, and climbed into bed. Effortlessly he fell asleep.

He was back in his California house watching helplessly as the ski-masked man ascended the stairs, gun in hand, then stood in the doorway of the bedroom. And there was Ellen, asleep in the moonlit bed. Dan tried to turn away, but couldn't. And then he was next to her, and she was on the floor, soaked in blood. He picked up her wrist and felt for a pulse.

She opened her eyes, and he woke up screaming.

He sat up in bed, soaked with perspiration.

"Why can't I get rid of that dream?" he shouted, knowing his neighbors must have heard.

The clock said 4:18 A.M. Dan knew he'd never get back to sleep. He got out of bed, slipped into his robe, and put on a pot of coffee. He turned on the lights, uncovered and opened Nevermore's cage, pulled out the envelope that Christy had given him, and began to read her handwritten narrative. He had almost finished when the smell of coffee reminded him that he needed a cup. He poured one and returned to the documents.

"Cocktail time!" Nevermore shouted from atop his cage.

"Shut up, Nevermore. I'm trying to concentrate."

Nevermore slunk back into his cage and tucked his head under his wing. Deciding sleep was a lost cause, Dan returned to his review of the narrative and the documents. After two more cups of coffee, he finished. It was 5:25 A.M.

Casey had pegged it—it was a Ponzi scheme. Fontaine had set up phony corporations and bank accounts for non-existent suppliers and customers. With the MBT Factors money, they made payments to phony suppliers, then moved the money into the phony customers' accounts, and paid back MBT Factors. But since they were only getting eighty-five percent of the phony invoice amounts back from MBT Factors, their sales had to dramatically increase to make up the difference. It was simple and elegant.

"Schwartz, I'm going to nail you," Dan vowed.

He chuckled. Over the years, he'd brought down some serious criminals—hit men, mob bosses who terrorized entire neighborhoods, major drug smugglers. Yet he knew he would get the same satisfaction over closing down one minor league jerk engaging in bank fraud.

Elated, he headed to the bathroom for a shower and a shave to get a head start on the day.

Eighteen

5:15 PM
January 10th
Manhattan, New York

Christy Marino left Fontaine, and began walking to the lot where she parked her car. She hadn't slept well, troubled by the meeting with the FBI. Remembering the alternative was going to prison, she felt better about it. Still apprehensive about cooperating, Christy knew there was no turning back.

* * *

The sun reflected off the windshield of the silver van as it emerged from the ramp onto the rooftop parking lot. The snow had melted, and cars were parked in their usual places. Driving around the double row of cars in the middle of the parking lot, he glanced ahead to where she always parked. He smiled wickedly when he saw her car, and then maneuvered the silver van into a space on the right side of it. He lowered the driver's side window, and listened for sounds of anyone else on the rooftop. He heard nothing.

* * *

Christy walked past the lot where Mary Lee Wen always parked and looked for Mary Lee's car. A lump formed in her throat, and tears stung her eyes. She continued to walk the five blocks to her own parking lot, aware of the hundreds of people around her, heading home to their families. She was envious.

* * *

The man quietly opened the driver's door and moved to the rear of the van. He looked right and left, scouring the parking lot for any sign of movement. He saw nothing. He quickly stepped around the rear of the car, did something, then returned, opened the door of the van, and slid behind the steering wheel. He adjusted both side rearview mirrors to provide him with an improved view of the ramp that people used to reach the rooftop lot.

* * *

Marino stood on the corner of Forty-sixth Street and Seventh Avenue, waiting for the light to change. She wondered if Dan had looked over the information in the envelope she'd given him. She was sure he had. That would make talking about Fontaine easier when she reached the FBI office. The light changed and she crossed Seventh Avenue.

* * *

The air was chilly, yet beads of perspiration formed on the man's upper lip. He wiped it with the sleeve of his jacket. He pulled the pistol out of his waistband, touched the magazine release button, and the bullet clip dropped out of the handgrip of the gun. Reassuring himself that it was fully loaded, he shoved it back into the pistol, hearing it click into place. With his right thumb he flipped off the safety. Holding the pistol in his right hand, with the thumb and first finger of his left hand he pulled back the slide, then released it. The pistol was now cocked, the first bullet chambered in the barrel, ready to be fired. Setting the gun on his lap, he looked in the rearview mirrors on both sides of the van.

* * *

Christy glanced up and down Broadway and saw the theaters that housed the shows she had never seen, and didn't care about. They weren't important. She asked herself what was important to her now. Sadly, she could think of nothing. She'd enjoyed her travel to Europe. Rome was nice, and she liked London. It seemed so long ago.

* * *

The man heard the noise of high heels as someone walked across the parking lot. In the mirrors he saw a woman walking towards the van. The man gripped the gun in his right hand and held it below the window, the barrel pointing toward the car. From behind the woman, he heard a man call out, and the woman turned and laughed. When the two of them reached one another, the man slipped his arm around her waist and they talked as they walked. He saw them get into a Ford Mustang in the center isle. Its engine started, and the car pulled away.

* * *

Christy crossed Eighth Avenue. She bought a warm pretzel and a cup of coffee from a street vendor. She ate part of the pretzel, then tossed the rest into a garbage can. Again, she began walking west along Forty-sixth Street. In the shadows of the concrete jungle, she felt a chill, so she threw away the coffee cup, pulled the coat around her, and put her hands into her coat pockets.

* * *

After hearing more footsteps, the man searched the rearview mirror to see who was coming up the ramp. He saw a man in a suit who got into a small white foreign car. The engine started, and the car disappeared down the ramp. Any minute now.

* * *

Christy crossed Ninth Avenue, and glanced at her watch. It was 5:30 P.M. She walked a little further to Tenth Avenue, and turned the corner. She began walking up the ramp to the rooftop parking lot, and gave a wave to the parking attendant in his booth between the up and down ramps. As she walked, the noise of her high heeled shoes echoed off the concrete walls and ceiling. She reached the top of the ramp. As she stepped into the bright sunlight shining on the rooftop, she put on her sunglasses. That morning, Christy had parked her car against the low wall furthest from the entrance, to keep other cars' doors from denting the sides of her car. As she walked a winding path between the middle two rows of cars, she saw a silver van parked close to the right side of her car. "Damn you!" she cursed, hoping it hadn't damaged her car.

* * *

The man had heard the sound of high-heeled shoes as it echoed up the ramp. He wiped the perspiration from his forehead and upper lip with the back of his coat sleeve. He scoured the images reflected in the rearview mirrors. It looked like her. She was slowly walking in his direction. He gripped the gun tightly in his right hand. She was between cars in the middle rows, and was getting closer. His eyes dilated. His breathing became rapid and shallow. His pulse sped up as adrenaline poured into his blood. She was behind the van, walking toward the car.

* * *

Christy fished the BMW key out of her purse. She stepped sideways between her car, and the Ford to the left of it, and tried to slip her key into the lock. It wouldn't go in. She looked at the key, thinking maybe she selected the trunk key by mistake. No, it was the right key. She tried again, but it wouldn't go in. A look of confusion crossed her face as she tried to understand what was wrong. Then she stepped to the rear of the car and looked at the license plate and made sure it was hers. She tried again to slip the key into the lock. It still wouldn't go in. She shook her head and walked to the passenger side of her car and was relieved to find the key slipped into the lock.

* * *

The man's left hand reached down for the inside door handle of the van. He saw her confusion, and pressed his back into the seat so she couldn't see him. He held his breath. He knew if she looked at the reflection in the BMW's window, she would have seen the gun barrel rise in the van's open window. The man's face filled the rest of the space above the gun. As he held his right arm stretched across his chest, he rested the barrel of the gun on his left forearm. The windowsill steadied the gun, and he pointed it at the back of her head. His right index finger slowly squeezed the trigger.

"Puft!"

Christy Marino heard nothing as the bullet penetrated her skull and everything went black. Her legs buckled. She was dead before she hit the ground.

The man quickly opened the door of the van. He stood, stuck the gun in his belt, and reached under both of her arms, and picked up her lifeless body, becoming covered with blood in the process. He dragged her inert body around the front of the silver van, and paused as he opened the right side sliding door with his left hand. He was shoving the upper part of her body into the van when he heard the first shout.

"Hey you! What the hell you think you're doing?"

The man turned and saw someone running toward him. "Shit!" He dropped Christy. When he looked up again, he saw a second man running toward him.

"Stop right there!"

And then he saw a third man. He couldn't believe it. He had just looked in the direction of the ramp, and saw no one. Where the hell had these guys come from, and what had they seen? He left Christy's bloody body, half in, and half out of the van. He pulled out the pistol, and held it out of sight behind his right leg. Then he ran straight towards the three men who were running towards him. The distance between the men vanished, as the first man came face to face with him.

The look of anger on the first man's face gave way to panic, as the gun appeared a few inches in front of his face.

"Puft!" Flames and lead spat out of the gun barrel. He fell to the ground, killed by a single bullet to the face.

As the man fell, the killer saw the second Good Samaritan who appeared momentarily confused as to what had happened. Seeing the gun, it became all to clear. But it was too late. He spun around to run, but slammed into a parked car.

"Puft!" The blood from his head, and the life from his body spilled out onto the ground.

The third potential rescuer might have gotten away if only he'd made a right turn toward the ramp instead of a left turn that took him to the corner of the rooftop. His error was fatal as he was cornered.

"Puft!" A bullet slammed into his head.

The man took a quick look around. He saw no one else. He stepped back to the van and shoved Christy's legs over her head, tumbling her body into the back of the van. He slid the side door shut with a noise that echoed across the parking lot. The man moved to the other side of the van and got behind the wheel. He heard a car engine start up, and then another. He took a moment for his breathing to slow down. He told himself to slow down, and not arouse suspicion. He backed the van out of its parking space, and slowly drove around parked cars to the top of the down ramp.

* * *

Gino Sorice, a CBS soundman, had been sitting in his car, waiting for David Waylon, his car pool partner to arrive, so they could drive home together. He had noticed the attractive woman in high heels pass his car and walk to a blue BMW. He had seen her first try to open the driver side door, and when she hadn't been able to, saw her move around to the passenger door.

Sorice saw the woman fall to the ground. He wasn't sure what had happened. Then someone got out of the van, and dragged the woman to the opposite side of the van. The man was shoving her into the side door of the van, when Sorice heard men's voices. Three men, whose voices he recognized, ran towards the man. The man dropped the woman and ran towards the three men. Sorice was terrified and began to tremble as he slid off the seat, onto the floor, hiding behind the dashboard.

He heard the sounds of men yelling; the sounds of running feet; the sound of the van's side cargo door being closed; and then he heard nothing. Sorice knew people had been killed, and peered over the dashboard.

He wasn't sure what to do. He knew if the man had seen him, he too would be killed. So he decided to drive off the rooftop lot ahead of the van. He started his engine and pulled into the lane. He heard the van's motor start up. In his rearview mirror, he saw the van back out. Sorice turned the corner around the middle two rows of cars. The van was following him. Sorice turned to start down the exit ramp. In his rear view mirror, he saw the van make the same turn. Sorice reached the booth at the base of the ramp. His mind raced, as he tried to figure out what to do. He was having trouble concentrating. Sorice pulled up to the booth and lowered his window. The attendant looked up from the book he had been reading. Sorice again looked in his rearview mirror and saw the van just behind him.

Sorice spoke to the attendant, but it didn't come out the way he wanted. "That guy in the van just hit three people." Then he stepped on the gas, and left a confused attendant wondering which cars had been hit, and how much damage had been done.

* * *

Michael Greenstreet, the nineteen-year-old attendant, decided he would ask the man in the van what had happened, but the man sped past him without stopping. Greenstreet shrugged his shoulders, but just to protect himself he started to jot down the van's license number, but saw the van had pulled out of sight—it was too late. He returned to his book.

* * *

115

Sorice pulled out into traffic and drove around the block, watching his rearview mirror. He didn't see the van, so he drove back up the entrance ramp to the rooftop parking lot just as William Jensen, another CBS employee, discovered the body of David Waylon.

"Gino!" Jensen yelled at him. "David's been hurt. Call 911 and get some help."

Sorice stepped out of his car and, like a zombie, walked toward Jensen. "There's two more over there." He mechanically pointed toward the bodies of Gould and Dombrowski, his eyes glazed over. "I think they're all dead." Sorice stood, solemn and immobilized.

Jensen nodded and pulled out his cell phone. He called CBS and told them to send a camera crew. Then he called 911.

* * *

Dan and Casey had waited for Marino at the FBI office. When she hadn't arrived by 6:30 P.M., Dan had made phone calls to her apartment and to Fontaine, but neither telephone was answered.

"Guess she had a change of heart," Casey said.

"That's what it looks like," Dan said sorrowfully as he shook his head. "But I find that hard to believe." He felt a wave of nausea come over him. A sinking feeling in his stomach made him suspect something was terribly wrong.

Nineteen

6:35 PM
January 10th
Manhattan, New York

Detective Jack Duffy stopped the car at the top of the ramp. Detective Richie LeBeau climbed out and surveyed the crime scene. Four RMP cars were on the roof, lights flashing. Emergency Services had set up klieg lights and generators. Uniformed officers held television camera crews at bay. It was a cross between an out-of-control movie set and a three-ringed circus. LeBeau had seen it all too often. He began to bark orders to the other detectives.

"Okay, Tom," LeBeau said, "Find out if we've got any witnesses. If so, get 'em over here. Find out if the attendant saw or heard anything. Jim, get those

television people off the roof. We don't need any of
their crap. Jack, come with me."

LeBeau and Duffy walked toward the uniformed
Sergeant who seemed to be the highest-ranking
uniformed officer on the scene. LeBeau recognized him
as Vern Dixon.

"Talk to me, Vern," he said. "What've we got?"

"Call to 911 at 5:58 P.M.," Vern said. "Caller said
that there were three dead in this parking lot. First unit
on the scene was 2918, Downing and McGrath. Arrived
at 6:03, confirmed three bodies. No pulse. Secured the
area. Called for an ambulance, a Crime Scene Unit, and
Emergency Services for some lights."

"Have they been pronounced?"

"EMS arrived at 6:09. EMT George Jones
pronounced them dead at 6:11."

Duffy and LeBeau jotted down the information.

"When they arrived, Officers Downing and
McGrath briefly talked with Sorice. He was pretty
shaken up."

"Back up a minute," LeBeau said. "Who's Sorice?"

"Witness. Knew the victims. Apparently saw
something."

LeBeau nodded.

"I think I see the CSU pulling up," Dixon said.
"Where do you want to start?"

"Where's Sorice?" LeBeau asked.

"In the front seat of my RMP. I've got Thelma
Woodson with him. She's pretty good at calming
people down."

"Good," LeBeau said. "Tell somebody to find
Johnson and let him know about Sorice. Take me to the
victims."

LeBeau and Duffy pulled on surgical gloves and
followed the Sergeant to the far aisle, weaving between

cars, ducking under the crime scene tape. When they reached the first body, LeBeau turned on his flashlight.

"Victim number one," Dixon said.

The body was lying face up, his right arm across his body, his left leg beneath him. His face and hair were covered in drying blood. LeBeau shined his flashlight around the body. He spotted a small shiny object and bent down to look at it. "Looks like we've got a cartridge casing. Probably a .22."

They walked toward the two rows of cars in the middle of the lot. Dixon stopped at the rear of a white Oldsmobile, and pointed at the second body. LeBeau shined his flashlight on the body of an overweight middle-aged man dressed in a suit, lying face down in a pool of blood.

"Jack," LeBeau said. "You see a shell casing?"

Both Detectives scanned the area with their flashlights.

"What's that by his right arm?" Duffy asked.

"Yeah, that's it," LeBeau said.

"Victim number three is over there," Dixon said.

They walked to the center of the parking aisle, where a third man on his back, his hands spread out to either side. Blood had oozed over his head and onto the ground then clotted. They saw the small hole in his face. LeBeau's flashlight illuminated another shell casing on the ground near the body.

"Anything else?" LeBeau asked.

"I'm not really sure what we have over here." Dixon led them to the empty parking space to the right of a blue BMW.

They all stood in silence and stared at a pool of dried blood, which looked like something had been dragged through it. Lying in the blood they saw a woman's red high-heeled shoe, a set of keys, an open purse with its contents spilled out, and a pair of sunglasses.

"Maybe Sorice can tell us what this is about," LeBeau said. "Was he the only witness?"

"Far as we know. A guy named Jensen showed up a few minutes after it happened. He called 911. Told me he knew the victims, as well as Sorice. Said they all worked for CBS, and had just come from work."

"CBS? That explains the media circus."

"It's worse than you know. Their camera crew was filming when we arrived."

"Great," LeBeau said. "Let's go see Sorice."

Thelma Woodson, a black police officer in her early thirties, sat in the front seat of a RMP car, talking quietly to a man sitting beside her, his eyes wide, staring into the night, yet seeing nothing. When she saw them approaching, she stepped out of the car.

"Gino Sorice," she said, nodding toward the man in the car. "He's in pretty rough shape. Apparently he was hiding in his front seat and saw what happened. He keeps blaming himself, saying he should have done something. I haven't tried to talk to him about what he saw. I wanted you guys to have first crack."

"Thanks, Thelma." LeBeau opened the passenger's side front door of the RMP. Both he and Duffy crouched in front of Sorice. "Mr. Sorice, I'm Detective LeBeau and this is Detective Duffy. How are you doing?"

"I should have done something," Sorice said in a barely audible voice.

"There is something you can do, Mr. Sorice," LeBeau said. "You can help us find whoever did this to them. That's the greatest help you can be to them at this point. Tell us what you saw."

"He chased them down and killed them. All of them. Now they're dead. I should have done something."

"You are doing something, Mr. Sorice," LeBeau said in a gentle voice. "You're helping us find whoever did this to them. They would want you to tell us. You know that, don't you?"

"Excuse me, Richie," Detective Jim Moore said. "Sorry to butt in, but can I talk to you for a minute?"

LeBeau stood and stepped away from the door of the RMP. "Do I need this now?"

"It might help," Moore said. "I've been talking to the parking attendant. Name's Michael Greenstreet. Told me Sorice here, drove down to the ticket booth just before six, and said something about a guy in a van right behind him hitting somebody. Greenstreet figured there'd been a fender bender, so he was gonna ask the guy in the van what happened. Before Greenstreet got a word out, the van flew past him and down the street. He was gonna write down the van's plate number, but he was too late."

"Did he get a look at the guy?" asked LeBeau.

"Male, dark hair, sunglasses."

"What color was the van?"

"Not sure. Said it was light-colored."

LeBeau sighed. "It's a little more than what we had."

"Right. I called it in, and asked them to put it out on the air. Told 'em to make sure the APB says the guy's armed and dangerous. I don't want to see some poor uniform pulling him over and getting killed."

"Good thinking," LeBeau patted Moore on the back, then walked back to the RMP. "Mr. Sorice, tell us about the van."

"It was a van." Sorice said in a shaky voice.

"How do you know?" LeBeau asked.

"I heard the sound of the sliding door being closed."

"What makes you so sure that's what you heard?"

Sorice looked LeBeau in the eye for the first time. "I'm part of a camera crew. We use vans like that. I open and close the sliding cargo door a dozen times a day. I'm sure that's what I heard."

"Did you see the man in the van?" asked LeBeau.

"He's the one who did it. He killed them, and left."

"Tell us what he looked like, Mr. Sorice."

"I don't remember. He killed them. He chased them down and killed them."

"Yes, Mr. Sorice, we know. Tell us what he looked like. Was he white, black, Hispanic, Asian?"

"He wasn't black."

"Good. You're doin' great. Was he young, middle aged, or old?"

"I'm not sure."

"You're doing just fine. Did he wear glasses?"

"No. Yes. I'm not sure. He may have. I don't remember."

"Very good, Mr. Sorice. See, you're helping your friends. They would have wanted you to help them, wouldn't they?"

"I don't know. Maybe. I can't believe they're dead. I should have done something, I just don't know what."

"You're helping them right now. You're doing a wonderful job. Now I need to ask you a few more questions. They're important. You can answer them, can't you? To help your friends, you can answer them, right?"

"I'll try."

"Good. What was the man wearing? A suit?"

"No."

"Jeans and a jacket?"

"Yeah! Jeans and a brown leather jacket. I remember!"

"Was he wearing a hat?"

"I don't remember. Maybe. No, I don't think so."

"Did you see the gun, Mr. Sorice?"

"He had a gun!"

"Yes, Mr. Sorice. He had a gun. Tell us what the gun looked like. Did it look like this one?" LeBeau pulled out his .38 caliber Smith & Wesson revolver.

"I don't think so, but I'm not sure."

Duffy pulled out his 9 mm Colt automatic and showed it to Sorice.

"Did it look like that gun?" LeBeau asked.

"Yeah. Sort of. I can't be sure. I think it was bigger. It didn't make any noise, you know. When he shot it, I mean. It just sort of went 'puff.'"

Duffy and LeBeau looked at each other. They were dealing with a professional.

"Which part of the gun was bigger, Mr. Sorice?" LeBeau said, trying to keep the excitement out of his voice.

"That part." Sorice pointed to the barrel of the automatic.

"How was it bigger, Mr. Sorice? Was it bigger around?"

"No, it was longer. It had something on the end of it, I think. I don't remember for sure. Maybe it did."

"You're doing just fine, Mr. Sorice. You're helping your friends. They'd be very proud of you."

"I'm really scared."

"I can understand that."

"No, I don't think you do. I'm afraid if the murderer finds out I saw him, he'll kill me."

"I see."

"There's something else. You've got to promise me that no one else at CBS finds out it was me who saw it happen."

"Why Mr. Sorice?"

"Because I didn't do anything. Nobody will trust me anymore."

"Okay, Mr. Sorice, I'll make sure no one finds out that you saw it. Nobody at CBS will learn it was you."

"Give me your promise."

"I promise, Mr. Sorice."

"Thanks. Do you really think I've helped you?"

"I'm sure of it," said LeBeau. "Now, just sit back and relax. We need to talk to the other policemen, and then we'll come back. Thelma, would you get Mr. Sorice's home phone number and call his family? Tell them he's okay but is going to be getting home a little late tonight. If he feels up to it, let him talk to them to reassure them. The news may already be out and they shouldn't be worrying about him. Would you do that?"

"Glad to," Woodson said.

"Not the greatest of witnesses," Duffy said as the two of them walked over to join Detective Jim Moore.

"No, but we've got a little more than we did." LeBeau turned to Moore. "Did you get anything else?"

"Nah," Moore said. "You guys get a description of the shooter from Sorice?"

"If you can call it that," Duffy said. "A not-black man in a brown leather jacket wearing maybe sunglasses and a maybe hat."

"This isn't getting any easier, is it?"

"Gun wore a silencer," LeBeau said. "Adds an interesting twist. So let's go take a look at the stuff on the ground next to the blood by the BMW. Maybe we'll get lucky."

The three Detectives ducked under the "Police Line Do Not Cross" yellow tape and walked toward the blue

BMW. As they approached, one of the CSU Detectives was taking photographs.

"How you doing, Manny?" LeBeau asked.

"Pretty busy tonight, thanks to you guys," answered Detective Manuel Garcia. "What do you think happened?"

"Not sure yet. We've got an eyewitness that tells us the shooter killed the three. He didn't tell us anything about what happened here. Maybe he didn't see it. Maybe he doesn't remember. You guys ready to dust for prints?"

"Almost. Something you want done first?"

"Yeah. Maybe it'll explain the whole thing." LeBeau pointed to the items on the ground. "I'd like to take a look in that purse and see if that key fits the BMW."

"I've got my pictures," Garcia said. "I'll call Scott over here and have him dust those items first."

A few minutes later the other member of the Crime Scene Unit finished and handed the keys to LeBeau. He tried the key in the passenger's door of the BMW. It slipped right into the lock.

"Okay," he said. "Why would anyone coming to get into their two-door car, open the passenger's door instead of the driver's door?"

Duffy was kneeling next to the driver's door, penlight in hand. "Because something's stuck inside this lock."

"Manny," LeBeau said. "Make a note to remove this lock once this vehicle gets towed to the evidence garage. Have 'em take out whatever's inside it and save it for me."

"You got it."

"Jim, while we're going through the purse, take down the plate on this BMW and run a check on it."

"Sure, Richie," Moore said.

The two detectives moved back to the passenger side of the BMW, stepping around the blood and the other items. LeBeau picked up the purse and took out the wallet.

"There's eighty-seven bucks in here, so it doesn't appear robbery was the motive," said LeBeau. "Okay, lady, tell me who you are."

Flipping through the identification, he found a New York driver's license bearing the photograph of an attractive, dark-haired woman. "Christina L. Marino. 613 Grandview Avenue, Ridgewood, Queens, New York. Jack, would you run her name through the computer and see if there's anything on her?"

"Sure."

Duffy stepped away as Moore reappeared with notes in his hand. "The plate on the BMW, New Jersey KBL-917, is registered to Christina L. Marino, 118 Winsom Road, Teaneck, New Jersey. No outstanding tickets, no wants. That help?"

"Yes, and no. Now we've got two addresses for her, one in Queens, and another in Jersey." LeBeau shook his head. "Jim, why don't you take a ride over to Queens and hook up with detectives from the 104th? Ask them if they'll go with you to that Queens address and see if she's there. Tom, go to Jersey and get a detective from the Teaneck PD to go with you to the other address, and see if she's there. Right now, she's the best lead we've got."

Twenty

8:25 PM
January 10th
Teaneck, New Jersey

"Here it is." Teaneck Detective Sam Boston looked at his computer screen. "Nothing on Marino. But the address comes back to a missing persons report. Mary Lee Wen. Disappeared on January 3rd, a week ago."

"A second disappearing body," NYPD Detective Tom Johnson said. "Same address. What a coincidence."

"From what I hear on the radio, you've got a few bodies that didn't disappear."

Johnson nodded. "Three to be exact. You got a suspect for Wen?"

"Husband. Don't have enough to charge him. Let's find out if he knows Marino."

"I'd appreciate it."

They drove to Winsom Road and rang the bell.

"Evening Mr. Wen. Remember me? Detective Boston, Teaneck PD. This is NYPD Detective Johnson. We need to ask you a few questions."

"Have you found my wife?"

"No."

"Oh, I was hoping . . . come in." Wen led the detectives into the living room and sat on a sofa. "What questions?" Wen's hand trembled and his eyes dilated.

"Do you know a Christina Marino?" Boston asked.

"She worked with my wife."

"What kind of car does Marino drive?" Johnson asked.

"A German car," Wen said. "Why are you asking me? What's happened?"

"We found a blue BMW on a rooftop parking lot in Manhattan tonight," Johnson said. "There were Jersey plates on it. Registration shows the owner as Marino, but lists your address. Any idea why?"

Wen reached for a cigarette, and lit it with unsteady hands. "No. She doesn't live here."

Car was in a parking lot on the west side of Manhattan," Boston said. "Why would it be there?"

"I don't know."

"Where does Marino work?" Johnson asked.

"At Fontaine Diamonds. Same as my wife." Wen took a long drag on the cigarette.

"Who owns Fontaine?" Johnson asked.

"I think his name is Schwartz."

Boston stood to leave. "Thanks, you've been very helpful."

"What happened to Christy?" Wen asked.

"Oh, so you know her," Johnson said. "When was the last time you saw her?"

"Just after Christmas."

"Before or after your wife disappeared?" Boston asked.

"Before."

"Have you seen her since?" Johnson asked.

"No."

"Okay," Boston said, moving towards the door. "If you hear from her, give us a call." The two detectives walked back to the car.

"We learned Marino wasn't there, and something else clicked," Boston said. "He said his wife and Marino both worked at Fontaine. When I worked the missing persons on his wife, I went to Fontaine with an FBI agent working a fraud involving Fontaine Diamonds."

"Fraud, huh? Did the Feebee say if Wen and Marino were subjects or witnesses?"

"Witnesses against Schwartz — a real dirt bag."

"Think he's capable of murder?"

Boston shrugged. "Maybe. Might be worth looking into. The FBI guy never told us how he knew Wen was missing."

"Typical FBI. Never tell you shit."

* * *

NYPD Detective Jim Moore fought through the tail end of commute traffic and finally reached the 104th Precinct in Queens. He put his shield on his coat pocket and walked in.

"Detectives upstairs?" he asked the desk sergeant.

"Yeah."

He climbed the stairs and opened the door to the squad room. Two detectives sat, feet propped up on their desks. They eyed him. "Can I help you?" one of them asked.

"Yeah. I'm Jim Moore from Midtown North. And you?"

"Rudolfsky. Jim Rudolfsky."

"We caught a triple homicide in Manhattan tonight. There's a possible fourth victim. Got a Queens address on her driver's license. Would one of you guys come along to check it out?"

Rudolfsky pulled out a pad. "Gimme the name and address."

"Christina Marino, 613 Grandview Avenue—"

"I don't need to look that up. I'll go with you, but I'm the wrong guy to talk to."

"Why?"

"Talk to the Feds," Rudolfsky said with a chuckle. "She told me she's a witness in an investigation they've got going."

"How'd you learn that?"

"Marino came in last week all upset and wanted to file a missing persons report on some Chinese woman. Think her name was Wen. Marino bugged the hell out of me, called, came by, plastered posters all over town, even offered a reward."

"Wen ever turn up?"

"No."

"When'd you last hear from Marino?"

"Couple of days ago. Called and asked if we had learned anything about Wen. Told her no, and didn't think we would."

"Shit," Moore said. "Ever find out what she was doing for the Feds?"

"Not really. Guess you'll have to ask them yourself. If they'll tell you. Think she was killed tonight?"

"Maybe. Found some blood and her purse next to her car."

They drove to Marino's building, buzzed her apartment and waited. No answer. They buzzed the apartment super.

"Whatta youse want?" a voice answered the intercom.

"Police," Rudolfsky said. "Buzz us in."

"Right. Who are youse guys, really?"

"We're the cops. Now get your ass up here, and open this fucking door!"

The intercom clicked off.

"People here say *youse*?" Moore asked.

"Only to impress the tourists."

A fat, middle-aged man dressed in an undershirt and dirty slacks appeared on the opposite side of the double door. The detectives flashed their gold shields, and got buzzed in.

"Does Christina Marino live here?" Rudolfsky asked.

"2-B."

"How long she lived here?" Moore asked.

"Maybe six years."

"Alone?"

"Hey, I don't stick my nose into tenants' business."

"Answer the question, asshole."

"Yeah, alone."

"Got a key for her apartment?"

"Sure." The super shrugged his shoulders. "Whatever youse guys want."

They rang the bell. No answer. They knocked. Nothing.

"Unlock it," Rudolfsky said.

"Ain't youse guys s'posed to have a search warrant or something?"

"Shut the fuck up, and open the God-damned door!"

He let them into the apartment. No one was home. Moore picked up envelopes full of photographs. He flipped through, pulled out one and showed it to the super. "This her?"

"Yeah."

Moore studied it, then picked up a framed photograph from the coffee table, and showed it to Rudolfsky. This the missing Chinese woman?"

"That's her. Used that for the posters."

Moore put the photos in his pocket and turned to the super. "Listen. If Marino shows up, call us. Don't let anybody into this apartment unless we tell *youse*. Got it?"

The super nodded. The detectives left while he locked up the apartment.

"*Youse*?" Rudolfsky asked with a chuckle.

"Hey, when in Queens . . ."

* * *

Johnson and Moore briefed everyone on what they'd learned.

"We're in for a lot of press," Chief of Detectives Michael Keenan said. "The media's already dubbed it, 'The CBS Murders.' So every night I need a progress update."

"Glad to, Chief," LeBeau said. "But can you do us a favor? Keep the press off our backs. Otherwise we might have a dead witness on our hands."

"I'll take care of it." Keenan headed towards the flock of cameras and reporters who were still being held at bay.

"Richie," Captain Bill Watson said. "We're under a lot of pressure to solve this quickly. I talked to Nick Thomas, the head of the New York FBI Office, and told him there's a good chance Marino is dead. They're investigating a multi-million dollar bank fraud case, and Marino was cooperating."

"Don't tell me you're turning this case over to the Feds! You can't."

"I'm not. Like it or not, our murder case is tied into their fraud case. It's going to be a joint investigation.

132

We'll bring in some detectives from the Homicide Bureau. The FBI's going to assist us—assist, not take over."

"Yeah, that'll be a first."

Twenty-One

6:30 AM
January 11th
Manhattan, New York

Dan was jolted awake by the phone. He fumbled for the receiver. "Hello?"

"Dan? Captain Bill Watson, NYPD. Nick Thomas told me to give you a call. I think we found her."

Dan fought his way out of a dreamless sleep. "What are you talking about? Found who?"

"That witness of yours—Marino."

"Christy?"

"Single shot to the head. Found her on Franklin Street, just off Broadway."

"On my way." Dan stared at the ceiling. It was a bad dream, a nightmare. Had to be. But the morning light seeping into his bedroom and the pain in his gut was real.

Had to get moving. Dan grabbed some coffee from the deli, and drove to Franklin Street, nursing the hope it was someone else. NYPD cars were everywhere, lights flashing. Yellow crime scene tape was strung. A crowd strained to see.

As Dan ducked under the yellow tape, he saw police photographers packing up their cameras, and technicians dusting for prints. A blue plastic sheet had been pushed away. The woman was sprawled on the ground, lying face down, her hair caked with blood and dirt. Her short red leather skirt was hiked up, only one shoe on. The clothes were unmistakably Christy's.

Two detectives were bending over the body. Dan couldn't see, so he edged forward for a closer look. They turned her head and Dan saw Christy's face.

It reminded him of when he found Ellen. He'd tried to wake her. He knew she was dead, the cold flesh, the blood. But staring at her slack-jawed face, the eyes frozen open—that face that had been on the next pillow so many mornings—he'd shaken her shoulder, said her name. Ellen. Waited for those eyes to blink, the lips to draw back into a slow, lazy yawn. Ellen? He'd seen her yawn like that so many times and never realized how absolutely perfect it was. Ellen! Since that night, he'd carried a deep hatred of the man who had done that to Ellen, . . . to him. Always there, part of his inner soul, like coals smoldering under the ashes.

But this was Christy. Christy Marino. His anger burned. He'd find who did this to Christy. Find him and make him pay.

He turned to the detective standing near him. "When was she found?"

"About 5:30 this morning. A guy out walking his dog. Dog must've picked up the scent of blood. Kept trying to get under that blue plastic. Guy pulled it back, found the body, called 911."

"You again!" a voice called from behind Dan.

Dan turned to see a detective in a Fedora stalking toward him. The same one from the Chinese restaurant.

"What the hell is it with you? What do you do? Listen for a homicide on a scanner so you can show up and look at the victims? You really are sick! Get the hell out of here. Next time you show up, I'll have you arrested."

"I've got a right to be here."

"Right," the detective said, then turned to the closest uniformed policeman. "Officer, escort this guy out of here."

Dan took one last look at Christy before he left.

* * *

Back at the FBI office, Dan sat with Thomas and Blackman.

"You've seen the headlines," Thomas said. "Press is calling it 'The CBS Murders.' There was a fourth victim—Christy Marino. She was a cooperating witness in the Fontaine investigation. The NYPD and the FBI are forming a Joint Task Force to solve these murders. Dan's been handling the Fontaine investigation. So he's going to head it up."

"I don't think he should," Blackman said. "Seems like every time we meet, it's because someone involved with Dan's investigation has been killed."

"Cut it out, Ike!" Thomas shouted. "You're way out of line!"

"Obviously a mob hit," Blackman said.

"Dan?" Thomas looked at Dan to get his attention. "What do you say?"

Blackman's idiocy was not going to squelch Dan's need for vengeance. "I . . . take it personally when one of my cooperating witnesses is killed. I want to run the investigation." He couldn't find Ellen's killer. He wasn't allowed to look for Sammy Ho's. He *wanted* Christy's killer. He was hungry for this case.

"Then it's yours," Thomas said. "I got a call last night from FBI Director Montgomery. He'd heard from Bradford Millbanks, Chairman of CBS. Millbanks told the Director that because three CBS employees were killed, he'd appreciate receiving daily briefings. The Director agreed. Not that we wouldn't push anyway, but this . . ."

"Understood," Dan said.

"Go to Midtown North. Find what they need and get it for them."

"And don't fuck up," Blackman said as he stood and walked out.

"Dan, stay a minute?" Thomas said. "We're under enormous pressure to solve this quickly. Have an email to me every morning by 8:00 A.M. Keep me up to the minute on what's happening."

Dan began to walk back to his office.

"Robertson, get in here!" Blackman shouted as Dan passed his doorway.

He stopped and looked into Blackman's office.

"I just wanted you to know," Blackman said. "I'm going to watch you every minute you run this case. At the first sign of a screw up, I'll hang you out to dry. You got that?" Blackman pointed a finger at Dan.

"Do whatever. I've got a case to solve." Dan continued to his office, determined to channel his energy into the task ahead.

He asked Casey and two other agents to come to his office. After they were settled, Dan said, "Did any of you catch the news about the murders on the west side parking lot?"

"Yeah," Casey said. "Awful. Papers say the police don't have any suspects."

"There's a little more to the story. A professional hit. Christy Marino was the fourth victim," Dan said, a catch in his voice.

"What?" Casey said.

"Her body was found this morning, dumped in an alley in lower Manhattan."

"Oh my God!" Casey said. "I can't believe it. What—"

"The FBI and NYPD are forming a Joint Task Force. The NYPD has the primary jurisdiction because of the homicides. She was our witness, so we have legitimate jurisdiction, but we're going to play a supportive role. In ten minutes we're going to Midtown North for a meeting with the detectives."

They began to file out, then Casey turned back. "Dan, are you all right?"

"Yeah." He became aware of his anger and loss. He forced his feelings back under control. "Don't worry. I'll be okay."

She nodded, but the look on her face said she didn't believe him.

The FBI agents drove to Midtown North, and found their way to the squad room. Dan easily picked Watson out of the crowd and introduced himself. While they were talking, a detective walked out of the men's room and stopped cold when he saw them.

"You!"

Everyone turned.

"I can't work with you!" LeBeau said. "First you turn up in Chinatown to look at the dead in the restaurant. Then you show up this morning where Marino's body was found. Do you get off looking at corpses?"

"I couldn't tell you then why I was in Chinatown," Dan said.

"Oh, I can't wait to hear this."

"The man I was looking for in that restaurant was an FBI agent."

"Why the hell didn't you tell me?"

"He was undercover. If I'd identified him, everything he'd done would've been lost, and others killed. I shouldn't have been there myself, but . . . I had to see . . . to make sure."

The silence stretched forever.

"I'm sorry about your agent," LeBeau said.

"Thanks. He was a good man."

"What about this morning?"

"Let me answer that," Watson said. "I called Dan. The victim was a cooperating witness in his FBI case. It's tough to lose a witness."

Everyone watched detectives move chairs to the conference table. They sat down and introduced themselves.

"Why doesn't Casey tell us about the fraud investigation," Watson said. "Then I'll have LeBeau fill you in on the murders."

After Casey and LeBeau had brought the group up to speed on both cases, Watson asked, "I realize the description of the shooter is pretty thin, but does it match anyone in your fraud investigation?"

"Hard to say," Casey said. "Certainly not Schwartz, and I'm pretty sure it's not David Wen. It sounds like a hired gun."

"Casey, I've got a question for you," LeBeau said. "How was Mary Lee Wen killed?"

"We're not sure. Her body was never found."

"Nothing ever turned up?"

"Well, her car was found over on the west side of Manhattan. I think it was on West Thirty-sixth Street. They found some blood. Oh, and a .22 shell casing."

"And you didn't think that was important enough to mention?" LeBeau said. "All the people on the rooftop

were killed with a .22. The women worked together.
One disappeared and a .22 casing was found in her car.
The other gets killed by a .22, along with three CBS
guys. The same guy may have killed all of them. We've
got shell casings I want to compare with the one from
Wen's car. Where's that shell casing?"

"I'm not sure if the 10th Precinct or the Teaneck PD
has it."

"We'll get it," Dan said. "Look, why don't we
divide up the work and get started. To keep track of the
paper, evidence and leads, I'd like to bring in some
computers, faxes, other equipment, and analysts to
operate them. Let's run a dozen or so telephone lines
into the squad room here, and give everybody a phone."

Knowing how the NYPD strictly watched costs,
and being accustomed to sharing a phone with others,
the detectives stared at Dan and at each other, their
mouths open.

"Okay!" LeBeau said. "Working with you Feds
may have some advantages."

Twenty-Two

2:15 PM
January 11th
Queens, New York

Dan drove LeBeau to Queens to execute a search warrant on Christy's apartment. When they arrived, there were a few police cars, but nothing that indicated there was anything major going on inside the building. Dan showed his credentials, and LeBeau his shield, to a uniformed officer in the lobby. Another officer stood at the door of Christy's apartment, and after signing the search log they stepped into the apartment.

Dan remembered the apartment from the last time he saw Christy in it, neat, if a little cramped and crowded. With detectives and agents now going through everything, it was a disaster. There was so little room to move among people and her possessions, Dan stood out of the way.

He felt Christy's presence in the apartment. He saw the cognac bottle he had brought. He remembered the emotional devastation on her face when he told her about Mary Lee's car.

Dan watched Agent Sydney Jackson go through Marino's desk. As he leafed through the papers in the drawers, something caught his interest, and he stopped to read it, then turned to Dan. "Come take a look at this."

Dan stepped over some papers, slipped on some gloves and read the hand-written letter.

> *My Dearest Christy,*
>
> *I can't begin to tell you how much I love you. Before I met you, my whole life was designed to make me to feel inferior. What was required and expected of me was total obedience— first to my parents' wishes, then to my husband's demands. I wasn't allowed to have an opinion different from theirs. An arranged marriage to a man I wouldn't love, even if I could.*
>
> *Sex was for his pleasure alone, and to provide him with children. Until I met you, I didn't know such pleasure could exist. I love you so much for loving me. Without your love and support, I don't think I could even write this letter.*
>
> *I'm still burdened by my Chinese cultural upbringing, but the life and love we've found together frees me*

*more and more. You told me how you
were disowned when your family
learned you didn't love men. I see your
pain whenever we talk about it. I've
experienced that same pain, even
though my family knows nothing about
our love. We can help each other
through the pain. I know we can.*

*As soon as I'm able, I want to live
with you, and love only you. Thank you
for your patience while I sort through
things. No one could ever ask for a
more sensitive, caring, and loving
relationship.*

Christy, I love you. ·

Mary Lee

Dan felt like he'd been kicked in the stomach.
Christy and Mary Lee were lovers. Why hadn't Dan
seen the women's relationship for what it was? Maybe
because he was attracted to Christy, and didn't want to
see it. It explained why Christy was street-tough and
never wanted to depend on anyone else—she didn't
have anyone except Mary Lee. And when Mary Lee
disappeared, he had used that as leverage to try to get
her to talk. No wonder she wanted nothing to do with
him. She'd known she was at risk, even then. From
who? David Wen? If David Wen had known about it,
he'd have a motive to kill Christy. Why hadn't she said
so? Because she would have had to tell Dan about their
relationship.

Finally, Dan looked up at Jackson. "Sidney, show
this to LeBeau, and tell him not to mention it to anyone
else."

Dan stepped over piles of paper from the desk to reach LeBeau.

"If I can catch a ride with you back to the station house, we can talk about the case on the way," LeBeau said.

* * *

They talked as they drove back to Manhattan.

"The only thing we established is a romantic link between Marino and Wen," LeBeau said. "Do you think it shed some light on who the killer could be?"

"When I heard Christy had been killed, first thing that came to mind was her boss at Fontaine was behind it. I thought Schwartz was the only one with motive for both killings."

"That'd make sense if somehow he got wind of her talking to the FBI."

Dan thought a moment. "I wonder if the two women teamed up against Schwartz and were ripping him off while he was ripping off MBT Factors."

"Why do you think that?"

"Marino drives a new BMW. I don't think she could afford one on a bookkeeper's salary. I saw photographs in her apartment of Wen and her in Europe. I doubt either of them could afford that kind of travel on their salaries."

"And maybe she used the FBI to put Schwartz in prison as the last move in her game," LeBeau said. "Possible. Gives him a motive."

"I don't completely buy it," Dan said. "Schwartz is certainly a jerk, but David Wen seems cold. That love letter gives him all the motive he needs to kill both of them."

"Or maybe pay somebody to do it. What do you know about Wen?"

"There's nothing in the FBI files. The Teaneck PD was going to see if the NYPD had anything on him. I'm thinking we should know more about him. Can you help me?"

"Sure. I'll have somebody run a check on him."

"This lesbian love between these two," Dan said.

"Yeah?"

"I don't want to see the media learn about it."

"Not a problem," LeBeau said. "I put the letter back into the drawer. Nobody at the PD will leak it."

As they pulled into Midtown North, they were surrounded by news photographers who prevented the car from moving until Dan touched the siren. They jumped back a little, but moved in again, cameras flashing. Dan worked the gas and brake pedals, lurching the car forward through the crowd. After they parked, more questions were shouted as they went up the stairs and into the squad room.

"It seems the feeding frenzy has begun," Dan said.

"Should have seen them during the Son of Sam murders."

"You worked that case?"

"I had a little something to do with it. Back when I was young and foolish." LeBeau raised his voice. "Okay, have you got this case wrapped up yet?"

There was a chorus of groans from the squad.

"Let me tell you about the parking lot," Bennett said. "Casey and I went over to Allied Parking Company. In order to park on that rooftop lot, you had to fill out a permit and become a monthly parker. No dailies. We asked for applications of all active parkers so we could match 'em against people who came for their cars last night. We learned something interesting. Since the New York parking business is the easiest rip-off around, the company wanted to be able to check on their employees and customers. Allied went high-tech. Instead of a sticker on the window, they issued plastic permits you hang from the rear view mirror. What they didn't say was that there was a computer chip embedded in the tag."

"What exactly does the chip do?" asked LeBeau.

"It gets read by electronic sensors when the car passes the attendant's booth—like E-Z Pass for tolls. The computer tracks when the car comes in, and goes out. Allied compares those times with the handwritten log the attendant submits, to make sure he's honest. They also try to stop the same permit being used to park two different cars, and—"

"All this is terribly interesting, but how does it relate to the murders?" LeBeau asked.

"We went through the applications looking for vans," Bennett continued.

"Hang on," Dan said. "If the parkers can move the permit from vehicle to vehicle, isn't it possible the killer got the permit for, say, his wife's Honda?"

"Thought of that. I believe the shooter got his permit in the last month or two, and I think it's for a van because he didn't want to arouse suspicion by asking too many questions about the rules. I've got five bucks says the application lists the van. Any takers?"

"I'll take the bet," Watson said from across the room. The entire Task Force was following the discussion.

"There's something else Casey came up with," Bennett said.

"Since the computer chips track the movements of everybody," Casey said, "we'll be able to track the times Marino came and went each day. I figure he stalked her. Arriving before she did, leaving right after."

"So we look for somebody whose movements parallel hers," Dan said.

"This is interesting," LeBeau said.

"How'd you guys make out on Marino's apartment?" Watson asked.

"Nothing much," LeBeau said.

"How's the artist's conception drawing of the shooter coming?"

"Talked to Gail this morning," LeBeau said. "She's just started, but may need more time. The witnesses keep changing their minds."

"Keep on her. We need it."

"Anybody know if the lab results are back?" LeBeau asked.

"Oh yeah," Sandoval said. "Remember the jammed lock on the BMW?"

"Yeah."

"Wooden matchsticks. That's what they found when they took it apart."

"Is that the best you can come up with?" LeBeau asked.

"Don't shoot the messenger."

LeBeau sat down and waved Dan into a chair across from him. "First day and I'm already exhausted."

"Looks like we've got a good team here. It will just take a little time to put it together."

"Star Wars parking garages and wooden matchsticks—really."

LeBeau fell silent, staring across the room and chewing his lip. "Dan, do you guys have the resources to back a long shot?"

"In this case? Yeah, sure. Why?"

"Who carries wooden matchsticks? Smokers use lighters. Only person I ever knew who carried wooden matchsticks was somebody trying to quit smoking who needed to put something in his mouth. I'd like to get the end of that matchstick checked for saliva and DNA typed. Can your lab do that?"

"Sure we can," Dan said. "Long shot is right, but why not? The payoff may be worth it. I think you may be on to something."

Twenty-Three

5:30 PM
January 11th
Manhattan, New York

The investigation was unfolding around him. Dan watched the agents and detectives gathering and sorting information, following leads, eliminating leads. The team was starting to click. There were so many areas which needed attention. Prioritizing was essential.

Dan walked over to Casey. "Call Len Weinstein. Tell him we want to search Fontaine tomorrow morning. Take the materials that Christy gave us and draft a warrant. Might mean an all-nighter, but it's important."

"Fontaine? I thought you wanted me to work on the murders."

"We can't forget we've got a fraud investigation that may be linked to these murders. The Fontaine case didn't get killed, just because our cooperating witness did. We need to be doing things."

"Dan, we are doing things. Everybody in this room is trying to solve this case, so don't—"

"And if the murder weapon is in Schwartz's desk, then what? Give him time to get rid of it? No way. Get a warrant and search Fontaine."

"All right." Casey gathered the materials she needed.

"Before you go, are the parking permit applications in alphabetical order?"

"Yeah."

"Would you see if there's an application for Schwartz?"

Casey quickly leafed through the applications. "Nothing. Found one for Marino. Hers was the only name I recognized. Anything else?"

"No. We've got to execute the warrant in the morning."

"You think it's worth our time?"

"If we find a .22 automatic, it'll be too good to be true. Publicity over Christy's murder might prompt Schwartz to get rid of evidence."

"I see," Casey said.

Dan left and went back to the FBI office to brief everyone. As he drove down the West Side Highway, he felt the anger starting to boil up again. At Schwartz, at David Wen, at the scumbag who killed Ellen, at all the self-centered bastards who destroyed lives for the sake of power, money, pride or whatever.

He learned that Thomas had been called to an urgent meeting at Headquarters in Washington, D.C., SAC Phillips was at firearms training, ASAC Wright was at Quantico, which meant his only superior in the office was Blackman. Oh well, he could deal with Blackman for ten minutes if he had no other choice. Dan drew a deep breath and knocked on Blackman's door.

"Yeah?" Blackman was leaning back in his chair, his feet up on the desk, talking on the telephone. He held up an index finger indicating he would only be a minute. Dan took a seat.

From what he could hear of Blackman's end of the conversation, the call had nothing to do with FBI business. Two minutes passed, then five. Dan started to get up, but Blackman motioned for him to sit back down. Dan did so, but didn't like being kept on hold.

Just when Dan had decided he'd waited long enough, Blackman hung up. "What's up?"

"I need to brief you on the CBS Murders case."

"Right," Blackman said. "So what have you learned about whoever murdered your cooperating witness?"

Dan bristled, but an argument would only prolong the meeting.

"We found wooden matchsticks in the door lock. Looks like the killer wanted her to come to the passenger side of her car."

"Mmm," Blackman said, reading a memo.

"We're going through parking applications, looking for a van."

"Find any?"

"Three. They're being run out. We searched Marino's apartment and—"

"Find anything?"

"No," Dan said, feeling he was being put on the defensive. "I take that back. We did learn something that may be relevant."

"What?"

"A letter from Mary Lee Wen. She's the Chinese woman who—"

"I know who the hell she is!"

"All right." Dan paused. "The letter talks about a lesbian love relationship between Christy Marino and Mary Lee Wen."

"What the hell does that have to do with the murders?"

"It may give David Wen a motive to kill the two women."

"Because his wife is a dyke? He could've divorced her."

"Sure, but there's the whole Chinese culture thing at play here."

Blackman examined his fingernails. "Bullshit! You're reaching."

"A .22 caliber shell casing was found in Mary Lee Wen's car. There were .22 caliber shell casings found on the ground near the three CBS employees."

"Does David Wen own a .22?"

"We don't know."

"Dan, these aren't difficult things to think of," Blackman said. "I hope you come across as a better investigator to the detectives than you are right now."

He wouldn't let Blackman get the better of him. He'd get through this. "The detectives and I agreed the information about the lesbian relationship wouldn't be shared with the press."

"Hmm," Blackman said. "Any other bright ideas for suspects?"

"We can't rule out Bernie Schwartz."

Blackman picked up a memo off his desk. "Who's he again?"

"He owns Fontaine Diamonds."

"Yeah, and what's his reason for wanting to kill these two dykes and three CBS guys?"

"He . . . may have learned the FBI was trying to get the women to talk about the fraud," Dan said. "To make sure nobody learned what they knew, he may have had them killed."

Blackman laid the memo back down and stared at Dan. "You mean you ran such a sloppy investigation, Schwartz may have found out what you were doing? Why didn't you just pick up the phone and tell him all about it?"

"There was nothing sloppy about our investigation!" Ike had found a way to get under his skin. "I don't know how he learned about it, if he learned about it at all. Someone else could've leaked this information. All I'm saying is that we can't eliminate him as a suspect."

"You don't have any idea how he learned? Just like you don't have any idea how the alleged undercover memo disappeared? I'm beginning to see a pattern here, Robertson. You got sloppy, and an agent got killed. You got sloppy again, and a cooperating witness got killed. You've got no business being in the FBI if you continue to put other people's lives—"

"You've got it all wrong, Blackman!" Dan shouted, rising to his feet. "I don't know what it is with you. Instead of focusing on getting the job done, you spend your time tearing good people down! You get off on that, don't you?"

"Get the hell out of my office right now!"

"Gladly!" Dan stalked back to his office, still seething. What the hell was going on? Blackman was trying to push his buttons, and was succeeding. Dan tossed a few things in his briefcase, snapped it shut, and headed home.

* * *

Dan ate carryout food from its Styrofoam container, sitting in the living room, watching television. Beside him on the table, he'd set out a bowl of grapes for Nevermore. Between grapes, Nevermore gave his comments and imitations of what he heard on the television, brightening Dan's spirits.

Dan finally calmed to the point where he could actually watch television. He began to channel surf, looking for anything worth watching. He saw flashes of movies he hadn't seen and hadn't missed. An infomercial tried to sell him something that would either tone his abdomen or straighten his spine, he wasn't sure which. Then he hit the beginning of the 11:00 news. The lead news story was about a flood in Africa, followed by a fire in Queens. He was ready to turn it off when he saw the newscaster with an image over her shoulder that said, "The CBS Murders." Dan raised the volume.

"While the police have made little progress in the CBS Murders, NEWS 2 has learned more details of what happened. Apparently, in addition to the three CBS technicians gunned down in the parking lot, a Queens' woman was also killed. Her body was discovered early yesterday morning in lower Manhattan," the newscaster said. "The police aren't speculating on how or why her body was moved."

"And in a further bizarre twist," the newscaster said. "The dead woman, Christina Marino, is alleged to have been the lesbian lover of a New Jersey woman who disappeared a week earlier, and is presumed dead. In other news, . . ."

"Son of a —!" Dan shouted at the television. Nevermore looked at him, and quietly stepped out of reach.

Dan stared at the television, but saw and heard nothing. Someone was giving away critical details about the case. His case. That had never happened to Dan before.

"I'll get you!"

Nevermore flew to the safety of his cage, landing and quickly climbing through the door, then onto a perch furthest away from Dan.

He'd heard there were leaks in the police department, but to see details of an active FBI case—his case—on the news. He had to talk to LeBeau, or maybe Watson. Or should he sic Thomas on them? No, that would be as much as admitting that he couldn't handle the responsibility of running the case. He knew he had to handle it. He'd start with LeBeau, and get to the bottom of it.

No, he'd start with Fontaine Diamonds. With Christy's name on the news, Schwartz was apt to bolt.

He dropped back onto the couch. Christy was so guarded about her relationship, and now it was on the news for all the world to see. He felt he'd failed her again.

Twenty-Four

10:30 AM
January 12th
Manhattan, New York

"Casey spent half the night drafting the search warrant for Fontaine. But it was an exercise in futility. When we got there, the place was empty—cleaned out," Dan said on his cell phone as he drove to Midtown North.

"Would it have made any difference if you had searched last night?" Nick asked.

"No. According to some neighboring merchants, Schwartz cleaned out the place over the last couple of days."

"Think someone tipped him off?"

"Hard to say. Coming so close after Christy's murder, there might be a leak at the PD," Dan said.

"I heard the two women were lesbian lovers. Was that a leak from the PD too?"

"I don't know, but I'm going to have a showdown with LeBeau when I get there. There's no way we can run a case if the media knows everything we learn."

"Take it slow. Let's not rush to judgment."

At Midtown North, Dan was mobbed by reporters, but fought his way through them. He opened the door to the squad room, spotted LeBeau, and quickly walked over to his desk.

"I've got a bone to pick with you, LeBeau!" he said.

"Yeah? Well, I've been waiting for you to show up too!"

The room got quiet.

"Somebody tipped off Schwartz before our search warrant and the media is reporting the lesbian relationship," Dan shouted. "Did you have anything to do with this?"

"This is a typical fed ploy!" LeBeau shouted as he stood up. "This is the reason we don't work with you guys!"

Captain Watson rushed out of his office. "What the hell—both of you, in my office, right now!"

LeBeau and Dan glared at one another as they followed Watson into his office. Watson closed the door. "Sit down. Tell me what this is about. Dan, you first."

Dan tried to rein in his rage. "Yesterday, LeBeau and I learned Christy and Mary Lee Wen were lovers. We agreed not to share the information with the media. Both of us agreed when we briefed our superiors, we would tell them that piece of information couldn't be let out."

Dan shot a look at LeBeau. "So while I'm watching the eleven o'clock news last night, what tidbit of new information did I hear them report? That Marino was the lesbian lover of a Chinese woman who disappeared the week before. You tell me. How did they learn that?"

LeBeau sat impatiently, his jaw clenched.

"Dan," Watson said, "that's a pretty strong accusation you've—"

"I'm not the one who leaked it," LeBeau said. "Take a hard look at your fellow Joe College Cops before you start throwing that kind of charge around. If you think—"

"Stop it, both of you!" Watson shouted. "Who else knew about Marino and Wen?"

"One of my agents found the letter," Dan said. "I trust him as much as I trust myself. Other than that, I told only my immediate superior."

"Who did you tell?" Watson asked LeBeau.

"I only told you. That's it."

"And what about the search team?" Watson asked.

"They might've found evidence that Christy was a lesbian, but nothing about Wen being her lover."

"You're sure?" Watson asked. "No letters, love notes, cards, anything?"

"Nothing," Dan said.

"Could anyone outside the task force have told the media?" Watson asked.

"Maybe," LeBeau said. "The building super is a sleazeball."

"To the right people, this information could be worth money," Dan said. "While we're on the subject, somebody tipped off Schwartz. We searched Fontaine but they had left, moved out."

"We didn't even know about Fontaine until two days ago," LeBeau said. "You're barking up the wrong tree."

"Okay," Watson said. "I don't know where the leaks came from, and neither do you. It's unfortunate, but it happened. And your verbal sparring isn't going to undo it. There's no basis for accusations here. We'll look into the leaks. You two go solve this case."

LeBeau returned to his desk. Dan followed him and said, "For the record, I don't believe you personally were the source of the leak."

"Same here." LeBeau shrugged. "Hell, the captain's right, it could have come from anywhere."

"Back to the case, have you guys turned up anything new?" Dan asked.

"We finally pried Wen's casing away from the 10th Precinct. Ballistics is comparing the three cartridge cases from the rooftop with the one from Wen's car to see if they match. The examiner thinks the gun was a .22 semi-automatic. Fits with our eye-witness's description of the gun."

"Anything else?"

"We've got a tire print from where Marino's body was dumped. Don't know for sure, but it may have come from the shooter's vehicle."

"The light-colored van," Dan said. "Richie, you've been working homicides for a long time. Can you profile the shooter?"

LeBeau took a deep breath. "In my opinion, it was a professional hit. The .22 semi-automatic is the gun of choice for a professional. He used a silencer. Plus, he took Marino's body away from the scene, and dumped it elsewhere."

"And the three CBS guys—what do you think was going on there?"

"My theory is that Marino was the intended victim. According to our eyewitness, the shooter was parked to the right of her car. I believe he jammed the lock on the driver's side door to force her go to the passenger's side where he could shoot her. He dragged her body around the van and shoved her through the cargo door."

Casey, at a nearby desk covered with neatly sorted stacks of parking permit applications, swiveled in her chair. "Why didn't he just park on the driver's side of the BMW?"

"In my theory, that's what he planned to do," LeBeau said. "But when he arrived on the rooftop, the space on the left was already taken—that car was still there after the shooting. So he had to park on the right and jam the driver's door lock. That forced her to come to him."

"And the three dead CBS employees—another modification of his plan?" Dan asked.

"Classic innocent bystanders. They saw him stuffing Marino's body into the van. They confronted him. Our eye-witness said there were shouts right before he chased them down and killed 'em."

"Boy, that *is* cold." Casey shivered.

"Just another mark of a professional. Can't leave witnesses. He probably had time to pick up the shell casing after shooting Marino, but after shooting the other three, he felt pressured to get out of there. That's when he got in a hurry and left the casings. If he'd seen our eye-witness watching over the dashboard of his car, we probably would've had five dead, and no clues."

"Richie, if I hear you right, you believe Marino was the target," Casey said. "But are you saying she was killed because she was found out to be a cooperating witness in a fraud case?"

"That's one explanation," LeBeau said. "The other explanation has to do with that other woman, Wen. You saw the news?"

"It's what everybody was talking about all morning. I guess killing your wife because she was having an affair is a lot more believable. But either way, do you think both women were killed by the same guy?"

"We'll know for sure once ballistics finishes comparing the shell casings," LeBeau said. "But my gut tells me the same gun was used to kill both women."

Twenty-Five

1:05 PM
January 12th
Manhattan, New York

"Casey, what makes you think this is the one?" Dan said as he looked over her shoulder.

"We checked the other parking applications that listed vans. No other vans could be described as light-colored. This one's silver. Another sixteen parkers own vans, but the DMV lists them all as minivans."

"David Spencer. That doesn't sound like an evil enough name to be our killer," LeBeau glibly said. "What's the plate number, Casey?"

"New York tag, 939-HGY. But that tag belongs on an Olds Cutlass, registered to a Malcolm Steele, reported stolen in December of last year. But wait a minute," Casey said as she held the application up to the light. "Looks like somebody wrote down one license plate then scratched it out and wrote another."

LeBeau put on his glasses, and gave it a closer look. "Looks like 53 something, then GH. Your eyes are younger than mine, Casey. Can you make it out?"

"No."

"Why list one plate and then scratch it out?" Dan asked. "You don't think he'd be stupid enough to write down the real plate number first, do you?"

"Hey, sometimes you get lucky," LeBeau said with a shrug. "Let's run the name that's listed on the application."

"Already did," Casey said as she picked up a computer printout. "Unfortunately, there are 247 David Spencers licensed to drive in the State of New York. Unless we can get a little more on him, this looks like a dead end."

"Dan, why don't we take this application down to One Police Plaza to have the lab try to raise the plate number that's been scratched out," LeBeau said. "While we're there, I want to ask ballistics how they're coming with the shell casings."

"Fine by me." Dan reached for his coat.

"You mind driving?" LeBeau asked as he slipped the application into a briefcase.

"Okay, let's go."

They left the Station House, got into Dan's car, and drove south. Once they were on the West Side Highway, LeBeau said, "There's something I've got to tell you that I didn't want to say in front of the others."

"What's that?"

"Remember when you asked me to check the NYPD files on David Wen?"

"Yeah."

"I heard back from the Intelligence Division and the Jade Squad," LeBeau said. "Both of them know your man's name."

"Oh yeah?"

"There's a restaurant in Chinatown where the natives play cards in a locked basement room," LeBeau said. "The game is guarded by members of the Jade Dragons Tong, and—"

"The shooters at the Chinese restaurant?"

"That's them," LeBeau said. "Intelligence isn't sure if Wen is actually a member, but him being around Tong members paints him with the same brush. One thing the Tongs offer is murder for hire."

"Really?" Dan said, thinking of Sammy. "Didn't you say there was a .22 used in the restaurant that night?"

"Yeah."

"You see where I'm going with this?"

"Sure. Murder for hire. Both with .22's. It could possibly tie in with Marino's murder."

"Problem is, I've been ordered not to get anywhere near the investigation into Sammy's murder."

"Why's that?" LeBeau asked.

"I'd gotten authorization to put Sammy undercover. Problem was, after the murders at the restaurant, the signed authorization memo disappeared. Now I'm under investigation."

"Hmm," LeBeau said. "Classic cover-your-ass move by the higher-ups. Something goes wrong, pick a sacrificial lamb, then develop facts to support the conclusion. But don't worry, you're not investigating Sammy's death. You're helping me investigate the death of Christy Marino. And if that should happen to lead us to the guy who gunned down Sammy, well, we can't help it."

Slowly Dan smiled. Although it had only been weeks, he felt like he'd been fighting for years against something bigger and stronger than himself. Now, out of nowhere, he'd hooked up with someone who was willing to bend the rules enough to support him. It was nice to feel like someone was on his side.

"You've interviewed David Wen," LeBeau said. "What's your take on him?"

"Not a nice man."

"Could he kill?"

"By himself, hard to say. But if you're talking about hiring somebody, yeah, I think so."

"Johnson saw him the night of the murders," LeBeau said. "He thinks the guy could have done it, but I'd like to size him up myself. Can you set it up?"

"Sure. Want to take a Teaneck Detective along with us?"

"I'd rather not."

"Okay. Up for a run over there tonight?"

"Yeah. Unless you've got something planned."

"I only wish," Dan said. "Any other leads on Sammy's murder?"

"I'm not working that any more," LeBeau said. "The Jade Squad took it. From what I hear, they've got no leads."

As they reached One Police Plaza, LeBeau flashed his shield and they were admitted to the parking garage. They rode the elevator to the second floor, LeBeau stopping along the way as he greeted friends and acquaintances. LeBeau led the way to the Firearms and Ballistics Examination section of the NYPD Lab, where he introduced Dan to Detective Howard Morioka. After the usual small talk, LeBeau asked about the shell casings in The CBS Murders case.

"I've just been working on those." Morioka turned back to the counter and adjusted the focus of the ballistics comparison microscope. LeBeau moved in closer, and looked over Morioka's shoulder.

"Excuse me, Richie," Morioka said. "But you're fogging up both my glasses and the microscope."

LeBeau laughed and stepped back.

"What's taking you so long, Howard?" LeBeau asked teasingly.

"This isn't a high school biology monocular, Richie. It's actually two microscopes, joined by prisms, which cause the two images that I see through the eyepiece to appear as a split screen image. Then, I rotate these dials to bring the cartridge casings to the same spot, which enables me to compare them. Are you following this?"

"No, and that's why we hired you."

Morioka turned back to the eyepieces. "Good decision."

"Probably. All those cartridges you're looking at, were they fired from the same gun?"

"Not cartridges, Richie. Cartridge casings," Morioka said. "Cartridges are what they're called before they're fired by a gun. Afterward, you're left with bullets and cartridge casings."

Dan laughed out loud.

"There are similar characteristics present in all three, due to the imprints left by the breech face, the firing pin, the extractor, and the ejector," Morioka said.

"All right, all right," LeBeau said. "Detective Morioka, in your expert opinion, is it likely that the three cartridge casings which you are comparing could have been fired, extracted, and ejected from the same gun?"

"Yes, they definitely were," said Morioka good-naturedly. "That's what I've been telling you. Furthermore, the cartridge casing found in Mrs. Wen's Pontiac bears similar characteristics."

Suddenly LeBeau became serious. "You mean she was shot by the same gun?"

"No, Richie. I haven't been comparing guns. I merely said the cartridge casing found in her car bore imprints of a firing pin, extractor, and ejector mechanisms that were consistent with those found on the cartridge casings located on the rooftop parking lot."

"I know that's your way of saying they match," LeBeau said. "So, apparently he likes the gun well enough that he doesn't want to get rid of it after a hit. Maybe this guy isn't as much of a professional as I thought. Howard, were you able to do anything with the slugs, I mean bullets the Medical Examiner dug out of the four victim's heads?"

Morioka picked up on the seriousness and intensity. "Not much. As you know, when a .22 penetrates the bone of the skull, it deforms and sometimes fragments. That's one reason pros like that caliber. From the little I could make out, I suspect the bullets were hollow points, and they had lands and grooves in a six-right pattern consistent with a High Standard .22 automatic. That's the gun you should be looking for."

"Terrific," LeBeau said. "I'll check to see if Wen has a pistol permit. Now, Howard, didn't you do the work on that shooting at the Chinese restaurant?'

"Yeah, I caught that one," Morioka said.

"Do you remember what guns were used?" LeBeau said.

"Some 9 mm I thought came from a Heckler & Koch. But I also seem to recall there was a .22 that may have come from a High Standard."

"Would you do me a favor?"

"I know. I'll dig out the Chinatown murders .22 cartridge casings and compare them to these. Whether they match or not, I'll give you a call."

"Thanks, Howard. Appreciate your help. Look forward to your report."

LeBeau led Dan down the hall to the Document Examination room.

"David Wen and The Jade Dragons Tong are looking better and better," Dan said.

"I know you'd like to see us pin this one on the Tong, and I'd like nothing better. But I can't picture a Tong member using an alias like David Spencer. Besides, there's still a possibility that your guy . . . what's the name of the Fontaine guy?"

"Schwartz. Bernie Schwartz."

"Yeah, Schwartz. Let's not forget he had a motive to keep the two women from talking."

"But Mary Lee Wen never did talk to us," Dan said. "For that matter, Christy Marino never told us anything before she was killed. If she hadn't given me that packet of information, we would have shut down our case on Fontaine."

"True, but didn't you try to get them to talk in public? You may have been seen."

"On a crowded street and in a crowded restaurant. We were careful. And killing them because of the possibility they might have talked? It feels thin."

"Well, how much did you say the fraud involved?" asked LeBeau.

"Somewhere around seventeen million."

"I've seen people killed for a lot less."

"I still like David Wen as the suspect," Dan said as they walked into the Document Examination Section.

A woman wearing a lab coat over a short dress and heels looked up as they walked in. "Well, look who the cat dragged in."

"Gorgeous Gail," LeBeau said. "How the hell are you?"

"Just fine. It's been a long time."

Gail stood up and walked over to LeBeau and shook his hand. Dan found himself more than interested. She was five-foot seven, blond, and in a dress which showed off her long shapely legs.

What can I do for you?" she said.

"What I want, and what I need, are two separate things," LeBeau said. "I'm afraid I'll have to settle for what I need. But first, I'd like to introduce you to FBI Agent Dan Robertson. Dan, Gail Thompson."

Thompson smiled, her gaze locked on his blue eyes. "How do you do?"

"The pleasure's all mine," Dan said.

"Excuse me, Gail?" LeBeau said, attempting to be noticed.

"Sorry, Richie, what's up?"

"I need your help on a document." LeBeau slid the document out of the paper envelope, and handed the plastic-encased parking application to Thompson. "I've got to get this processed for prints, but right now I need to know what license number was written then crossed out."

She held the document up to the light. "Does this have anything to do with The CBS Murders, Richie? I heard you caught that one."

"Right there in your hands, you may well have the key to unlocking the true identity of the killer," LeBeau said melodramatically.

Thompson rolled her eyes. "Let's see what we're able to do with this."

She slipped the application into the Foster & Freeman VC2000 Full Spectrum light box. As she turned out the lights in the room, and turned on the machine, light shone through the application onto a glass surface. She adjusted the focus, and the enlarged letters became readable, even though their edges were fuzzy. Thompson maneuvered the document until the license plate information was displayed, and began making adjustments that changed it to ultraviolet light. After about ten minutes of fiddling, she said, "There it is, Richie."

LeBeau looked over her shoulder. "It looks like 538 YGH." He wrote down the number. "Gail, I can't thank you enough. This is probably our best lead. We've got to get back uptown and run this out."

Thompson extended her hand to Dan and shook his, gently wrapping her long fingers around it. "If there's ever anything I can do for you, all you have to do is whistle," she said in a passable Lauren Bacall.

Dan smiled and said, "Thanks."

LeBeau had watched them with a mix of jealousy and disgust. "Dan, I can't take any more of this. Let's go."

Twenty-Six

4:15 PM
January 12th
Manhattan, New York

"Looks like the media has given up for the day," Dan said as he pulled into the Midtown North parking lot.

"Only because they've got deadlines to meet," LeBeau answered. "They'll be back bright and early tomorrow morning."

They climbed the stairs and walked into the Squad room.

"How'd you guys make out?" Casey asked.

"538 YGH," LeBeau said. "Somebody run that puppy. Wen and Marino were killed by the same gun."

The normal buzz of the squad room became quiet. All eyes went to one of the IA's who was tapping away at a keyboard.

"Got it," the clerk said, "It's not a New York plate. It's New Jersey."

"Please tell me its David Wen," LeBeau said.

"No. Bart O'Reilly of Keansburg. Plate should have been on a Ford Escort. Hasn't been reported stolen, so he may be the owner."

"Maybe he's swapping plates between vehicles," Sandoval said. "Any Chevy vans registered to him?"

"No," LeBeau said, scanning the screen. "But there's a Ford Econoline. If he's our guy, maybe he's playing games with the make as well as the plate."

"Does it list the color?" Sandoval asked.

"Yeah," LeBeau said. "Silver. That light colored enough for you?"

"All right!" Sandoval yelled, to a chorus of cheers.

"Hey, hey, hey," LeBeau said. "Slow down. All this depends on our killer listing the correct plate from his own vehicle. It's possible, since he crossed it out for some reason. But if someone made up the plate, it may have nothing to do with Bart O'Reilly. This is what we're going to do. Bennett, you and Clements go over to that outfit that owns the parking garage. Find out who would have touched the application, fingerprint them, and bring back their prints."

"Okay," Bennett and Clements said.

"Erik," LeBeau said to Sandoval. "You and Casey do a complete work-up on O'Reilly. Find out if he's got a record either in New York or Jersey. Get his photo from his rap sheet if he's been busted, otherwise from his driver's license. If he's got a record, get his fingerprint card. It may be a long shot, but we've got to know if we're heading down the right path."

"You got it," said Sandoval.

"Oh, speaking of long shots," Casey said, "our lab called while you were gone. The matchstick tested positive for saliva, and they think they've got enough for DNA typing."

LeBeau laughed out loud. "Today the world's my oyster. Listen, somebody hired this guy, so Dan and I are going to take a run over to have a chat with David Wen. Dan, would you . . ."

"Yeah, I'll drive."

The rush hour traffic was bad, and it was 7:30 PM when they reached Wen's door.

"Mr. Wen?" LeBeau said. "I think you've met Agent Robertson from the FBI. I'm Detective LeBeau from the NYPD. Can we come in?"

"No, I don't think so."

LeBeau and Dan looked at each other. "We need to ask you some questions about some similarities in the way your wife and Ms. Marino were killed," LeBeau said.

"They're both dead, so what could we possibly have to say to each other?"

Wen's attempt to shut the door was momentarily blocked by LeBeau's foot.

"Get the hell off my property right now or I'll have you both arrested for trespassing!" Wen screamed.

Just before he forced the door shut, Dan got a glimpse of Wen's contorted face. LeBeau and Dan found their way back to their car in the dark.

LeBeau shook his head. "Did you see his face? I would definitely call that a murderous rage."

"Casey and I saw that same fury."

"He's a suspect in my book. We need to do a work-up on Wen to find out what he was doing, both the night his wife disappeared, and the evening Marino was killed. He probably wasn't the shooter, but you never know. I also want to see if he's spent a lot of money recently that could've been paid to a hit man."

Dan nodded. He quickly made it all connect. That would nail the shooter and tie him to Wen, and then Wen would lead them back to the Jade Dragons Tong who killed Sammy.

* * *

Back at Midtown North, Dan and LeBeau found Bennett and Clements at their desks.

"Looks like we're not going to be able to print everyone at the parking company until tomorrow morning," Clements said.

"By the time we got to the parking outfit, everybody had gone home," Bennett said.

"On the bright side," Sandoval said. "O'Reilly was busted in New York, not long ago."

"Murder?" LeBeau said. "Assault with a deadly weapon? I don't want to hear about a speeding ticket."

"Oh," Sandoval said.

LeBeau dropped into a chair. "All right, what?"

"Well," Sandoval said. "As best as I can make it out, he cloned a taxi."

"He what?" LeBeau asked. "Erik, I swear, if you're yanking my chain—"

"No, that's what I said," Sandoval said. "According to what's on the computer, he bought an old Ford, painted it taxi yellow, and rigged an in-service light on the roof. Then he made casts of another taxi's license plate and medallion—they go for a half-million you know—and created copies for his cloned taxi."

"And that's all you came up with?"

"Afraid so," Sandoval said. "You want me to run down to records and pull the prints and photo?"

LeBeau thought about it for a moment. "No, it's getting late. Besides, somebody who goes to the trouble to clone a taxi doesn't sound like a killer to me. I think it can wait."

LeBeau stood up and clapped his hands. "Okay everyone, let's call it a day. Jim, tomorrow morning, why don't you and Jackson take a run back to the 104th in Queens and see if they've got anything more in their files about either Wen or Marino. I don't want to overlook something that's already been done."

"You got it," Detective Jim Moore said.

"Jack," LeBeau said to Detective Duffy. "Tomorrow I want you to run down some information on David Wen, Bernie Schwartz, and Bart O'Reilly. Have any of them purchased a .22 caliber High Standard pistol? I don't know anything about licensing a pistol in New Jersey, so you can become our expert, okay?"

"Sure thing," Duffy said.

"Dan, why don't you get on an extension? I got an idea I'd like to try." LeBeau leafed through his notes until he found what he was looking for, picked up the telephone, and punched in a string of numbers. The phone rang five times before it was answered.

"Hello?" answered a groggy voice.

"Mr. Sorice?" LeBeau asked.

"Yeah. Who's this?"

"This is Detective LeBeau from the NYPD," LeBeau said. "Remember, we talked after the . . . after your friends were killed?"

There was silence on the other end of the line. "Oh, it's you."

"I'm really sorry to bother you. I know it's late, but I need to ask you a question. Okay?"

"I guess."

"When I talked to you before, I asked you about the man who killed everybody," LeBeau said. "Do you remember?"

175

"Yeah."

"You said the killer wasn't black," said LeBeau.

"Yeah."

"Is there any chance the killer could have been Asian? You know, Chinese or something."

"I . . . don't know."

"Okay, let me put it another way," LeBeau said. "Could you say the man who shot your friends was definitely not Asian? Like you were sure he was Caucasian or white."

"I'm not sure anymore. I know he wasn't black, but I can't recall if he was white or Chinese. Sorry, I just can't remember."

"Mr. Sorice, this is really important."

"I know, but I just can't remember."

"Okay. Thank you for your time, and I appreciate your help." LeBeau hung up the telephone receiver. "Son of a bitch!"

Dan hung up more quietly. "Did you expect anything else?"

"No, but . . ." LeBeau glanced at his watch. "Okay, guys, it's a quarter after eleven and I suspect we've already been given our quota of break-throughs for a half-day's work. Let's knock it off and hit it again first thing tomorrow morning."

Twenty-Seven

8:30 AM
January 13th
Manhattan, New York

"Okay, Barry, pull the plug on it. I'll talk to you later," LeBeau said on the phone. Dan had just arrived at the squad room at Midtown North and found it empty since the agents and detectives were out handling their assignments.

"What's cooking?" Dan asked.

"That was the police artist. Been working with our eyewitness," LeBeau said as he hung up. "Going nowhere. Gonna quit trying to come up with a drawing of our shooter. The artist thinks our eyewitness might be sandbagging us, and a convenient memory lapse will keep the killer from coming for him. What've you been doing?"

"I had to go by the FBI office for my obligatory email summary. Unfortunately, the AD was there, so I got an earful about how the Director was getting real tired of taking calls from the Chairman of CBS, and couldn't we wrap this up a little faster. Is there any coffee?"

"With the troops out early, you ought to be able to get a cup."

Dan helped himself to a cup, and came over and sat down. "Remember our conversation about trying to find out if David Wen had taken a chunk of money out of the bank to pay a hit man? Let's find out where he banks, and get a federal subpoena for those records."

"Why federal?"

"If a detective lays a DA's subpoena on a bank, how long does it take for you to get a response?"

"I don't know. Depends. Three, four weeks."

"We've got pretty good leverage with the banks," Dan said. "If they don't help us on this, we don't help them when they've got an embezzlement or wire fraud. We should get something back the next day, or the same day if we told them it was a rush."

"By all means, get a federal subpoena." LeBeau shook his head.

Dan made some calls to put the bank subpoena into motion and reviewed the interviews of the parkers the night of the murders. The squad room door burst open, and Jackson and Moore came in, both smiling broadly.

"Bingo!" Moore said.

"Well, don't just stand there gloating," LeBeau said. "Spit it out."

"We went over to the 104th and talked with Rudolfsky."

"He told us that Marino had tried to file a missing persons report on Mary Lee Wen," said Jackson.

"Mary Lee visited Marino the night she disappeared," Moore said.

"Afterwards, Marino plastered fliers all over the neighborhood, offering a reward for anybody who had information about what happened to her."

"Apparently there were two college kids making out in a car across the street," said Moore. "They saw a woman they think was Mary Lee, come out of Marino's apartment building, and walk down the sidewalk to her car."

"Just as she reached this little station wagon, a man jumped out of a silver van, and pushed her into her own car. Then he got behind the steering wheel and drove it away, followed by whoever was driving the silver van."

"Did they see the man shoot her?" LeBeau asked.

"I asked Rudolfsky," Moore said. "He said they were too far away to see, and they didn't hear a gun."

"He likes a silencer," LeBeau said. "And now we know he sometimes uses an accomplice."

"I wonder if his accomplice owns a Heckler and Koch 9 mm?" Dan said.

"Good question," LeBeau said. "Did the kids give any kind of description of the men?"

Jackson shook his head. "The one who pushed her into her car was wearing a ski mask. They never got a look at the other guy."

"Build? Short, tall, slim, husky?"

"Happened so fast they really didn't notice," Moore said.

"Dammit, why didn't Rudolfsky tell us about this the night Marino was killed?"

"Want to know what he said when we asked him?" Jackson said.

"Yeah," Dan said.

"He said that we asked him about Marino. If we wanted to know something about Wen, we should have asked about her." Moore said.

LeBeau threw his hands in the air. "And this guy made detective?"

Moore shrugged his shoulders.

"Nice job, guys," Dan said.

"So don't stand around here with your thumb up your ass," LeBeau interrupted. "Get back out there and find those kids. See if there's anything else they forgot to mention. Ask them about the license plate on the van. Ask them if they'd be willing to be hypnotized to see if we could learn anything else they can't remember. Do I have to solve this one all by myself?"

Dan laughed when he saw Moore reach the door, then turn and give LeBeau the finger.

"Have you heard from anybody else?" Dan asked.

"Casey and Sandoval were in earlier," LeBeau said. "They went down to records to pull everything on O'Reilly's taxi scam. I told them to call me before they came back. Clements and Bennett went to pick up a set of O'Reilly's fingerprints, and see if the lab can lift prints from his parking application. With any luck, they'll find O'Reilly's."

"Problem is, if we find his prints, it only tells us he didn't use his real name when he signed up for monthly parking," Dan said. "That's not a crime. For all we know, he might have a little squeeze on the side."

"I know you like David Wen and the Tong, but—" The telephone rang, and LeBeau grabbed it. "Midtown North. Detective LeBeau . . . Yeah, Howard . . . Sure, why not go ahead and ruin my day . . . You're sure? . . . Well, thanks. I appreciate the call." LeBeau hung up. "Our shooter wasn't at the Most Elegant Golden Dragon. Or at least his gun wasn't. The .22 casings don't match."

"But if he was a pro, he might own more than one gun."

"Come on, Dan," LeBeau said. "You're starting to reach a little here. Remember, we still don't have a decent Chinese suspect unless Wen himself was the killer."

"Can you imagine a hit man who clones taxis in his spare time?"

The phone rang again, and Dan picked it up. "Task Force. Agent Robertson . . .Go down to records and hook up with Sandoval and Jackson. Give us a call once the lab has raised the prints and made comparisons. We can use some good news." Dan hung up. "Maybe I am a little too hungry for David Wen. Shouldn't we take O'Reilly just as seriously?"

"What do you mean?"

"There was a lot more information on that application besides that scratched out plate," Dan said. "We ran only his name through DMV. There was an address on the west side of Manhattan, not too far from the parking lot. There was a telephone number. We've got a lot more work to do."

"But if O'Reilly's prints turn up on the application, we don't need to head in other directions," LeBeau said.

"With a case this high-profile, we can't afford not to run out every lead."

LeBeau sat quietly for a moment. "Goddamned Joe College cops. All right, what do you want to check out first?"

Dan got a copy of the application from the IA's. "The address listed was 436 West Forty-Fifth Street. Let's get a photo of O'Reilly, take it over there and see if anybody recognizes him."

"Okay," LeBeau said. "I'll call Sandoval and have him put a copy of his photo in an RMP car and run it up to us, red lights and siren."

In about fifteen minutes, the photo was in their hands. LeBeau opened the envelope, as Dan looked over his shoulder at a swarthy, dark haired man with a hard look to his eyes.

"Looks like a thug," Dan said.

"Yeah," LeBeau said. "If I had a daughter, I'd sure as hell never let this guy come around. Let's take a ride over to Forty-Fifth Street. I just remembered, all our cars are being used. You mind driving?"

Dan sighed. "No problem, Richie."

LeBeau put on his Fedora, and he and Dan drove to the garage. A Hispanic man stood on the sidewalk smoking a cigarette.

"You work here?" LeBeau asked the man.

"What's it to you?"

LeBeau flashed his shield. "I'm a NYPD Detective, and I ask people questions for a living. Got a problem with that?"

The hand holding the cigarette began shaking.

"I don't got no problem with it," the man said in a soft, hoarse voice. "I'm the super here."

Dan showed his FBI credentials. "What's your name?"

"Diego Chavez."

"Diego," LeBeau said. "Let's go inside and have a little chat. Okay?"

Chavez turned and led them into the garage. Nothing was parked there, but there were plenty of tire marks on the floor. In the front of the garage, there was a small office, a desk and chair visible through the door. Another desk and chair out in the open in the rear, a telephone on the desk.

"Who owns this place, Diego?" LeBeau asked.

"Tartaglia," Chavez said. "Vince Tartaglia."

"What's he use it for?" Dan asked.

"He runs a catering business," Chavez said. "He sends food for the people when they make movies or television shows in New York. This is where he keeps the wagons and stuff."

"Where are they are today?" Dan asked.

"Up in Harlem shooting *Law and Order*."

"Is his the only business run outta here?" LeBeau asked.

"Yeah," Chavez said.

Unconvinced, LeBeau let his eyes wander around the garage until he focused on the desk in the rear. "What's that?"

"Just a desk they use sometimes."

"Don't jerk us around, Diego!" Dan said. "Who uses it?"

"Anybody who needs it."

LeBeau fixed a stare on Chavez.

"What?" Chavez asked.

"Tell us about O'Reilly," LeBeau said, his stare unflinching.

"Who?"

LeBeau took the photo of O'Reilly out of his pocket and showed it to Chavez. "Now are you going to tell us about him, or do we need to take you back to the station and talk to you about him for the next three or four hours?"

Chavez tried to take a drag, but his hand was shaking so badly the cigarette slipped out of his fingers and dropped to the floor. Dan stepped on it. Chavez silently considered his options. "Look, I gotta be here when they come back. If I ain't, I get fired."

"So you're telling us you'd rather talk here about O'Reilly," Dan said. "Right?"

"Okay, he rents that desk over there." Chavez pointed his thumb toward the desk in the rear.

"How long's he been doing that, Diego?" LeBeau asked.

"I don't know. A few months."

"Who pays for the phone?" Dan asked. "O'Reilly?" Chavez nodded.

Dan walked over to the desk in the rear, and used the phone. A computerized voice said, "Two one two five six five nine one four seven." He wrote it down.

"Why does O'Reilly rent space here?" LeBeau asked.

"Sometimes he's got work here in Manhattan," Chavez said. "He uses it like an office."

"What kind of work does he do, Diego?" LeBeau asked.

"I'm not sure. I think all kinds of work, but something to do with cleaning filters, maybe from restaurants and air conditioners."

"Did he use this garage on Monday," Dan asked.

"I don't know," Chavez said. "I gone to the doctor that day, so maybe he have. He got his own key. Maybe he come and go and I never seen him."

"Doctor?" LeBeau asked. "I'm sure he'll be able to confirm you were there. What's his name and address?"

"I . . . I . . . ah, I don't remember," Chavez said.

"You never went to a doctor did you, Diego?" Dan said.

"You were here all day, because you didn't want to get fired, right?" LeBeau said.

"All right, all right, O'Reilly come here on Monday."

"Day, evening, both?" LeBeau asked.

Chavez didn't answer immediately, but got quiet and looked down. Finally in a soft voice said, "Both."

"What does he drive, Diego?" Dan asked.

"A van."

"It's silver, isn't it?" LeBeau asked.

"Yeah."

Twenty-Eight

11:10 AM
January 13th
Manhattan, New York

"I've always found people who aren't busy stick their noses into other people's business," LeBeau said, "and Chavez isn't busy. I'll bet he knows everything about O'Reilly's comings and goings."

"What are you getting at?" Dan asked.

"If O'Reilly had just killed four people, he'd be crazy to go driving around with one of the victims bleeding all over the back of his van. As quick as he could, he'd get that van off the street and into the garage until things settled down. Later that night, he'd drive to lower Manhattan and dump her body."

"Okay," Dan said. "I can understand him getting the van out of sight, but I'm still having trouble understanding why he took Christy's body with him. He's only going to dump it later. Why didn't he just leave her in the parking lot?"

"Because it slows down the cops when the killer makes the body disappear. Then the cops aren't investigating a murder, they're investigating a missing person, if and when somebody finally reports that person missing. Look how long it took us to get onto Mary Lee Wen."

"But he left three bodies behind."

LeBeau shrugged. "She's the only one he planned to kill. He already had her in the van and he could buy some time by taking her body. He figured the cops would be left wondering why somebody wanted to knock off three CBS guys. Plus he had to get out of there."

"Okay, I can see that. But it still leaves him in the van, on the street, a body in the back. Isn't that risky?"

LeBeau shook his head. "Not really. What would it take, five minutes tops, to make the run over to the garage? He probably figured it'd take the cops longer than that to get a description of his van."

"But when he gets to the garage, he runs into Diego Chavez. Now, does he admit to him he's just killed four people, one in the back of the van? Or does he not tell him, hoping his behavior won't give him away?"

"Good question," LeBeau said. "Ever consider becoming a homicide cop?"

Dan smiled. "Might be interesting."

"It has its moments. Anyway, I think he'd opt for telling Chavez. It's risky, but by telling him about it, O'Reilly turns Chavez into his accomplice. Chavez might not even be aware that's what's happened. When he does figure it out, he'd realize he's got a lot to lose if he decides to talk."

"Okay," Dan said. "But you still haven't convinced me he needs to dump her body in Manhattan."

"I'm not finished," LeBeau said with a smile. "The more he thinks about it, the more O'Reilly begins to give the police more credit than they deserve. Paranoia kicks in. Video cameras watching all the bridges and the tunnels. Cops in RMP cars ready to pull over and search every silver van heading out of Manhattan. He can't risk it. So he waits in the garage for three or four hours, takes side streets, and finds a dark alley where he can dump her body, not far from an exit out of Manhattan. After he gets rid of her body, he takes the Holland Tunnel and drives home to Keansburg."

"Or Teaneck."

"Still pushing Wen, are you?"

"Not so much as the shooter, but rather the one who paid the shooter. We can't rule him out."

"I don't think we should rule him out," LeBeau said. "But I'm really leaning toward our taxi cloner."

"True he cloned a taxi, but so far all we've got is that he sort of lied on his parking application—fake name, phony plate number, real address, and a phone number that doesn't square with the one on his desk—that's something else we need to run out."

"Yeah, all right," LeBeau said, "I'll admit—" The phone interrupted them. LeBeau grabbed it. "Midtown North, Detective LeBeau . . . What you got for me, Erik? And don't tell me anything I don't want to hear . . . Well that's good news, Erik . . . Any of them match O'Reilly's prints? . . . Look, I told you not to do that . . . Come on back."

LeBeau hung up the receiver. "The lab found ten partial prints on the application they believe are O'Reilly's. But they need eight to twelve matching reference points before they're willing to definitively say they're his."

"Rats! Well, let's take another approach. Remember the telephone in the back of the garage?"

"Yeah?"

"I used the telephone company's code numbers and learned the number of the phone is different from the one he listed on the application."

"So, what've you got in mind?" LeBeau said.

"If O'Reilly is our man—and at this point I'm not ready to concede that he is—then in your scenario he's stuck in that garage for three or four hours while he waits for the heat to die down. So, why don't we find out if he used the phone while he was waiting?"

"Not a bad idea, but how are we going to know for sure it was him using the phone?" LeBeau asked. "If the people who work for Tartaglia's catering business are in and out of there all day, any of them could have used the phone."

"I didn't say my theory was perfect, but why don't we get the phone records and see what we come up with?"

"Can you pull your subpoena magic on this one too?"

"Yep, we'll have them in a day or two." Dan called and put the subpoena in motion. Afterwards, he called the Investigative Analyst who handled subpoenas for bank account information, gave him the information about David Wen, and asked the IA to locate all the checking and savings accounts in his name and look for any large cash withdrawal since the first of the year. He asked the IA to do the same for O'Reilly, but to look for a large cash deposit during the same time period.

"Why don't you run O'Reilly's name and license plate through the FBI files, and see if you guys have ever had him turn up during one of your investigations?"

"Good idea."

"I haven't given up on Wen by any stretch of the imagination," LeBeau said. "After all, it was a silver van at the Chinatown shooting. And whoever shot Mary Lee Wen wore a ski mask and had a wheel man, just like in Chinatown."

"And the .22's that don't match?"

"No reason whoever killed Wen and Marino couldn't have had more than one High Standard .22 pistol. After all, there were at least three or four different guns in Chinatown. Who's to say that the driver of the silver van didn't have our gun stuck in his waistband?"

Dan smiled. "I knew you'd come around sooner or later."

"I haven't come around, I'm just keeping the door open."

Twenty-Nine

8:30 AM
January 14th
Manhattan, New York

"Robertson—See me ASAP—Thomas," said the phone message.

Dan had barely arrived in the FBI office. He took the shortcut through the men's room to the AD's office, and stuck his head through the open doorway of Thomas' office.

"Nick? Looking for me?"

"Come in and sit down." Thomas' tone wasn't cordial.

Dan set his briefcase and topcoat on one chair and sat in another. The AD had every New York newspaper lying on his desk in front of him.

"Have you seen these?" Thomas asked.

January 14th

"Yes, I have."

"Who's talking to the press? You?"

"Nick, you know me better than that. I don't know who's talking, but it's got to be somebody with inside knowledge. We only found out yesterday the cartridge casings matched."

"The part that bothers me the most is where they say . . ." Thomas picked up the newspaper. ". . . 'the Task Force has enough information to make arrests, but for some unknown reason, they haven't.' Is that accurate?"

"No it's not. Sure, we've got the cartridge casings matching and O'Reilly's partial prints on the parking application, but that's all. That isn't enough probable cause to get a search warrant, much less an arrest warrant. We're quickly developing evidence, but as of now, we just don't have enough."

"If the leak isn't you, then who is it? LeBeau?"

"He says he's not. The story's got too many details for it to be someone outside the Task Force."

Thomas paused, as if to carefully phrase his next words. "Dan, I'm aware of the previous leak to the press."

"What leak?"

"The lesbian relationship of the two women. I didn't say anything at the time, but there was talk that you were the source of that leak. Were you?"

"No way!" Dan shouted, then fought to gain control. "I was livid when I heard that on the news. I had an agreement with LeBeau that neither the FBI nor the NYPD would let out that information. You and I both know we haven't worked with the NYPD that much because of our concern that information would get leaked to the press."

"This leak may have come from our side just as easily as theirs."

"So what are you saying?" Dan said in astonishment.

Thomas fixed his stare on Dan. "What I'm going to do is make sure that nobody within the FBI is the leak. That includes you."

"In other words, you no longer trust my word?"

"I didn't say that. But I need to have more than just the word of our agents that they're not the source of the leak. If you aren't the source, then you've got nothing to worry about."

Dan felt himself relax a bit. There was sense in what Thomas said. "So, how are you going to go about it? That is, if you're willing to tell me."

"I don't mind telling you," Thomas said. "I'm on a first name basis with most of the TV and print journalists. I'm going to ask them to tell me, on a confidential basis, who the leak is. Once I know who it is, somebody's head is going to roll."

"But what if the leak came from someone on the NYPD side of the Task Force?"

"I've already talked to PC Donovan. He's ready to take quick severe action against anyone in the NYPD found to be the source of the leak. Until we know who it is, neither one of us is taking sides, if that's your concern."

"Thank you for that," Dan said. "Anything else?"

"Just one last thing," Thomas said. "You're a good man. I don't want to see your career destroyed. But if you're not being straight with me, I won't hesitate to pull the trigger." Thomas picked up the next phone message to return a call. The meeting was over.

Dan nodded. He hadn't done anything wrong, but he hadn't done anything wrong in the Tong case either. His being accused of things he hadn't done was becoming a pattern. Dan walked away feeling both stunned and angry that Thomas might consider him the leak.

Sometimes the press was far afield. But when they were on the money, like the stories about the investigation of The CBS Murders, it unnerved him. Somebody was talking.

Dan found his way to the garage and drove to Midtown North, not even aware of the world around him. At least not until he turned into the courtyard of the station house and the media surrounded his car like a swarm of bees.

"Have you found the gun used to shoot the people?" someone screamed through his closed car window.

"How soon before you arrest your prime suspect?" another yelled.

The reporters were shoved around by their peers. Microphones were stuck towards him. Camera flashes went off. He began lurching the car forward, and slamming on the brakes. He kept repeating it, making a foot of headway each time.

"Are the FBI and the NYPD able to work together?"

Lurch forward. Brake.

"Why were these women killed?"

Lurch forward. Brake.

"How did you learn about the love relationship between the two women?"

Lurch forward. Brake.

Finally Dan was rescued by uniformed officers who had come out of the Station House to get into their RMP car. They became crowd control officers, and like Moses parting the Red Sea, formed a corridor for Dan. He gave them a wave of thanks, drove to the back of the courtyard, parked, then walked up the stairs to the squad room.

"You got the media welcome too?" Watson said as he turned away from the window.

"Yeah." Dan dumped his briefcase and coat and poured himself a cup of coffee. He spotted LeBeau, and walked over and leaned against the edge of his desk. "I was called on the carpet regarding the news leak about the matching cartridge cases." Dan took a sip of coffee.

"You too?" LeBeau answered. "I was given the third degree this morning. Anything new since last night?"

"Not on my end."

"Son of a bitch!" Casey shouted as she slammed down the phone. "The bastard!"

"What is it?" Dan asked.

"That was Weinstein. Fontaine filed for bankruptcy yesterday!" She stood and began pacing.

"What does that mean for your fraud case?" LeBeau asked.

"It means that if I don't get moving, MBT Factors won't recover a thing."

Dan mentally chastised himself for focusing solely on the murders and letting Schwartz jerk the FBI around. "What does Weinstein plan to do about it?"

"He wants to put me into the grand jury today. He'll ask for an indictment so we can arrest Schwartz before he stashes whatever's left. I've got to go meet with Weinstein now. He's going to put me on the stand right away."

"Anything we can do for you?" Dan asked.

Casey gathered papers from her desk and shoved them into her briefcase. "If you've got the time, would you take a run up to New Rochelle and make sure Schwartz is still around?"

"Yeah, I can do that," Dan said. "Anything in particular you want me to ask?"

"Nah, just waltz him around and let him know we haven't forgotten him. I've got to go. The IA's can give you whatever you need." Casey stormed out the door.

"You gonna head up there now, Dan?" LeBeau asked.

"Sure, why not?"

"Mind if I come along? If O'Reilly's our killer, Schwartz might be the person behind the killer. I really ought to look at the guy."

"It's not a pretty sight." Dan got Schwartz's address from the IAs and picked up his briefcase and coat, and he and LeBeau walked to the car. "You want to drive, Richie?"

"No. You better."

"Why's that?"

"Because if you don't drive, I won't solve this case for you."

The two men got the FBI sedan, with Dan behind the wheel. "Richie, I don't think I've ever seen you drive."

"That's not only keenly observant, but also correct."

"Why's that?"

"I can't," LeBeau said with a straight face.

"Why, some kind of disability?"

"No, I don't have a driver's license, and I don't know how to drive."

"You're kidding," Dan said as they crossed the Triboro Bridge.

"No."

"How do you get around?"

"Subway, cabs, or having some nice person, like you, drive me," LeBeau said with a smile.

"Didn't the NYPD require you to have a driver's license?"

"Not when I joined the force."

Dan continued driving north up the Bruckner Expressway. "Didn't you have to drive a patrol car?"

"No, I walked a beat," LeBeau said proudly.

"That's incredible!" Dan said as he headed north on Interstate 95.

They made it to New Rochelle in forty minutes. Dan turned off I-95 onto the Boston Post Road and soon reached a section of New Rochelle known as "Larchmont Woods." Harding Street was just two blocks east of the Post Road, and they easily found number 59.

The unpretentious red brick colonial house was situated on a small lot. Although the grass needed to be cut, the house appeared to be well maintained. There was no response when they rang the doorbell. They saw some movement of the front window curtains. Dan walked over to the window and waited while LeBeau rang the doorbell again. The curtains moved again, and when they did, a teenage boy found himself looking out the window at Dan and his FBI credentials.

"Be a nice young man and open the door for us," Dan said in a loud voice through the glass. "Would you do that for us, please? Otherwise we'll break it down!"

The door opened a crack, and LeBeau shoved the door open with such force that it knocked down the young man in the process. Hearing the commotion, a second teenager joined his brother.

"I'm Detective LeBeau from the NYPD," LeBeau said as he showed the boys his gold shield, "and this is Agent Robertson from the FBI. Thank you for opening the door. I hope you didn't hurt yourself."

The teenager was nursing a bloody lip and a reddened nose with his right hand. "Like, what do you want?"

"Since we've been nice enough to tell you who we are, why don't you tell us who you are?" LeBeau said.

"I'm Daniel Schwartz. That's my brother Jacob. Like, what do you want?"

"Is Bernie Schwartz your father?" LeBeau asked.

"Yeah. Why? What's it to you?" Daniel Schwartz said. Jacob said nothing but watched and listened.

"Would you be kind enough to tell him we'd like to talk to him?" LeBeau asked.

"Like, he isn't here."

"Then you won't mind if we look around."

"Sure, if you've got, like, a search warrant, or something. But even then you'll only find out he's not here. You know?"

"So you know about search warrants," LeBeau said. "You've had experience with them?"

"No."

"Where's your father?" LeBeau asked, more forcefully.

"I told you," Schwartz said. "He's not here."

"You already told me that, and that's not what I asked you," LeBeau said, losing his patience. "Where is your father?"

"He and my mother went to Israel."

"When was that?" Dan asked.

"A few days ago."

"And when are they coming back?" LeBeau asked.

"Hey, I don't know," Schwartz said. "Like, they didn't say."

"Where are they staying?"

"They didn't tell us, you know?"

"Are you telling me, they left you and your brother home alone, and didn't tell you how to get in touch with them?" Dan said. "Who's taking care of you?"

Schwartz glanced at his brother then said defiantly, "We can take care of ourselves."

"I don't believe you," Dan said, then turned to LeBeau. "Do you believe them?"

"Sure, I believe them," LeBeau said. "You know what I think? I think their parents abandoned them. They're both minors, so we have no choice but to call Child Welfare and have them put into foster homes. When their parents get home, they can go to court, that is, if they want these two back."

"Hey, come on," Schwartz said. "Please, mister. Don't do that. We're, like, okay. Look, they left us some money."

"How much?" LeBeau asked.

"A thousand bucks."

"Sounds like they abandoned you for a long time," Dan said.

"Nah. They're coming back."

"I wouldn't be so sure," LeBeau said.

"Really, they'll be back."

"Do they call you? "Dan asked.

"Yeah."

"How often?" asked LeBeau.

"Like, every couple of days."

"Listen, Daniel, and this goes for you too, Jacob," LeBeau said as he looked sternly at the teenager. "The next time your parents call, tell them the FBI and the New York City Police Department want to talk to them. Have you got that?"

"Yeah."

"I'm going to give you a business card, and so will Mr. Robertson. Those cards have the telephone numbers where your parents can call us. Have you got that?"

"Yeah."

"One more thing," LeBeau said. "Are you going to be able to remember all this, or do you need to write it down?"

"I can remember it," Daniel said with annoyance.

"Good. The last thing is, if they don't call Mr. LeBeau or Mr. Robertson in the next forty-eight hours—that's two days—Child Welfare will come take you and your brother, and put you both in foster homes. Have you got all that?"

"Yeah, I'll tell them."

"Listen, Daniel, this isn't a game," Dan said. "We're not kidding."

"Like, okay, I got it."

"Good," LeBeau said. "Want to add anything, Dan?"

"No, I think you, like, covered it."

The two men turned and walked back to the car. The front door of the house didn't close until they were out of sight.

"Smart-assed little kids, wouldn't you say, Richie?"

"You got that right. Spoiled rotten. If they were mine, they'd learn some manners."

"Think the Schwartzes really are in Israel?" Dan asked.

"I wouldn't be surprised. I also wouldn't be surprised if they didn't come back."

"Really?"

"Really!" LeBeau said. "They know they're guilty of fraud, and know what'll happen if they come back. Do you know anybody at Immigration?"

"Sure. Why?"

"I think it'd be worthwhile to put young Daniel's and Jacob's names in Immigration's computer in case they decide to join their folks," LeBeau said. "That'll keep them from leaving the country. Plus, it'll give us leverage to get their parents back. I'd also like to be ready to grab Mr. and Mrs. Schwartz, if and when they try to come back into the country."

"I'll handle it when we get back to the office and let Weinstein know what I've done," Dan said.

"Sounds good."

LeBeau and Dan drove back to Manhattan. As they walked into the squad room at Midtown North, Kim Soo, one of the IAs, approached them.

"Mr. LeBeau, Mr. Robertson. I have telephone messages for both of you," she said. "Also, Mr. LeBeau, I was asked to give this to you." She handed him a computer printout.

LeBeau looked at the computer printout and then shouted, "Holy cow!"

"Hey, Richie!" Sandoval said as he turned toward LeBeau. "That was a great imitation of Phil Rizzuto," referring to the former New York Yankee shortstop, famous in their '50's championship team. "Were you and he friends in grade school?"

"Knock it off Sandoval, or I'll take away your tamale!" LeBeau shot back. Then he turned to Dan and said, "Hey, Dan. Come take a look at this. There's an outstanding arrest warrant for O'Reilly!"

"No kidding? What for?"

"It's that cloned taxi thing. It says here he was supposed to have begun serving a jail sentence three days ago."

"You mean the judge gave him jail time for that?" asked Dan.

"I guess so. Probably wouldn't have gotten any more than a fine, but he didn't make his court appearance, so the judge must have gotten pissed off and stuck it to him. He's ours whenever we want to pick him up."

"Mr. Robertson?" said the IA on the switchboard. "You have a call on line three."

He picked up the receiver. "Robertson."

"Dan, this is Casey."

"Hey, Casey! Where are you?"

"Ready to go out the door of the FBI office, but I thought you'd want to hear this as soon as possible," she said excitedly.

"So tell me!"

"We ran O'Reilly's name and all of his license plates through the FBI files. They just handed me the results."

"What'd you find?"

"Nothing on O'Reilly, but the license plate on his silver van was spotted by an Organized Crime surveillance team two weeks ago."

"Where?"

"In the Ridgewood Section of Queens . . . about half a block away from Christy Marino's apartment."

"Good work! I'll see you when you get here."

Dan hung up and told LeBeau. "Things are looking up, don't you think?"

"Yeah!" LeBeau said. "I told you if you were good to me I'd solve this case for you."

Thirty

1:40 PM
January 14th
Manhattan, New York

"Dan, this is Lou Piazza. You asked the IAs to handle some bank subpoenas for you?"

"Right Lou, any luck?" Dan said as he cradled the phone and grabbed a pen.

"Yeah. I located two accounts at Citibank for this guy Wen. There's nothing much in the checking account, just the usual monthly bills being paid, but the savings account shows a big cash withdrawal at the end of December—five grand."

"That's a lot of Christmas shopping."

"Maybe he was hitting the after-Christmas sales. He withdrew it on the 28th."

Dan thought about it. "Any deposits back into the account afterwards?"

"Not in the stuff I've seen. But I can't get access to the latest information until his new monthly statement next week."

"Nice work Lou. I sent another request on a guy named O'Reilly. Anything come back on him?"

"Oh, him. That guy must either be as poor as a church mouse, or he's living beyond his means. He's constantly overdrawing his checking account. He pays more in overdraft fees than his average monthly balance."

"Does he have a savings account?" Dan asked.

"Yeah, but I don't know why he bothers. His last statement shows a balance of $42.75, and that's the most he's had in it for six months."

Dan thought about it. On one hand, there was David Wen able to pull out enough money to pay a hit man. On the other, there was O'Reilly desperately in need of money. Maybe so much so that he took on a job of murder for hire. Maybe Wen didn't go to the Tongs. Maybe O'Reilly moonlighted for the Tongs—it was a silver van at the restaurant in Chinatown.

"Terrific. I also sent you guys a telephone subpoena for O'Reilly's business phone. Will you see if you can give it a little push? We can use all the help we can get."

Dan walked over to LeBeau, and told him what he had learned about Wen's and O'Reilly's bank accounts. "Would five thousand pay for a hit?"

"I know a guy who did it for a grand. His specialty was ugly divorces. But we don't have anything that tells us Wen and O'Reilly have been in contact with each other. Besides, if Wen is tight with the Chinese Tong, why would he take a chance with a down on his luck Irishman? It doesn't seem to fit."

"Unless O'Reilly does hits for the Tong."

"You're not suggesting the Tongs are into equal opportunity employment are you?" asked LeBeau.

"Why not? The more I think about the silver van and the ski masks, the more I'm beginning to like O'Reilly as the restaurant shooter. As to whether they've been in contact, don't forget we've got a subpoena in the works for O'Reilly's telephone in that garage. To cover it both ways, I'll get subpoenas for both Wen's and O'Reilly's home telephone records. While I'm at it, I'll learn where Wen works and see if he's got a direct telephone line. If he does, I'll go for it too."

"Yeah, that may give us our connection." LeBeau thought a moment. "At this point, even though I'm not working it any longer, unless we can think of something else, that may be our only way to link these two together. I told the PC the Chinatown shootings weren't moving as fast as I'd like. But the truth is, the case isn't moving at all. Unless we can crack Wen or O'Reilly—assuming O'Reilly is our man—we won't solve it." LeBeau paused. "Sorry, Dan."

"I know. So we'll just have to get Wen to crack. But in the meantime I've got some loose ends I need to tie up."

Dan called AUSA Weinstein's office, and left a message. Then he called Steve Newsome, the District Director of the Immigration and Naturalization Service.

"Hey Steve, this is Dan Robertson at the FBI. How are you?"

"Not bad," Newsome said. "Just got back from a week's vacation in the Dominican Republic."

"Poor baby, while the rest of us government grunts were working away, shoveling snow, and putting up with the usual bureaucracy. I hope you at least got sunburned."

"That I did, my friend. What's up?"

"We're about to indict a guy named Bernie Schwartz and his wife for bank fraud, but we just learned they're in Israel."

"If you want him extradited, talk to the guys at State Department."

"If it comes to that, we will," Dan said. "But we're hoping they'll come back for their two teenaged boys they left here in the States. Hopefully, they don't have a clue that arrest warrants are waiting for them."

"What can I do to help?"

"I need an INS stop on him and his wife, so we can grab them when they come back into the country."

"No problem. Fax over a request with all the particulars."

"And we don't want their sons to try and slip out of the country to join their parents."

"Only thing I'd be able to do there, would be an INS alert," Newsome said. "We wouldn't have any legal reason to stop them. But I can set it up so if they book a flight out of the country, we'll call you and let you know they're getting ready to leave."

"That'd work out just fine. I'll fax you the details, and copies of their parents' arrest warrants as soon as we have them."

"Do that, and I'll take care of it on our end. Just make sure you tell me to remove the stop or the alert once you no longer need it. People get bent out of shape if you grab them when there's no longer a reason."

"Thanks, talk to you later."

Dan asked one of the IAs to pull the information together in a fax to INS.

"So when did the OC surveillance spot O'Reilly's van?" Dan asked Casey as she came into the Squad Room.

"January 3rd," she said. "They'd staked out a bakery just down the street from her apartment building. The Lucchese family meets there to get their kickbacks."

"In a bakery?" LeBeau asked.

"Yeah," Casey said. "Good cover, huh?"

"They probably won't think so when they learn about our surveillance," Dan said. "So how'd they happen to spot the van?"

"The surveillance guys weren't sure they'd gotten there before the mob guys," Casey said. "So just to make sure they hadn't missed them, they wrote down all the license plates of the cars parked up and down the street."

"I like the idea that we've got O'Reilly in the vicinity of Marino's apartment," LeBeau said. "But couldn't there be another explanation of why he was there? Maybe he was doing some filter cleaning for the bakery, or a nearby restaurant."

"When they spotted the van, it was 7:30 at night," Casey said. "Unless O'Reilly works all kinds of weird hours, I doubt he was cleaning filters."

Dan smiled as Casey defended her discovery. She was good.

"Mr. Robertson," the switchboard IA said. "Mr. Thomas calling for you."

Dan grabbed the phone. "Robertson."

"Dan, this is Nick. Come back to the office right away."

Dan was still smarting from his morning meeting with Nick Thomas, and didn't relish an afternoon edition of the same thing. "Can you tell me what it's about?"

"We'll talk when you get here."

"Right." Dan hung up. What was going on? Why did he get the feeling he was about to be told he wasn't doing enough to solve the case?

"Is something wrong, Dan?" Casey asked.

"Casey, please." He gathered his things. "I'm expecting a call from AUSA Weinstein. I want you to take it for me, and tell him that Bernie and Sarah Schwartz are in Israel. Get a copy of their arrest warrants, and add them to the stuff the IAs have pulled together to get faxed to INS."

"Okay," Casey said. "Anything else?"

"Not that I can think of right now, but I guess I'm a little preoccupied."

"What did Thomas say?" she said, a look of concern on her face.

"It's not so much what he said," Dan said snapping his briefcase shut, "as what I'm afraid he's going to say."

As he drove to the FBI office he thought of the embarrassment he'd feel at being pulled off a major investigation. "But I'm doing a good job!" he shouted, and saw people on the sidewalk giving him sidelong glances.

He parked his car in the basement and rode the elevator to the office in silence.

Minutes later, he was standing in Thomas' office.

"Have a seat, Dan," Nick said.

Dan sat down, trying to interpret Nick's mood. He didn't seem annoyed or angry, maybe distracted. Something was going on.

"It's been four days since the shooting," Nick said. "The NYPD and the FBI have committed a significant amount of resources to the case, but the fact remains, the murders haven't been solved. I'd hoped the media feeding frenzy would die down, but it hasn't. I've held back the reporters the best I can, but they sense we're not making much progress. And they're right."

"Nick, we're doing everything—"

"The Mayor and the Police Commissioner are livid. But that's understandable since it's an election year. The FBI Director has the Chairman of CBS breathing down his neck, but that's understandable too."

"What's this all about, Nick?"

"Level with me, Dan. Do you know who the killer is?"

"We've got two suspects," Dan said, "David Wen and Bart O'Reilly. Wen is, or was, the husband of the missing Chinese woman—"

"Why him?"

"His wife was having an affair with another woman. He's possessive, violent, and jealous. Rage is a pretty powerful motive. He knew where Marino lived, worked, her daily routines, and the car she drove."

"Do you think he did it?"

"Yes, and no. He may not have done it himself, but if he wanted his wife and Marino dead, he could have paid someone to do it. We discovered a five thousand dollar withdrawal from his savings account about a week before his wife disappeared. He knows members of the Jade Dragons Tong, and that they're quite capable of—"

"Hold on . . . Did the witnesses describe a Chinese killer?"

"No, they didn't, but—"

"Then tell me about O'Reilly."

Dan took a breath and continued. "We know Bart O'Reilly applied for a permit to park on the rooftop lot. His prints are on the application. He owns a silver van similar to what was seen by the witness on the rooftop, and matches the vehicle seen by witnesses where Mary Lee Wen was grabbed. But he's just a small-time hood. He was supposed to appear in court on a charge of cloning a taxi. He didn't show up and the judge issued a bench warrant."

"And you have him in Christy Marino's neighborhood less than a week before she was killed."

"How did you—"?

"Come on, Dan. You're not the only one I talk to about this case. And you've got O'Reilly in the neighborhood of the parking lot on the night she was killed. In spite of all that, you want me to believe he's not the killer?"

Dan took another deep breath. It unnerved him to brief someone who already knew so many details about the case. "I'll admit that it appears O'Reilly is our best candidate for the shooter."

"So, who hired him to do it?"

"It could have been Wen. We haven't ruled him out. But Wen would have gone to the Tong. And the Tong wouldn't have touched O'Reilly."

"What about Bernie Schwartz—the target of our Fontaine investigation?" Thomas asked.

"He left the country with thirteen million of stolen money. We're still considering him."

"So why do you keep focusing on O'Reilly and Wen and ignoring the O'Reilly—Schwartz connection?"

"Because nothing has connected Schwartz and O'Reilly. We're waiting on some phone records, but so far, there's nothing to link them with one another."

"Maybe you can't admit it could've been Schwartz," Thomas said. "I won't let you use this case as a means of getting back at the Tong for Sammy's murder."

Dan glared at Thomas, angry he'd been accused of using the case as a vendetta. "Are you pulling me off the case?"

"No, it's still your investigation. You're capable of running and solving this case," Thomas said. "But starting immediately, put a full-court press on O'Reilly.

At the same time, pull out all the stops to find out if Schwartz hired him."

"LeBeau might not—"

"LeBeau can do whatever he wants to with the NYPD resources, but I forbid you to expend any more of our resources on Wen. Put a surveillance on O'Reilly. I want it round-the-clock, in place no later than tomorrow morning. We'll monitor the surveillance from the Command Center if we need to," Nick said.

Dan nodded. He realized there was no room for negotiation.

Thirty-One

4:25 PM
January 14th
Manhattan, New York

Dan was going 75 miles an hour, weaving in and out of traffic on the West Side Highway, and nearly missed the turnoff for West Fifty-fourth Street. He was seething as he drove back to Midtown North. He turned right from the middle lane, cut off a taxi, and was given a chorus of honked horns and digital gestures. He was out of control and could care less. It made sense to focus on the connection between O'Reilly and Schwartz. But why completely drop David Wen a suspect? To suggest Dan was using the investigation as a vendetta against the Tong made him furious.

He was grateful the media wasn't surrounding the Station House, or he might have ended up with a reporter as a hood ornament. He slammed the door, stomped up the stairs, and nearly knocked down Sandoval as he threw open the door.

"Watch it!" shouted Sandoval.

"Get stuffed!"

"You can't talk to me like that!" Sandoval shouted. "If you think you're so tough—"

Donnie Bennett put his arm around Sandoval and pulled him out the door. "Come on Erik, let it go."

Dan was oblivious as he stormed into the room and slammed down his briefcase on his desk. Everyone was watching.

"Having a bad day, are we?" LeBeau asked.

"Damn straight I am!"

Casey stood and walked over to Dan's desk. "What's the matter, Dan?"

"First I'm accused of being a news leak. Then Thomas orders me to drop David Wen as a suspect!"

"Did he tell you why?" LeBeau asked.

"He said after four days we haven't solved it. That reporters are eating him alive. The Mayor's trying to get re-elected. The FBI Director's tired of hearing from the Chairman of CBS. And, of course since our eyewitness didn't see a Chinese killer, so it couldn't possibly be Wen, or the Tong."

"What does he think we should be doing?" asked LeBeau.

"Begin a surveillance of O'Reilly tomorrow morning and try to find his connection to Schwartz."

"What about the cash withdrawal from Wen's account—"

"He didn't care!" Dan shouted. "Just didn't care. And I thought he didn't get caught up in the political nonsense!"

"Dan," Casey said. "Don't take this personally."

"The hell I can't." Dan slammed his fist on the top of his desk.

"You know," LeBeau said thoughtfully. "It wouldn't hurt us to keep an eye on—"

"I know how to run an investigation," Dan yelled.

LeBeau was on his feet. "Dan, shut up a minute and listen to me! Since the FBI is springing for the surveillance on O'Reilly, the NYPD can pony up for a closer look at Wen. Unless your boss wants to tell me what I can and can't do with NYPD resources. In that case, I'll suggest that he go perform upon himself, something that has been suggested as anatomically impossible."

Dan smiled and caught his breath. "Are you sure you want to do this, Richie?"

"Look, Wen is still a suspect. Besides, I'm eligible to retire right now. Thomas can't hurt me."

Dan looked at LeBeau, and shook his head in disbelief. "Thanks, Richie."

"Hey, can I see you guys a minute?" LeBeau called out to Detectives Jim Moore and Tom Johnson as they came back into the squad room.

The three of them huddled in the corner of the room, but Dan heard them.

"I want you to go down to the Fifth Precinct and talk to whoever heads up the Jade Squad," LeBeau said. "We need to know about Wen's relationship with the Jade Dragons Tong. He plays cards where they provide protection. We need to know if he paid the Tong five grand for a hit on his wife and Marino. We've got to know as soon as possible."

As they left, LeBeau walked back to his desk, sat down, and pulled out a well-worn NYPD telephone directory. He found a number, and called. "Hey, Dan, pick up the extension, but pretend you don't hear me use Wen's name."

Dan heard a gravelly voice say, "Intelligence, Detective Walker."

"Ben, this is Richie LeBeau. How are you?"

"Hello, you old geezer. I thought by now you'd be dead. How the hell are you?"

"Well, I'm not dead, so I must not be too bad," LeBeau said. "Ben, have you been following this CBS Murders thing?"

"Who hasn't?" Walker said. "You catch it?"

"Yeah. Me and a Feebee named Dan Robertson. He's on the extension."

"Nice to meet you, Ben," Dan said.

"Same here, Dan," Walker said. "What can I do for you, Richie?"

"Keep a lid on this, Ben," LeBeau pleaded. "We've got a problem with news leaks and at this point we can't afford for anything more to get out. Would you run a couple of names through the Intelligence files and computer and see if anything comes up?" LeBeau asked. "Bart O'Reilly and David Wen. Can you get back to me as soon as possible?" LeBeau gave Walker everything he had on the two men.

"Of course, Richie. Glad to help."

LeBeau had just hung up his telephone when it rang. He motioned for Dan to listen in again. "Detective LeBeau."

"Is this Detective Richie LeBeau?"

"Didn't you hear how I answered the phone?"

"Oh yeah, sorry. This is Detective Al Dawson. I worked a case on a guy who cloned a taxi. Name's O'Reilly. My Lieutenant told me you're interested in him."

"That's right, Al," said LeBeau. "Tell me what you've got?"

"Two months ago, Ibrahim bin Salim reported his hack license stolen from his cab in Manhattan. Happens all the time. Six weeks ago, Salim was sitting in a line of cabs on Park Avenue. He spotted a cab in front of him that had the same taxi number on the roof light as his."

"You're kidding!"

"It also had a license plate with the same number on it. Salim looked at the medallion on the hood, and sure enough, same as his. And the hack license even had the same number as his. All of this was on a Ford sedan, painted taxi yellow with fare rates on the door. A complete forgery."

"A cloned taxi." LeBeau said.

"Right. By then, Salim was really pissed. Medallions sell for over half a million. So he found a uniform, and demanded the cop arrest the guy. It was O'Reilly."

"What are the odds of getting caught by the very cab you cloned?" LeBeau said.

"About the same as hitting the lottery. Can you imagine the work that must have gone into it? No way you could tell it was fake. Even up close, it looked real. I got the call from the uniform. Boy, you talk about having to dig deep into the New York Penal Code to find out which law he broke."

"So what happened?"

"I took him to night court. O'Reilly pled guilty. The judge told him to appear on Tuesday morning for sentencing. O'Reilly was a no-show, so the judge issued a bench warrant for his arrest. This helpful?"

"It could be," LeBeau said. "Fax me a copy of the warrant. You got a good address and phone number for O'Reilly?"

"I think so," Dawson said. "Hold on a second. Okay, here it is, 436 West Forty-Fifth Street."

"We've already got that one, he doesn't live there."

"Then the phone number's probably bad," Dawson said. "It's 212 565-9147."

LeBeau recognized it as the one from the desk in the back of the garage. "We've already got that one too, but thanks for your help."

The phone rang again. "Task Force, Detective LeBeau."

"Richie, this is Ben Walker."

"Boy, that was fast. What have you got?"

"Wen was spotted with the Jade Dragons Tong in Chinatown. We don't think he's a member, but he knows them."

"Great," said LeBeau. "What about the other guy?"

"O'Reilly may be a part of the West End Irish Gang—the 'Westies', but they haven't sent us their latest membership list."

"Smart ass. What do you know about him?"

"Been arrested for burglary, assault, and fencing stolen items, but he beat the rap every time. He's never done time."

"Anything about him packing?"

"Not known to carry a gun, as far as our files show. But that information is about eight years old."

"Have you got anything on where he lives, his family, that sort of thing?" LeBeau asked.

"No, I gave you all we've got. I don't even have a good date of birth or Social Security number for him. If you come up with anything, send me a copy so I can update our file."

"Sure. From what I remember, the Westies used to hang out near the old piers on the west side of Manhattan and hire out for anybody who had the bucks. Even did hits for the Mafia, right?"

"That's right."

"Anybody saying they're doing hits for the Tongs?" LeBeau asked.

"Hmm," Walker said. "Nothing in the files about that. It's possible, but the Tongs were always a tight group—never had much to do with outsiders."

"Thanks for the help, Ben. I owe you."

"You'll get my bill."

LeBeau hung up the phone and leaned back. "What've we got for O'Reilly's address?"

"Driver's license that says he lives in Keansburg, New Jersey," Dan said, "but we don't know for sure that information is still valid."

"Mr. Robertson?" said one of the IAs. "This just came for you."

Dan took the manila envelope and opened it. "'Ask and it shall be given' . . . Records for O'Reilly's phone at the garage. Looks like we've got four calls to Keansburg, New Jersey after 6:00 P.M. on January 10th, the night of the murders."

"All to the same number?"

"Two different numbers." Dan wrote them down and handed them to the IAs. "Would you get me the subscriber and street address for both these numbers?" Dan turned back to LeBeau. "I'm supposed to put a surveillance on O'Reilly tomorrow morning, and I don't know where he lives."

"That could be a problem," LeBeau said with a laugh. "But don't worry, we've got about fifteen hours before you'll need it."

The IA handed Dan a printout.

"One number comes back to a Bob Miller on Forrest Place, and the other one to an A. Glenn on Creek Road. Nothing for O'Reilly."

"Creek Road?" LeBeau said. "What was the address on O'Reilly's driver's license?"

Dan leafed through the papers on his desk, and finally found the one he was searching for. "Eighty-one Creek Road, Keansburg."

"All right," said LeBeau.

"Dan?" Casey said. "I didn't mean to listen in on your conversation, but I heard you asking about O'Reilly's phone number."

"What I need is a good address and phone number for O'Reilly."

"Maybe I can help. The number he put on the application was 212 972-3414. But when I tried it, I found out that 972 isn't a Manhattan exchange. So I tracked down the Keansburg area code—608—and put it in place of the number he listed. Then I made a pretext call, and found it was a working number. I think it matches the called phone number from that telephone bill."

Dan compared the phone number on the parking application to the phone numbers called from the phone in the West Forty-Fifth Street garage. "Well I'll be," he said. "Gotcha. Thanks Casey." He put down the papers, picked up the telephone, and called the FBI Surveillance Supervisor. While he waited he said, "I'm going to nail you."

Thirty-Two

9:05 PM
January 15th
Keansburg, New Jersey

Barbara Lindsay answered the knock on the back door of her Keansburg, New Jersey home. Four men dressed in leather jackets and blue jeans stood on her back porch. Two held small gym bags. They looked like members of an aging rock group.

"May I help you?" she asked warily.

"Are you Mrs. Lindsay?" said the one in the middle.

"Yes. Who are you?"

"We're FBI agents," he said as he showed her his credentials. "My name is Frank Halloran, and I'd like to introduce Vern Sanchez—he's the short guy on the end. Pete Benicia next to me, and this other guy's Rich Nally."

"I'm pleased to meet all of you. It's just . . . I'm sorry, but you don't look like FBI agents."

"That's okay, ma'am—we're not supposed to."

"Oh, I see . . . Won't you please come in?" She opened the door and led the men into the house. "My husband made all the arrangements—he's the dispatcher for the Keansburg Police Department."

"We understand ma'am," Sanchez said with a sympathetic smile. "I'm sure you don't often have FBI agents using your house to watch somebody. Do you mind if we turn off the lights in the living room and pull the curtains?"

"Sure. Whatever you need."

Sanchez pulled binoculars out of his bag. Benicia set up a camera on a tripod in front of the slit in the curtains of the living room's picture window.

"We're watching the O'Reilly house across the road," Halloran said. "Have you ever seen a silver van at their house?"

"Oh, sure."

"When was the last time you saw it?"

"Bart usually takes it to work during the week, and he leaves real early," she said. "It was here last weekend, but I haven't seen it this week."

"Where does he work?" Halloran asked.

"I think he does some kind of contracting work."

Sanchez was looking out the window through the binoculars. "Hold on, guys, I've got two white males coming out of the house!"

"Vern, stay here, keep an eye on them, and talk to us on the radio," Halloran said. "Rich, Pete, grab your camera. Let's roll. Thanks for your hospitality, Mrs. Lindsay, but, we've got to run."

* * *

"This is SO-4. Just want you to know we're listening here at home," Surveillance Squad Supervisor Sal Delano said from the Command Center in the Manhattan FBI Office. He pressed a button, and the overhead lights dimmed as a New Jersey map was projected on a screen on the far side of the room. "We use a Global Positioning System transmitter in the team leader's car, which causes a tiny red laser dot to appear on this map. The dot identifies the location of the surveillance team leader. Let's see where they go," Delano said to LeBeau and Dan, who were sitting behind him.

"Boy, when you guys throw resources at a case, you really do it right," said LeBeau.

"That's right," said Delano. "The surveillance agents are all driving nondescript vehicles—a Ford station wagon, a newer Camaro, and a Ford panel truck. While they look ordinary on the outside, each vehicle's engine had been replaced with a high-performance V-8 that can move it at almost any speed. They've got fictitious license plates from the states surrounding New York and they swap them from time to time. And the agents have an assortment of hats, glasses and jackets that allow them to disguise themselves."

* * *

"This is S0-4-11," Sanchez radioed, using a radio code that indicated he was Special Operations, Squad Four, Unit Eleven. "Subject number one is getting into a reddish orange jellybean, along with a second white male, approximately thirty, five-ten, one-sixty. He's now known as subject number two."

"Roger that, 4-11," Halloran said. "Direction of travel?"

"Card number one," Sanchez said. "Direction is Omega."

* * *

"They're following a jellybean?" asked LeBeau.

Without turning around, Delano answered, "Means the vehicle's a sedan. The media use scanners to follow police and FBI activities. We got tired of them following us, so we came up with a means to assure a news crew wasn't following us. Each week, new surveillance code cards were prepared. The numbered cards have code names for major streets, highways and compass directions. If any surveillance unit believes it is being followed, the surveillance team switches to another code card while the one unit stops and 'dry cleans' itself. Today, I-95 is Los Angeles, I-78 is Florida, I-278 is Oregon, Omega indicates west, Gamma is east, Beta is south, Athens means Manhattan, and the pan handle is the Holland Tunnel."

* * *

"Good morning. This is SO-5. We are 5-10 and 5-12. En route."

* * *

"Okay, who's that?" asked LeBeau.

"It's our surveillance aircraft," said Delano. "They're based in the Linden, New Jersey Airport. Today the two-man crew is flying a wing-over, single engine Cessna 182 that can fly quietly at speeds from 70 to 145 knots and at altitudes from 2,000 to 5,500 feet."

"How can they tell which vehicles are which?" asked LeBeau.

"The pilots use infrared binocular goggles. The surveillance vehicles have their car numbers painted on their roofs with infrared paint. While the paint is invisible to the naked eye, the numbers stand out boldly with infrared goggles."

"This is too much, Dan," LeBeau said. "When you said you would support our investigation, I had no idea."

"Yeah, we've got some neat toys," Dan said.

* * *

"The package has stopped," Brown said from the airplane.

"Does anybody have a visual?" Halloran asked.

"I can see them through the glasses," Sanchez said. "Subject number one has exited the vehicle, and is walking into the Newark Airport Long-Term Parking Lot. Subject number two is still sitting in the jelly bean."

"Roger that, 4-11," Halloran said. "Tell me what you see."

"This is 4-11," Sanchez said. "I have a black, repeat, black box coming out of the lot. He stopped for a minute beside the jelly bean, made a U-turn, and is coming Delta, away from the airport."

* * *

Dan looked up at the speaker on the wall and said, "What the . . .?"

"Box?" LeBeau asked. "I don't see box on my code card."

"It means van," Delano said over his shoulder.

Dan turned to Delano and said, "Sal, why are they following a black van? Our witness said a light-colored van, and the DMV says O'Reilly has a silver van. Nobody said anything about a black one."

"I wish I knew," said Delano. "We've got the right man. At least I think we're on O'Reilly."

"If it's O'Reilly in the black van, then where's the silver one?" Dan asked. "And who's in the car?"

"This is not good," said LeBeau, his eyes never straying from the moving red dot.

"We know O'Reilly cloned a taxi," Dan said. "It wouldn't be much of a stretch to create a black van out of a silver one."

* * *

"Now the jelly bean is following the box," Sanchez said. "Both are on Oregon, heading Delta."

"Okay, men, we've got two packages," Halloran said. "If they split, 4-13 and 4-12, take the jelly bean. You and I've got the box, 4-11."

"Both packages are now turning Gamma on Florida," said Sanchez. "Both targets are pulling into the rest area at exit forty-one! I'm too close! I've got to fly by! Can anybody else pull over and keep an eye?"

"I'm right behind you," said Benicia. "I'm pulling over."

"Can you see what they're doing?"

"Affirmative. They're transferring camping gear from the jelly bean to the box."

"Roger that," said Halloran. "Everybody get ready. They're getting back into their vehicles. Did you get the plate number on the box, 4-13?"

"Affirmative," said Benicia. "As soon as we know what's happening, I'm going to switch to channel four and call it in."

"Roger that," Halloran said. "I won't lose it."

"This is 4-11. I'm now on Omega-bound Florida."

"The box just flew by me, 4-11," said Halloran. "Are you on him?"

"Ten-four, 4-14."

"How fast is he going?" Halloran asked.

"My speedometer reads one hundred, and he's pulling away from me," Sanchez said.

"This is 4-12," said Nally. "The jelly bean is heading into Athens via the pan handle."

"All units, this is 5-10. We've got to pull off. There's a massive thunderstorm moving in from the

Omega, and we're useless when we're wet. Good luck. We'll re-join if and when we can."

"Roger that, 5-10," Halloran said. "We can see dark clouds ahead. Thanks for the help. Well, it looks like it's just you and me, 4-11. Let's not lose him."

* * *

Delano turned to Dan and said, "We're running a four unit surveillance, rather than our usual six. Now we're down to two units on the van. From what you've told me, that's our most important target, so I'd like to pull off the two units from the car and have them join in on the van. O'Reilly's not in the car. Shall we let the car go?"

"Do it," was the quick answer from Dan. "But somebody better quickly tell me its O'Reilly in that black van."

Thirty-Three

10:45 PM
January 15th
Manhattan, New York

"The car has New Jersey 187-TNL, and the van has New Jersey 987-QFT," Delano said to Dan.

Dan handed the page with the two license plates to the IA. "Run these plates ASAP! I need to know the owner, and which vehicles these plates should be on." The IA nodded and left.

"Think O'Reilly painted the van?" LeBeau asked.

"Maybe," Dan said. "Let's see what we get from the DMV checks."

The door to the Command Center opened, and Casey walked in, wearing the smile that always meant she'd made a breakthrough. "Hi Dan, Richie. How's it going?"

"You don't want to know," Dan said. "What have you come up with?"

"I'm pumped! I've been working on the parking lot data with Sandoval and Bennett. We're on to something. We see a pattern of arrivals and departures for Marino and O'Reilly."

"Meaning?"

"In the two weeks before the murders, O'Reilly either arrives at the parking lot just before Marino does, or right afterwards. On other days, he leaves just before she does, or right after. So it looks like he was—"

"Stalking her!" Dan said. "He's got to be our shooter, unless . . . Did any of the other parkers have a similar pattern?"

"No. Not only that, we've been through all the parking records for everyone who parked on the lot on Monday. Three vans have permits, O'Reilly was the only one that parked that day."

"Nice work, Casey," Dan said.

"Thanks. So why aren't you jumping for joy?"

"O'Reilly's heading west in a van full of camping gear. A black van."

"Why a black van?" She paused, then exclaimed, "He painted it!"

"Yeah, that's what we figure."

"Dan, this is great! We've got him stalking Marino, disguising his van, and fleeing. He's got to be the one. Did he have the van at home?"

"No, he had it stashed in the Newark Long Term parking lot," Dan said. "Got anything else?"

"Yeah. Late yesterday afternoon, we got the telephone records of O'Reilly's home phone. The phone service was in the name of A. Glenn. I ran a DMV check on that name, and it comes back to a forty-five year old white female who lives at that same address on Creek Road in Keansburg."

"O'Reilly keeps his name off everything possible," LeBeau said. "Smart. I'm liking him better and better."

"Well, maybe not that smart," Casey said. "He made a bunch of calls he charged to her home telephone from pay phones in New York. At first we didn't think much of it, but we found a guy over at Verizon who helped us find locations of those phones."

"What'd you come up with, Casey?" LeBeau asked, becoming interested.

"Some were from the phone in the garage on West Forty-Fifth Street, but you already knew about those from phone records. Then, about a week before the murders, he used a pay phone on Grandview Terrace in Queens. Some of the other calls came from a pay phone on West Forty-Sixth Street in Manhattan."

"Those locations are near Marino's apartment, and near the rooftop parking lot."

"Right! Just to make sure, we took a ride over to Queens, and from the pay phone on Grandview Terrace, you can see the front of her apartment building. The phone here in Manhattan is on the wall of the rooftop parking lot."

"All right!" Dan said.

"It gets better," Casey said. "The calls from Grandview Terrace were made before she would have left for work, and those from the rooftop parking lot, just before she would have come to get her car."

"Great stuff, Casey!" LeBeau said.

"And now for the pièce de résistance," Casey said proudly.

"Didn't know you spoke French," Dan said.

"There's a lot of things you don't know about me," Casey said with a smile.

"Ooooh," LeBeau said and laughed.

"One phone call is really significant," Casey continued. "He made it on January 10th from a pay phone on Broadway here in Manhattan at 8:15 PM. The pay phone is two blocks from where Marino's body was dumped, and the time fits with our theory about O'Reilly's activities that day."

"Excellent," Dan said. "Here's what I want you to do. Put together everything you can on O'Reilly and the van. We've got to know if we're following the right van. Find a judge who'll give you a search warrant for it. Get Clements to help, and ask Sandoval and Bennett to pitch in. Tell them LeBeau said they've been goofing off too long."

Casey left, and the IA came in from the computer room and handed a printout to Dan that he read. "When are we going to get a break in this case? Whenever we get answers in this investigation, we're left with more questions!"

"Let's see, Dan," LeBeau said, then read aloud, "New Jersey 187-TNL is registered to a Nissan owned by Robert Miller from Keansburg, New Jersey. New Jersey 987-QFT from the van is a newly-issued plate." LeBeau looked up. "It isn't in the computer yet. I'm gonna call Midtown North, and get the VIN from the van we know was registered to O'Reilly. When the surveillance guys check it out, we'll know if it's the right van."

"Makes sense," Dan said. "Why not send somebody over to New Jersey DMV?"

"It's Saturday," LeBeau said.

Dan closed his eyes and shook his head. He'd lost all track of time.

"Sal?" Dan asked. "I want you to have the surveillance agents get the VIN from the dash of the van. And I want them to take a pocketknife and scrape the black paint to see what's underneath. And if I'm not here or at Midtown North, have them call me at home, no matter what time it is."

At 3:30 P.M. Casey returned, and her eyes immediately went to the screen. Her face didn't have the enthusiasm that it had that morning.

"How'd you make out, Casey?" Dan said.

"Not good," she said as she sat down in a nearby chair. "We laid it all out for the judge—the license number, fingerprints on the parking application, eyewitness on the rooftop, garage where O'Reilly went after the shootings, parking lot and phone records that showed he was stalking her, plus the phone call around the time her body was dumped."

"And?" Dan said.

"He said it was all circumstantial, and not enough to compel him to sign the search warrant. He said that making a mistake on a parking lot application wasn't a crime, and that since O'Reilly worked in the city, the phone calls and parking times could easily be a coincidence, rather than a pattern of stalking. I asked if he'd go along with a search of O'Reilly's home in Keansburg, but he wouldn't go for that either. He said he'd really like to help us, but to wait and come back when we've got more."

"In other words we're out of luck," said LeBeau who had been listening.

"Right," Casey said.

"Then the surveillance guys better give us something when they check out the van tonight," said Dan.

"I'm really beat," LeBeau said. "Think I'll find somebody to drive me home. Can I interest you in that, Dan?'

"Nah, I think I'll stick around for awhile. Maybe I'll come up with some brilliant idea. See you tomorrow." Dan watched the others walk out of the Command Center, and was left with his thoughts, but only for a moment. He answered his phone. "Robertson."

"Dan, Nick. I've got a message to call the Director. Would you come down to my office and give me an update so I'll have something to tell him?"

"Sure, Nick. Be right there." Then Dan turned to Delano. "Sal, I'm going to stop by Thomas' office, then head home."

"'Night, Dan."

Dan stuck his head into Thomas' office, saw he was alone, and walked in.

"You look tired, Dan. Let's make this quick so you can leave."

"Sure," Dan said, then updated him about the day's events.

"Good. That ought to give me enough to keep them happy for at least another day. But on another point . . . I've always thought of myself as a kind and gentle superior—sort of a benevolent dictator—slow to anger and abounding in steadfast love."

"Oh, yeah, that's what everybody says about you."

"Pay attention. It's because of the way I am that I'm only going to say this once. But I am also human, so I'm going to say it. I want you to listen carefully."

"Yeah, sure."

"Good. Here goes. *I Told You So.*"

Dan couldn't help himself, and smiled. "You did at that, Nick."

Thomas stood and clapped his hands. "Okay, that's all. Now, get out of here and get some rest. Tomorrow you can solve this case."

Dan slowly made his way down to the garage, and got into his car. For a long time, he sat staring at the cinderblock wall in front of him. O'Reilly was the shooter, it seemed almost certain. Despite what the judge thought, the pattern was just too clear. But who hired him?

It was a long shot that David Wen found and hired Bart O'Reilly, but he needed to be sure.

He drove out of the garage and headed for Teaneck, rationalizing that he was on his own time and not countermanding Thomas' directive.

There was no answer when he rang David Wen's doorbell, but there was the noise of children in the backyard. He made his way around a hedge and through a small wooden gate to the rear of the house. He saw Wen's children playing some complicated game involving a strangely out-of-season beach ball and two plastic kiddy-sized shovels. The thick winter snowsuits added to the hilarity of the game. David Wen was seated on a folding lawn chair, bundled in a parka, reading a Chinese-language newspaper.

"Mr. Wen?"

The children stopped playing, stared at him, then ran and clung to their father. Wen dropped the newspaper and held them close. Glaring at Dan, he said, "You're trespassing. Get out."

"The gate was open and I've got a few more questions for—"

"You're not welcome. Go. Now."

"Mr. Wen, I'm trying to find your wife's murderer."

Wen muttered something under his breath that Dan couldn't understand. He said something to the children and they ran into the house.

"Ask your questions."

"When did you first meet Bart O'Reilly?"

There was no change in Wen's expression—no hint of recognition. "I don't know who you're talking about."

"Did the Tong put you in touch with him?"

"I don't know him."

"How long had you known your wife and Christy Marino were lovers?"

That evoked a reaction. It wasn't the rage that Dan expected. For just a moment, Wen's stoic expression slipped and Dan saw the pain and the embarrassment. Then the moment passed and Wen's placid expression returned.

"What do I have to say to make you leave?" Wen asked.

"The truth, Mr. Wen," Dan said. "I will leave when I hear it."

Dan could see Wen's jaw muscles working. He was bracing for a tirade, but Wen quietly said, "I learned of my wife's . . . relationship to that . . . Marino when I read of it in the papers." He paused. "It didn't come as a surprise."

He paused again and Dan waited.

"Since Mai Li and I were married," Wen said in an even, tightly-controlled voice, "there was always a . . . distance between us. I learned to live with it. She was a good mother, a good housekeeper, a dutiful wife. I was prepared to live with it all of my life. And with her."

Dan saw Wen's pain resurface. David Wen fought it back by sheer force of will.

"Then I learned from you she allowed herself to be led into crime. The papers . . ."

"I know what was in the papers, Mr. Wen. And I'm sorry it happened that way."

Wen nodded. "And now she is gone, and my children are without a mother. I thought I had lost her long ago. I was wrong. I have lost her all over again." Wen raised his eyes to Dan's. "Now you have your truth."

Without another word, Wen started to walk toward the house.

"One last question. Why didn't you say this before?"

Wen paused and seemed to give serious consideration.

"Because my grief is my own. Why demean it by revealing it to a *gwai loh*?"

The back door slammed. Dan thought, "Foreign devil. I've been called a lot worse."

Thirty-Four

1:03 AM
January 16th
Manhattan, New York

"Where are you?" Dan asked, awakened from a sound sleep.

"The lovely bridal suite of the Howard Johnson Motor Inn in Lancaster, Pennsylvania," said Vern Sanchez of the surveillance squad. "O'Reilly stopped driving hell bent for leather through the rain, and took a room for the night."

"What've you got?"

"Couldn't see the van's VIN. An envelope on the dashboard covered it."

"Think it was intentional?"

"Hard to say. A bunch of crap all over the dashboard. I scraped the van's black paint with my knife. Couldn't tell if the paint underneath was silver or gray primer."

"And you woke me up for this?"

"Saved the best 'til last. Spotted a cartridge casing on the floor near the driver's seat. Might be a .22."

"You didn't pop the lock, did you?"

"No way! Used my flashlight and binoculars."

"Nice work."

"What's happening at your end?" Sanchez asked. "How long are we going to follow this guy?"

"Things are nuts here. Tried to get a search warrant, but a judge shot us down. That cartridge casing may help, but for now keep following him. Delano rolled out a second surveillance team to let you guys catch some rest."

"Okay, we'll keep at it."

"Hang in there. We're pushing as hard as we can on our end."

Dan hung up, wide awake, staring at the ceiling. They had to justify a search of the van. That evidence would tie O'Reilly to the murders. Unless O'Reilly spotted the casing and tossed it out the window. That thought made it hard to sleep.

* * *

It had been one week since the murders. Dan was listening to the surveillance team radio traffic. Clear, sunny, and better weather allowed the FBI Air Force to fly again.

Blackman walked in and stood listening for a few minutes, then sat down beside Dan. "Where are they?"

"Just west of Hagerstown, West Virginia."

"Why don't you just stop him and search the van?"

"The judge nixed our request for a search warrant. We're still not positive he's driving the van used in the murders. The plate doesn't match, and we haven't been able to look at the VIN. We could stop him, but we couldn't search the van."

"You're burning up a lot of manpower and piling up costs. You better pray you're doing the right thing."

"You know Ike, it's interesting that whenever things look good, your sentences have a lot of 'I's and 'we's'. But if things are going badly, all your sentences have a lot of 'you's' and 'they's'. Ever notice that?"

"The difference between you and me is that I'm a team player, and you're not."

"But whose team are you on, Ike?"

Blackman stood up, and spoke through clenched teeth. "You better hope you're right. If you're wrong, I'll lead the effort to get you fired. You're nothing but a goddamned out-of-control cowboy."

"And you've got no balls. You avoid making decisions so you can't be blamed if something goes wrong."

Blackman started to say something, but noticed LeBeau walk in. He glared at Dan, nodded to LeBeau, then left.

"What's going on, Dan?" LeBeau asked.

He told LeBeau about the phone call from Sanchez, the bad news about the VIN and the paint, and the good news about the cartridge casing.

"Damn! We've got to crack this thing open. We haven't done much on the van we know is registered to O'Reilly. It might be the same one. Let's put somebody on that."

"I'll send somebody over to retrieve the parking stub O'Reilly turned in when he pulled out in the black van. That would tell us when he first put the van back into the lot. It may tell us whether or not we're following the right van."

The surveillance radio traffic resumed. LeBeau asked, "Where are they now?"

"Somewhere around Morgantown, West Virginia."

A file clerk handed Dan a large manila envelope.

Dan tore open the envelope and read its contents.

"Anything good?"

"Maybe. "It's from Lou Piazza. Bank account information about O'Reilly and Wen. The statement just went out, and shows a deposit of $5,000 back into Wen's savings account."

"What's the date?"

"January 11th."

"The day after the murders. Contract killers don't give refunds. Especially when it's successful."

"I know. Something else makes Wen a lot less attractive as a suspect." He told LeBeau about his visit to Wen the previous evening.

"What if he paid the Tong to kill the two women, but somebody else got to them first?"

Dan thought for a moment. "I don't know. After what Wen said last night, it doesn't fit quite as well."

"Let's learn a little more," LeBeau called Ben Walker from Intelligence at home. "Ben, Richie LeBeau. I'm still working this CBS murders thing, and there's something I need . . . Yeah, I know the Nets have got a shot, and couldn't possibly do as well if you're not there, but this is really important. Help me out." LeBeau told him the details of David Wen's bank transactions, and included a lot of please's, I know's, and I owe you's, then hung up.

"We're going to have to score a couple of Nets tickets for Ben, but he'll do it." LeBeau told Dan what he put into the works.

"What are you thinking?" asked Dan. "Go ahead and use the bench warrant from the cloned taxi, and have O'Reilly arrested?"

"We could, but we'd only be able to latch onto his body," said LeBeau. "We'd have no legal right to search the van. And we've got to have the van to link O'Reilly to the murders."

"If it's the right van."

"I wasn't convinced until I heard about the cartridge casing."

"What makes you so sure now?"

"Because I think I know how it got there. The van was parked on the right side on Marino's BMW. O'Reilly's sitting behind the wheel in the van. He holds the gun in his right hand with his right arm across his chest, pointing it out the driver's window, towards Marino and the BMW."

"Yeah?"

"He squeezes one off. But remember, he's shooting a High Standard automatic. That means the spent cartridge casing is ejected to the rear and to the right of the gun. It bounces off the dashboard then onto the floor of the van where your surveillance agent spotted it, and where it still may be. That will tie O'Reilly to the murders."

"Unless he spots the cartridge casing, realizes it could put him away, and chucks it," Dan said.

"If he does that, we're screwed."

Thirty-Five

11:15 AM
January 16th
Manhattan, New York

"What's that radio traffic, Sal?" Dan asked over the din from the speakers in the Command Center. "They didn't pull him over, did they?"

"Nah," Delano said. "The second surveillance squad finally caught up with them. Glad we're finally switching to a full six-unit team and a new bunch of cars. It'll make it less likely he'll spot them."

LeBeau answered his phone and said, "Tell me something good, Ben . . . Oh, yeah? . . . Sure, terrible habit. Terrible . . . That much? . . . Too rich for my blood . . . Your snitch is certain about those dates? . . . Yeah, I know, two Nets tickets to a game of your choice . . . Thanks. You too Ben."

"What'd you learn about Wen?" Dan asked.

"Played in a high-stakes poker game on the twenty-ninth. Took a grand to get into the game, and everybody settled in cash at the end of the night. No markers. Wen lost his shirt, but had the balls to get them to commit to a return game. Played the night Marino got hit, and won back all his losses. Must've banked it the next day. Some guys have all the luck. Looks like Wen has an alibi."

"Looks more and more like the murders are related to the Fontaine fraud," Dan said. "But Schwartz was in Israel, and his lawyer put the company into bankruptcy."

"Doesn't mean Schwartz didn't hire O'Reilly to take out a couple of people who could've hurt him by working with the feds. "You've indicted him. What about extradition?"

"I was hoping his kids would convince him they were headed for foster homes."

"You mean you weren't serious about that?"

"Let's focus on the surveillance. As long as the media doesn't get wind of O'Reilly, we stay on him long enough to figure some way to arrest him and search the van. Then Schwartz panics about the two little Schwartzes and flies into New York to save them from big bad foster homes, only to get arrested at the airport by the FBI. When he realizes we've got him on the fraud, he sings and gives up O'Reilly to save his own hide."

"You've been watching too many cop shows. Never happens like that in real life. We're going to have to use a lot more shoe leather. Make our own luck. Put a case together on O'Reilly. Arrest him. Search the van. Find enough to convict him. Once he realizes he's looking at the death penalty, we let him plead to murder two in return for a life sentence."

The door to the Command Center opened and Casey, Bennett, and Sandoval walked in carrying a large cardboard box.

"What have you got there?" Dan asked.

"The last two weeks of used tickets from the airport long-term parking lot." Bennett said.

"And videotapes," Casey said as she shot a look at Bennett.

"Videotapes . . . of the van going into the parking lot?" Dan asked.

"That's right," Casey said. "Somebody could have parked it in the lot after using it for the murders. Later they took it out and painted it." She turned back to Dan and LeBeau and said, "The key question is where was the van from Monday evening through Saturday morning?"

"We still don't know for sure that the black van is the same one used in the murders," LeBeau said.

"Yeah, but we're about to solve the mystery," Casey said.

LeBeau shook his head. "You never seem to suffer a lack of confidence. How do we learn which ticket belongs to the van?"

"Two ways," Casey said. "First, the attendant writes the vehicle's license number on the back of the ticket as the vehicle leaves. Second, we have security camera videotapes that are time and date stamped. The video camera is angled to catch license plates as vehicles leave."

"So, what are you waiting for?" LeBeau said.

Casey and the detectives began to sort and organize the parking tickets. Dan and LeBeau pitched in.

"What are we looking for, Casey?"

"We're trying to find four license numbers." Casey picked up a marker and wrote them on the board. "New Jersey plate 538-YGH. The plate from the parking lot application. The one O'Reilly crossed out. It was supposed to be on his Ford Escort. The next one we probably won't find is New York plate 939-HGY. It was written on the application after the other plate was scratched out. The DMV computer says it belongs to Malcolm Steele for an Olds stolen last year. Then there's New Jersey plate 218-RSL—registered to O'Reilly for his silver Ford van. The last is New Jersey plate 987-QFT—the license plate on the black van that the surveillance team is following. It may be a good plate number, but so far, it isn't in the DMV computer."

They each took a stack of tickets, sat down at desks, and began to sort through them. An hour had passed before Bennett said, "All right!" He held up a parking ticket and read from it, "New Jersey plate 987-QFT coming out of the lot on Saturday January 15th at 10:47 A.M. and entered the lot on Thursday the 13th, at 4:18 P.M."

"Great!" Casey said. "Put it aside and keep going."

"Wait," Dan said. "If the van only went into the lot on the 13th, that's five days after the murders. Where's it been?"

"If it's the silver van, it was being painted black," LeBeau said. "Keep looking for the other tickets."

After two hours, they hadn't found parking tickets, which matched the other license plates.

"If O'Reilly didn't put it in the lot right after the murders, where was it?" Bennett asked.

"How about this" Dan said. "He takes Marino's body to the garage on the west side after the murders. He stays there for a while, then takes the van, paints it black, then puts it in the Newark lot on Thursday, and takes it out on Saturday. But it doesn't quite fit. If he hid it to paint it, why not leave the van in that hiding place until he runs?"

"Yeah, why risk moving it?" Casey said.

"All good questions for which we have no answers," LeBeau said. "Casey, can we look at those videotapes?"

Fifteen minutes later Casey and Sandoval returned with a television and VCR.

"Okay, Casey," said LeBeau. "Let's start with the tape from the night of the 10th. We know O'Reilly made a phone call from lower Manhattan at 8:15 P.M."

Bennett pulled out the tape and handed it to Casey. She put it into the VCR, and fast-forwarded it until she found 8:30 P.M. Casey set it to run faster than real time, causing vehicles to move jerkily.

"Wait!" LeBeau shouted. "Go back a little bit."

Casey rewound the tape and played it on real time. After a few cars and SUVs went in, a light-colored van pulled up to the entrance of the Long-Term lot, and the driver reached for the ticket. The time stamp said 8:47 P.M.

"Freeze it, Casey!" LeBeau got up, walked to the television screen, and stared at the vehicle. He glanced back and forth from his pad of paper to the screen. "Gotcha, you bastard!"

"That's the license plate for the Escort," Casey said. "He *is* swapping plates."

"Why don't we have a ticket that matches it?" Dan asked. "Did we miss it?"

"God, I hope not," Sandoval said. "I don't want to go through those tickets again."

"We've got them in numerical ticket order," Dan said. "Casey, find a ticket for someone else who entered the lot about the same time. Then see if there's any tickets missing that would correspond with 8:47 P.M."

It didn't take long. Ticket 62941 was missing.

"What does the parking outfit do when somebody loses a ticket?" LeBeau asked.

Bennett was already flipping through his notes and reaching for the phone. "Let's find out," he said.

"Casey and Erik," Dan said. "Look at the videos and see if you can spot the van leaving."

Bennett hung up the phone and said, "They've got a list of people who can't find their tickets. The attendant records the time they leave, and whatever time they tell him they came in. Then he charges the maximum parking fee."

"That could get expensive," Casey said.

"Yeah. Even though it's Sunday, the guy agreed to come in and give us the log. Let's go, Casey." As he started for the door, Bennett looked over his shoulder and said, "I'll be right back to solve this case for you."

"You're sounding more like LeBeau every day!" shouted Sandoval.

In an hour, they were back with the logs. Everyone was looking over Bennett's shoulder as he ran his finger down the page.

"Here it is. The van exited at 9:34 P.M. on Tuesday the 11th. But the entry time doesn't match. This log says the van entered the lot at 11:15 A.M. on Monday the 10th. That's six hours before the murders."

"Don't you see?" said LeBeau. "That's what O'Reilly told him. He's cloning an alibi. He was willing to pay a wad of money to claim the van was in the lot six hours *before* the murders until four days afterwards. If he'd used the parking ticket they gave him when he drove in, it would've shown the van entered the lot on Monday at 8:47 P.M, two and a half hours *after* the murders. He couldn't afford to do that. So he told the attendant he'd lost the ticket. Smart move, but didn't realize he was being videotaped."

"He thought he could fool us if he created a phony paper record of when the van arrived," Bennett said.

"Then he tried to confuse us by using the Escort's plates on the van the day of the murders," said Casey, "and again by switching plates on the van."

"Not to mention the color change," LeBeau said. "A silver van comes out of the lot on Tuesday night, and a black one goes in on Thursday afternoon. Presto change-o. This guy ain't stupid."

"But he didn't outsmart us," Casey said.

"So he enters the lot in a silver van the night of the murders," Dan said. "He takes it out, paints it, put it back, then takes it out on Saturday morning."

"I'm gaining some new respect for his planning," LeBeau said.

"Great theory, but we still have to come up with evidence to prove it," Dan said.

"Anybody want to take my bet the missing parking ticket is stuck above his sun visor?" Bennett asked.

"No, but I'd like the opportunity to personally remove it, if that's where it is." LeBeau said.

"We can speculate all we want," Dan said. "But we still haven't answered the question of whether the silver and black vans are one and the same. Casey, let's get back to the videotape so we can find out."

Thirty-Six

2:40 PM
January 16th
Manhattan, New York

Clements burst into the Command Center, a smile on his face, and some paperwork in his hand. Detective Moore was right behind him, also smiling.

"Hi Rob, Jim. What's up?" Dan said.

"Remember how you wanted us to check out O'Reilly's van?" Clements answered. "Well, it's stolen."

"Sort of stolen," said Moore.

"What are you guys talking about?" Dan asked. "Is it stolen, or not?"

"I'm not sure," Clements said and sat down. "We did a couple of things with the van. First, we ran it through the New York and New Jersey DMV computers."

"O'Reilly didn't always own this van," Moore said.

"Who'd he buy it from?" Dan asked.

"A guy named . . ." Clements looked in his notes. "Here it is. Name is Bob Miller. He lives in . . ."

"Keansburg, New Jersey," Dan said.

"How'd you know? "Clements asked.

"Because the surveillance guys followed his Nissan when it left O'Reilly's house. Miller and O'Reilly made a few stops, then went to the Newark Airport parking lot where O'Reilly picked up the black van."

"This guy could be O'Reilly's accomplice," Moore said.

"Right," Dan said

"On January 2nd, Miller reported the van stolen to the police who entered the information in the National Crime Information Center computer," Clements said.

"The next day, the van was recovered in the Bronx by officers of the 45th Precinct and returned to Miller," Moore said. "You'd think when your stolen van's recovered, you'd be happy, but when Miller picked up the van, he was not a happy camper. The guys at the 45th, thought he was pulling an insurance scam."

"According to the computer, Miller sold the van to O'Reilly on January 4th," Clements said.

"The night after Mary Lee Wen disappeared," said Dan. "Clever. If you kill somebody, and your van's spotted, you claim it was stolen, so it couldn't possibly be you. But you said that the van was 'sort of stolen.'"

"After the guys from the 45th recovered the van, they called the Palisades Park Police, told them they'd located the van, to notify the owner, and remove it from NCIC," said Clements.

"But when we checked NCIC, it was still there," said Moore. "They forgot to remove it. It's still listed as stolen."

"Hmm," said LeBeau.

"I've seen that look before, Richie," said Dan. "What are you thinking?"

"Well," said LeBeau as he finished putting his thought together. "If we need some justification to pull over O'Reilly, we've now got a second reason for doing it. The first one is that taxi clone bench warrant. But, I like this stolen van idea better because it gives us a legitimate reason to search the van."

"Wouldn't someone quickly learn the stolen van ploy was nothing more than bad information?"

"Maybe. But in the time it would take to sort it out, we could search the van and grab that .22 caliber cartridge casing," said LeBeau. "Once we've got it, we could hold O'Reilly on the warrant, and take our time putting together a murder charge."

"We couldn't talk a judge into a search warrant" said Dan. "What makes you so sure we've got enough evidence to charge him with murder?"

"That was before we knew about the van going in and out of the parking lot. Besides, you went for a federal search warrant. The New York Supreme Court judges give the NYPD a lot of leeway. Once we've got the cartridge casing, we won't have a problem."

"If you say so," said Dan, not completely convinced. "I'm going to brief Thomas."

"I better do the same with Captain Watson," said LeBeau with a smile. "Isn't it nice to have something to tell them?"

"You can say that again," Dan said as he headed for the door.

"Hey, Dan. Before you go, I want to show you something," said Casey. "Come here a second." She stood in front of the television and VCR, pressed the remote, and the silver van moved into the shot. She pressed a button, and the frame froze.

"Look right here," she said, using her pen to point at the van's fender, just above the front bumper. "See that dent on the silver van? And now," she said as she ejected the videotape and replaced it with another. She played the tape and a black van pulled up to the booth on its way out of the parking lot. She froze that frame, and pointed to the same spot on the black van. She turned and faced Dan and LeBeau, a smile on her face. "Same dent—same van."

"Well I'll be damned," said LeBeau.

"I can't believe you noticed that," said Dan. "It's a black and white picture. It's nighttime. The van itself is pretty small in the picture. How'd you pick up on that?"

"When I first learned to drive, my dad let me drive the van he used for the restaurant he owns. When I was making a right turn, I misjudged the right front corner of the van, and put a dent in that same spot," Casey said. "After he finished ripping into me, there was no way I'd ever forget it."

"You done good, Casey!" said Dan as he nodded his head and smiled. He gave her a "high-five" and walked out the door.

The breaks he and LeBeau had been looking for were beginning to show up. They were following the right van. Dan felt good as he walked to Thomas' office, and the Sunday quiet of the office felt relaxing, rather than depressing.

Thomas put down the memo he was reading when Dan walked through the door. He saw Thomas' somber face and looked forward to its change once Thomas heard the news.

"What's up, Dan?" Thomas asked.

"We've had a couple of good developments. We located the parking ticket O'Reilly used when he put the black van into the lot."

"When did he put it in?"

"On Thursday afternoon," Dan said.

"Damn!" said Thomas, realizing it didn't match the murder time sequence.

"Wait. There's more." Dan told Thomas about the Newark Long-Term Parking lot videotape, the light-colored van entering on Monday evening, about two and a half hours after the killings, and Casey spotting the same dent on the fenders of both the silver and black vans.

"That's great," Thomas said.

Dan told him about the van being listed as stolen and the justification it provided to stop and search the van.

"You think you can pull that off?"

"I think so. Once O'Reilly's arrested for the stolen van, and held in jail by the failure to appear warrant, it'll give us the time to put together a search warrant for the van. We can then recover the .22 caliber cartridge casing, and anything else he didn't get rid of."

Thomas leaned back in his chair. "Yeah. That could work. A little risky, hanging our hat on a stolen van report that we know is bullshit. Another problem is the van's got new plates on it. So anyone running the plates to see if it's stolen would learn it wasn't."

"So we've got to find a way to look at the VIN to prove it's the same van."

"Got any ideas?"

"Maybe have a state trooper pull the van over, but unless O'Reilly's breaking the law, he wouldn't have any reason to do that."

"Wasn't he driving real fast, like a hundred miles an hour?"

"The first day he was, but he seems to be having a problem with one of his tires being low on air. He's driving slower," said Dan with a smile.

"What happened to it?"

"Not a clue," said Dan, unable to keep a straight face.

"Think about how to pull him over. We've got to do something pretty soon. The Director keeps getting calls from the Chairman of CBS. We're getting crucified by the press. I'm getting more pressure from the Mayor and Police Commissioner."

"We're all feeling it," said Dan. "I want to send everybody home to get at least one good night's sleep. I've got a feeling once we stop O'Reilly, it's only going to get worse."

"Right. You get some sleep, too! You look like a raccoon."

Thirty-Seven

7:05 AM
January 17th
Manhattan, New York

Dan drove to the FBI office, buoyed by the beautiful day, breakthroughs in the case, and a firm belief that they were going to arrest O'Reilly. Even the occasional cab driver who cut him off wasn't enough to dampen his spirits.

* * *

The sun rose on the black van, parked at a rest area just outside Huntington, West Virginia.

"This is 4-17," said Vic Padilla. "We've got movement. The cargo door just opened, and the subject exited the box."

Padilla watched O'Reilly glance around at semi tractor-trailer rigs, motor homes and cars, also parked at the rest area. Apparently satisfied, he began walking.

"Looks like he's heading for the can. Why don't you follow him, 4-18?"

"Ten-four. Out of the unit."

A few minutes later, O'Reilly emerged.

"This is 4-17. Subject's headed back to the van. Getting in. I see brake lights and exhaust. He's ready to roll."

"The box is moving. Heading Delta on four six," said Padilla.

The other surveillance team members had left the volume on their hand-held radio high enough so any radio traffic would wake them. They started their cars, and fell in behind the van.

Outside Greyson, Kentucky, O'Reilly took exit 173 and pulled into the parking lot of The Old Rebel Truck stop and Diner. Padilla pulled into the lot and walked into the diner, right behind O'Reilly. In a Peterbilt baseball cap, blue jeans, and a plaid shirt, he looked like every other truck driver in the diner. The other units spread out to watch the van and cover all exits.

* * *

Dan arrived at the Manhattan federal building, went to the Command Center to check on the surveillance, then to a meeting in the FBI conference room next to Thomas' office. He poured himself a cup of coffee, pulled out a chair, and joined Watson, LeBeau and Thomas around the conference table.

"Where's O'Reilly this morning?" Thomas asked.

"Just west of the West Virginia-Kentucky state line," said Dan.

"Any indication he's spotted the surveillance?"

"No."

"Bill, I doubt we're going to gain anything more by continuing to follow O'Reilly," Thomas said.

"I agree," said Watson.

"This morning, we're supposed to hear from the New Jersey DMV about the VIN," Dan said. "We've got to have something irrefutable."

"Yeah," said Watson. "But, I've got to tell you, I'm hearing concern that O'Reilly might somehow slip away before we hear about the VIN."

"Let's have the Kentucky State Police set up a roadblock to get a first-hand look at the VIN," Dan said.

"I'll call Mark Littleton, the Agent in Charge of the Louisville FBI office, and ask him to broker it with the Kentucky State Police," said Thomas. "Former FBI AD Gary McDaniels retired and got the job as Commissioner of the KSP. He'd enjoy getting in on this."

Thomas put the call to Littleton on the speakerphone.

"Hey Mark! How's your golf game?"

"Got a nine handicap. How about you?"

"I haven't had much of a chance to get out on the links. I guess it's easier when you head up a 'Sleepy Hollow' office like Louisville. They probably even force you to attend the Kentucky Derby, right?"

"Yeah, it's a dirty job, but, somebody's got to do it. What's up, Nick?"

"Seen anything on the news about The CBS Murders?"

"Sure, who hasn't? A real tragedy. What makes you ask?"

"I've got a surveillance team following a guy we think did it. I need some help from you and Gary McDaniels. I was wondering if you'd call him."

"He'd love it. I saw him last week and he said he missed the day-to-day action of the Bureau. What do you want him to do?"

"Let me have the supervisor who's running the case tell you about it," said Thomas, motioning to Dan.

"Mr. Littleton, this is Dan Robertson," he said, and briefed him on the case.

"This guy armed and dangerous?" asked Littleton.

"Most definitely."

"Want him arrested?"

"When they check the VIN, no," said Dan. "But eventually, yes. Tell them we've got a couple of warrants on the guy. When it comes time to arrest him, we'll have them do the honors."

"Dumb question, but why not arrest him now?"

"Long story," said Dan.

"I'll call McDaniels. When you're ready to arrest this guy, let us know. What do you want the FBI to do?"

"Put a couple of agents with the state police so we'll have some radio communications to and from the scene to coordinate."

"Where do you want the roadblock?"

"We'd like to keep it away from major cities and populated areas," said Dan. "Try and set it up before Lexington. But if they can't, let's see which way he heads."

"Okay. Give me the details of the vehicle and the driver."

After doing so, Dan turned to the other three men. "Well, we're asking the Kentucky State Police to set up a roadblock on a four-lane Interstate highway. Other than bringing all traffic and interstate commerce to a virtual halt, and pissing off a hundred or so people, this ought to work just fine," he said with a trace of a smile.

The New York FBI office faxed a picture of O'Reilly and a copy of the radio code card to the Louisville FBI office to enable their agents to translate the radio traffic.

* * *

The surveillance reached the far side of Lexington, Kentucky.

"The box is turning Miami on zero-six," said Padilla.

Where U.S. Route 60 merged with Interstate 64, the surveillance agents looked ahead, and saw the state police roadblock.

"He's pulling off to avoid the roadblock," said Padilla. "Wait. Maybe not. No, he's pulling into that Amoco station. Maybe he needs gas."

* * *

Thomas, Dan, Watson and LeBeau had moved to the Command Center to listen in on radio traffic of the surveillance squad.

"Well, here's our moment of truth," said Dan. "I hope we've got the right van."

"Me too, because we've got no back-up plan," said LeBeau.

* * *

"Okay," said Padilla. "Here we go. The subject just paid for the gas, and got back into the box. Now he's pulling onto zero six. Okay, he spotted the roadblock and is slowing down. Now he's merging into a single lane. He's the second car in line behind a Pontiac." After a moment, Padilla continued, "He's pulling up. Now he's stopped and the trooper's talking to him."

* * *

"Good morning. May I see your driver's license?" the trooper said as he tensed, ready to use his gun, if necessary.

"Sure, Officer," said O'Reilly as he dug his wallet out of his back pocket.

* * *

A few minutes later the phone rang in the Command Center, and Dan put it on speaker.

"Robertson," he said.

"This is FBI Agent Ron Peters from the Lexington, Kentucky Resident Agency. I'm on a cell phone at the state trooper barracks in Lexington. Is this the New York FBI's Command Center?"

"Right. You're on the speaker phone so everybody can hear."

"Okay. The state police just checked the van, and the driver is Bart O'Reilly, address 81 Creek Road, Keansburg, New Jersey."

"We know that. What's the van's VIN?"

There was a pause on the telephone.

"Peters? You still there?"

"Yeah, there was a little screw up. The trooper didn't get the VIN. The captain says he's sorry and he'll make it right."

"Sorry!" screamed Dan. "What's wrong with that guy? It was a simple request. Read the VIN. Tell us what it is. How can you screw that up?"

"Sorry. The captain has another trooper following behind the van. Should he pull him over to get a look at it?"

Dan put the phone on mute so that Peters couldn't hear the conversation in the Command Center. "I say we go ahead and have them arrest O'Reilly on the stolen van charge. If they don't, he may get away. It's the only thing that'll give us the authority to search the van."

"Watson?" asked Thomas.

Watson nodded his head in agreement.

"Do it. I can't take any more incompetence," said Thomas just before he stormed out the door.

Dan released the mute button and said, "Peters, this is Robertson. The van that O'Reilly's driving is stolen. It's in NCIC if they want the details. Have the state troopers arrest him for possession of a stolen van, and impound it in some kind of indoor garage. And nobody, I mean nobody, touches the van, or gets it released from impound. Got that?"

"Yeah, I'll take care of it. I'll call you back when it's done. Sorry about the mix-up."

"Just don't let this guy get away." Dan disconnected.

"I feel sorry for that trooper," said LeBeau. "I've got a feeling he's going to be pulling some awful shifts in some rotten places for quite a while."

* * *

The four State Police cruisers converged on O'Reilly. Evans' cruiser screeched to a stop cross-wise in front of the van. Tice boxed him in on the driver's side. Simmons pulled his up to the rear of the van, while Van Doren's prevented O'Reilly's escape to the right. The troopers leaped out of their cruisers, guns drawn, and surrounded the van.

"Get your hands up where I can see them!" ordered Evans.

"Now with your left hand, reach out the window and open the door with the outside handle," ordered Tice, staring down the sights of his 9 mm.

Seeing he was surrounded by the four troopers, O'Reilly complied and stepped out of the van. "What the hell's going on?"

Evans pointed his .9 mm Browning automatic at O'Reilly, and barked orders. "You're under arrest for possession of a stolen vehicle. Lie face down on the ground, and put your hands straight out to the sides."

"What?" O'Reilly said, laughing while he complied. "You're making a mistake here. This van's not stolen. I bought it from my nephew awhile ago."

"Shut up!" Van Doren shouted.

Evans quickly searched him, handcuffed him, read him his rights, then led him to the patrol car.

After O'Reilly was shoved into the patrol car, he leaned towards Evans and said, "Look, this is all a mistake. You'll know pretty soon. But can you at least get me my glasses? They're in the front seat of the van."

Van Doren heard O'Reilly's request. He opened the driver's door and spotted a .22 caliber cartridge case on the floor of the van, just under the driver's seat he had been told about by the FBI. "Hold on a minute," Van Doren said to Simmons. "Get a camera and a piece of tape. I want that photographed before the van is moved. At this point, we can't afford to lose it, or screw this up any more than we have already." They photographed and taped the cartridge in place.

"Simmons, close and lock the van doors, call for a wrecker to tow it to the Barracks in Frankfort," Van Doren said to his sergeant. "Make sure all doors are sealed."

* * *

"Mr. Robertson," the switchboard operator said, "I've got a call for you."

"Dan, this is Peters in Lexington. The VIN matched your silver van. O'Reilly was arrested, and the van's being towed to the state police barracks where it's impounded under lock and key."

"Thank God!" Dan said. "Where's he being held?"

"The Franklin County jail, in Frankfort, Kentucky."

"Did he have a gun on him when they arrested him?"

"Not on him, but there might be one in the van. The troopers found the .22 caliber cartridge casing on the front floor of the van, just like you said."

"Great. Anything interesting turn up when he was booked?"

"Not really," said Peters. "He said he didn't want to talk, but kept saying the stolen van charge was all a big mistake. Oh yeah, there was one thing."

"What was that?"

"He had a lot of money on him."

"How much?"

"Let me look at my notes," said Peters. "Okay, here it is. There was $2,679.32."

"Wow. That is a lot for a guy who doesn't have a job."

"Yeah, I'd say so, and $2,600.00 of it was in brand new $100 bills."

"Thanks." Dan hung up the phone and turned to LeBeau. "Richie, would you call uptown, and get everybody from the Task Force down here as soon as possible. We've got to put together a search warrant for the van—tonight."

Thirty-Eight

5:00 PM
January 17th
Manhattan, New York

Dan called Assistant D.A. Patrick Bergen and Assistant U.S. Attorney Leonard Weinstein, and asked them to come to the Manhattan FBI office. "Thanks for coming on such short notice," Dan said. "The Kentucky State Police arrested O'Reilly."

"On what charge?" asked a concerned Weinstein.

"Driving a stolen van," LeBeau said with a smirk.

"You've been following a stolen van for three days?" asked Bergen.

Dan told the prosecutors about the van's history, the stolen report, it's recovery, and the sale of the van from Miller to O'Reilly. "We think it was never removed from the NCIC computer."

"I don't like it," said Bergen.

"It wasn't planned," said LeBeau. "Things were happening fast. This was the only way we would have legal authority to search the van."

"I'm not crazy about this either," said Weinstein. "Didn't you tell me you had a 'failure to appear' warrant for O'Reilly?"

"Yeah, and I faxed a copy of it to the KSP to make sure they don't cut him loose," said LeBeau.

"Down the road, there could be problems with this," said Bergen.

"The most urgent task is to put a warrant together so we can search the van tomorrow," said Dan. "We've got to persuade a Kentucky judge to let us look for evidence of the murders."

"Alright," Weinstein said. "I think it should be a federal search warrant."

"I agree," said Bergen. "The New York State statutes might be a little tough to use outside the state."

"Okay, our theory is Christy Marino, a federal witness, was murdered, and O'Reilly, the prime suspect, fled the state to avoid prosecution." Weinstein stroked his beard as he wrote on a legal pad. "Which Judicial District?"

"O'Reilly's in jail at Frankfort and that's Eastern," said Dan. "The Chief Federal Judge is Milton P. Arnold, III."

"Let's list the criminal offenses that justify the warrant," Weinstein said.

"Murder, New York Penal Code Section 125.25," said Bergen. "That's second degree murder."

"Federally, we've got Unlawful Flight to Avoid Prosecution," said Dan. "Section 1073, Title 18 U.S. Code, and Obstruction of Justice."

"That works. We'll make it Obstruction of a Criminal Investigation. That's Section 1510. Let's throw in Section 1512," said Weinstein, "the Federal Witness Tampering statute. Okay, that's sufficient legal reasons to request a search warrant. Now for the affidavit, we need to say what specifically leads us to believe we need to search the van. Who's going to be the affiant?"

"Casey Brody knows more about the case than anyone, so I'd like to make her the affiant." said Dan.

"Get her in here, and ask her to bring all the files," said Weinstein. "I've got a million questions to ask her. What was the vehicle?"

"It's a Ford Econoline," Casey said as she came through the door and sat down. "The VIN is CGD15A7140819."

"Which plate is on the van now?"

"New Jersey 987-QFT."

"Who has custody of the van?" Weinstein asked.

"The Kentucky State Police in Frankfort, Kentucky," Casey said.

"We need all the reasons why we should search the van. We'll start with the murders. Day, time, place, all the particulars."

"Happened on Monday, January 10th, at about 6:00 P.M.," said LeBeau, "on a rooftop parking lot operated by the Allied Parking System. The exact address was 618 West Forty-Sixth Street, between Eleventh Avenue and the West Side Highway. Across from Pier 84."

"Did you have an eyewitness to the murders?" asked Weinstein.

Everyone looked at LeBeau.

"That's a delicate subject," said LeBeau. "Yes, we've got an eyewitness, but we really don't want to identify him."

"We don't have to name him. What did he see?"

"Saw Marino walk to her car, and get stuffed into the van," said LeBeau. "Saw three CBS guys run toward the van and get shot. He saw the van one last time as he left the lot."

"This is good stuff," said Weinstein. "Marino's body wasn't found on the rooftop. How'd you learn she'd been killed? While you're at it, tell me everything you found at the crime scene that led you to her."

LeBeau told him about the blue BMW and everything else they found. "We checked who owned the BMW, and looked in the purse. Christina Marino was the victim."

"When did you find her body?" asked Weinstein.

"The next morning, on Franklin Street," said LeBeau. "Shot once in the head. Tire tracks near the body."

"What about evidence at the crime scene?" asked Weinstein.

"Three .22 caliber cartridge casings near the bodies."

"None near the BMW?"

"It's in the van," said Casey. "One of the surveillance agents spotted a spent cartridge through the van's window."

"Hold on," said Weinstein, "what do we know about the bullets?"

"All were .22 caliber, probably hollow-points. Most likely from a .22 caliber High Standard automatic."

"Anything specific from the Medical Examiner's autopsy findings we should be searching for?"

"Yeah," said LeBeau. "'Unidentified metal particles,' as well as particles of substances identifiable as straw, Styrofoam, and cellophane."

"That's the kind of specificity I need," said Weinstein.

"There's something more from the ballistics examination of the cartridge casings found at the parking lot. The gun was a High Standard automatic.

They matched a cartridge casing from Mary Lee Wen's Pontiac, with those found at the parking lot."

"Wait a minute," said Weinstein. "Who's Mary Lee Wen? She wasn't one of the CBS victims. Where did she come from?"

Casey explained.

"This guy may have killed five people," said Weinstein.

"Casey, tell them how we got on to O'Reilly," Dan said.

Casey told the prosecutors about how they had traced the parking application to the car, the phone and the home of O'Reilly.

"We think O'Reilly was stalking Marino," said LeBeau. "We compared all the different dates and times O'Reilly either entered or exited the parking lot with the dates and times Marino entered and exited."

The drafting of the search warrant continued on into the night. Hundreds of suggestions for revising and editing the document produced twenty-seven drafts of the affidavit. The relevance of each shred of evidence was discussed, debated, and decided upon before it was added to the affidavit. They included the insurance scam by Miller, and the FBI surveillance near Marino's Queens apartment.

They concluded by listing each piece of evidence they hoped to find—hairs, blood, body and everything else.

At 2:15 A.M., they finished and it was time to go home. Thomas appeared in the conference room and informed Casey, Weinstein, LeBeau and Bergen that an FBI airplane would be at the Linden, New Jersey airport at 6:00 A.M. to fly them to Kentucky. Hopefully, Judge Milton P. Arnold III would sign the search warrant so they could search the van.

Thirty-Nine

10:15 AM
January 18th
Manhattan, New York

Dan raised his head off the pillow and looked at his alarm clock. It didn't seem like he'd slept. The familiar battle between mind and body began. His mind said to get up and go to work, but his body refused to listen. Coffee was needed.

He padded into the kitchen only to find there was none. Desperate for caffeine, he opened the refrigerator and spotted the solitary can of Coke. It was a godsend.

He uncovered Nevermore's cage and turned on the television. "Sorry about neglecting you. I'll make it up to you."

"Nevermore!" the parrot squawked.

He found his way to the bathroom, and after a shower, the process of becoming human was underway. A large cup of coffee from the neighborhood deli helped the process.

By the time he arrived at the office, Dan had finished the deli coffee and went searching for more. When he reached the coffee machine, he saw Clements waiting for the machine to finish filling his cup.

"I left about ten last night," Clements said. "What time did you finish up?"

"After two," Dan said as he pushed the buttons on the coffee machine. "At least we were able to catch a little sleep. I pity everyone who had to catch that early flight to Kentucky."

"I told Casey I'd cover for her in a meeting with the Immigration guys who are trying to catch the Schwartzes. Heard anything from Kentucky?"

"Not yet," Dan said. He pulled the cup out of the coffee machine and took a sip. "It's a little early yet. I've got to make a few calls to headquarters to get a forensic team to search the van."

"Let's catch some lunch after you do." Dan returned to his office and placed a call.

"Mr. Green's office," said a perky woman's voice in a Virginia drawl.

"Hi, this is Dan Robertson in the New York office returning his call. We missed each other yesterday."

"I'll put you through," said perky Virginia.

"Green," said the Assistant Director in a gruff voice.

"Good morning. This is Dan Robertson in New York."

"What's up?"

"I'm calling to ask if you can send a forensic team to Kentucky to help us on a case."

"If they're needed in Kentucky, why isn't the Agent in Charge of the Louisville office calling me?" said Green.

"I can have Mr. Littleton call you if you want, but this is a case that New York is running." Dan gave Green a little background of the case.

"If this guy is the dangerous killer you say he is, why didn't you arrest him when you spotted him in New Jersey? Using a couple of surveillance teams and aircraft support sounds to me like a waste of bureau resources."

"Mr. Green, this case is being monitored by the Director, and he told us to pull out all the stops to solve this one. If you'd like to check with him, I'm sure he would support our use of your forensic team."

"Don't tell me what to do! The Director's out of the country. I'm not about to call him there. You'll have to rely on the New York and Louisville FBI Agents to take care of this. Didn't we train them in evidence collection when they went through New Agents' training?"

"Mr. Green, I'm aware of what was included in New Agents' training," said Dan, his voice going up a notch in volume and force. "I also know that there's a lot of Agents who haven't processed a crime scene in ten to fifteen years. We need a top-notch team who deals with serology and trace evidence on a daily basis. This case is too important to risk screwing it up."

"Then don't. I can't just sit here and continue to tell you I won't send a team to Kentucky. What is it about NO that you don't understand?"

Dan was seething by the time he had hung up the receiver. He called another number.

"Mr. Van Pelt's office," said a voice that had to be perky Virginia's sister.

"Dan Robertson in New York calling. Is he available?"

"Just a moment," she said and put him on hold. "Yes he is, Mr. Robertson. I'll put you through."

"Van Pelt," said a man in a voice that could've been a brother to perky Virginia and her sister.

"Dan Robertson in New York. I need you to send a couple of fingerprint experts to Frankfort, Kentucky to process a van that's a part of The CBS Murders case we're working in New York. Can you help us out?"

"Of course," said Van Pelt. "I've read about the case in the Daily Briefing Book that all the ADs receive. You've had a break in the case?"

"Maybe," Dan gave Van Pelt a quick update of what had happened, and why they needed the fingerprint experts.

"When I first read about the case I had serious doubts you guys would ever solve it. Tell me where to send my fingerprint men, and I'll get them on their way."

Dan passed the information on to Van Pelt and thanked him. No sooner had he hung up, the phone rang. Nick Thomas wanted to see him right away.

Forty

11:30 AM
January 18th
Manhattan, New York

Dan stepped into the AD's office. Thomas motioned for him to take a seat.

"I just got a call from Ben Green at headquarters," said Thomas as he stared at Dan. "He told me you got a little testy when he wouldn't send a forensic team to Kentucky. That right?"

"Not really. I asked for a team, and told him why we needed it. He said, no, I pushed a little harder. He said no again and I dropped it. Was I pissed? Yeah. But respectful, not testy."

"Ben can be a real jerk from time to time. Let's drop it. On the brighter side, I got you another forensic team."

"Great! Where from?"

"The Kentucky State Police. I called McDaniels and told him that FBI Headquarters was being a horse's ass. He said he'd get a good team to help us out. By the time the judge signs the search warrant, the team will be in Frankfort."

"I wasn't sure what I was going to do. Thanks for the help."

"Keep me up to date. I was caught off guard when Green called me."

"I hear you. Anything else?"

"No. I know there's a lot to be done, so get back to work."

Dan walked back to his office feeling good that one problem was solved. At the same time, he was annoyed Green tried to backdoor him with Nick. Too many snakes in this outfit.

Dan called the Lexington Resident Agency to have Casey call him once she landed. He had just hung up when Clements appeared in his doorway, looking very excited about something. "What's up?" Dan asked.

"Just got a call from Immigration," Clements said. "The Schwartzes are on a flight from Geneva that lands at 2:40 this afternoon."

"Get some more agents and hightail it out to JFK to arrest them," Dan said and then paused. "But I don't want to sit here for hours, waiting to hear what they find when they search the van. I'll join you. Let's go."

They pulled onto Broadway, made the loop around the park outside City Hall, took Park Place to the ramp of the Brooklyn Bridge, and swung onto the Gowanus Expressway to take the Shore Parkway to JFK airport.

"We're cutting it close," Clements said as he looked at his watch. It's 2:30. We've only got ten minutes."

"Which airline?" Dan asked as they walked through the terminal.

"Swissair from Geneva," They stopped in front of the screen listing arrivals and departures. "There it is. Flight 138. I hope to hell it isn't early! It arrives at Gate R-34. That's way down at the end of the concourse."

"Slow down. We don't need to go to the gate. They have to go through Passport Control. That's where we'll go. It's a lot closer."

Dan led the agents to the arrival level of the International Terminal, showed his credentials to the Customs Agent, and was shown to the small office out of which the Immigration and Naturalization Service operated. Dan told the INS agent why they were there and showed them the arrest warrants. The INS agent typed on the computer, then turned around and smiled.

"What was that?" asked Clements.

"Modern day crime stopping. The Schwartzes will be detained, no matter which immigration booth they come through."

"Great way to arrest somebody," said Clements. "You just wait for them to identify themselves."

The INS agent changed screens on the computer, and brought up airline arrival information. "The plane is on the ground, but hasn't yet reached the arrival gate."

"Do you get a lot of these?"

"We get a fair number of arrests, mostly drug dealers."

Through the windows of the small office, everyone saw a burst of activity as passengers arrived to clear Immigration.

"All right," the INS agent said. "It's showtime!"

The passengers came down the ramp to the INS booths, some walking, some running, wanting to be first. The seasoned travelers only had carry-on luggage and avoided waiting for their luggage once they'd cleared Immigration. Both Clements and Dan were looking for the Schwartzes. The other agents were glancing at the people lined up behind the yellow line painted on the floor. The INS Agents emerged from their break room, and slowly made their way to the booths from where they would process the passengers.

After a few minutes, a low-tone buzz sounded, and the INS computer started flashing.

"It looks like your guests have arrived," the INS agent said.

The people in the INS control booth watched as two INS Agents walked over to booth three and told Bernie and Sarah Schwartz to follow them to the small detention room. Although they couldn't hear what was being said, both Bernie and Sarah Schwartz clearly made their objections known.

The INS agent pushed back his chair and stood up. "Let's go get acquainted with Mr. and Mrs. Schwartz."

They wove their way through the people to the closed door where the shouting couple had been taken.

When they entered, the two INS Agents walked out. In clothes wrinkled from the long plane ride, Bernie Schwartz was bathed in perspiration, his face contorted, and red with rage. Sarah Schwartz carried a Louis Vuitton handbag and wore a designer sweat suit. Her face was immobile, jaw clenched, and she stood with hands on both hips. "What the hell do you mean by this?" she screeched. "We've got to get home to our children! Just who do you think you are?"

"I'm gonna fucking see to it that you're out of a job for this!" Bernie shouted. "I'm gonna call my lawyer right now!"

"Mr. and Mrs. Schwartz, my name is Roger Clements. I'm an FBI Agent," he said as he showed his credentials. "You're both under arrest for bank fraud.

Turn and face the wall, spread your feet, and place both hands on the wall above your head. We're going to search you before we handcuff you."

"You're going to do no such thing!" shouted Sarah Schwartz.

"Like hell I'm not!" Agent Jude FitzGibbon said as she grabbed Sarah in an arm lock and shoved her against the wall. "Now you can do as I say, or I'll add a charge of Obstruction of Justice to the other charges!"

"Get your hands off my wife!" Bernie Schwartz shouted as he lunged towards FitzGibbon.

"Not a good idea!" Tom Matthews said as he grabbed Bernie Schwartz by the arm and swung him away from FitzGibbon.

"Don't do anything stupid!" Agent Sidney Jackson said, as his hands pinned Bernie's other arm, and the two agents shoved him against the wall and began frisking him.

Dan stood with his back to the door, making sure the only exit was blocked. He smiled as he watched his agents make the arrests. FitzGibbon had one of Sarah's arms behind her back and snapped on the handcuff. Bernie's arms were wrenched behind him, his corpulent body making cuffing more difficult.

"You're under arrest. Anything you say can be used against you ..." FitzGibbon said as she ticked off the points of the Miranda warnings. "... Do you understand your rights?"

Sarah had begun to cry, and between sobs she said, "Uh huh."

"Was that a yes, Mrs. Schwartz?" FitzGibbon asked.

"Yeah," came her frightened answer.

"I ain't got nothing to say to you fuckers," Bernie said.

FitzGibbon finished frisking Sarah, and Matthews did the same on Bernie. Both of the Schwartzes complained loud and long about everything that was being done to them.

"Listen up," Clements said to the Schwartzes. "We're going to take you to the Manhattan FBI office. You'll be fingerprinted and photographed. If you want to call your lawyer, that'll be the time to do it. You'll either be put in jail at the Metropolitan Correctional Center, or be set free on bail. Any questions?"

Forty-One

8:45 AM
January 19th
Manhattan, New York

"I got a call from Casey around midnight last night," Dan said as he sat opposite Thomas in the AD's office. "The search of the van went well. They recovered the .22 caliber cartridge casing, what looks like blood, hair, a partially-empty box of Remington Peters .22 caliber hollow point bullets, and some little white specks of Styrofoam."

"Was the cartridge casing from the van compared with those from on the rooftop parking lot?"

"Yes. They match."

"What about the other evidence?"

"We're waiting for the lab to analyze the blood and hair."

"Do you have enough for an arrest warrant on O'Reilly?"

"Not yet."

"Where is he now? Is he talking?"

"In the Frankfort jail. The judge denied bail. O'Reilly hired a local attorney but he's not talking."

"Did he hire a mob lawyer?"

"Not that anyone knows. Name is Cleveland."

"Where's the evidence from the van?"

"Here in New York. The NYPD lab will compare the blood and hair by noon today."

"Who's talking to the press about the arrest?"

"I don't know," Dan said. "It's not coming from our side. I saw the news and papers this morning. They don't have the whole story."

"You don't know how bad it's going to be now they've had a whiff of it. What else is happening?"

"We arrested Bernie and Sarah Schwartz yesterday afternoon when they came through Immigration."

"Good. What have you got planned for today?"

"Since we didn't find a pistol in the van, I want a search warrant for O'Reilly's house in Keansburg."

"You better move quickly. That would be the nail in the coffin for O'Reilly."

"It could be," said Dan. "If you and I have covered everything, I need to get at it."

Back at his desk, Dan picked up the phone and called the Surveillance Squad Supervisor, Sal Delano. Benicia had gotten the best look at O'Reilly's home, so Dan called him.

"Not too far from town. Sort of out in the country," Benicia said.

"What's the house like?"

"Small white clapboard, pitched roof, screened-in porch."

"Any garage?"

"Yeah. Detached one-car. Same clapboard and roof."

"Did you get a look around the outside of the house?"

"Not really. We had barely set up when they took off. But the map shows an estuary from the Atlantic running behind the house."

"Really! Nice place to get rid of a gun."

"Or a body. No idea how deep it is, but the tide is probably strong enough to carry a body. You might check with the guys in air surveillance and see if they shot any photos of the house on the first day."

Dan called and the eight by ten inch black and white photos arrived on his desk ten minutes later. Photos showed the house, the garage, and the estuary.

Dan called Ray Russell, the Senior Resident Agent in the Newark FBI's Red Bank Resident Agency had arranged for the surveillance team to watch O'Reilly's house. "How you doing, Ray?"

"Not bad. I see you guys arrested O'Reilly for The CBS murders. A nice piece of work."

"Thanks, but I'm afraid it's only the beginning. Sorry to do this, but I've got to ask you for another favor. We're putting together a search warrant for O'Reilly's house, the garage, and the estuary behind his house."

"You mean the Waackaack Creek?"

"Is that what they call it?" asked Dan. "Ray, would you pull together information about the house, its legal description and stuff? We're going to need it for the search affidavit, and I need somebody to search the creek."

"Maybe I can help," said Russell. "We've got a good relationship with the Ocean Township Police Department, they've got a decent scuba team. I could ask them to help."

"That would be great! Do it."

"When's the search?"

"Tomorrow. Gotta run. Talk to you later." Dan hung up the phone, and gathered papers. A young man in a suit appeared in the door of his office.

"Are you Dan Robertson?"

"Afraid so."

"You running The CBS Murders investigation?"

"The FBI's end of it, yeah. Why?"

"I was just talking to Tim Mahoney in Special Operations. He told me you might be doing a search over in New Jersey."

"Damn it! Can't anybody in this place keep their mouth shut?" Dan shouted.

"Sorry. I was just trying to be helpful. Mahoney said you might need to search a river. I formed an FBI scuba team about six months ago. We've been practicing quite a bit, diving in lakes and the ocean. If you need to search that river over in Jersey, I'd like to ask you to use us."

"Tell me ... what's your name anyway?"

"Tim Roban. I'm on Squad 18."

"That's a foreign counterintelligence squad. Is this your way of trying to get transferred to a criminal squad?"

"No, I'd just like a chance to help."

"Have you talked to your supervisor about any of this?" asked Dan.

"Yeah. He says it's all right if you need us."

"How many search warrant evidence dives have you guys made?"

"Well, ...actually, this would be our first," said Roban.

"Do you have any idea how many millions of people are watching everything we do on this case? Can you imagine what would happen if we screwed up even the smallest aspect of this investigation? And you want me to risk it all, with a scuba team that's never made a dive, searching for evidence?"

"We can do it," Roban said pleadingly. "We won't mess up."

"How many agents on your team?"

"There's four of us."

Dan stood staring at the young agent, remembering what it was like to be young and optimistic. "What the heck! Tell you what I'll do. If you and your scuba team agree to take directions from the Ocean Township Police scuba team, you can dive. Do you agree to that condition?"

"Yes!" Roban's face broke into a wide grin. "All we want is a chance."

"Then have your team suited up and ready to go tomorrow."

"Thanks! You won't be sorry." Roban turned and literally ran back to tell the others.

Dan smiled as he watched him go.

When he got out of his car at Midtown North, cameras started taping, and photos were being taken. He fought his way through.

"How do you like today's media feeding frenzy?" asked Sandoval.

"Not my cup of tea," Dan set his things down and turned to Casey. "Welcome home. How you doing on the search warrant?"

"It's coming along, but not too fast. Bergen and Weinstein are home sleeping."

"If they can't be here, get other ADAs and AUSAs to help. Casey, you're going to be the affiant on the affidavit, and direct this search warrant. We execute the search warrant tomorrow," Dan said. "If we get lucky, we might find the gun. Let's get cracking on this affidavit. I'd rather not face another all-nighter."

The pace of the investigation had increased. The media's story about the arrest sped up the need to search before any evidence was moved or destroyed. ADA Gloria Thurman, and AUSA Tom Renfro appeared at Task Force headquarters.

About 2:00 P.M., Bergen, Weinstein, and LeBeau, joined the group. After five cups of coffee, LeBeau and Casey returned to life. LeBeau and Clements went to the men's room, and stood side-by-side as they used urinals and continued to discuss the affidavit. Behind them, they heard the sound of a toilet being flushed, and the stall door being opened.

"How you doing fellas?" came the voice of Casey, who had just exited the stall.

Both men were in shock, and for the moment, speechless. They pressed their bodies against the urinals in an attempt to gain a modicum of privacy in the situation.

"Sorry for the intrusion, but the toilet in the women's room is out of order. I really had to go and nobody was in here when I first came in," Casey said, unable to keep from smiling.

"Casey, you really shouldn't have ..." LeBeau finally blurted out.

Casey, washed and dried her hands, checked her hair, and smoothed her skirt. Then she stepped over to the two men and stood behind them.

"Hey, its been nice going with both of you," she said as she simultaneously patted both men on their butts, then turned and walked out the door, laughing the whole time.

"You've really got to do something about her," LeBeau said with a laugh.

Forty-Two

2:00 PM
January 19th
Frankfort, Kentucky

The Franklin County, Kentucky Courtroom was filled with the regular court watchers, an attorney or two, and the public defender. The prisoners were led in and the sheriff's deputy removed handcuffs from the four men and one woman, and instructed them to sit in the chairs along the wall behind the defense table. The prisoners whispered back and forth, except for O'Reilly who spoke to no one, his eyes watching everything around him.

"All rise," The bailiff called out. "The Franklin County Superior Court is now in session, the Honorable Marcus T. Green, presiding."

Judge Green, a dark haired, heavy-set man stepped up to the bench and sat down. "Please be seated." Green slipped on his reading glasses and turned to the bailiff. "Please call the first case."

"Case 4281, The People of the State of New York vs. Bart O'Reilly."

"Bailiff, is Mr. O'Reilly present in the courtroom?"

"Yes, your Honor, he is."

"Is Mr. O'Reilly represented by counsel?"

A slender, blond-haired man of thirty-five, stood and answered the judge. "Yes, your Honor. Jeffrey S. Cleveland, on behalf of Bart O'Reilly."

"Let the record show that the defendant is present in the courtroom, and is represented by counsel," the judge began. "The purpose of this hearing is to provide Mr. O'Reilly an initial court appearance following his arrest by the Kentucky State Police, and to address the issue of his extradition to the State of New York. Is that correct, counselor?"

"Yes, your Honor, we—"

"According to the Kentucky State Police, Mr. O'Reilly was arrested based on a bench warrant issued in New York on, let me see . . . January 11th, for failure to appear to begin serving a criminal sentence. Is that correct, counselor?"

"Your Honor, there is an issue we would like to raise before this court. We contend that Mr. O'Reilly was falsely arrested by the Kentucky State Police for possession of a stolen vehicle. It was only after that illegal arrest, that Mr. O'Reilly was actually charged under the provisions of the 'failure to appear' warrant to which you make reference."

"What exactly are you proposing Mr. Cleveland?"

"That the court release Mr. O'Reilly, since he was arrested illegally."

The few people in the courtroom chuckled.

"Order in the court!" Judge Green shouted as he rapped his gavel. "Mr. Cleveland. This court has been provided with a copy of the Kentucky State Police report regarding Mr. O'Reilly's arrest. Do you have a copy of that document, counselor?"

"Yes, your Honor, I do."

"In my reading of it, it would appear to me that Mr. O'Reilly was arrested on reasonable belief that the van he was driving was stolen. The Kentucky State Police, on their own initiative, and made further inquiries regarding the status of the van Mr. O'Reilly was driving."

"Yes, your Honor, but—"

"Those inquiries, made with the, let me see . . . Palisades Park, New Jersey Police Department, resolved the question of the stolen status of the van."

"That addresses the van, your Honor, but not the arrest. You see—"

"And subsequent inquiries, regarding Mr. O'Reilly, made by the same Kentucky State Police, determined the existence of an outstanding bench warrant for the arrest of Mr. O'Reilly, issued when he failed to surrender to begin serving a jail sentence."

"Yes, your Honor, but getting back to his arrest—"

"Counselor, are you attempting to make a motion to this court, to throw out the arrest of Mr. O'Reilly?"

"Yes, your Honor."

"Fine. Motion denied! Now, regarding the extradition of Mr. O'Reilly back to New York, does the defendant waive his right to a judicial hearing?"

"Your Honor, the defendant does not wish to proceed with a judicial hearing, but has a request—"

"Fine, the defendant waives extradition, and is therefore remanded to the custody of the New York City Police Department, represented by, let me see . . .

Detectives Jack Duffy and James Moore. Gentlemen, are you present in this courtroom?"

"Yes, your Honor," Moore said, as the two men stood. "We're right here."

"Very well. This court remands Mr. O'Reilly to your custody, for the purpose of transporting him to the State of New York. Now, Mr. Cleveland, is there any other issue you want this court to address?"

"Yes, your Honor. When arrested, Mr. O'Reilly had in his possession, cash money in the amount of $2,679.32. That money is currently being held by the Kentucky State Police. We request that such monies be released to Mr. O'Reilly to enable him to pay any and all expenses he might incur."

"And could those expenses, perhaps, include your fee, Mr. Cleveland?"

"Well, yes your Honor, in part, but—"

Judge Green shifted his focus to the defendant. "Mr. O'Reilly, you are here in my courtroom, having failed to appear to begin serving a sentence. I am not aware of your being gainfully employed, yet when you were arrested you had over $2,600 in your possession. You could have been represented by a public defender, yet you retained the services of Mr. Cleveland. Would you please inform this court how you came to select him as your counselor?"

"Your Honor, after I got arrested, I looked up attorneys in the phone book. I saw Cleveland's name. I remembered that I had a good time in Cleveland, once. So I hired him."

"Surely you are not serious, Mr. O'Reilly."

"Oh yeah, your Honor. I had a real good time."

"Never mind. Can you explain how you came into possession of this much money?"

"A guy I know paid it to me."

"For what reason?"

"He owed me."

"What was his name?"

"Can't remember."

"You can't remember the name of someone who owed you, then paid you over $2,600?"

"No sir."

"Do you have any kind of receipt or document which could confirm this was the source from which you obtained this money?"

"Nah. We just shook hands on it."

"And now you can't remember his name?"

"Nope."

"Mr. O'Reilly, your story is incredulous, as was your story regarding your rather unusual attorney selection process. This court has not been convinced that you did not come into possession of those funds through illegal means. Therefore, it is the ruling of this court that said money may constitute evidence of a crime, and as such, will be turned over to these New York Police Detectives. Any decision regarding release of those funds will not be made by this court, but rather, it will be made by the court in New York. Mr. O'Reilly, you are ordered extradited back to New York, and are remanded to the custody of these detectives, to be so removed." The judge struck his gavel. "Next case!"

* * *

In the custody of Detectives Duffy and Moore, Bart O'Reilly arrived at Standiford Field airport in Louisville, Kentucky at 1:45 P.M. They returned their rental car, and went to the U.S. Air check-in counter and filled out the forms required when armed law enforcement officers transport a prisoner on a commercial flight. After setting off the metal detectors, both detectives showed the airline security people their

NYPD shields and the completed forms, and were allowed to continue to the gate.

Duffy held a handcuffed O'Reilly while Moore went through the whole story again with the airline gate agent.

The Boeing 737-300 was configured into three seats on each side of a center aisle. The three men took their seats on the left side of the first row behind the bulkhead seats. For the flight, they re-handcuffed O'Reilly's hands in front of him, and sat him between them, the narrow seats wedging them tightly, shoulder-to-shoulder. To prevent their handcuffed prisoner from becoming too much of an attention-gathering spectacle, the detectives covered the handcuffs with a newspaper.

The other passengers boarded a half-full flight and took off just after the scheduled 3:10 P.M. departure time. After an hour and a half, the aircraft landed in Roanoke, Virginia, the flight's only scheduled stop. The aircraft was on the ground for forty-five minutes while passengers and luggage were offloaded, and new passengers and luggage were taken on board. While they waited, Moore phoned Midtown North Precinct station house, and told Captain Watson of their progress.

"Everything went real well with the judge." said Moore. "We could use one or two judges like him in Manhattan."

"Anything in the Kentucky local newspapers about the case?" asked Watson.

"Didn't see anything. Why?"

"Well, somehow the press here learned about O'Reilly's arrest, and the cartridge casings matching. Don't be surprised if reporters meet the plane when it lands."

"Okay, I'll keep an eye out for them."

"Remember, you aren't authorized to talk to the media."

"I know. They're calling my flight. Gotta go."

Moore re-boarded the flight and sat back down beside O'Reilly. He wanted to share the information from the phone call with Duffy, but couldn't without O'Reilly overhearing, so Moore decided to wait until O'Reilly had to use the toilet.

The aircraft taxied down the runway, took off, and climbed to its 24,000 feet cruising altitude on the final leg of their journey to New York. The captain turned off the seatbelt sign, and told everyone they were free to move about the cabin. Moore saw a number of passengers leave their seats, but wasn't ready for what happened next.

Passengers began to take still cameras, video cameras and tape recorders out of their carry-on luggage, and quickly surrounded Duffy, O'Reilly, and Moore.

A microphone was shoved in Duffy's face, and a cameraman's light illuminated all three men. Questions were hurled at them.

"Is this Bart O'Reilly, that you're taking back to New York?" a female reporter asked.

"How did you learn about O'Reilly?"

"Are the reports in the newspapers correct?"

"Have formal charges been filed against him?"

Finally, as all cameras and microphones were pointed at him, Duffy held up his hands, asking them to stop. "Look, all we're doing is transporting a prisoner," he said. "We've got instructions not to talk to anybody, and I seriously doubt our prisoner will have anything to say to you."

The cameras and microphones immediately switched to O'Reilly.

"Were you surprised at your arrest?"

"Can you tell us the details of where and how you were arrested?"

"Have you seen today's newspapers?"

Flashes from still cameras and lights from video cameras had temporarily blinded him. Microphones were shoved toward his face, yet O'Reilly sat stoically, eyes staring straight forward, not saying anything until he heard the next question.

"What is your reaction to the news about the bullets matching?"

O'Reilly's head snapped toward the reporter. "What bullets?"

"The ones from the parking lot matching the one from your van."

Once O'Reilly heard that, he immediately shut up, his eyes dilated, his breathing became rapid, and his face turned red.

O'Reilly didn't speak again, and withdrew into himself, seemingly not hearing the additional questions, or seeing the reporters.

"Okay folks, that's enough," Duffy said to the reporters. "Please return to your seats and leave us alone."

The flight attendants ushered the reporters back to their seats, amid unrelenting protestations and complaints.

When the plane landed at LaGuardia Airport in Queens, the reporters on the plane took as many photos as they could before the detectives led O'Reilly away. When O'Reilly and the detectives reached the end of the gangway, the reporters from the airplane were joined by at least a dozen of their colleagues, and the media frenzy rose to a new height. It didn't stop until the detectives and O'Reilly climbed into Sandoval's sedan, and the car pulled away from the curb.

The sedan wove its way in traffic through Queens and south into Brooklyn until it reached the Brooklyn House of Detention. O'Reilly was booked, photographed, fingerprinted, issued an orange jumpsuit, and put in a cell by himself. The steel-barred door slammed shut, its noise echoing through the cellblock.

Forty-Three

9:00 AM
January 20th
Keansburg, New Jersey

Annie Glenn, O'Reilly's common-law wife, answered the door of her house wearing her bathrobe and slippers. Holding her newborn baby, her daughter, Patsy Eberly, stood behind her in the living room. "What is it?" Annie asked, her eyes darting back and forth among the cars and people gathered in her front yard.

"Ma'am, I'm Special Agent Casey Brody from the FBI. We have a search warrant for your house, garage, and the creek behind it. Go ahead and read the warrant if you want, but we're going to get started." Annie didn't say anything as Casey talked, and only glanced at the copy of the warrant.

"You can stay in the living room while we search the house," Detective Donnie Bennett said. "We can't let you interfere."

Annie merely nodded her understanding. She numbly turned on her television, sat on the sofa, and began to watch morning television game shows.

"Sidney, Erik, and Jack, hook up with Monty and search the house." Casey said. "Sidney, keep the log of the house search."

Casey checked the clipboard that contained the names of the detectives and agents participating in the search. She wanted to ensure equal participation by the New York FBI, the NYPD, and the Red Bank FBI. Casey assigned detectives and agents to search the garage.

"Hey Dan, did you spot the Ford Escort over there behind the garage?" Casey said as she motioned in that direction. "I'll have somebody get its VIN, and see if it matches the one from the DMV computer."

"Sounds good," Dan said.

"Tom, I'd like you to keep a log of the scuba search," Casey said.

The Ocean Township Police scuba team had arrived, and was looking at the Waackaack Creek to plan their dive. The FBI scuba team arrived in several cars, and introduced themselves to the Ocean Township divers.

As a large NYPD van pulled up, Dan and NYPD Lieutenant Hank Murray turned to look.

"Who's that, Hank?"

"Not sure."

Casey and the others walked toward the van and saw six trim, muscular men climb out. All wore baseball caps and one-piece blue jumpsuits with NYPD patches on one shoulder, a scuba patch on the other, and their names embroidered above the left breast pocket. Two wore sergeant's stripes.

"Morning!" said Murray as he, Dan and Casey reached out to shake the newcomers' hands.

"How you doing?" came the reply. "I'm Sergeant Milt Dunn," and he introduced the others.

"I'm Lieutenant Murray from Midtown North," he said and introduced Casey and Dan.

"Chief of Detectives Keenan said you had a scuba search," said Dunn. "Told us to come help."

"We're beginning to have more divers than we have river," said Casey. "We've got three Ocean Township Police Department divers, and four from the FBI."

"You don't need them," said Dunn. "You can go ahead and cut 'em loose." The NYPD scuba team was unloading their diving equipment, ignoring the conversation.

"Who the hell do you think you are, mister?" shouted Murray.

"Probably the best fucking divers here," Dunn shot back. "We wrote the book on police dives. We teach police divers the way it's supposed to be done."

"Dunn, I don't much care for your attitude."

"Departmental policy. The NYPD doesn't dive with anyone else." Dunn and the other NYPD divers began suiting up.

"I need a phone," said Murray. He made a call, had Dunn speak to someone. Dunn then spoke to the other NYPD divers who reloaded the equipment into the van, climbed in, and drove off.

"Who'd you call, and what did they say?" asked Casey.

"Captain Watson at Midtown North. Told him what was happening, and that we needed somebody with more clout than the Chief of Detectives. He conferenced the Police Commissioner in, and Dunn was told to leave."

"Let's get those divers in the water," Casey said, and headed into the house.

"Not much here, Casey," said Sandoval. Some bank statements and phone bills. Name on the phone bill was A. Glenn."

Casey walked outside and entered the garage. "How's it going?" she asked LeBeau.

"Looks like the van was painted here," LeBeau said pointing to a rectangle on the floor surrounded by black paint. "We took paint scrapings from the floor, and found a few empty cans of black spray paint. We also found some rags with what looks like dried blood on it."

"There's something wrong here," said Moore, as he suspiciously looked around the outside of the garage.

"What?" asked Casey as she stepped into the bright sunlight to talk to him.

"I'll tell you in a minute," he said and began measuring. "Ah ha! Gotcha!"

"What are you doing?" Casey asked.

"I suspected the outside of the garage was bigger than the inside. The width was okay. But the length was way off. By at least six feet."

"What are you saying?" asked Dan.

"I think there's a hidden room in this garage. My measurements tell me I'm right. Now I have to find a way into it."

Moore began pushing panels of plywood, looking for a door. He picked up a hammer and tapped twice, then moved over a few inches and tapped again. Finally, the tapping made a hollow sound. "Okay! Here's the door. Let's find a way to open it."

It took some doing, but the men found a two-by-four at the bottom of the wall that had to be swung out of the way, and then, using a knothole as a latch, with a slight pull the door swung open. Moore shined his flashlight into the small room. He stepped in and saw an overhead light with a pull chain. He pulled and two light bulbs went on.

Moore's measurements were fairly accurate. The room was a little less than six feet wide, and ran the entire width of the garage. The two light bulbs were equally spaced across the ceiling, but provided adequate illumination for the room. A small table was at one end of the room. Other things were tossed about haphazardly. At the far end of the room, Moore saw a number of small spots of light. When he reached the wall, he discovered they were caused by sunlight as it shone through small holes in the wall. He shined his flashlight on the holes and touched them with his fingers.

"What have you got?" asked Casey.

"I think these might be bullet holes."

As she entered the small room, Casey stepped on a small object. "Jim, shine your flashlight on the floor over here. I need to see what I stepped on."

Moore walked back toward her, his flashlight illuminating the floor. As he shone the light around her feet, she reached down and picked up the object from under her shoe.

"Would you look at this?" Casey said as she picked up the object. "Gentlemen, I hold in my hand, a .22 caliber cartridge casing. What do you think about that?"

Moore wasn't looking at Casey or the cartridge casing. He was looking at the floor of the room near her feet, where he was directing the light.

"Casey, don't move," he said, and reached down to pick up a small object.

"Find another one?" Casey asked.

"Yeah, I did. Those are bullet holes in the wall over there," Moore said as he gestured toward the wall. "I think O'Reilly used this room to try out the silencer on his .22 caliber High Standard automatic."

"I can't wait until we compare those cartridge casings to the ones from Wen's car, the parking lot, and the van. Are they Remington-Peters?" asked LeBeau.

Moore shined the flashlight at the end of the casing. "Yep! Sure are!"

"Let's have the search team carefully go through this whole room," said Lt. Murray. "Maybe we'll find the gun."

Dan, Murray and Casey walked outside to check on the progress of the scuba search. The seven divers had suited up, and five of them were in the water, holding onto a rope stretched across the creek. The other two were beside each riverbank, at either end of the rope, ready to accept items found by the men in the middle of the creek. One at a time they submerged, while the others waited their turn.

"How's it going guys?" Casey asked the group.

Johnson, the only one who didn't have an aqualung regulator in his mouth, answered for the group. "The water's so muddy they can't even see their hand in front of their face. They're doing a grid search, using their hands to feel along the bottom of the riverbed."

Graham Dean, one of the Ocean Township Police divers burst from beneath the water, his right hand in the air. He pulled off his mask, and let the regulator drop out of his mouth.

"I've got one!" he shouted.

"One what?" asked Johnson.

"A .22 caliber cartridge casing."

"Get a shot of that, would you?" Johnson said as he turned to the FBI photographer.

Terry Hall of the Ocean Township Police scuba team, emerged from the water with a large brown object in his hands. He lifted his mask, and dropped the regulator from his mouth.

"What have you got, Terry?" asked Agent Carl Dickerson.

"I'm not sure, but whatever it is, it was weighted down, and tossed into the creek." All of the divers watched while Hall wrestled with the object. He untied the bundle, and something fell out.

"Hey, Keith! Dive down and get that, would you?" asked Hall.

The water was filled with bubbles as Agent Keith Hopkins submerged. He came back up in a minute, holding a large rock. "This is the only thing I could find," he said after pulling off his mask and regulator. "Is this what you dropped?"

"I think so," said Hall.

"What have you got?" asked Hopkins.

"A leather jacket. It looks like it's in pretty good shape. Now why would anyone want to wrap a good leather jacket around a rock, and throw it in the creek?"

"Maybe it was covered with blood that wouldn't come off. It isn't exactly the kind of thing you bring to your local dry cleaners," said Johnson who had been watching and listening from the creek bank.

LeBeau walked over to the group.

"I'm not sure we can link O'Reilly to that particular leather jacket, but it sure is another nice piece of circumstantial evidence."

"You think we've found enough to charge O'Reilly with murder?" Casey asked Dan.

"I don't know. When you put it together with what they found in the van, it just might be."

Dan thought of the promise he made to Christy Marino. "We're almost there."

Forty-Four

9:30 AM
January 21st
Manhattan, New York

The telephone rang in the US attorney's office. "This is Leonard Weinstein."

"This is Leo Traub, an attorney with Selig, Levine and Traub."

"What can I do for you?"

"I've been retained by Bernie and Sarah Schwartz. I'd like to meet with you to discuss the possibility of cooperation in return for a deal."

"That might be a little bit difficult since the only other possible defendants in the case, Mrs. Wen and Miss Marino, are both dead. Under those circumstances, I'm not quite sure how the Schwartzes cooperation might be useful."

"I think it would be worth your time to talk with them," said Traub. "Why don't we allow you to question them about their trip to Europe, and go from there. If the information demonstrates that the events leading to the bankruptcy were the unfortunate circumstances which I have been led to believe they were, then I'd entertain the possibility of a plea agreement."

Weinstein thought about the offer for a moment. He looked at the tall stack of case folders on his desk, and admitted to himself that any chance to reduce the workload was worth considering. "I'll agree to an initial interview by the FBI. But until you place something substantial on the table, I'm not interested in a plea."

"Very well," said Traub, annoyed with the response. "How about this afternoon?"

"I'll set up an interview for one o'clock. But there's no way I can be there. I'm booked solid for days."

"Then one it is," said Traub. "Where shall I bring my clients?"

"The FBI office at the Jacob Javitz Federal Building. I'll have the FBI set it up." Weinstein finished the call, then picked up the receiver again, and called Dan. "I just had a curious call." Weinstein told him about it, and asked him to handle the interview.

At 1:00 PM, in a small interview room in the FBI office, Traub introduced the Schwartzes to Casey and Dan. They were read their rights and the interview began.

"Tell us about your trip to Europe," said Casey. "When did you leave, and where did you go?"

"Our trip?" said a perspiring Bernie Schwartz. "Well, we left on January 12th on El Al Airlines for Tel Aviv, Israel. We got there on the 13th. We stayed at the Tel Aviv Hilton."

"How long were you there?" Casey said, noticing Bernie's twitching hands.

"How long? Oh, I'd say about a week," said Bernie.

"And what did you do while you were there?" asked Dan, glancing back and forth between Bernie and Sarah.

"What didn't I do?" said Bernie, making hand gestures. "I met with some of my diamond suppliers, and paid them the money I owed."

"Where'd you get the money to travel and pay them?" Casey asked sharply. "Fontaine Diamonds is in Bankruptcy."

"The money?" Bernie stammered. "I, ... ah, ... you see, my wife had some of her jewelry with her. We, ... ah, ... sold her diamond ring in order to pay some of the people."

"The Bankruptcy Trustee told me that you wire transferred $200,000 to yourself out of the Fontaine bank account," Casey said, becoming angry. "Tell me about that."

"Oh, that?" Bernie said, his perspiration having increased so much that he wiped his forehead with his handkerchief. "Well, ... I, ... ah, ... didn't want to travel with cash to pay my suppliers. The Middle East can be dangerous, you know. So ... I, ... ah, ... wire transferred the money to myself, so it would be there, you know ... waiting for me."

"If it was Fontaine money, why didn't it stay in a Fontaine account?" Dan asked.

"Why? Well, you see, ... I thought it was going to be transferred from the Fontaine account at MBT in New York, to be held by Bank Leumi in Tel Aviv. The bank must have screwed it up, made a mistake, and transferred it into my personal account in New York. It would have taken too much time and trouble to reverse it out, so I just left it in my personal account, and paid the debts to the suppliers in cash."

"In cash!" said Casey. "First you tell us it's dangerous to carry cash in the Middle East, and now you tell us that you're paying your suppliers in cash! Which is it? And did you get paid receipts from those suppliers?"

"Receipts? No, ... that's not the way it's done in the diamond trade."

"Well, it's the way the tax and bankruptcy people in this country work!" said Dan, his patience being sorely tried. "Where'd you go next?"

"Where?" Bernie said, wiping his forehead again. "Let's see, I think it was Munich, Germany. We really wanted to go to Geneva, but couldn't get on a flight. So we flew to Munich, rented a car, and drove."

"Why'd you go there?" asked Casey.

"There? We, ... ah, ... visited an old friend," said Schwartz, fidgeting.

"What's the friend's name?" asked Dan.

"It's ... ah ... Cohen. Samuel Cohen."

"You can give us his phone number, can't you?" asked Casey.

"Oh, sure."

"How long did you stay there?" asked Dan.

"Let me think," Bernie said as he glanced at Sarah and saw her sitting still as a statue, only her eyes moving. "One or two days, I think. Then we flew home and got arrested."

"Very little of this is supported by the stamps that were made in your passports as you came and went from these countries," said Dan. "How long did you ... never mind. Let's change directions. How did Fontaine Diamonds come to have a relationship with MBT Factors?"

"How? Michael Goldman at Westchester Savings and Loan recommended we use Wallace Goldstein as accountants for Fontaine," said Bernie. "We did, and they recommended we talk to MBT Factors at Manhattan Bank and Trust about trade finance."

"Trade finance?" asked Dan.

"Yeah, business funding, you know," said Schwartz, slipping into business jargon with his slick con pitch. "They told me that MBT Factors lent money against outstanding accounts receivable. Fontaine had grown rapidly, but we needed additional capital to fund our expansion. Rather than bring in an equity partner, we decided to pursue trade financing."

"And who from Fontaine managed the relationship with MBT Factors?" Casey asked.

"Who?" Bernie said, his eyes flitting rapidly back and forth. "We needed someone experienced in trade finance. We asked Wallace Goldstein if they could recommend anyone, and they suggested Christy Marino. We interviewed her, liked her, so we hired her."

"What exactly did she do for Fontaine?" asked Casey.

"What did she do? She handled the deposits of money coming in, and paid the bills. Every day, she put together a list of new receivables, and sent them to MBT Factors."

"Were there ever any problems?" asked Dan.

"Were there? I should say! Just before Christmas, I found out she had been sending invoices to MBT before shipments went to the clients. I asked her what she was doing, and she said it was called an early acquisition method, and everybody did it. Business was good, so I didn't worry about it. Then I saw a lot of odd charges on her American Express Card bill."

"You were opening her mail?" asked Casey.

"No, she had a Fontaine Corporate American Express card. But on the bill, there were a lot of her personal charges. She said that she'd pay the company back for all her personal shit."

"Did she?" asked Dan, becoming angrier.

"No. Not only that. I took a business trip to California and when I got back, she said she'd been diagnosed with cancer, and needed to see some damn specialist in Switzerland."

"When they performed an autopsy on her there was no cancer found," said Dan.

"See what I mean? She was a lying little cunt!"

"Let's get back to MBT Factors," said Casey. "Who from Fontaine dealt with their audits?"

"Christy Marino. And another thing. In July, there was about four grand worth of gold chains bought from All That Glitters. Fontaine's never done any fuckin' business with them. So I asked around, and Golda Hillberg, our office manager told me that All That Glitters called and asked if somebody would come pick up the gold chains. That goddamn Christy told Golda that she'd handle it," Bernie said, working himself into a frenzy.

"So what did you do about it?"

"I hired a fuckin' private investigator. He followed her, and checked into what she was doing. He said he couldn't prove it, but he was sure she was stealing from Fontaine. The little bitch! You bust your ass to build a business, and your ungrateful employees stab you in the back!"

"What about the invoices sent to MBT Factors for Fontaine sales to clients who claim they never did business with you?"

"That fuckin' bitch was puttin' in phony invoices, then pocketing the money. I don't know how, but she was doing it."

"And you knew nothing about it?" asked Dan incredulously.

"No. Then one day I go into the vault to get some loose diamonds," Bernie said, spittle flying out of his mouth. "The damn things weren't there! They were fucking gone! So I confront the little cunt, and she tells me she needed surgery for her cancer, and if I gave her $100,000.00, she'd tell me where they were. Can you imagine that?"

"So what did you tell her?" asked Dan with total disbelief.

"Nobody's going to fuckin' shake me down. I knew I had to talk to my lawyer. I told Marino that's what I was gonna to do. So I told my lawyer about it, and he said he'd negotiate with her for the return of the diamonds while I was in Israel. Not Traub, here. Our corporate attorney, Isaac Jonas. But before he could do it, she got whacked."

"Yeah, that was unfortunate," Casey said sarcastically. "How much do you think she stole from Fontaine?"

"The best I can figure, that little bitch ripped me off for about two and a half million!"

"Do you have anything that would prove what you've been alleging?" asked Casey.

"I had some of these things written down, but she fuckin' stole that too! I guess just to cover her tracks!"

"I've had enough of this!" shouted Dan as he stood up. "I've got better things to do with my time than to listen to this self-serving drivel!"

"Are you fuckin' calling me a liar?" Bernie screamed.

"Calling you a liar doesn't come anywhere close to what you really are!"

"Hey everybody, let's just calm down," said Traub. "There's no need to turn my client's cooperation into an adversarial confrontation."

"This isn't cooperation!" said Dan angrily. "It's called getting jerked around by a sleazeball, and I'm not going to put up with it!"

"Okay, okay," Casey said and took a deep breath. "Continuing this way isn't going to get us anywhere. I think it would be best if we wrap it up for today."

Bernie was still seething, and Dan stood over him, literally daring Bernie to give him a reason to hit him.

"Mr. Robertson, Miss Brody?" said Traub. "Would you please give me a few minutes alone with my clients before we call it a day?"

"Sure," said Dan, staring at Bernie. "We'll wait in the hall."

* * *

Once the door was closed, Traub sat in a chair opposite Bernie and Sarah. "Bernie, that wasn't a smart thing to do. You're not in a very good bargaining position to begin with, but if you piss off the FBI and the United States Attorney, they'll hurt you."

"Fuck 'em," said Bernie. "They don't have shit on me. Just a bunch of trumped up charges so they can put me out of business. I want you to sue the feds for what they're doing to me!"

"Bernie," Traub said in a pleading voice. "Don't do this. It won't work. Just tell them you were trying to keep your business afloat, and things just got out of hand. Tell them you've learned your lesson, plead guilty to one or two counts, and in return you ask for probation."

"Why should I plead guilty?" Bernie asked, coming out of his chair. "I didn't do anything wrong, I tell you. They're out to get me because I'm a successful businessman, and they're nothing but stupid bureaucrats trying to make a name for themselves."

"Bernie, I think you should listen to Leo," Sarah said with a desperate tone to her voice. "He's trying to keep us ..."

Bernie spun around, his face contorted in rage and said, "Shut the fuck up you stupid cunt! You don't know shit about what's going on here! You can't let people like this take advantage of you. Once you do, they ..."

"Bernie, you've got to listen to me," Traub said. "If you continue with that attitude they'll put you in prison for a long time. The grand jury had indicted both of you on forty-two counts of fraud, saying that you defrauded MBT out of thirteen million dollars. That's not just some FBI Agents out to get you! Snap out of it!"

* * *

"Can you believe that line of crock he was spitting out?" Casey said to Dan.

"It was all I could do to keep from strangling him."

"What do we do now?"

"Tell Weinstein that all we got out of him was a pack of lies, and to tell Traub either they plead or we go to trial! Schwartz doesn't deserve a break."

* * *

"Yes, Leonard, Bernie Schwartz made some major judgment mistakes, but only in an effort to keep his business afloat to provide for his family," said Traub, trying his best to negotiate a plea agreement for Bernie and Sarah.

"Come on, Leo," said Weinstein. "His motivation was nothing more than pure greed. He stole from MBT Factors and spent lavishly on himself, purchasing luxury items, belonging to a country club, a second home in Florida, and vacation travel."

"Be a mensch. Leave Sarah out of it. Let him plead guilty to a couple of counts of fraud, and agree to probation."

"Leo, I don't have to do anything. The best I'll offer is to let Bernie plead to thirty-five of the forty-two counts of mail fraud, wire fraud, interstate transportation of stolen property, tax evasion, and agree to pay a major fine. Bernie is going to prison. Sarah has to plead guilty to five counts of tax evasion, and agree to a lesser fine. That exposes her to a maximum prison term of nineteen years. As far as Sarah's prison time, the government won't make any recommendation. It'll be up to the judge. If we go to trial, I'll go for the maximum on both. Bernie and Sarah will each be looking at 250 years of prison time."

"Is that your bottom line?" Traub asked.

"That's it. Take it or leave it."

"I'll discuss it with my clients, and get back to you," sighed Traub.

* * *

Neither Bernie nor Sarah believed they had done anything wrong, but they were intimidated enough about going to prison that they finally agreed to plead, hoping the judge would go easy on them.

On their day in court Bernie and Sarah Schwartz stood in the courtroom before Judge William J. Buchanan, of the Southern Judicial District of New York, in lower Manhattan.

"Very well, let's begin," the judge said. "I have before me a report prepared by Mr. Weinstein, outlining the details of the crimes with which the defendants are charged. I am also in possession of a formal written agreement between Mr. and Mrs. Schwartz and the Government of the United States of America. Was this agreement entered into without coercion, threats, or promises on the part of the government?"

Bernie Schwartz stared at the judge, almost holding his breath as he awaited the judge's sentencing decision.

"Yes, your Honor, it was," said Traub.

"Mr. Schwartz," the judge began reading from his prepared text, "Your actions caused a financial institution to suffer a thirteen million dollar loss, and cease operations. You destroyed the careers, and eliminated employment of fifty individuals. You conducted your business in a wanton and reckless manner, causing financial losses and bankruptcy of two suppliers. You took money and property, converted it to your own use without regard to others."

Bernie Schwartz squirmed in his chair as he listened to the judge.

"You have concealed your fraudulent activities and involved your wife. As a result, you have placed her at risk of criminal penalties."

Sarah Schwartz winced when the judge mentioned her, and began to sob quietly.

"Your actions have deprived both the federal and New York tax authorities of revenue. You have shown no remorse whatsoever. You made no effort to assist investigating officers to assist in their resolution of this matter. You have made no offer of restitution. You may still be in possession of significant monies and jewelry that could mitigate others' losses, but have steadfastly refused to divulge its whereabouts. In all my years on the bench, I have never seen such a blatant disregard for other human beings, others' property, or the laws of this country."

"Mrs. Schwartz," the judge continued, shifting his eyes to her, "You were an active participant with your husband in these criminal activities, and cannot hide behind a claim of pseudo-innocence. You personally benefited through home remodeling, expensive cars, a home in Florida, and a lavish lifestyle. You participated in the fraud, as well as in actions to cover-up your criminal activities. Your request to avoid prison because of the need to raise your sons, falls deafly on this court. Abandoning your teenaged sons while you and your husband vacationed in luxury in Europe, could hardly be called the actions of a concerned mother."

"Mr. Bernard Schwartz, would you please rise as this court passes sentence on you?"

Bernie Schwartz and Leo Traub both stood.

"This court sentences you to a term of twenty-eight years, to be served in the Federal Penitentiary at Leavenworth, Kansas."

Bernie Schwartz's knees went weak at the judge's words. He wasn't going to a "country club" prison, but would be jailed with the most dangerous federal criminals.

"In addition, this court imposes on you, a monetary fine in the amount of $1,752,000. Lastly, this court orders the forfeiture of your homes in both New York and in Florida."

Bernie's head was spinning, but his anger continued to increase.

"Please be seated Mr. Schwartz," said the judge. "Mrs. Schwartz, please rise."

Leo Traub helped a weak and shaky Sarah Schwartz to her feet.

"Mrs. Schwartz, this court sentences you to a term of three years, to be served at the Federal Correctional Institution for Women at Alderson, West Virginia."

"In addition, this court imposes on you, a monetary fine in the amount of $350,000. Lastly, this court orders the forfeiture of your homes in both New York and in Florida, owned jointly with your husband."

Sarah Schwartz was shocked. The sentence meant she'd go to jail. She nearly fainted, but Leo Traub quietly spoke to her as she continued to stand and sob.

LeBeau, Dan and Casey shook hands.

"The defendants are remanded to the custody of the United States Marshals. Court adjourned." Judge Buchanan struck his gavel.

Forty-Five

5:20 PM
January 21st
Manhattan, New York

"I'm sure Bernie Schwartz hired Bart O'Reilly to kill Christy Marino, but I can't prove it," Dan said in an outburst to LeBeau and Casey. They sat in McDougall's bar, a block away from the federal building.

"You don't have to convince me, Dan." LeBeau took a pull from his long-necked beer bottle. "You guys talked to Mary Lee Wen, then she disappeared. You talked to Christy Marino, and she got killed. They were the only people who could've hurt Schwartz with their testimony. Have you considered the possibility that the private detective Schwartz hired might have followed her to the FBI office?"

"I've thought about that. I've thought about her murder every day," said Dan as he stared into his glass of beer. "I didn't know if David Wen or Bernie Schwartz was behind it. After we were sure Schwartz was involved, we couldn't figure what prompted him to have them killed. Christy told me both she and Mary Lee helped with the fraud, but until Schwartz mentioned he hired a private eye to check on Christy, I wasn't sure what freaked him out enough to have her killed. I'm still not sure how he got onto Mary Lee. But there've been so many leaks in this investigation, it could have come from somebody else."

"Maybe somebody at Fontaine overheard a conversation between the two women," said LeBeau.

"Or maybe somebody from Fontaine saw us the morning we tried to talk to May Lee on the sidewalk," said Casey.

"I know it bothers you, Dan, but don't be so hard on yourself," LeBeau said. "Remember you guys put Schwartz away so he can't do any more damage."

"I know that," Dan said. "But I want to nail Schwartz for murdering those women." He slowly twirled his glass between the fingertips of both hands, making wet rings on the tabletop.

"First things first, Dan" LeBeau said. "We've got a tough but winnable case against O'Reilly. So we convict him of the murders. Then we get him to cooperate with us, and in return for his cooperation, tell the judge how much he helped. Then we get Schwartz."

"You're right, but nothing's nailed down."

"True," said Casey. "Our only eyewitness has developed a case of amnesia. We don't have a murder weapon. And, so far, all the other evidence is circumstantial. If we can't convict O'Reilly of the murder and get his cooperation, I don't see how we can convict Schwartz."

"We've got to," said Dan in a soft voice, momentarily lost in his thought, unaware the others were looking at him until he raised his eyes. "What?"

"What were you thinking?" LeBeau asked.

Dan stared into his glass. "I was remembering three people close to me that were killed. Aren't you two a little concerned for your own safety?"

"Not as long as I've got my rabbit's foot with me," LeBeau said.

"Wasn't good luck for the rabbit," said Casey with a smile.

Dan looked at each of them, and a hint of a smile appeared at the corners of his mouth. "Thanks, I guess I needed to hear that. Some days I feel like Sisyphus. For every foot he pushes the rock up the hill, it rolls back two."

"I may know that guy," said LeBeau with a smile. "Do you remember which precinct he works out of?"

* * *

8:20 AM
January 22nd
Manhattan, New York

Bart O'Reilly was ushered into the New York State Supreme Court courtroom, dressed in his orange jail jumpsuit, wearing manacles and leg chains. He shuffled to the defense table where the sheriff's deputy removed his restraints. He rubbed the deep red marks the manacles had left on his wrists. When he saw the courtroom's leather-padded doors swing open, O'Reilly smiled.

Walter Lowenthal walked down the aisle of the courtroom in long, confident strides. He was impeccably dressed in a thousand dollar suit, and in a hand with manicured fingernails, carried a rich brown leather briefcase. He carried himself with an air of confidence one does after having battled in the courtroom, and more often than not, come away the victor. Lowenthal smiled as he let himself through the gate and reached out to O'Reilly, as if to pass on some of the confidence he exuded.

Lowenthal's grand entrance wasn't missed by ADA Bergen who turned to his colleague, ADA Gloria Thurman, and said, "I wonder who's picking up the tab. There's no way O'Reilly could afford Lowenthal's legal fees."

"You know Lowenthal?" Thurman watched the heads of O'Reilly and Lowenthal bowed in whispered conversation.

"I've come up against him once or twice. He handles all the criminal work for the 'Westies.' LeBeau told me O'Reilly is part of the Westies. Lowenthal showing up to defend him shouldn't surprise anyone."

"Is he a good attorney?" asked Thurman, as the bailiff came through the door from the judge's chambers.

"He knows the law, and what's more important, he knows all the loopholes to get his clients off. Never underestimate him."

Dan and LeBeau stepped into the courtroom and slid into one of the rows of benches behind the prosecution table.

"All rise!" the bailiff belted out. "Oyea, oyea, oyea! The New York Criminal Court in and for the County of New York is now in session, the Honorable Jason V. Patton, presiding! All ye who have business before this court, stand near, and you will be heard."

The judge walked to the bench, took a seat and rapped the gavel. "Be seated." Judge Patton slipped on his reading glasses, turned to the bailiff and said, "Please call the first case."

"Docket number 23144-A, The State of New York versus Bart O'Reilly."

The judge ensured the prosecutor and defense attorneys were in the courtroom. Judge Patton looked over the tops of his reading glasses. "It's been awhile since you graced my courtroom, Mr. Lowenthal. Good to see you again."

"Thank you, your Honor," Lowenthal said with a smile and a slight nod of his head. "It's always a pleasure to be here."

"What an ass kisser," Thurman whispered.

"Let's get started," Judge Patton said. "This is a preliminary hearing to determine if there is sufficient evidence to charge the defendant with murder. This is not a trial, nevertheless the rules of evidence apply, and this proceeding will be conducted with the decorum of a trial proceeding. Now are there any motions?"

"Yes, your Honor," Lowenthal said. "The defense moves to suppress any and all evidence collected by the Kentucky State Police when they searched a van owned by the defendant. The defense also moves to suppress any and all evidence collected by the FBI during their search of the defendant's home."

"What?" said Thurman, shocked at the thought.

"Don't worry," Bergen whispered. "It's usual for the defense to try and eliminate all the incriminating evidence. He'll probably also enter a motion to dismiss all the charges."

"May I approach, your Honor?" asked Lowenthal.

"Yes, you may," said the judge.

Lowenthal stepped out from behind the defense table, walked to the judge's bench, and handed him copies of both motions.

After a few minutes of reading, the judge said, "The court has read your motions, Mr. Lowenthal. Rather than dragging this out, and ruling on the motions at some later date, the court will hear oral arguments today."

"Objection, your Honor!" Bergen said as he stood. "The prosecution has only now received copies of these motions. The government respectfully requests time to research the motions, draft responses, and subpoena rebuttal witnesses."

"Objection overruled. At the end of Mr. Lowenthal's oral argument, the court will take a noon recess. That will allow the prosecution one and a half hours to prepare their rebuttal."

Bergen and Thurman whispered for a moment. Then Thurman picked up the copies of the motions, and walked out of the courtroom.

"Please begin, Mr. Lowenthal," the judge said.

"Thank you, your Honor," Lowenthal said as he gathered his notes, stood, and began pacing as he talked.

"On January 17th of this year, the defendant, Bart O'Reilly, was driving his Ford Econoline van to visit his sister," Lowenthal said in a deep melodious voice that filled the courtroom. "At a roadblock on Interstate Sixty-four, near Lexington, Kentucky, established by the Kentucky State Police at the request of the FBI, the defendant was asked for his driver's license. He provided it to the trooper as requested. The driver's license was valid. It was examined, found to be in order, and returned to the defendant."

"A short time later, the defendant was arrested by the Kentucky State Police," Lowenthal continued. "When he was arrested, the trooper told him it was for the crime of possessing a stolen vehicle. The defendant attempted to explain to the trooper it was a mistake, but the trooper did not want to hear the truth. Mr. O'Reilly was transported to jail and incarcerated, charged with possession of a stolen vehicle. The alleged stolen vehicle was taken to the State Police garage and stored for a length of time sufficient for the FBI to have a friendly federal judge sign a search warrant."

Lowenthal reached over and took a sip of water.

"Later that day, three events took place. An arrest warrant was lodged against the defendant. It charged Mr. O'Reilly with failure to appear to begin serving a jail sentence. The defendant does not contest that charge. Then the Kentucky State Police dismissed the possession of a stolen motor vehicle charge, upon which they arrested the defendant. How could a vehicle become 'not stolen'? We'll get to that in a moment. The third event was the search of the 'not stolen' van. Three events of which at least two were flawed."

Lowenthal took a moment to sip some more water.

"The search of the defendant's van provided the prosecution with evidence which they allege, link the defendant to a murder which took place in Manhattan on January 10th. But the Manhattan's District Attorney's Office was concerned that there was insufficient evidence from the van to charge the defendant with this crime. So, using the evidence they discovered in the defendant's van as justification, they searched the defendant's Keansburg, New Jersey home. During that search, they found other evidence which allegedly links the defendant to the murders of January 10th."

"But wait a minute!" Lowenthal said dramatically. "What about that van which was stolen one minute, and not stolen the next? What happened to bring about the change? For that information, we needed to look to the Palisades Park Police Department where the stolen report was filed. It had been reported stolen on January 2nd. When stolen, the van was owned by Tom Miller, a neighbor and nephew of the defendant. The stolen information about the van was entered into the FBI's

National Crime Information Center computer. But two days later, the van was recovered in the Bronx and returned to Miller. But the computer information that listed the van as stolen was never removed. Miller sold the van to the defendant on January 5th, and it has been in his possession ever since."

"But according to the Kentucky State Police, they were informed by the New York FBI the van was stolen. They acted on that information and arrested the defendant. But the Kentucky State Police were not totally trusting of the FBI, so they checked the stolen status of the van. They learned the van was not stolen when they arrested the defendant. The defendant was not violating any traffic laws, and his driver's license and vehicle registration were valid."

Lowenthal paused for emphasis, then said, "The Kentucky State Police had no legal right to stop the defendant! It was an illegal stop, an illegal arrest, and therefore the search of the defendant's van was illegal! And because the search of the van was illegal, the search of the defendant's home was illegal! Therefore, any evidence obtained as a result of either of those two searches must be ruled inadmissible, and the charges against defendant must be dismissed!"

Lowenthal turned and walked back to the defense table, a smug, self-satisfied look on his face. A beaming O'Reilly stood, and vigorously shook Lowenthal's hand. Bergen, Dan, and LeBeau were stunned.

Judge Patton rapped his gavel repeatedly, and over the din shouted, "Court is recessed for one and one-half hours! Court will reconvene at two o'clock!"

There was a buzz in the courtroom as the reporters sensed that Lowenthal had delivered a knockout blow to the case against O'Reilly.

Forty-Six

12:30 PM
January 22nd
Manhattan, New York

Lowenthal had delivered a stunning argument. Dan and LeBeau remained seated as the courtroom emptied.

"I can't believe it!" Dan said. "Can Lowenthal get O'Reilly off?"

LeBeau took a deep breath and exhaled. "He just might. His argument was persuasive and factually correct."

Patrick Bergen passed Dan and LeBeau as he headed out of the courtroom. He gave them a contemptuous stare.

Dan thought about the man-hours and money spent trying to find, follow, and arrest the killer. It had been his idea to use the stolen van ploy. He remembered

Blackman's threats and Thomas' warnings. Dan would be blamed. He had failed Christy. It was too much. He felt a hand on his back, and turned to see LeBeau.

"We need to talk with Patrick Bergen and see if there's anything we can do," LeBeau said reassuringly.

"I doubt he'll talk to us."

"Come on," LeBeau said, and pulled Dan to his feet. "Let's go."

As they walked out of the courtroom, the media surrounded them.

"In light of Lowenthal's motions, how do you feel?" asked a blond reporter.

"We can't comment," LeBeau said pushing his way through the reporters.

A video camera light came on, and a television reporter stuck a microphone in Dan's face. "Would you care to comment about the effect today's development might have on the successful prosecution of O'Reilly?"

Silently Dan pushed his way past both the reporter and cameraman and continued down the hall. Other questions were shouted, while still and video cameramen walked backwards to get shots of them. It wasn't until they got into the elevator that the hounding by the media ended. They rode in silence to the sixth floor and walked down the hall to Bergen's office. The door was ajar. LeBeau knocked and pushed open the door. Bergen sat behind his desk, Thurman stood to his side, the two of them poring over Lowenthal's motions. They looked up as LeBeau and Dan walked into the office.

"We wanted to ask what we could do," LeBeau said, trying to be as upbeat as possible.

"You've done enough already," said Bergen icily. "If there's a way out of this, it'll be a legal way, not another bumbling effort orchestrated by you two."

"Just a minute!" shouted Dan.

"No, you listen to me," shouted Bergen. "If Lowenthal is successful in suppressing the evidence from O'Reilly's van and house, that leaves us with some phone calls and parking records which may, or may not, show him stalking Marino. It sure as hell won't show him killing her. Then we've got the long-term parking videos that show a van coming and going, but still don't link him to the murders. Judge Patton may dismiss the murder charges against O'Reilly, but even if he only suppresses the evidence, it doesn't leave me enough to put together a credible prosecution, much less get a conviction. I might as well drop the charges against him. Can you help? Nobody can help at this point! Get out of here."

Dan and LeBeau walked out of Bergen's office, feeling lousy. They went outside to find a bright sunlit gorgeous day. They each bought a hot dog and a soda from a street vendor and sat on the granite steps of the courthouse.

After taking one bite out of the hotdog, Dan realized he had no appetite and pitched it into the trashcan. "I keep hoping for an inspiration, but nothing comes. I'm not sure I want to be in the courtroom this afternoon. Any ideas?"

"No," LeBeau said as he broke off part of his hotdog bun and tossed to a pigeon that was quickly joined by others, "but we'll come up with something."

"I think I'll go for a walk. I need to sort this out. I'll see you back in the courtroom at two."

"I better get on the phone. Captain Watson always wants to know bad news fast . . . as soon as I finish feeding the pigeons."

* * *

Judge Patton rapped his gavel, and the courtroom quieted. Everyone was anxious to see how Bergen would counter Lowenthal's blows to the case against

O'Reilly. Bergen tried to sound convincing, using numerous citations to support his argument that the arrest was legal, and the search evidence shouldn't be suppressed, but it was readily apparent he couldn't repair the damage. After an hour and a half, Bergen finally concluded and sat down.

Judge Patton took off his glasses. He spent a moment in contemplation, then said, "The argument set forth by the defense in support of suppressing the evidence from the search of the van and the defendant's home is compelling. The prosecution has not adequately shown why the evidence should not be suppressed. Therefore it is the ruling of this court that the motions to suppress the evidence from the two searches are granted. Furthermore, in the absence of strong evidence to the contrary, the court does not believe there is sufficient reason to support the defendant being charged with the crime of murder. Should the prosecution, at some time in the future, develop admissible evidence which would show a reasonable belief the defendant should be charged with this crime, the court will take under consideration, a charge of murder. Until such time, the murder charges against the defendant are dismissed."

Bergen slid down in his chair and slowly shook his head. Dan closed his eyes and clenched his teeth. LeBeau sat impassively, staring into space. Lowenthal and O'Reilly stood, grinning broadly, and embraced. Reporters jumped from their seats and rushed out of the courtroom, anxious to meet their afternoon deadlines.

"Mr. O'Reilly," Judge Patton continued. "You are remanded to the custody of the City of New York to begin service of the sentence previously imposed upon you. Court is dismissed." Patton rapped his gavel once, and quickly stepped down from the bench.

"One of the worst days of my life," Dan said.

"We gave it a good shot, Dan. I'll go uptown and tell the brass what happened. Give me a call later, will you?" LeBeau stood, put his hand on Dan's shoulder, and gave it a squeeze.

"Okay. I've got to go back to the office and face the music. I hope I still have a job after they finish with me." Dan stood and followed LeBeau to the back of the courtroom. On his way out, he took one last look over his shoulder, then pushed open the door and left.

The beautiful day was lost on Dan. In the short walk from the Criminal Courts Building on Center Street to 26 Federal Plaza, he went over and over why he had pushed to use the stolen/not stolen van ploy to arrest O'Reilly. That it sounded like a pretty good idea at the time was an excuse he knew wouldn't cut it with Thomas. But there was no other way to stop the van. He hoped Thomas wasn't available, but he was. He took a deep breath and walked in to Thomas' office.

"Dan, I was just going to call you," Thomas said. "Sit down. You look terrible. What's wrong?"

"The judge threw out the evidence from the searches of O'Reilly's van and house, then dismissed the murder charges."

Thomas sat back and contemplated what he heard. "Plenty of people are going to be angry over that and looking for a scapegoat."

"I know," Dan said, fearing what was coming.

"Maybe someone else's head will roll."

"What do you mean?"

"Some things happened today. First, I got a call from the Administrative AD at headquarters. He told me the OPR issue over the Chinese Undercover Operation, which involved you, had finally reached his desk. He was about to recommend to the Director that you be busted back to the bricks."

"Terrific," Dan said sarcastically.

"I told him that he couldn't because some new information has just come to light. I told you I was going to find out who was leaking information to the media about The CBS Murders investigation. After going through quite a few media people, I learned who was doing it."

"Good! Who was it?"

"The person who had been talking to them said his name was Dan Robertson."

"What?" Dan said, as his mouth dropped open. "That's impossible. I never spoke to anyone in the press about this case! There's got to be a mistake!"

"I had the same reaction. One reason it took so long, was because I did some further checking. What I'm about to tell you doesn't leave this room. The FBI continually monitors the telephone calls being made into and out of this office. It's a legal overhear, authorized by the Director of the National Security Agency."

"What?"

"We can review the dialed numbers of outgoing calls, the telephone numbers from which incoming calls are received, or the taped conversations of any of those calls when it's a matter of national security, or potential breaches of security. I had our people do a computer search for calls to the phone number of the reporter who first leaked the stories."

"They couldn't have found a call placed by me, because I never made any," Dan said, pleading his case.

Thomas continued. "They found a number of calls placed from this office to that reporter's telephone. We found the conversations and listened to the tapes. There were definitely leaks from this office. The call was placed from extension 4208. The voice print from the caller was compared with yours, and the voice of the person assigned that extension."

"Wait, that's not my extension. Sounds familiar. Whose is it?"

"Ike Blackman. After leaking information about the progress of the investigation and the lesbian relationship, he told the reporter that his name was Dan Robertson. I confronted him. He admitted it."

"Why would he do it?"

"He didn't explain. We'll probably never know. He may have been jealous of you and the work you've done. Ike would have had a hard time matching your accomplishments. Since he couldn't out-shine you, he set about to destroy you. He almost pulled it off."

Dan shook his head. "Sure, we didn't always agree. But—"

"There's more. We searched Blackman's office, and found the memo authorizing the use of Sammy Ho in the undercover operation. I told the AD at headquarters he couldn't take administrative action against you. You were set up by Blackman."

"I hope they nail him," shouted Dan. "He deserves to be fired!"

"Don't worry about that. I told the Deputy AD in the Office of Professional Responsibility I personally wanted to handle the Blackman matter quickly and quietly. After Blackman goes a month without pay, he'll be demoted to a street agent and transferred. Now, getting back to the CBS Murders, remember I told you headquarters would be looking for a scapegoat over O'Reilly, and one had been found?"

"Yeah."

"I know Blackman did some terrible things. He demanded you have O'Reilly pulled over and arrested on the basis of his driving a stolen van. You tried to tell him that it was a mistake, but he was your superior, and you had to do what he said. When I learned about it I was furious, but by then it was too late." Thomas paused, looked at Dan, and said, "Got it?"

Dan's face broke into a broad grin. "You are devious."

"Moi?" Thomas said as he reached for his next message, and picked up the phone. "Get out of here."

Dan walked the halls to his office. As he rounded a corner, he found himself face-to-face with Blackman. Their eyes locked on each other in hateful stares. Their jaws clenched. Neither spoke as they passed.

Dan headed home, calling it a day. Tomorrow, he'd figure out how to nail O'Reilly.

Forty-Seven

9:20 AM
January 23rd
Manhattan, New York

Dan sat beside LeBeau's desk as the two men drank Starbuck's coffee.

"Pretty good," LeBeau said, the look on his face affirming his appreciation of the coffee. "What'd you pay for it?"

"Two-fifty."

"My God! I can buy a whole can for three bucks. It's good, but not that great."

"What's the problem? It didn't cost you anything."

"Which means next time, it's my turn, and I can't afford to play in your league."

"What do you mean? With the overtime pay you guys get?" Dan gave LeBeau a wink.

"And now you're winking at me. Hey, I'm not that kind of a guy. Besides, what the hell are you so happy about? Didn't it sink in that O'Reilly walked?"

"Yeah, it sunk in. But I'm in a good mood because there were some favorable resolutions to some issues that had been hanging over me."

"What the hell is that supposed to mean?"

"Never mind." Dan saw Casey and Clements carrying large cardboard boxes. "What have you got there?"

"Boxes to pack up things. The charges against O'Reilly were dismissed. I figured the Task Force would be dismantled, and we'll be moving back to the FBI office," Casey said, an exasperated tone to her voice.

"I haven't told you to move back to the FBI office. We aren't done. We've got to nail O'Reilly."

"Good luck. Ever hear about double jeopardy? If we tried to come after O'Reilly again, we'd be laughed right out of the prosecutor's office."

"Dan, let it go," said LeBeau. "We got beat. Accept it."

"No! I don't agree."

"Dan, after Judge Patton threw out the good stuff, we've got squat for evidence," said LeBeau. "There's no way Bergen is gonna take another stab without something new."

Dan glanced at the Task Force members. "Would you hang in for one more week?"

"A week won't make a difference," said Casey. "For that matter, a month won't either."

"If I showed you a way to get O'Reilly, would you give me one more week? Yes, or no?"

The investigators looked at one another and shrugged their shoulders.

"I don't know, Dan," LeBeau said, and turned to the agents. "Is he always this stubborn?"

Without hesitation, Casey and Clements said, "Yes."

"If you've got a brilliant idea, I'll consider it," said LeBeau. "But, if you're refusing to give up because you can't admit defeat, then forget it."

"Here's the idea I came up with last night. When O'Reilly was arrested in Kentucky, he had—"

"Dan, the judge ruled the arrest was illegal," LeBeau said.

"Please hear me out! When he was arrested, O'Reilly had a bunch of money on him, right?"

"Yeah," said Casey. "Twenty-six hundred and change."

"What did the money look like?" Dan asked.

"What do you mean, what did it look like?" asked LeBeau. "It looked like money. You know, green with pictures of dead presidents."

"That's not what I mean. Was it old, beat up bills, or crisp new bills?"

"Dan, you had too many scotches last night," said LeBeau.

"New, or old?"

"New bills," said LeBeau.

"Hundreds?"

"Yeah."

"Consecutively numbered?" Dan asked.

"Does this guy ever give up? Yeah, I think they were consecutively numbered. Do you remember, Casey?"

"I think so. Where are you going with this?"

"Richie," Dan said to LeBeau. "I want you to go get the money, okay?"

"If it'll make you happy, I'll get it," said LeBeau. "But I don't see how it's going to give us another shot at O'Reilly."

"Casey, do you have an extra set of Bernie Schwartz's fingerprints?" Dan said.

"Sure. You know we always take two sets."

"Go get them and bring them to the NYPD fingerprint experts where LeBeau and I will be waiting with the money."

"All right," said Casey.

"Dan, would you drive me to pick up the money?" said LeBeau. "It'll only take a minute."

Dan shook his head as they got into the car and shot over to the West Side Highway.

As they headed South, LeBeau said, "Will you tell me what you're up to?"

"I want to see if Bernie Schwartz's fingerprints are on O'Reilly's money."

"You don't really think Schwartz is stupid enough to personally hand the money to O'Reilly, do you?"

"Only one way to find out, isn't there?"

Casey picked up the fingerprint card, and by the time she reached the NYPD's Bureau of Criminal Identification, LeBeau and Dan were waiting. LeBeau flashed his shield, and they went to the Fingerprint Lab on the third floor.

"Robert!" LeBeau said from across the room.

A technician wearing a gray lab coat, surgical gloves, and goggles, turned around. Seeing LeBeau, he broke into a broad grin and quickly walked over to him.

"Richie LeBeau! I haven't seen you since the Son of Sam mess."

"Good to see you, too, Robert." LeBeau motioned towards Dan and Casey and said, "These are FBI Agents Dan Robertson, and Casey Brody. Robert Hazen, NYPD fingerprint expert."

Hazen took off his gloves, and they shook hands. "But somehow, I don't think this is a social call. What's up?"

"The NYPD and the FBI have hooked up to try and solve The CBS Murders," said LeBeau.

"But didn't I read in the paper that the judge dismissed the charges against the guy you arrested?"

"True, but Dan has an idea," LeBeau said. "Go ahead and tell him."

"My theory is that Bernie Schwartz paid Bart O'Reilly with this money," Dan said. "I want to know if any fingerprints show up on these hundred dollar bills."

"That's easy enough," said Hazen.

"And if they do, I need to know if they match Schwartz's prints."

Hazen put on his gloves and spread the money on the counter. He slipped on a mask, and took a spray can out of a cabinet.

"I always knew that you could check for prints on paper, but I never saw it done," said Casey.

"There are traces of perspiration on our fingertips. Perspiration contains amino acids. In this spray can is a solution of ninhydrin. It's a chemical that interacts with amino acids. After we spray the evidence, we apply heat from an iron, and wherever there's amino acids, they interact with the ninhydrin generating a purplish color, and the fingerprint ridges appear."

"I knew that," said LeBeau.

Hazen gave LeBeau a look, shook his head, and began to spray the bills. Nothing was visible when he finished spraying, but as he applied the hot iron to them, fingerprints began to appear.

"That's what I wanted to see," Dan said as he leaned forward and watched.

The process took a few minutes, but when Hazen had finished, you could see fingerprints on most of the bills. Hazen picked up Schwartz's fingerprint card and looked at it for a moment.

"Okay, it looks like Schwartz has a tented arch on his right thumb. That's the print that's most likely to appear. Let's see if we have any tented arches on the bills."

Hazen rapidly looked through the bills, and then turned to the others. "Its just first glance, but I'm not coming up with any tented arches. Let me take a look at O'Reilly's prints, and see what he's got on his right thumb." Hazen took a quick look, and said, "He's got a whorl, so let me take a quick look at the bills again." On the third bill he looked at, Hazen stopped. Using a magnifying loop, he looked back and forth between the bill and O'Reilly's fingerprint card. "We definitely have O'Reilly's thumbprint on this bill, but that's not surprising."

"You didn't see any tented arch prints on the bills?" asked Dan.

"No, but that doesn't mean one or more of Schwartz's other prints aren't on them." Hazen leaned back on his stool, took off his mask, and said, "Let me ask you a question about Schwartz. How big of a man is he?"

"I guess he's about five-five or five-six," Casey said.

"No, that's not what I mean," said Hazen. "Is he small-framed? Skinny?—"

"Oh," said Casey. "I guess you'd call him fat. Let me see his fingerprint card." She lifted the card, and looked at the weight, listed under physical description. "When we arrested him, he weighed in at two hundred forty-five pounds."

"What makes you ask, Robert?" asked Dan.

"I'm seeing a repeated print on these bills. It's a radial loop, so it's not Schwartz's right thumb. It just looks a little small for a man of that size. I'll take a closer look to compare all of Schwartz's prints to the ones that show up on the bills, but it'll take a little time. Why don't you give me a call in a couple of days, Richie?"

"I'll do that," said LeBeau. "Thanks a lot for your help."

"I'm sorry I didn't come up with what you needed," said Hazen.

The men shook hands, and LeBeau led the others out of the building. They stood on the sidewalk, and talked for a moment.

"Might not pan out, but it was a great idea, Dan," said LeBeau.

"If Schwartz paid O'Reilly to do it, we've got to find a way to get them both," said Dan.

A ringing cell phone interrupted their conversation. Casey answered.

"It's the office," she said as she looked at the caller I.D. After a short conversation, she said, "The head of the Metropolitan Correctional Center wants me to come see him immediately. I'll meet you back at the Task Force office as soon as I'm done."

"Any idea what he wants?" asked Dan.

"No. It wasn't something he was willing to talk about over the phone."

"Okay, Casey," said LeBeau. "See you later." Turning to Dan, LeBeau said, "Dan, would you mind giving me a ride to—"

"I know, Richie, I'll drive. Have you ever considered getting a driver's license?"

LeBeau thought for a moment, then said, "No. Why?"

* * *

About an hour and a half later, the door to the Detectives' Squad Room at Midtown North flew open, and Casey burst in, quickly walking over to Dan.

"Dan, I need to get authorization for a body recorder."

"Sure, we can do that." Dan said. "What's going on?"

"I got down to the MCC, and they told me that one of the jailhouse snitches had something important to tell, and it was an emergency. The prisoner said he needed to talk to whichever FBI Agent had put Bernie Schwartz in jail," Casey said, having finally caught her breath. "The guy who wanted to talk was Louis Kirwan. He was arrested by the Secret Service for masterminding a multimillion-dollar credit card operation. He hasn't come to trial yet, so the jailers were pretty sure he was looking for anything he could use to help him cut a deal for less jail time."

"What did he want?" asked Dan.

"Kirwan told me once Bernie Schwartz learned he too was a white-collar crime prisoner, Schwartz wanted to become his best friend. I guess Schwartz wanted to associate with a better class of felons," Casey said with a laugh.

"Either that, or Schwartz wanted to find someone to help him make sure he didn't become another prisoner's 'boy toy'," said LeBeau.

"Maybe," said Casey. "Anyway, Schwartz is housed at the MCC while he's waiting for the U.S. Marshals to transport him to Leavenworth. After getting to know Kirwan over a week or so, he asked if Kirwan could arrange for a hit man to kill somebody."

"What!" shouted Dan. "So far, Schwartz thinks he's gotten away with having Christy Marino and Mary Lee Wen killed. Who does he want to have killed now?"

"Two people, actually. Mike Westerfield from MBT Factors and AUSA Len Weinstein who convicted him."

"My God!" said LeBeau. "So, what did Kirwan tell him?"

"Kirwan told Schwartz he could arrange it, no problem," Casey said. "He told him it would take a couple of days, and that Kirwan would get the 'right person' to visit him."

"So Kirwan is willing to wear a wire to get it on tape?" asked Dan.

"Of course," said Casey. "He'd do anything to cut a deal for himself."

"Did you talk to the Secret Service Agent who arrested him?" asked Dan.

"Yeah, I did. The guys at the MCC had called him, too, and I ran into him while I was there. He said he didn't personally have a problem with Kirwan wearing a wire, but he needed to get it okayed by his supervisor."

"Terrific, Casey," said Dan. "Call a different AUSA for the body recorder authorization, since Weinstein himself is the target. Get the recording equipment from the techs back at the office. Let's see if we can get it on tape today." Dan turned and said, "Roger, would you notify Weinstein and Westerfield that they're targets of a hit man? There's always the chance that Schwartz may have found somebody else at the MCC who's also willing to hire a hit man for him. Casey, Rob, get moving quickly."

Dan turned to LeBeau, and said, "We'll own Schwartz, then pressure him to give up O'Reilly."

Forty-Eight

7:03 PM
January 23rd
Manhattan, New York

The Task Force members sat around the conference table. The tape recording of Louis Kirwan's conversation with Bernie Schwartz had been dubbed from the tape of the small, compact body recorder. They heard the sound of Kirwan walking to the "common room" of the MCC, then Kirwin's voice was heard.

Hey, Bernie? How the hell you doin'? Come on over and have a seat. We gotta talk.

Yeah, Lou, we gotta take care of this little problem of mine pretty fuckin' soon. I don't know how much longer I'm gonna be

338

in this goddamned place before they ship me out to Leavenworth. Did you talk to your guy?

Yeah, I did. Keep your voice down, Bernie. You gotta be careful around here. There's always a jailhouse stool pigeon nearby, ready to sell you out to cut a deal for himself. You can't be too careful.

Yeah, I hear you.

Are you sure you wanna go ahead with this?

Damn straight, I am. Those two fuckers are the goddamned reason I'm here. I want them to pay. Your guy can kill them both?

Of course he can. What do you think I am? A guy who'd rip you off and not deliver?

Okay, I didn't mean no disrespect.

All right, tell me again who you want whacked.

What the hell's wrong with you? You getting fuckin' senile on me, so's you can't remember?

No, that's not it. I just want to make sure I know who the hell you want killed. You wouldn't want the wrong guys to be taken out, would you?

I see what you mean. Okay. Mike Westerfield. Vice President at MBT Factors. Got an office on Park Avenue. Shouldn't be too hard to find.

Who's the other guy?

Name's Leonard Weinstein. A fuckin' federal prosecutor, and a goddamned snake! The bastard!

Hey, Bernie, chill out. You'll give yourself a heart attack, and then you might not be around to enjoy hearing the news, once its done.

Yeah, what the fuck does it matter? I'm looking at twenty-eight years, and I'm beginning to have serious doubts I'll even be fuckin' alive by the time I've finished doin' that nut.

Okay, okay. Let's get back to the job. I don't mean no disrespect, but I gotta be sure you're gonna be able to come up with the scratch to pay this guy. He don't come cheap, and if you try to stiff him, you'll get dead, and the same will happen to me.

How much are we talkin' about?

He gets twenty-five grand for a hit. So that's fifty to you. Can you handle the freight?

Of course I can!

You sure?

Damn it! My goddamned wife is in the joint down in West Virginia. I've spent a fuckin' fortune on her, making sure she doesn't have a tough time of the three years she's doin' there. She bitches about everything. She couldn't stand her cellmate, so I paid to have her put in a cell by herself. Then she couldn't stand the goddamned food, so I paid to have Kosher brought in every day. And I have to come up with bucks, so she can pay the other inmates to let her use the phone to call our kids. For what I've paid to keep her happy, it would've been cheaper to just have her fuckin' killed. And, now you want to know if I can afford a hit?

Sorry. I meant no disrespect, but I hadda ask.

Yeah, okay. So how does it work?

The guy gets everything up front. You have somebody put the cash together, and send it by Federal Express to my cutout man. He sends it along to the hit man. The hit man decides when and where he's gonna take 'em out. Once he's finished with the first hit, he sends you a postcard and tells you how great his vacation to Aruba is. Get it? First hit, so the code word starts with an 'A.' Then after the second one, you get a postcard telling you how much he's enjoying Bermuda. And the picture postcards are really mailed from each of those places, so the jailers don't get suspicious.

Fuckin' A! Give me your cutout man's address, and I'll make a call to the guy that has my goddamned money.

I'll give it to you tomorrow. They just made the call, and right now we've got to go back to our cells.

Dan snapped off the tape recorder.

"Schwartz has no conscience whatsoever," said LeBeau. "The very idea that he'd consider having his own wife killed!"

"I thought Kirwan did a pretty good job of selling Schwartz on the idea that he could pull it off," said Casey. "How far do you want to take it, Dan?"

"Let Schwartz send the money," said Dan. "That'll strengthen our case against him for conspiracy to murder a federal prosecutor."

"And if for some reason that doesn't fly, we'll try him in State court for the same thing," said LeBeau.

"Where will we have him send the money, Dan?" asked Casey.

"I'll call the Undercover Unit at headquarters and get a name of someone who they've already set up as a mail drop. That way we can control it, and after all is said and done, we recover fifty thousand dollars." Suddenly, Dan stopped, and the expression on his face indicated that he had just thought of something important. He smacked himself on the forehead with the palm of his hand.

"What is it, Dan?" Casey asked.

"Clements, you and LeBeau run back to the office and pick up a set of Sarah Schwartz's fingerprints."

"You mean that you think Sarah Schwartz's fingerprints are on the money?" Casey asked. "Bernie Schwartz isn't that stupid."

"You're right that he's not stupid," said Dan. "But, who else could he could trust to pay O'Reilly to do the murders?"

"What about double jeopardy?" said Casey.

"First things first," said Dan. "Get her fingerprints. Casey, I want the techs to dub the part of the tape where Bernie says it's cheaper to have his wife killed. Not the whole tape, just that one section. Get a battery-operated portable tape recorder."

"Dan, it's seven thirty at night. I doubt there's any techs around."

"Then have one come in. We need this tonight."

"You want me to have Hazen come in?" LeBeau asked.

"Yeah, Richie. This is really important. We need to know if we've got her prints on that money. If I'm right, and her prints show up, find two or three bills with her prints on them."

"And what are you going to be doing, Dan?" asked LeBeau.

"Lining up an FBI plane for tomorrow morning."

"Want to tell me why?" asked LeBeau.

"Let's find out about the prints, first."

"Okay," LeBeau said. Then he turned to Clements, and said, "Would you mind driving—"

"Sure, Richie," said Clements, shaking his head. "Let's go."

* * *

Dan nervously paced back and forth in the Detectives' Squad Room. He glanced at his watch again for the umpteenth time, 9:30 PM. "What could possibly be keeping them?"

"Maybe Hazen wasn't home, and they had to find somebody else to do the comparisons," said Casey.

"I shouldn't get my hopes up, but I can't help myself. We need a break. Kirwan helping us was a godsend, but it only takes us part way."

"We'll get there, Dan," Casey said reassuringly. "Want more coffee?"

"If I had any more, you'd probably have to scrape me off the ceiling. Did you put fresh batteries in the tape recorder?"

"Yeah, I did. I've got a back up set, and a second copy of the dubbed portion of the tape. It's all here. Make sure to keep the recorded tape away from the batteries. It could act just like a magnet and erase—"

The door burst open, and LeBeau strutted in, a broad smile on his face. He was closely followed by Clements who definitely had a spring in his step.

"How did you know, Dan?" LeBeau asked. "Hazen found Sarah Schwartz's prints on every single bill! And he found O'Reilly's prints on eight of them, so I brought all eight back with me."

Dan was elated, and offered a silent prayer of thanks. He looked at the faces of LeBeau, Casey, and Clements, slowly nodded his head and said, "We really pulled this one out of the hat."

"So where do we go from here?" asked LeBeau.

"Right now, go home and sleep. Tomorrow morning at six o'clock, we'll get a ride on an FBI plane down to Alderson, West Virginia to visit Sarah Schwartz."

"Dan, you have no idea what a treat you can look forward to," Casey said. "After the little ride I took out to Kentucky, I can honestly say I have no problem whatsoever in missing this trip. Besides, I've got to get Schwartz charged with attempted murder."

"But it doesn't bother you in the least to see me go again," said LeBeau.

"Have you ever flown on any of the FBI's little planes, Dan?" Casey asked.

"No, I haven't."

"Boy, are you in for a treat!" said LeBeau.

"Okay," Dan said. "Let's go home. Six o'clock comes real early. Richie, need a ride home?"

"No. I'll ask one of the uniforms to run me home in an RMP," LeBeau said. "See you in the morning."

Dan slowly drove home and parked the car. He let himself into his apartment and turned on the light.

"Squawk! Hello Gorgeous!" came the voice from across the room.

"No, Nevermore, not Gorgeous. Only me."

Dan walked over, turned off the television, and opened the African gray's cage door. The parrot let himself out, and using his beak and claws, worked his way to the top of the cage and perched.

"Nevermore, you wouldn't believe what a son-of-a-bitch Ike Blackman turned out to be!" Dan said, shaking his head in disgust. "But in spite of him, I'm going to solve this case, and send the bad guys to jail."

The parrot cocked his head, listening to what he was being told, then said, "Cocktail time!"

"I agree, Nevermore. I can certainly use a drink." Dan walked into the kitchen for a glass and some ice. and looked for a snack for the bird. "We're out of grapes. How about some figs?" He carried some back into the living room, poured himself a scotch, and selected a cigar from his humidor.

He set four figs in a shallow bowl on the coffee table. Nevermore flew from his cage, skidding as he landed, knocking some magazines to the floor. Nevermore held the first fig in one claw and bit off pieces with his beak, as Dan smoked his cigar.

He was looking forward to tomorrow's meeting with Sarah Schwartz. He leaned back, blew smoke towards the ceiling, and smiled.

"I'm going to nail that . . ."

"Son-of-a-bitch!" said Nevermore.

Forty-Nine

6:00 AM
January 24th
Linden, New Jersey

The morning sun peeked over the eastern horizon as the Cessna 210 taxied down the runway, its engines increasing in speed. The weight of four men made the plane a little heavier than usual. As the plane neared the end of the runway, Dan and LeBeau both held their breath and braced themselves. At the last minute, the pilot pushed the engines to full throttle and the plane responded by gently lifting off the ground, clearing the trees at the end of the runway by a few feet.

The pilot turned his head, looked over his right shoulder at them, and in a voice loud enough to be heard over the engine noise said, "What's wrong? Didn't think I could get it up?" Then he broke into a smile. "It's a well-known fact that I can always get it up. You won't be able to move about the cabin during the flight. We don't have attendants, so forget about cocktails or indigestible meals. I hope you visited the restroom because we don't have one of those either. Our flying time to West Virginia will be approximately two hours and twenty minutes. Sit back, relax, and enjoy."

Dan wasn't quite sure what to make of this cowboy FBI pilot who seemed to be having a great time. After the previous long day and short night, he didn't relish the thought of the long flight to West Virginia. Dan and LeBeau sat behind the pilot and co-pilot, both exhausted but keyed up for the interview of Sarah Schwartz. From behind sunglasses, they closed their eyes even though they knew that sleep wouldn't come.

The only positive thing was the gorgeous scenery. At 6,000 feet, Dan and LeBeau saw picturesque New Jersey below. To the southeast was Philadelphia, surrounded on the north and west by forestland and bordered on the southeast by the Delaware River. The plane flew in a fairly direct path towards West Virginia.

For the first hour and a half, the flight was fairly uneventful as they traversed Pennsylvania and Virginia. They had just crossed into West Virginia when things began to change. As the westerly wind came up against mountain ranges, it created updrafts and turbulence that affected their small prop plane.

When they crossed the Appalachian Mountains, the pilot told them to buckle up. The small aircraft bounced and pitched with each gust of air. Feeling like rodeo bronco riders, Dan and LeBeau gripped anything they could find.

Then the Allegheny Mountains took their turn. It was worse. Dan turned a shade of green. LeBeau seemed oblivious, but saw the look on Dan's face.

"Boy, I'm sure glad they gave me this parachute," LeBeau said, speaking loudly over the sound of the engine.

"What parachute?" Dan said.

LeBeau pointed down at a flight bag wedged between his feet. "This one. You mean they didn't give you one?" LeBeau looked out the window, then turned back to Dan with a straight face. "Don't worry, we're not all that high up."

Dan realized LeBeau was yanking his chain, and managed a laugh.

The plane landed at Lewisburg, West Virginia, and everyone got out and stretched. Dan turned to the pilots and said, "We'll see you in three hours or less." Dan and LeBeau got into the FBI car that had been left for them and headed to the prison. A twenty-minute drive on Interstate 64 took them through the town of Alderson. They came to a massive stone front gate and a parking lot outside a chain link fence topped with razor-sharp concertina wire. They walked to the visitors' entrance of the red brick two-storied building where a guard led them to a room on the second floor of the administration building. They were told that Sarah Schwartz was being brought there.

"All prisons look alike," said LeBeau.

"This one's a little different," said Dan. "Only female prisoners are housed here. No smart quips, LeBeau. There's a number of inmates as well as guards who'd pound you into the ground if you said the wrong thing."

They heard the sound of the large steel door being opened, turned and saw a small, dark-haired woman in a khaki shirt and pants hobble in, her progress impeded by the leg irons and manacles. The female guard removed the restraints and Sarah Schwartz stared with a crazed look.

"Prison regulations require a female guard to be present at all times during a meeting between a female inmate and male visitors," the guard said. "You will sit on opposite sides of this table. You may not pass anything to the inmate without first showing it to the guard. You are not permitted to touch the inmate at any time. Do you understand and agree to these conditions?"

"Yeah."

"Schwartz, you sit on that side of the table. You two sit on the other side. I'll be standing so I can see all three of you."

Dan and LeBeau sat on the bench bolted to the floor, and noticed the table was also bolted down.

Sarah Schwartz remained standing. "Who are you? I don't know you!"

"Sit down, Schwartz!" shouted the guard.

Sarah Schwartz quickly complied, even though it was obvious that she didn't want to. Again, she asked, "Who are you?"

"I'm an FBI Agent. My name's Dan Robertson," he said as he showed her his credentials.

She had trouble reading until she put on her glasses. Her lips moved as she read. Then she turned to LeBeau.

"I'm Richie LeBeau, an NYPD Detective." He showed his shield and identification. "We've come here today to ask if you'd help us nail the man who killed Christy Marino."

"Why should I talk to you? You guys put me here."

"Because if you do, we'll see if we can get you out of here a little sooner," said Dan.

"What?"

"Or," LeBeau said. "If you don't help we'll indict you for accessory to murder."

"You can't ... I didn't ... What?" was all that came out of Sarah Schwartz's mouth.

"Maybe this will help you understand," said Dan. "Richie, have you got those bills?"

Out of his briefcase, LeBeau pulled a plastic sleeve containing the eight hundred dollar bills. LeBeau slipped on surgical gloves and spread the bills on the table between them.

"Mrs. Schwartz," Dan began, "these are eight of the twenty-six one hundred dollar bills Bart O'Reilly had with him when he was arrested."

She might have been listening, but her eyes were locked on the money in front of her.

"Do you see these purple marks on the bills, Mrs. Schwartz?" asked LeBeau, who pointed to the fingerprints. "These marks tell us that Bart O'Reilly handled this money. When he did, he left his fingerprints."

"But Bart O'Reilly's weren't the only fingerprints we found on the money," said Dan. "Do you know whose fingerprints we also found on this money?"

Sarah Schwartz said nothing, as her eyes darted back and forth among the bills.

"You know, don't you?" said LeBeau. "You know we found your fingerprints. You handled it, because you paid Bart O'Reilly for the murders. Your husband made the arrangements, but you handed over the money. That way he could say he never paid Bart O'Reilly to murder anyone."

"But, where does that leave you?" said Dan. "You can be charged with murder, even though you didn't shoot the gun, because you paid to have it done. Your husband sure put you in a terrible position."

Sarah Schwartz seemed to implode. She put her face in her hands, and began to sob. Her body shook and she made plaintive cries like an animal that had been caught in a trap.

"We didn't come here today to tell you we know what you did," LeBeau said. "We came to provide you with a once-in-a-lifetime opportunity. As things now sit, you can be charged with murder. The average prison sentence for murder is twenty-five years."

But if you agree to help us, we'll see to it that you won't do another day of jail time," said Dan. "And we'll pull some strings to have you released for the time you've already served."

"Twenty-five more years, or no more years," asked LeBeau.

Sarah Schwartz's head rose slightly. She didn't make eye contact with LeBeau or Dan. "What do I have to—"

"Simple," said Dan. "Agree to testify against Bart O'Reilly, and tell the court that, at your husband's insistence, you paid O'Reilly to commit murder."

"But Bernie . . . he'd never let me get away with it," she said, her tear-filled eyes finally making contact with theirs.

"Do you actually think that Bernie would care if you were charged with murder?" asked LeBeau. "Do you think he cares so much about you he'd do anything to make sure you were okay?"

"Well, yeah he . . . I know he wouldn't let me stay in jail for another twenty-five years. Sure, he's done some bad things, but he loves me," she said, tears streaming down her face.

"Then he's really got a strange way of showing it," said Dan.

Dan pulled the tape recorder out of his briefcase, and set it on the table in front of him and Bernie Schwartz's voice was heard.

Damn it! My goddamned wife is in the joint down in West Virginia. I've spent a fuckin' fortune on her, making sure she doesn't have a tough time of the three years she's doin' there. She bitches about everything. She couldn't stand her cellmate, so I paid to have her put in a cell by herself. Then she couldn't stand the goddamned food, so I paid to have Kosher brought in every day. And I have to come up with bucks, so she can pay the other inmates to let her use the phone to call our kids. For what I've paid to keep her happy, it would've been cheaper to just have her fuckin' killed.

She stared at the tape recorder with a look of rage on her face. Her nostrils flared. Her eyes were wide and dilated. Her breathing was rapid. Sarah Schwartz looked up and said, "That bastard of a husband of mine can rot in hell for all I care."

Fifty

2:15 PM
January 24th
Manhattan, New York

When they opened the door to the squad room, the other members of the Task Force turned, not knowing what the news would be. Neither LeBeau's nor Dan's face gave any clue.

"How'd it go?" Casey asked tentatively.

Dan looked at LeBeau, then to the others. He balled his right hand into a fist at eye level, brought it straight down and shouted, "Yessss!" He sat on the edge of a desk, and related the story. LeBeau chimed in with any detail that Dan had left out.

LeBeau returned some calls, then abruptly stood up, grabbed his fedora, and walked over to Dan.

"Come on, Dan, let's go," LeBeau said as he pulled on Dan's elbow. "There's someplace both of us need to go. Don't ask. You'll thank me later."

"Why can't you tell me now?" Dan asked in protest, even though he was standing and putting his suit coat back on.

"Just trust me, damn it!" LeBeau snapped. "Come on!"

The two of them went back out the door, down the stairs, and got into Dan's car.

"Well, if I'm driving, you're going to have to tell me how to get to wherever we're going."

"Go south on the West Side Highway," LeBeau said as he snapped his seatbelt.

Dan gave an annoyed glance at LeBeau. "That's a start."

As they had reached Lower Manhattan, LeBeau said, "Okay, swing over and go east on Houston Street."

Dan wove around double-parked cars and trucks.

"Turn right on Elizabeth Street," LeBeau said. "Park anywhere you can find a spot."

Dan spotted a space, pulled in, and put his FBI parking placard on the dashboard. He turned to look at LeBeau, and in an impatient tone, asked, "Richie, where are we going?"

"NYPD's Fifth Precinct," LeBeau said as he got out of the car and closed the door.

Dan got out and caught up as LeBeau ascended the five steps into the station house. LeBeau flashed his shield at the desk sergeant, and headed up the stairs with Dan right behind him. LeBeau walked directly to one of the desks, and stopped, with Dan right by his side, he saw Detective Jimmy Lee.

"What?" Dan's gaze shifted back and forth between the two detectives.

"Richie, Dan, please have a seat," Lee said as he motioned at the two chairs.

"Will somebody please tell me . . ." Dan said, his patience completely gone.

"Dan," LeBeau said. "I didn't want to tell you, because you'd probably have some questions that I couldn't answer."

"And it wasn't something I wanted to tell you over the phone," said Lee.

"For god's sake, what is it?" shouted Dan.

"It has to do with Sammy Ho's murder," said Lee. "There was a young Chinese man who tried to extort money from a merchant in Chinatown. He played cat and mouse, avoided us for a week, but we finally arrested him last night."

Dan watched Lee, wondering how this conversation would lead to Sammy Ho.

"He was a member of the Jade Dragons Tong," said Lee. "We had members of the Jade Squad interviewing him for hours last night, while the ballistic experts were comparing the slugs and casings from the guns he had in his van."

"Did they match up with those from the restaurant where ..."

"They did, Dan," Lee said. "He had eight different weapons in his van. It was that old Tong ploy of having the youngest member hold onto the weapons, so if he's arrested as a juvenile, he'd have the best chance of avoiding jail time. The lab was able to match slugs and casings from four of those weapons with those from the restaurant. More importantly, one of the four guns matched the slug that killed Sammy."

Dan exhaled, closed his eyes, and tilted his head back, sending the news to Sammy. He sat for a moment, thought about it, then stood, walked over and looked out the window.

"What about the killers?" Dan asked. "Was this kid there that night?"

"He was driving the van," said Lee. "At that point, they didn't trust him enough to put a gun in his hands to kill somebody, and not fall apart from the pressure."

"Did he tell you who the others were?" Dan asked.

"Not at first," said Lee. "But then the ballistics reports came back. And we pulled out the crime scene photos and showed him what had been done to Sammy and the others. He tried to act tough, but it wasn't long before he sang like a canary. We've been all over Chinatown, trying to find the others. So far we have two of them. We should have the rest in a day or so."

"Did the kid say what the shootings were about?" asked Dan.

"Pretty much what we had initially picked up from our informants," said Lee. "The Ghost Shadows Tong had tried to take over one block of Chinatown that the Jade Dragons owned. The Jade Dragons wanted to send a message—let them know what it would cost. They spotted two Ghost Shadows Tong members in the restaurant, called in the artillery, and shot up the place. It was nothing personal toward Sammy. Nobody realized he was an FBI Agent. He was just in the wrong place at the wrong time. A tragedy, but that's all it was."

"I'd like to be in the courtroom when they're arraigned," said Dan. "I want to get a look at them."

"Sure, Dan," said Lee. "I'll give you a call once I know."

"Thanks, Jimmy," Dan said as he stood and shook his hand.

As Dan and LeBeau walked to the car, LeBeau said, "Sorry about all the secrecy."

"It's okay, Richie. You did the right thing."

"You're not going to do anything stupid at these guys' arraignment, are you, Dan?"

"No, I won't. I don't know what I'll do, but tonight I'm going to go home and write a letter to Sammy's widow. She needs to know."

They returned to Midtown North, and Dan went to Casey's desk. "I was thinking about Schwartz and his plans to have Weinstein and Westerfield killed. Have you had a chance to sit down with an AUSA?"

"I talked it over with Diane Denton, who gave me authority for the body recorder. She talked it over with ADA Bergen and he's supposed to be arraigned tomorrow morning in state court."

"What about Kirwan? Once Schwartz learns he turned state's evidence against him, it might get ugly if both are still in the MCC," said Dan.

"Got that covered. Bernie Schwartz has been put into solitary. They made up a story that somebody had threatened to kill him."

"Did he believe them?"

"He bought it," Casey said. "Schwartz is even proud of it. Convinced that if somebody wants to kill him, he must be pretty important."

"When is that guy going to start living in the real world?"

"Probably never. He's having too good of a time."

"Let me know how Schwartz's arraignment works out."

"Sure. How are you holding up, Dan?"

"I feel like a human pinball, bouncing from one thing to another. Changing the subject for a minute, would you like to go to dinner tonight?"

"I had planned to do a few loads of wash and vacuum my apartment."

"So you're not interested?"

"I might be able to postpone those tasks for one more day. I'd love to go."

"Let's make it eight, and wear something nice."

"See you then," she said.

* * *

Dan picked up Casey, and they went to Fifty-First between Avenue of the Americas and Seventh Avenue. As they rode the elevator to the street, Dan looked over at Casey, and wondered why he hadn't ever really noticed how attractive she was.

She caught his gaze.

"I was thinking how pretty you look."

She blushed and lowered her eyes.

"I didn't mean to embarrass you."

"I'm not used to compliments. But thanks for saying so."

The awkward moment was broken as the elevator stopped. The doors opened and they walked out onto the sidewalk.

As Casey walked close beside him, she slipped her left hand around his right upper arm and leaned into him. He turned to look at her and smiled.

She returned the smile. "Where are we going?"

"Oh, I don't know," he said. "Maybe we should just keep walking until we find a restaurant and when we look through the window, we spot an empty table."

She gave his upper arm a playful punch, and then laughed.

"Actually," he said as he looked up at the canopy that had "Le Cité" emblazoned in white letters on the green canvas. "I believe we're here."

"Ooooh! Heard about this place."

"Let's hope it lives up to expectations."

"We'd prefer that table by the window," Dan said, pointing across the room while pressing a twenty dollar bill into hand of the maître d'.

The maître d' broke into a smile, slipping the twenty into his pocket. He led them to the table and handed them menus. "Could we have a bottle of Clicquot, please?" Dan said.

Casey laughed and said, "You handled that well."

"Thanks. I wanted to share a couple of things with you."

Their waiter appeared, poured the champagne and insisted on telling them the evening's specials that didn't appear on the menu.

"Remember the OPR mess? Guess what happened?"

"It went away," she said, smiling.

"That's right," he said as he raised his glass in a toast. "Here's to overcoming a big one."

She raised her champagne glass and touched his. "Amen."

Both of them took a sip, and after setting her glass down, she said, "Tell me what happened."

"In a nutshell, Ike Blackman was trying to sabotage me, first by removing and hiding the signed undercover authorization memo. And then by leaking information about The CBS Murders investigation. When he called the media, he told them his name was Dan Robertson, and again tried to torpedo me."

"That bastard!" Casey said.

"I've been sworn to secrecy. So you can't pass it on."

"I won't," she said. "Everybody wondered what Blackman had done to get demoted and transferred. What a rat! To think he almost got away with it! What else is going on?"

Dan paused, took a deep breath and said, "Sammy Ho's murder was solved."

She gasped, her hand going to her mouth. She reached out, took his hand in hers, and said, "That's got to be a load off of you. Who killed him?"

He told her the story.

"Dan, I'm so sorry," she said. "But it's good to have closure." There were tears in her eyes.

He was moved by her empathy. "Thanks Casey. You're right. I had felt responsible for his death."

She looked at him. "Dan, you need to find a way to quit blaming yourself for what happens to others."

"What do you mean?"

Casey slowly turned the champagne glass twisting its stem between her fingers. She raised her eyes and said, "You feel guilt about Christy Marino and Sammy Ho. Do you think you've subconsciously connected this to your wife's unsolved murder? Your wife's death wasn't your fault. Neither was the deaths of the others. Let go of that guilt. Get on with your life."

He considered her words for a moment. "You may be right. I appreciate your telling it like you see it. Maybe I have held onto those feelings for too much time."

"Don't wait too long to sort these things out." She let go of his hand, picked up the menu, and began to look it over. Then she lowered it so she could see him, and said, "In the meantime, let's have dinner."

Fifty-One

9:45 AM
January 25th
Manhattan, New York

Schwartz was reading a newspaper when the guard opened his cell and handed him a suit. "Put these on."

"Why the fuck should I?"

"You've got an 11:00 A.M. court appearance."

"What the hell for?"

"How should I know?" said the guard as he started to leave.

"Where?" Schwartz asked warily.

"New York Supreme Court."

"My case was in federal court," Schwartz said. "This is a fuckin' mistake."

"Put on the clothes. You leave in fifteen minutes."

Schwartz dressed and waited for the U.S. Marshals, but was surprised when LeBeau and Sandoval cuffed him and led him out.

"What the hell is this?" Schwartz asked.

"Shut up!" said LeBeau.

Schwartz was led into the courtroom in the Manhattan Criminal Courts Building and joined Leo Traub at the defense table.

"Leo, what the fuck is going on?" asked an anxious, perspiring Schwartz in a whispered voice.

"You're being arraigned for conspiracy to commit murder."

"Murder!" Schwartz shouted, loud enough to cause everyone in the courtroom to turn and look at him.

"Give it up, Bernie. They know all about it. You tried to murder Westerfield and Weinstein. You're digging yourself a deeper hole."

"How the hell... Who told them?"

"Kirwan was wearing a wire when you hired him for the murder."

"That lousy fuck! I thought I could trust that son-of-a-bitch! I'm gonna have somebody cut off his nuts and feed 'em to him."

"Bernie, if you keep this up, you're going to have to find another lawyer."

"So you're bailing out on me, too?" said Schwartz. "You make a ton of money off of me, and when I really need you, you quit? Is that how you fuckin' lawyers work?"

"Bernie, shut up!"

The bailiff came out of the judge's chambers, followed by the judge.

"All rise!" the bailiff belted out. "Oyea, oyea, oyea! The New York Supreme Court in and for the County of New York is now in session, the Honorable Marie

Vanderlee, presiding! All ye who have business before this court, stand near, and you will be heard."

Judge Vanderlee sat down, struck her gavel, and said, "Please be seated. Bailiff, please call the first case."

The bailiff said, "The People of New York versus Bernard Schwartz."

"This is an arraignment for the purpose of informing the defendant of the charges which have been filed against him, and permitting him the opportunity to enter a plea," the judge said. "Is that understood?"

Traub stood, said, "Yes, your Honor." Then he sat down.

"Will the defendant please rise?"

Both Schwartz and Traub stood.

"Bernard Schwartz, you are charged with violation of Section 125.25 of the New York Penal Code, namely, Conspiracy to Commit Murder. Mr. Traub, does the defendant waive the reading of the charges?"

"Yes he does."

"How does the defendant plead?" asked the judge.

"Not guilty, your Honor," Traub said quickly.

"Very well," said Judge Vanderlee, and she set the dates for the filing of motions, and the date the trial would begin. "This proceeding is adjourned. Bailiff, call the next case."

Schwartz looked up at the judge and said, "You fuckin' bitch! I ought to—"

Judge Vanderlee rapped her gavel and said, "Mr. Traub, one more outburst from your client, and I'll find you both in contempt! Do you hear me?"

"Yes, your Honor. My deepest apologies to the court."

LeBeau and Sandoval walked from the back of the courtroom and snapped the cuffs on Schwartz.

"You lousy fucks," Schwartz said with a sneer.

"Bernie, I don't want you to say another word to either of these men," Traub said. "Is that clear?"

Schwartz gave Traub one last furious look as he was led away.

* * *

At Midtown North, the members of the Task Force listened as Dan told them how he planned to build the case against O'Reilly for murder.

"Like I said before, that's double jeopardy," Casey said. "We can't go after him because we'd be charging him with the same crime, a second time."

"I'm not suggesting we charge him with the murders of Marino and the three CBS employees," Dan said. "We're going to charge him with the murder of Mary Lee Wen."

"Do we have enough evidence?" Casey asked.

"I think so," Dan said. We've got the .22 caliber cartridge casing that was found in Wen's car, along with blood and hair that matches hers. Then we've got O'Reilly stalking Wen at Marino's apartment."

"Wasn't he stalking Marino?"

"Not if we're going to charge him with Wen's murder," said Dan. "We can interpret O'Reilly's actions any way we want. He's never going to take the stand in his own defense. Even if he did, do you really think he'd say, 'No, I wasn't stalking Wen. I was really stalking Marino.'"

"True," said LeBeau. "But we're going to need a lot more than that. After all, we don't have a body."

"We may not need one," said Dan. "In addition to O'Reilly stalking Wen, we've got those two teenagers who saw the silver van and the man who followed Wen after she left Marino's apartment. We have that FBI surveillance near Marino's apartment, and they took down the license number of O'Reilly's van. We'll say that O'Reilly was there, stalking Wen, looking for a chance to kill her. There's nobody who's going to refute it."

"It's all circumstantial evidence, and it sounds pretty thin to me," said LeBeau.

"If that's all there was, I'd agree," said Dan. "But we've got Sarah Schwartz, ready to testify she personally paid O'Reilly to kill Mary Lee Wen. And that can be confirmed since her fingerprints are on the hundred dollar bills that she used to pay O'Reilly. And of course, he had those bills in his possession when he was arrested in Kentucky."

"But that was money she paid O'Reilly to kill Christy Marino," said Casey.

"That's not what Sarah Schwartz recalls," Dan said. "Just like the stalking, O'Reilly isn't going to get on the witness stand and say, 'Oh no, that wasn't money she paid me to kill Mary Lee Wen. It was money she paid me to kill Christy Marino.'"

"Clever," said LeBeau. "But I'm still not convinced that we can link the .22 caliber cartridge casing from Wen's car to O'Reilly. After all, the evidence from the search of the van was thrown out by the judge."

"Then we'll use the .22 caliber cartridge casings we found in the garage when we searched O'Reilly's home," said Dan.

"That was part of the evidence from the search of his home that was ruled inadmissible," said Casey.

"So, we'll get a new search warrant for O'Reilly's home, based on the different probable cause that I've been talking about," said Dan. "Then, the same evidence from the search of his home becomes admissible."

"I don't know, Dan," said LeBeau. "Sounds pretty iffy to me."

"Let's run it past Bergen, and see if he thinks the DA's Office will go with it," said Dan. "When I asked you to hang in there another week, you agreed. My week isn't up."

"Okay," said LeBeau. "I'm in. Run it past Bergen, and see what he thinks. Let's take a ride downtown, and see him. Dan, would you—"

"Yeah, I'll drive."

* * *

The next day, Bart O'Reilly was brought before Judge Vanderlee. As he sat down next to Lowenthal, O'Reilly said, "Hey, Walt, will somebody tell me what the fuck is going on? I've got two days left on my twenty-day sentence, and then I'm out of here. Now I get dragged down here for a goddamned arraignment."

"You've been charged with murder," said Lowenthal, not looking up from the criminal complaint he was reading. When he had finished, he looked up at O'Reilly, and said, "Who is Mary Lee Wen?"

"How the hell should I know?"

"Bart, this isn't the time to be jerking around your attorney. If I'm to put together any kind of defense, you have to level with me. Who is Mary Lee Wen?"

"I don't know," O'Reilly looked away, not making eye contact with Lowenthal. "It's some trumped up charge."

"Somebody thinks you killed her, and this complaint charges you with her murder. Are you sure you don't know her?"

"She's just some stupid Chink."

"So you do know her. Okay, Bart, I'm going to plead you not guilty, but when we're out of this courtroom, you and I are going to talk. Don't play games with me."

"Yeah, sure."

"All rise!" the bailiff belted out, and went through his announcement.

The bailiff stood. "The People of New York versus Bart O'Reilly."

"Mr. O'Reilly, you have been charged with murder in the second degree," said Judge Vanderlee. "The charge stems from the death of one Mary Lee Wen, having been killed on or about January 3rd of this year. How does the defendant plead?"

"Not guilty," Lowenthal said. "Your Honor," said Lowenthal. "I would respectfully request that bail be set at a reasonable amount, so that the defendant might be able to earn a living to support his family while awaiting a trial, the outcome of which will undoubtedly exonerate my client."

"Mr. Bergen?" the judge said.

"Your Honor," Bergen said as he stood. "This is a capital offense, and as such, requires that the defendant not be freed on bail. Furthermore, the defendant is currently serving a twenty-day sentence on a much lesser charge. Rather than surrendering himself to begin serving that sentence, the defendant fled the State of New York where he had been charged. He also fled the State of New Jersey where he resides. If it hadn't been for the successful efforts of the Federal Bureau of Investigation, who located him in the State of Kentucky, I have no doubt that even today the defendant would be a fugitive from justice. The prosecution vigorously opposes bail in any amount."

"Thank you, Mr. Bergen," said Vanderlee. "Mr. Lowenthal, do you have anything to say in opposition to the prosecution's argument?"

"Yes, your Honor," said Lowenthal as he stood. "The prosecution is obviously uninformed about the motives of my client, and opts to distort the situation to support their argument. Mr. O'Reilly was merely mistaken about the date he was required to surrender. That was the reason he failed to appear. At the same time, Mr. O'Reilly's only living sister, who resides in the State of Kentucky, became gravely ill. The motivation for his driving to Kentucky, was to be with her in her time of need. It was nothing more than his love for his sibling. Furthermore, the Federal Bureau of Investigation did not act in accordance with the law when they had Mr. O'Reilly arrested. In an appearance before Judge Patton, the arrest of my client was ruled to be illegal, and the trumped up murder charges against Mr. O'Reilly, similar to those with which he is now charged, were dismissed. It is plain to see that today's charges against my client, are nothing more than the Manhattan District Attorney's Office petulant attempt to even the score. I have no doubt that these charges will also be dismissed, and accordingly, request the defendant be released on bail, set at a reasonable amount by this court."

Lowenthal sat down, and Judge Vanderlee removed her glasses, rubbed her eyes, and pondered her decision.

"Thank you both. While the court is certainly compassionate to the defendant's sibling's plight, the defendant, or at the very least his attorney, cannot flaunt the legal requirements of the court. In light of the seriousness of the crime for which the defendant is charged, and his previous disregard of the court-imposed surrendering appearance he was required to make, this court rules that the defendant be held without bail." Vanderlee set the date for the filing of motions, and the date for the commencement of the trial. Then rapped her gavel once, and said, "This proceeding is adjourned. Bailiff, call the next case."

Lowenthal turned to O'Reilly. "Bart, we are going to have that talk and you will tell me why they think you killed her."

Fifty-Two

1:00 PM
January 26th
Monmouth County, New Jersey

ADA Bergen, LeBeau, and Dan sat in green leather chairs in Judge Vincente Benedetto's chambers, in Monmouth County, New Jersey.

After having read the affidavit, the judge looked up at the men and asked, "The probable cause in this affidavit before me, uses none of the evidence located in the van?"

"No sir," said LeBeau, who then got a look from Bergen that told him not to answer any more questions. LeBeau gave a slight shrug of his shoulders.

"Based on what I see before me, it seems to me that you have sufficient probable cause for the search," said the judge. "But I'm having trouble understanding why you didn't go this route the first time. I'll sign the warrant. But let me ask you something. Are you going to go back to the house and search it again, or legally use the evidence you located when you previously searched the house?"

"We plan to now use the evidence previously seized," said Bergen.

"Very well, gentlemen," said the judge as he signed the warrant and handed it back to them. "Good luck to you."

"See now, that wasn't so hard," said LeBeau, teasingly taking credit for the idea. "Didn't I tell you it would work?"

"LeBeau, you're something else," said Dan, shaking his head.

Fifty-Three

10:30 AM
February 25th
Manhattan, New York

O'Reilly's murder trial began in Manhattan.

"Call your first witness, Mr. Bergen," said Judge Vanderlee.

"The prosecution calls Doris Morales," Bergen said.

"I was sitting in the front seat of my boyfriend's car as it was parked on Linden Avenue on the night of January 3rd," testified the Queens teenager.

"Thank you, Miss Morales," said Bergen. "At approximately 7:45 that night, what did you see?"

"A Chinese woman came out of the apartment building, turned right, walked to the corner, and started to get into a maroon car."

"Did you see anyone else?"

"Yeah, there was this guy. I think it was a guy wearing one of those ski masks like bank robbers wear."

"Objection, your Honor," said Lowenthal. "Implying that the ski mask is the exclusive apparel of bank robbers paints the defendant with a broad brush. Move the characterization of the ski mask be stricken."

"Sustained," said the judge. "The court reporter will strike that portion of the witness's response."

"What was the man in the ski mask doing?" asked Bergen.

"He got out of this silver van and started following this Chinese woman down the street, and around the corner. When she got to that maroon car over on Linden Avenue, it looked like he pushed her into the car. She screamed, and he got in after her. Then both the maroon car and the silver van drove away."

"Could you see what the man was wearing?"

"It was a short leather jacket, one of those brown bomber jackets."

"Thank you, Miss Morales, no further questions."

"Your witness, Mr. Lowenthal," said Judge Vanderlee.

"Miss Morales," said Lowenthal. "What were you and your boyfriend doing in the car?"

Morales looked down at her hands. "Kissin' and stuff."

"It would seem that you're more interested in watching others than kissing your boyfriend. Do you expect us to believe you stopped that activity entirely, so you could watch these things?"

"Right then, we was having an argument," said Morales.

"Oh, I see," said Lowenthal with a grin on his face. "And when you argue, you don't look at one another?"

"No we don't!" Morales said angrily.

"And at 7:45 in the evening, you can see a car, half a block away and tell its maroon in color?" Lowenthal said mockingly.

"Yeah, I could! There was a street light right above it!"

"There's only two streetlights on that street and they're both very dim. No further questions," said Lowenthal.

"The prosecution calls Eve Jenkins," said Bergen.

"I'm a Vice President with Verizon," said the middle aged, attractively dressed woman.

"Would you please a look at this document and tell me what it is?" Bergen said as he handed it to her.

"This is a copy of a Verizon bill for telephone number 608 972-3414."

"At what address is this telephone located, Mrs. Jenkins?"

"At 81 Creek Road, Keansburg, New Jersey," she said.

"And this bill covers what time period?"

"December 23rd to January 22nd."

"I direct your attention to a call made at 7:17 P.M. on January 3rd, placed from telephone number 718 764-1828, and charged to this number. Can you tell us the exact location of the telephone which was assigned number 718 764-1828?"

"Yes. It's a public payphone, located on the sidewalk at the corner of Grandview Avenue and Linden Street in Queens."

"Ms. Jenkins, would you tell me the subscriber of the telephone, to which that call was charged?"

"Yes, telephone number 608 972-3413 is the number assigned to A. Glenn at 81 Creek Road, Keansburg, New Jersey."

"Thank you Ms. Jenkins, no further questions."

"Mr. Lowenthal?" asked Judge Vanderlee.

"Ms. Jenkins, have you conducted a search to determine if that particular telephone was in working order on that date?" asked Lowenthal.

"No, I haven't. I wouldn't normally—"

"Thank you Ms. Jenkins. No further questions.

"The prosecution calls Stuart Anderson," said Bergen.

"I'm a Teaneck, New Jersey Auxiliary police officer. When I was on my way to my regular job in Manhattan, on January 6th, I saw an abandoned maroon Pontiac station wagon parked at the curb on West Thirty-sixth Street, between Tenth and Eleventh Avenue. I recognized a Teaneck voter district parking decal on the rear window of the Pontiac. I pulled over to take a look at it, and when I looked inside the vehicle, I saw blood on the front seat. I called the Teaneck Police dispatcher, and learned the vehicle was owned by Mary Lee Wen, who had been reported missing. Then I called the NYPD."

"Mr. Anderson, to the best of your knowledge, was Mary Lee Wen ever found?"

"Never."

"Thank you, Mr. Anderson," said Bergen. "No further questions."

"Mr. Lowenthal?" said Vanderlee.

"Mr. Anderson, when you first spotted this Pontiac parked in Manhattan, were the windows rolled up, and the vehicle locked?" asked Lowenthal.

"No, the windows weren't rolled up, and no, the vehicle wasn't locked."

"And isn't the area, where this vehicle was located, frequented by drug dealers and prostitutes?"

"Yeah."

"No further questions, your Honor."

"The prosecution calls Detective Barry Flynn," said Bergen.

"I'm a Detective in NYPD's 10th Precinct. On the 6th of February, my partner, Jake Shea and I met with Stuart Anderson, an auxiliary policeman from the Teaneck, New Jersey Police Department, on West Thirty-sixth Street, where a maroon Pontiac station wagon with Jersey plates was parked."

"Detective Flynn, did you request a forensic examination of the interior of that vehicle?"

"Yeah, I did."

"And what was found?"

"A Remington Peters .22 caliber cartridge casing on the left rear seat, and a whole lot of bloodstains on the seats, dashboard, and carpet. We found some hair, on the dashboard, and some that had been caught in the rain guard above the driver's door."

"Thank you, Detective Flynn, no further questions."

"Your witness, Mr. Lowenthal," said the judge.

"Detective Flynn, did you obtain a search warrant, authorizing you to search this Pontiac?" asked Lowenthal.

"No, we didn't," said Flynn. "We asked ADA Bergen about it, and he said, based on the circumstances of the missing woman, the blood, and all, we had sufficient probable cause to search it without a warrant."

"A short time ago, I asked Mr. Anderson if the area where the vehicle was located, was populated by drug dealers and prostitutes," said Lowenthal. "He told me that was true. Do you agree with that answer?"

"Yeah, I guess you could say that."

"So would it be theoretically possible, that the blood and hair and cartridge casing found in that

Pontiac, could have been left there by any number of persons?" asked Lowenthal.

"Yeah, I guess, but—"

"Thank you, Detective Flynn. No further questions," said Lowenthal, walking back to the defense table.

"The prosecution calls Dr. Herbert Mallot," said Bergen.

A bespeckled gentleman in a brown tweed jacket took the stand.

"Dr. Mallot, you are an MD, the chief serology examiner for the NYPD crime lab, and qualified as an expert witness, are you not?" asked Bergen.

"Yes, I am."

"Would you tell us what qualifies you as an expert witness?"

Lowenthal stood and said, "The defense stipulates that this witness is qualified as an expert witness."

"Very well," said Bergen. "Were you requested by Detective Flynn to examine the bloodstains and other evidence which were found in a Pontiac station wagon owned by Mary Lee Wen?"

"Yes, I was," said Mallot.

"My examination determined that all of the bloodstains located were consistent with blood group A negative. The hairs had been forcibly removed from the head of a person of the Asian race."

"Dr. Mallot, did you obtain hairs from a hairbrush owned by Mary Lee Wen, and compare them to the hairs found in the Pontiac?"

"Yes, I did. I also had DNA tests performed on the blood and hair from the car, which compared it to the blood and the DNA from the hair on the brush."

"Objection, your honor!" shouted Lowenthal. "The existence of blood on the hair from the brush has not been established!"

"Sustained. Mr. Bergen, establish the basis for the statement."

"Very well, your honor. Dr. Mallot, when you received the hairbrush owned and used by Mary Lee Wen, did you examine the hair on it?"

"Yes, I did."

"And what did you find," asked Bergen.

"I found human blood. It is not uncommon for a human being, while brushing their hair, to pull individual hairs out of their scalp," said Mallot. "Most people aren't even aware that they've brushed out any of their hairs. Sometimes these hairs have a tiny drop of blood on the follicle, or root of the individual hair. This was the case with Mrs. Wen's hairbrush. There were a number of hairs that had microscopic amounts of blood on them. That provided me with a baseline blood sample, against which I could make comparisons."

"What were the results of your comparisons, Doctor?"

"The hairs from the car matched the hair from the brush. The blood from the car matched the blood group A negative, a tiny drop of which I found on a hair follicle from the brush. Tests conducted by an independent lab in California demonstrated that, for all comparative purposes, the DNA from the hair and blood matched."

"Dr. Mallot, how rare would this particular DNA match be?"

"One in nine hundred eighty-four million."

"Thank you doctor, no further questions at this time. Your honor, the prosecution reserves the right to recall this witness."

"Your witness, Mr. Lowenthal," said Judge Vanderlee.

"No questions, your honor."

"The prosecution calls Gary Edwards," said Bergen.

"I'm an FBI agent. I'm part of an Organized Crime investigation surveillance team."

"Agent Edwards, would you tell us where you were, and what you were doing on the night of January 3rd?"

"On the evening of January 3rd, at approximately 6:50 P.M., as a part of our investigation, I recorded all the license numbers of vehicles parked on the street along Grandview Avenue in Ridgewood, Queens."

"Did you happen to see a silver van during your exercise that night?" Bergen asked.

"Yes, I did. Among those plates I recorded, was New Jersey license 218 RSL, which was attached to a silver Ford Econoline van. I obtained DMV information which indicated it was registered to Bart O'Reilly."

"Was Mr. O'Reilly the target of your Organized Crime investigation?"

"No, he wasn't."

"Thank you Agent Edwards," said Bergen. "No further questions."

"Your witness, Mr. Lowenthal," said the judge.

"No questions, your honor."

"Ladies and gentlemen, we've had a long and very busy morning. Before we break for our noon recess, I want to remind members of the jury that they should not talk about this case, or the testimony they have heard, with anyone else. We will reconvene at two o'clock this afternoon. This trial is in recess," Judge Vanderlee declared, as she struck her gavel.

Fifty-Four

2:00 PM
February 25th
Manhattan, New York

When the trial reconvened, Bergen wasted no time in picking up where he had left off that morning.

"The prosecution calls Kathleen Carter Brody," said Bergen.

"I'm a Special Agent of the Federal Bureau of Investigation."

"And in that capacity, on January 20th of this year, authorized by a search warrant, did you direct a search of the home of Bart O'Reilly at 81 Creek Road, Keansburg, New Jersey?"

"Yes, I did."

"Objection!" Lowenthal said. "Evidence from that search has been ruled inadmissible. It cannot be introduced here."

"Your honor, Mr. Lowenthal is in possession of a second search warrant issued by Judge Benedetto on January 26th," Bergen said. "Based on the second search warrant, the evidence is admissible."

"Objection overruled. Continue Mr. Bergen."

"Agent Brody, tell me what you found there."

"In a hidden room in the back of the garage, we found a number of Remington Peters .22 caliber cartridge casings scattered about on the floor."

"Agent Brody, was there also a search conducted of a creek which runs behind Mr. O'Reilly's house?"

"Yes, there was," said Casey. "A scuba search was conducted of the Waackaack Creek."

"What, if anything, was located during that search?"

"A man's bomber style brown leather jacket was found in that creek."

"Was there anything unusual about the condition of this jacket when it was located?" asked Bergen.

"Yes, what was unusual was that the jacket was wrapped around a large rock, almost as if it had deliberately been weighted to sink to the bottom."

"Objection!" shouted Lowenthal. "The second part of Agent Brody's sentence is speculation. Move it be stricken."

"Sustained," said Vanderlee.

"No further questions, your Honor," said Bergen as he sat down.

"Your witness, Mr. Lowenthal," said the judge.

"Agent Brody," said Lowenthal. "Let me see if I understand this correctly. You searched Mr. O'Reilly's home?"

"Correct."

"And you searched his garage?"

"That's right."

"And you even searched the creek behind his home?"

"Yes."

"And did you locate any handguns?" asked Lowenthal.

"No, sir."

"Any guns at all?"

"None."

"So the only evidence of any relevance which you located was some .22 cartridge casings in a secret room of the garage, the very existence of which, the defendant might not have even been aware. And a brown leather jacket that could have been thrown away by anyone, before it got tangled up with a rock. Is there any evidence of significance, Agent Brody?"

"The significant evidence which we located was the jacket and the cartridge casings."

"No further questions," said Lowenthal.

"The prosecution calls Howard Morioka," said Bergen.

"I'm an NYPD Detective assigned to the Ballistics Section of the Laboratory," said Morioka.

"Detective Morioka," said Bergen. "Did you compare a .22 caliber cartridge casing which had been located in a Pontiac station wagon owned by Mary Lee Wen with numerous .22 caliber cartridge casings which were located in a garage of a house owned by Bart O'Reilly?"

"Yes, I did."

"And what were your conclusions when you compared them, Detective Morioka?"

"I found that the cartridge casing from Mrs. Wen's vehicle bore imprints of a firing pin, extractor, and ejector mechanisms, consistent with those found on the cartridge casings located in Mr. O'Reilly's garage."

"In other words, you believe they match?"

"What I concluded was that all of the cartridge casings had been fired, extracted, and ejected from the same gun," said Morioka as he pushed his glasses back up his nose.

"No further questions," said Bergen.

"Mr. Lowenthal?" asked the judge.

"I have no questions for this witness," said Lowenthal.

"The prosecution calls Robert Hazen," said Bergen.

"I am a Fingerprint Technician at the NYPD Laboratory," said Hazen.

Bergen took a plastic bag over to the witness chair, and said, "Mr. Hazen, do you recognize this?"

"Yes, I do," Hazen said as he leafed through the contents of the bag. "These are hundred dollar bills which I examined. I conducted an examination to determine if those hundred dollar bills bore any latent fingerprints," said Hazen, who then went on to describe the ninhydrin process of raising latent fingerprints.

"And were you able to locate any fingerprints?"

"Yes, I was," said Hazen. "There were two people whose fingerprints consistently appeared on those hundred dollar bills—Bart O'Reilly and Sarah Schwartz."

"Thank you, Mr. Hazen," said Bergen. "No further questions."

"Your witness, Mr. Lowenthal," said Vanderlee.

Lowenthal collected his thoughts, then slowly stood and walked towards the witness chair. "Mr. Hazen, isn't it possible that there are any number of reasons these hundred dollar bills could have come into Mr. O'Reilly's possession at some time after they had been handled by Mrs. Schwartz?"

"Objection!" said Bergen. "Calls for speculation."

"Sustained," said Vanderlee.

"In what kind of condition were these hundred dollar bills when you examined them?" asked Lowenthal.

"I would say nearly brand new," said Hazen. "There was a very slight bend to the center of the bills which is usually caused by them being kept in a folding wallet. Other than that, they were pristine."

Lowenthal paused as if to ask another question, but then said, "No further questions of this witness."

"The prosecution calls Sarah Schwartz," said Bergen. Murmurs were heard, and those in the courtroom turned to look at her.

Sarah Schwartz was led by a jail matron through the defendant's doorway, dressed in a simple navy blue skirt and jacket, with a white cotton blouse. She wore no makeup or jewelry.

"Order!" shouted Vanderlee as she rapped her gavel.

Court artists immediately began capturing her likeness for television and newspapers.

"Mrs. Schwartz," Bergen began. "You are here not only because of a subpoena, but also because of a writ. Is that correct?"

Sarah Schwartz nodded.

"Mrs. Schwartz, you must give verbal responses to the questions," said Vanderlee.

"Yes," she said in a quiet voice.

"Where are you residing at the present time, Mrs. Schwartz?"

Not looking up, she said, "Alderson Federal Penitentiary."

"And why are you there, Mrs. Schwartz?"

"I'm serving a three year sentence for bank fraud."

"Was there anyone else convicted for the same crimes?"

"My husband, Bernie."

"So you assisted your husband in the fraud?"

"Yes, I did."

"Did you also assist your husband in anything else?"

Sarah Schwartz again lowered her head, and once again contemplated her hands, and in a voice that could hardly be heard, she said, "Yes, in a murder."

"You'll have to speak up, Mrs. Schwartz," said Vanderlee.

"A murder."

"Who was murdered, Mrs. Schwartz," Bergen asked, as gently as he could.

Sarah Schwartz began to sob, her whole body racked with anguish. Finally, she looked up, and with tears streaming down her cheeks, she said, "Mary Lee Wen. He had Mary Lee Wen murdered!"

Bergen brought a box of tissues to the witness stand.

"Take your time," Vanderlee said. "Compose yourself, and once you have, we'll move on."

After drying her eyes and wiping her nose, Sarah Schwartz looked up at the judge and nodded that she was ready to continue.

"What role did you have in the murder of Mary Lee Wen?" asked Bergen.

"According to my husband's instructions, I took five thousand dollars out of the bank, and paid it to the man that he hired to kill her."

"When you got that money at the bank, was it in brand new hundred dollar bills?"

"Yeah."

"And to whom did you pay the money, Mrs. Schwartz?"

Sarah Schwartz bit her lower lip, hesitated, then with her eyes downcast, said, "Bart O'Reilly."

There was a burst of noise in the courtroom. Vanderlee pounded her gavel, and shouted, "Order or I'll have the courtroom cleared!" The din slowly subsided, and Vanderlee held her hand up, instructing Bergen to wait until the room was quiet. When it was, she lowered her hand, and nodded to him.

"Mrs. Schwartz," Bergen said. "Is the man to whom you paid five thousand dollars to kill Mary Lee Wen, in this courtroom? If so, please point him out."

Slowly, Sarah Schwartz's eyes came up, and she turned her head so that she looked at the defense table. She raised her right arm until it was outstretched, then with her index finger, she pointed directly at Bart O'Reilly and said, "Yes. That's him."

"Let the record show that Sarah Schwartz has identified the defendant, Bart O'Reilly as the man to whom she paid five thousand dollars to kill Mary Lee Wen," said Bergen.

"No further questions, your Honor."

Vanderlee looked at her wristwatch, and then over at Lowenthal. "I could either recess for the day, or let you begin cross-examination. How much time do you think you'll need for your cross, Mr. Lowenthal?"

"I think I could wrap it up in the next thirty minutes, your Honor," said Lowenthal. "And I respectfully request the court allow me that time."

"Very well, counselor," said Vanderlee. "Your witness."

Lowenthal stood, and noticed O'Reilly staring at Sarah Schwartz, a stare that spoke volumes of malevolence. Lowenthal leaned over and whispered something into O'Reilly's ear, but it had no effect on him. Lowenthal walked over to the witness stand.

"Mrs. Schwartz," Lowenthal said. "I'm not sure if we should believe a word that you've said. After all, you are a convicted felon. You defrauded a bank of over thirteen million dollars. And from what you've said here today, it sounds like you are the one who should be on trial for murder."

"Objection, your Honor!" said Bergen. "Defense counsel is using this as his closing argument."

"Sustained. Mr. Lowenthal, ask questions. Don't make speeches."

"Yes, your Honor. Mrs. Schwartz, has the prosecution given you immunity from prosecution for the murder of Mary Lee Wen?"

"Yes," said Sarah Schwartz, again studying her hands.

"And has Mr. Bergen promised to get you out of prison for giving this testimony?"

In a quiet voice, she said, "He agreed to tell the parole board what I'm doing, and recommend they consider paroling me."

"So in order to keep from being prosecuted for murder, and to get out of jail free, you're willing to say anything they want you to say! Isn't that right?"

"No, what I said is the truth!" Sarah Schwartz said defiantly.

"Objection!" shouted Bergen. "Mr. Lowenthal is badgering the witness."

"Sustained," said Vanderlee. "Mr. Lowenthal, if you cannot manage to conduct yourself as a responsible officer of the court, I'll find you in contempt, and we'll recess immediately. What will it be?"

"I have no further questions of this witness, your Honor."

"Thank you, counselor. This trial is recessed until nine o'clock tomorrow morning."

Fifty-Five

4:15 PM
February 25th
Manhattan, New York

Once court had been recessed for the day, Patrick Bergen gathered his notes and papers at the prosecution table. He felt good about the presentation of the case. He would have preferred to see Lowenthal cross-examine Sarah Schwartz the next morning, but on balance, the case against O'Reilly hadn't suffered for it.

"Pat?" the voice said, startling Bergen.

Bergen saw Lowenthal standing beside the prosecution table. The look on Lowenthal's face didn't have its usual self-confidence or arrogance. "I was wondering if I could see you in your office in about an hour," Lowenthal said.

Bergen glanced at his watch, then said, "About five? Sure."

Lowenthal nodded and walked away as Dan and LeBeau approached Bergen.

"Lowenthal wants to talk to me in my office at five," said Bergen. "Can both of you be there?"

"Sure we'll be there. What's up?"

Bergen shoved his papers into his briefcase. "I don't know. He usually just mows you down in the courtroom and gloats about it afterwards."

At five o'clock, LeBeau and Dan sat in Bergen's small office, their knees scraping the front of Bergen's desk.

"I'd think with you being such a great prosecutor and all, you'd manage to find yourself a larger office," LeBeau said.

"Like with Congressmen and Senators, it's all based on seniority. I just have to wait until enough prosecutors leave the DA's office or die. Then I'll get a larger office."

The intercom buzzed. Bergen said, "Lowenthal's here."

"I would go get him, but I'm afraid if I left, I might lose my good seat," LeBeau said with a smile.

When he walked in, Lowenthal's expression made it clear that he wasn't pleased to see LeBeau and Dan.

"Have you met NYPD Detective Richie LeBeau and FBI Supervisor Dan Robertson?" asked Bergen.

"Do they really need to be here?" said Lowenthal. "I mean after all, it's a legal issue, and I don't believe either of them are attorneys."

"I asked them to sit in on our meeting," said Bergen.

"And being a lawyer doesn't give you an exclusive understanding of the legal process," said Dan, angered by Lowenthal's insinuation.

"What's your problem?" asked LeBeau, who had developed an instant dislike for Lowenthal. "Are you uncomfortable talking in front of the men who've put your client in jail?"

"Look, Walt," said Bergen who fixed a stare at the defense attorney. "It's my meeting. I'll decide who's included. End of discussion. Take a seat or leave."

Lowenthal sat down in the last empty chair, and pulled out a legal pad. "The case you put on today was impressive," said Lowenthal.

"Thanks for the compliment, but I can't believe you wanted to meet with me just to express your admiration of my legal acumen."

Lowenthal chuckled and said, "You're right. I think it's time to save us some time and money. I want to see if we might be able to negotiate a plea bargain."

"What do you have in mind?" asked Bergen, who had shifted into a predator mode.

"O'Reilly pleads to accessory to murder, and you recommend five years."

Before Bergen could respond, Dan exploded, "No way in hell am I going to let your scumbag client off that easy, after killing five people in cold blood!"

"Well put," Bergen said to Dan. Then to Lowenthal, he said, "I drop the death penalty. I go with second degree murder, and life imprisonment without possibility of parole."

"Murder in the second degree, and twenty years," said Lowenthal.

"No!" LeBeau shouted. "If that's your best offer, I say Bergen finishes it off in the courtroom, and we all watch as the jury returns a guilty verdict after less than an hour of deliberation."

"I think LeBeau has a point, Walt," said Bergen. "You haven't put enough on the table. What else can you offer?"

"What do you want?" asked Lowenthal.

"O'Reilly admits that he was paid by Bernie Schwartz to kill Mary Lee Wen and Christy Marino," Bergen said. "And he agrees to testify against Schwartz. In addition, O'Reilly isn't sentenced on his second-degree murder plea until after he testifies. If he reneges on the agreement and doesn't testify, or he doesn't testify as he agrees, then we go back to second degree murder with the death penalty."

"I'm not sure Schwartz paid O'Reilly to kill those women," said Lowenthal. "How can I agree to something like that, when it depends on factors of which I'm not certain?"

"Cut the crap, Lowenthal!" said Dan. "You know that's the way it happened. That's the only bargaining chip O'Reilly has to offer."

Lowenthal thought about the offer. Finally, he looked at Bergen. "It's not a deal that I can easily sell my client."

"Would you rather take your chances with the jury?" asked Bergen.

"No," said Lowenthal.

"Then I think you'd better be a terrific salesman," said Bergen.

"There's another point that needs to be included," said Lowenthal. "In return for his testimony, O'Reilly also receives immunity from prosecution in the murders of Christy Marino and the three CBS guys."

"No way!" said Dan, remembering his silent promise to Christy. "Pat, this guy has killed five people! He's got to pay!"

"I've got to make sure that once O'Reilly has testified, Schwartz doesn't turn around and testify that O'Reilly killed the others," said Lowenthal.

"Walt is right, Dan," said Bergen. "It's a reasonable request."

"Dan, we talked about this," said LeBeau. "We want to see Bernie Schwartz pay for what he did to those two women. Without O'Reilly's testimony, we'd have a tough time proving our case. Let it go, Dan. O'Reilly wouldn't get any more prison time for killing five people, than he'd get for killing one. This deal locks O'Reilly into a life sentence, and gives us what we need to convict Bernie Schwartz."

"Done, Walt," said Bergen, as he quickly moved to make sure that the deal didn't become unraveled.

"I've got a question for you before you go," Dan said to Lowenthal. "What prompted you to come looking for a deal."

"Well, the trial wasn't going well for my client. After listening to witness after witness, it dawned on O'Reilly that if he didn't do something pretty soon, he'd end up taking all of the blame for something that Bernie Schwartz had a big hand in bringing about. He didn't want to take the whole fall for it." Lowenthal stood and left.

"It's a good deal, Dan," said Bergen.

"Can you convict Schwartz for murdering Christy Marino and Mary Lee Wen?" asked Dan.

"Yeah, I'll get a conviction," said Bergen. "Don't forget we've already charged Schwartz with conspiracy to murder Westerfield and Weinstein. This two-count murder conviction will probably tack on at least one life sentence to the twenty-eight years he's already looking at."

"That sounds a lot better," said Dan.

"Well done, guys," Bergen said with a nod of his head. "You made me look good."

Fifty-Six

10:00 AM
March 24th
Manhattan, New York

"The New York Supreme Court in and for the County of New York is now in session, the Honorable Hector Benvinides, presiding!"

The short Hispanic judge walked to the bench, sat down and said, "Please be seated. Bailiff, call the case."

"The State of New York versus Bernard Schwartz."

"Mr. Bergen," said Benvinides, "you may proceed with your opening argument."

"Members of the jury, you will hear how Bernard Schwartz schemed, planned, and paid for the murders of Mary Lee Wen and Christina Marino. The prosecution will show the defendant was motivated by only one factor. Greed! It wasn't enough to just make a living. No, he wanted it all, right now. He concocted a scheme to defraud a bank out of thirteen million dollars, crimes for which he has been sentenced to twenty-eight years in prison. While Mr. Schwartz was fraudulently acquiring this money, he became concerned the FBI might find him out. So he hatched a plot to have Mary Lee Wen and Christina Marino killed, for no reason other than these two women might have exposed his crimes."

Bergen paused and took a sip of water, then returned his gaze to the jury.

"Had Mrs. Wen betrayed him? No, she hadn't. She kept his secret all the way to the grave in which she lies, wherever it may be. Mr. Schwartz hoped that this heinous crime would be sufficient warning to Christina Marino not to betray him by cooperating with the FBI. But rather than being cowed by the murder of her friend and coworker, Miss Marino was incensed, and wanted to see Bernard Schwartz pay for what he did. She agreed to cooperate in the FBI's investigation into the Fontaine Diamond fraud. She met with them once, and at that time gave them copies of Fontaine records to assist in their investigation. But for some reason, Bernie Schwartz became suspicious these women were betraying his secret to the FBI. So he hatched a plot. But, as John Steinbeck said, quoting Robert Burns, 'best laid plans oft go astray.' But things did not go as planned. In order to conceal his murder of Christina Marino, the hit man killed three CBS employees who were eyewitnesses to his crime. And so, Bernard Schwartz became responsible for the murders of five people. Five innocent people, two of whom were his employees. And why did he want these two women killed? He had them killed because he feared they betrayed him to the FBI. A deadly betrayal."

Bergen paused, and looked at the faces of the jurors whose attention was riveted on his every word.

"During the course of this trial, the prosecution will let you see and hear from several witnesses. In chilling detail, two of them will tell you of his plot to carry out these murders. You will hear how he located and hired a hit man. You will see and hear Bernard Schwartz's own wife tell you how, at his direction, she took thousands of dollars in cash, and personally paid the hit man. And then ... and then, you will see and hear the hit man, himself, tell you about the murders. That's right. Although he's already been convicted of murder, he'll tell you how Bernard Schwartz hired him to kill two women. Two women whom Schwartz feared had betrayed him."

The courtroom was silent as Bergen took one last long look at the jurors, making eye contact with each of them. Then he turned, walked back to the prosecution table and sat down.

"Thank you Mr. Bergen," said Judge Benvinides. "Mr. Traub, your opening argument?"

"Thank you, your Honor," said Traub who stood, and looked over at the jury and saw interested, expectant faces. He took a breath and began.

"Ladies and gentlemen of the jury. If Mr. Bergen prevails, we will not see justice done, but, rather so the bruised ego of an Assistant District Attorney can be assuaged. Initially, the court rebuffed Mr. Bergen when he tried to bring murder charges against Bart O'Reilly, the hit man to whom he referred. The court dismissed the charges against Mr. O'Reilly, because in his zeal to make a name for himself, Mr. Bergen forgot that everything has to be done in accordance with the law. He tried to use an illegal arrest and two illegal searches to support his case. But his case was only a house of cards that came tumbling down. And now, in part, Mr.

Bergen hopes to somehow redeem his reputation by finding someone else to convict so he can see glowing words about himself written in this city's newspapers. Bernie Schwartz didn't commit murder. We already know that it was Bart O'Reilly who did that. And we know that Sarah Schwartz paid him to do it, since she testified to that fact in court. A hit man gets paid to murder people. A woman pays him to do it. So you've got to ask yourself why isn't she charged with this crime? We have her word, and only her word that Bernie Schwartz told her to pay Bart O'Reilly. And what about her word? It's the word of a woman who has been convicted of fraud. Would you trust her to tell the truth? Oh, the prosecution will dress it up, nice and pretty, so it will look plausible for you. But, it is nothing more than a vain attempt to shift the blame from Sarah Schwartz to Bernie Schwartz. And the reason? A prosecutor's bruised ego. Nothing more. Bernie Schwartz should not even be sitting in this courtroom, charged with this crime."

Traub sat down, and murmurs were heard throughout the courtroom.

"Order!" Benvinides said as he rapped his gavel repeatedly. "We'll take a fifteen minute recess before the prosecution calls the first witness."

A short time later, Benvinides rapped his gavel, and said, "Mr. Bergen, please call your first witness."

"The prosecution calls Isaac Jonas,"

"Issac Jonas, were you retained by Fontaine as a corporate attorney?" asked Bergen.

"Objection to this witness," said Traub. "As Fontaine's corporate attorney, anything that he knew, or conversations to which he was a party, would be privileged and inadmissible."

"Your Honor," said Bergen. "The testimony which I intend to elicit from this witness is beyond the scope of privilege, even when taken to the extreme."

"Objection overruled," said Benvinides. "But if it appears to me that you're heading into forbidden waters, I won't hesitate to stop you."

"Thank you, your Honor," said Bergen. "Mr. Jonas, in December of last year, were you asked by the defendant, Bernard Schwartz, to do something for him that was beyond your legal responsibilities?"

"Yes I was," said the overweight, balding man.

"What exactly did he ask you to do?"

"To locate somebody to murder one of Fontaine's employees."

"Do you recall exactly what Mr. Schwartz said to you?"

"I think it was, 'Izzie, find me a hit man to rub out the Chink.'"

"And what was your understanding of the meaning of his words, 'rub out the Chink?'" asked Bergen.

"To have the Chinese woman killed."

"And you knew to whom he was referring, when he said 'the Chink?'"

"Sure," said Jonas. "There was only one Chinese person working at Fontaine. That was Mary Lee Wen."

"And how did you go about finding a hit man?"

"I do some legal work for Vince Tartaglia who's got a catering business over on the west side of Manhattan."

"Was it to him you went, looking for a hit man?"

"No, it was a guy who works for him, Diego Chavez."

"Why would Diego Chavez know a hit man with whom you could arrange a murder or two?" asked Bergen.

"Because he knows a bunch of Irish guys that hang out in the neighborhood," said Jonas. "They're part of the West End Irish Gang, or 'Westies'."

"And what name did Diego Chavez give you?"

"Bart O'Reilly. One day I was in my office, and Chavez calls, says the guy's interested, and to come meet him."

"Did you hire him?" asked Bergen.

"No. Bernie did in a later meeting."

"How do you know that meeting actually took place?"

"Because Bernie told me he hired him to kill Mary Lee Wen."

"Did you have any further contact with Mr. O'Reilly?"

"Yeah, when Bernie decided to have Christy Marino killed, he asked me to tell O'Reilly to kill her too."

"Did you?" asked Bergen.

"Yeah."

"As an attorney, licensed to practice law in the State of New York, are you aware that what you did is accessory before the fact to second degree murder, a felony? And because of that criminal act, your license to practice law can be revoked?"

"Yeah."

Bergen began to walk to the prosecution table, but then stopped, turned, and walked back to Jonas. "How did Mr. Schwartz learn his employees were talking to the FBI?"

Jonas looked down, picked at his cuticles and mumbled something.

"I'm sorry Mr. Jonas. I couldn't hear your response. Could you repeat it, perhaps a little louder?"

"Because I told him they were," Jonas said in struggled words.

Bergen's expression showed shock. "And how did you learn this information?"

Jonas continued to look into his lap as he said, "There's another attorney who works in the same building I do. He's the uncle of a federal prosecutor who told him that two women had signed cooperation agreements with the FBI."

"And who is this person related to?"

"Leonard Weinstein."

Audible gasps were heard and conversation began throughout the courtroom.

"Order," Judge Benvinides said as he repeatedly rapped his gavel.

The conversation and noise died down.

"You conveyed this information to Bernie Schwartz who in return told you to find someone to kill them?"

"Yes."

"Are you now aware that Mary Lee Wen never signed any such agreement?"

"I know," Jonas said as he began to sob.

"No further questions at this time, but I reserve the right to recall this witness," said Bergen, who walked to the prosecution table and sat down.

"Your witness, Mr. Traub," said Benvinides.

"Mr. Jonas, you have made some incredible statements about murder for hire. You have even pointed the finger at one of your clients who, you say, involved you in this nefarious scheme. And admittedly, you knew that what you were doing could very well end your ability to practice law, and thus generate any income. It brings me to the point where I have to ask you, why did you do it?"

"Well, I ... ah ... you see, Bernie and I have been friends since we were kids. And as long as he's been in business, I've done legal work for him. So when he asked me to help him out on this, well, ... you know ... I went along."

"Did you go along because you wanted to get involved in a modern day version of Murder Incorporated? Or, was it because you didn't think you'd be caught? Or was it just the old excuse that, the money was just too hard to pass up?"

"Objection, your Honor!" said Bergen. "Counsel is badgering the witness, and not permitting one question to be answered, before he asks another. Counsel, in effect, is making statements, rather than conducting a cross-examination of the witness."

"Sustained," said Judge Benvinides. "Counsel will allow the witness to answer each question that you ask."

"Mr. Jonas, why did you do it?" asked Traub.

"I needed the money," Jonas said, his shame obvious.

"You needed the money," said Traub, mockingly. "How much money did your law firm generate in billing fees last year?"

"Oh, I don't know exactly."

"It doesn't have to be exact, Mr. Jonas. Just a round figure."

"About a hundred thousand," said Jonas.

"I see. And, of that hundred thousand, how much was generated in fees from Fontaine Diamonds?"

"Around seventy thousand."

"So you couldn't really afford to antagonize Bernie Schwartz, could you? You'd do whatever he wanted you to do, wouldn't you?"

"Objection, your Honor!" said Bergen. "He's doing it again."

"Mr. Traub," said the judge.

"Sorry, your Honor," said Traub, who then turned back to Jonas and asked, "Mr. Jonas, what was the arrangement you made with the District Attorney's office, which resulted in your testifying on behalf of the prosecution?"

"That they would not prosecute me for accessory to murder if I testified."

"Is that all?"

"No. I also agreed to voluntarily surrender my license to practice law."

"So, since Bernie Schwartz is no longer in a position to retain your legal services and provide you with seventy percent of your income, and you didn't want to go to prison, you agreed to sell him down the river. Is that correct?"

"Objection, your Honor!" shouted Bergen.

"I withdraw the question," said Traub. "I have no further questions for this witness."

Fifty-Seven

2:30 PM
March 24th
Manhattan, New York

The prosecution calls Randy Reynolds," Bergen said.

"Mr. Reynolds," Bergen said. "Do you own and operate a private investigative business whose services were retained by Bernard Schwartz of Fontaine Diamonds?"

"Yes, he wanted me to check out Christina Marino, one of his employees that he thought was stealing from him."

"And what did you do to try and find out if she was stealing?"

"I did an arrest check, pulled her credit bureau information, talked to some of the outfits she had credit cards from. You know, that kind of stuff."

"From that investigation, were you able to reach a conclusion about whether or not she was stealing from Fontaine Diamonds?"

"No, I wasn't," said Reynolds.

"When you discussed your findings with Bernard Schwartz, was he satisfied that everything had been answered, and did he tell you to conclude your investigation?"

"No way! I mean the guy was really pissed off when I told him. He told me that he didn't believe that I'd really done what I'd said, and if I didn't come up with something he wasn't going to pay me."

"So what did you do?"

"Told him I didn't know what else to do, so he told me she had stolen some records from his business and he wanted them back."

"And did Mr. Schwartz tell you what he wanted you to do?" asked Bergen.

"Yeah, he said he wanted me to break into her apartment and steal them back," said Reynolds.

"Did you agree to do that?"

"I told him I wouldn't do it. I don't need that kind of trouble."

"Did Mr. Schwartz ever pay you for your time and expenses?"

"No, he didn't. He stiffed me for two thousand bucks."

"Thank you, Mr. Reynolds," said Bergen. "No further questions."

"Your witness, Mr. Traub," Benvinides said.

"Mr. Reynolds," Traub said. "You have been a private investigator for eight years, and during those eight years, have you ever been the subject of a criminal or civil suit?"

"Yeah. It comes with the territory."

"Two years ago, as a result of your investigation, were you not sued for providing false information which resulted in a person being fired from their job?"

"Yeah, that's right."

"And last year, suit was brought against you for misrepresenting yourself as an insurance investigator?"

"Hey, in this business, you've got to get creative. That time, it didn't work out."

"And six months ago, based on numerous complaints, weren't you advised that you were under investigation by the New York State Licensing Bureau, and told there was a possibility that your private investigator's license might be suspended?"

"Yeah."

"No further questions of this witness," said Traub.

"The prosecution calls Sarah Schwartz," said Bergen, and buzz began in the courtroom.

"Mrs. Schwartz, thank you for agreeing to testify," said Bergen. "Before we begin, I would like you to take a look at this document." He handed it to her. "And do you still want to testify against your husband, even though you don't have to?"

"Yeah, I do."

As she answered the question, Bergen saw Sarah Schwartz's eyes widen in fear, and following the direction of her stare, turned quickly enough to see Bernie Schwartz make a throat-slashing gesture with the index finger of his right hand.

"Your Honor!" Bergen said, twirling towards the judge. "The prosecution respectfully requests that the court immediately direct the defendant to cease making gestures at the witness in an attempt to intimidate her!"

"Mr. Schwartz," Benvinides said angrily. "You will refrain from making any such gestures. If it happens again, I will cite you for contempt. If it happens again after that, I will have you restrained, or removed from these proceedings. Do you understand what I expect from you?"

Schwartz lifted himself a couple of inches off his chair, and without making eye contact with the judge, said, "Yeah."

Bergen composed himself, then turned back to the witness, and asked, "Mrs. Schwartz, at the present time, are you serving a three year sentence in a federal penitentiary as a result of a financial fraud case in which you and your husband were involved?"

"That's right."

"When you and your husband owned Fontaine Diamonds, were Mary Lee Wen and Christina Marino employed there?"

"Yeah."

"Are those two women dead, Mrs. Schwartz?" asked Bergen.

Sarah Schwartz began to sob, and quietly answered. "Yeah, they're both dead 'cause Bart O'Reilly killed them," Sarah Schwartz said with a catch in her voice.

"Who decided that O'Reilly should kill both of these women? Was it Bernie Schwartz?"

"Yeah, because he was afraid they'd talk about the thirteen million dollar fraud going on at Fontaine."

"How do you know, first hand, that Bart O'Reilly was hired and paid five thousand dollars?"

"Because, I paid him when I was in Jonas' law office."

"How did you know for sure that Mr. O'Reilly was going to murder someone in return for the cash you had given him?"

"Because right after I gave it to him, he said to me, 'Don't worry about a thing. She's as good as dead.' Then I saw it on the news."

"No further questions of this witness, your Honor," said Bergen.

"Your witness, Mr. Traub," said the judge.

Traub stood, and slowly walked over to the witness stand.

"Mrs. Schwartz," Traub began. "You could very well be on trial here today, couldn't you, because you paid a hit man to have someone killed, didn't you?"

"Well, no, it was Bernie who hired O'Reilly to kill her. I only paid him, like Bernie told me to. I didn't want those women killed. I was just doing what Bernie told me to do."

"And now that you've had a change of heart, you want everybody to believe it wasn't you, but rather it was your husband who was responsible for hiring a hit man. Is there a reason why you aren't a defendant in court today? In other words, were you given immunity from prosecution for murder in return for testifying against your husband?"

Sarah Schwartz looked down at her hands as they lay in her lap, and said, "Yeah."

"I have no further questions for this witness," said Traub.

"The witness is excused," said Judge Benvinides.

As she stepped down from the witness stand, Sarah Schwartz threw the finger at her husband, and her face contorted in rage, she screamed, "Cheaper to kill me, huh!"

Fifty-Eight

3:40 PM
March 24th
Manhattan, New York

Those in the courtroom strained to see O'Reilly. For many of them, it was their first opportunity to see this swarthy, tattooed, real live hit man.

"Mr. O'Reilly," Bergen began. "In December of last year, when you were contacted by Diego Chavez, did he ask you if you were interested in getting paid for murdering someone?"

"Yeah, I was really hurting for money at the time, so I told him if it paid enough, I'd do it."

"What did you talk about when you met with Bernard Schwartz?"

"He wanted me to whack some broad who worked for him."

"By 'whack', do you mean murder?"

"Yeah."

"Did he say why?"

"Nah," said O'Reilly. "I didn't ask. He didn't say."

"Did you agree to kill the woman?"

"Yeah. Like I said, I needed the money. I mean my daughter got knocked up and moved in with me and my woman."

"Was the first woman you killed Mary Lee Wen?"

"Yeah, I followed her when she went over to her friend's apartment in Queens. When she came out of the building, I followed her and popped her as she started to get into her car."

"By 'popped her', do you mean kill?"

"Yeah."

"What did you do after that?"

"First I put her body in the van, then got rid of it. I dumped her car over on the west side of Manhattan."

"Did someone ask you to kill Christina Marino, another employee of Fontaine?"

"Yeah. Jonas called me and says there's another job, just like the first one. Schwartz wanted Marino killed."

"How did you go about killing this woman?" asked Bergen.

"She was tough. I camped outside her place in Queens in the morning. That didn't work, so I followed her after work and found out where she parked her car in Manhattan. Got a permit to park there. She came for her car, and I popped her."

"Now, let me make sure of your testimony," said Bergen. "You were paid by the defendant, Bernard Schwartz, to kill Mary Lee Wen and Christina Marino?"

"He paid me for one of them. His wife paid me for the other. I can't remember which."

"That's all the questions I have for this witness," said Bergen.

"Mr. Traub. Your witness," said Benvinides.

"Mr. O'Reilly," Traub said. "You readily admit to having killed two people, yet the judge threw out the murder charges against you for the murder of Christina Marino, as well as CBS employees, David Waylon, Yuri Dombrowski, and Tom Gould. Is that true?"

"Yeah. Guess I got lucky."

"But you have pled guilty to the murder of Mary Lee Wen, and now in your sworn testimony, you admit to murdering Christina Marino, as well. Is that correct?"

"I guess," said O'Reilly.

"I believe that is what you said. If you are unsure of your testimony, we can have the court reporter read back what you said. All I'm asking is that you answer the question of whether or not you admitted to having murdered Christina Marino. Which is it?"

"Yeah, I killed her."

"So now, you want everyone in the jury to believe that you, an admitted murderer, only did it because the defendant paid you to do it?"

"Yeah."

"Oh, come on now, Mr. O'Reilly," said Traub. "You know very well the defendant had nothing to do with these murders. You were recruited by Diego Chavez, hired by Isaac Jonas, and paid by Sarah Schwartz. The only reason you're telling us these lies is because that's what Mr. Bergen wanted you to say!"

"Objection, your Honor!" said Bergen. "Defense counsel is supposed to be asking questions of the witness, not making speeches."

"Sustained," said Benvinides. "Mr. Traub, you will save your speeches for your closing argument."

"Mr. O'Reilly," said Traub. "Isn't it a fact that you are trying to pin the actions of yourself, Isaac Jonas, and Sarah Schwartz, on the defendant?"

"No! Bernie Schwartz hired me to kill those two women."

As he looked at O'Reilly, Traub shook his head, then turned to the jury and did the same thing. Finally he looked up at the judge and said, "No further questions of this witness."

Bergen stood, and said, "The prosecution rests, your Honor."

The judge made a note, turned to Traub and said, "Mr. Traub, you may call your first witness."

"The defense calls Dr. Daniel Goldschmidt," Traub said.

The elderly man took the stand.

"Dr. Goldschmidt, as a doctor of ophthalmology, did you perform an eye test on Bart O'Reilly in September of last year?"

"Yes, I did, and based on my tests, Mr. O'Reilly is legally blind."

"So would he be able to shoot a gun or do anything which requires close visual concentration?"

"No, he would not."

"No more questions."

"Dr. Goldschmidt," said Bergen. "If someone is legally blind, would they be able to drive a motor vehicle?"

"Oh, I don't think so."

"Or pass the test to obtain a driver's license?"

"Definitely not."

"But Mr. O'Reilly not only passed his eye test for his driver's license, but also drives a motor vehicle. How is that possible, Dr. Goldschmidt?"

"I don't know."

"No further questions."

Traub stood and said, "The defense rests, your Honor."

The gasps of people were heard throughout the courtroom.

"Order!" Benvinides said as he pounded his gavel. "Order in the courtroom!"

When the noise finally subsided, Benvinides looked at Traub and said, "Is it my understanding that you do not intend to call any furthur witnesses on behalf of the defense?"

"That is correct your Honor."

"What the fuck do you mean that's your only defense witness!" shouted Bernie Schwartz. "I'm paying you these big bucks to get me off! You better come up with something!"

"You're out of order, Mr. Schwartz!" shouted Benvinides while rapping his gavel continuously.

"Yeah, well I want another fuckin' lawyer 'cause the asshole I've got isn't worth shit!"

"Mr. Schwartz, you will sit down and shut up!" screamed Benvinides. "If you don't, I'll have you removed from this courtroom!"

"Oh, yeah?" shouted Schwartz. "Well you can go fuck yourself, too. This is nothing but a kangaroo court, and you're the biggest kangaroo here!"

"Bailiffs, remove the defendant from this courtroom!" said Benvinides as he stood pounding his gavel. "Mr. Schwartz, this court finds you in contempt!"

"What are you gonna fuckin' do, send me to jail?" yelled Schwartz as he was handcuffed and dragged from the courtroom.

Once Schwartz had been removed, and the commotion in the courtroom had died down, Benvinides looked at Traub, and said, "Mr. Traub, before we continue, are you sure you do not wish to call any defense witnesses?"

Traub ran his hand through his hair, and without looking up at the judge, said, "No, I'm finished."

Both Bergen and Traub made their closing arguments, Bergen's was impassioned, while Traub's was understandably flat. Both were brief, concluding in just under an hour. The judge instructed the jury, and gave them the case. After two hours of deliberation, they sent word to the judge they had reached a verdict. The jurors were led back into the courtroom, and took their seats. Bernie Schwartz was brought back into the courtroom, and Benvinides watched him like a hawk.

"Ladies and gentlemen of the jury, have you reached a verdict?" asked Judge Benvinides.

The jury foreman stood, faced the judge, and said, "Yes we have, your Honor."

The clerk of the court retrieved the sheet of paper from the jury foreman and carried it to the judge, who read it and handed it back to her.

"Would you please read the verdict?" asked the judge.

"We, the jury," began the clerk, "find the defendant, Bernard Schwartz, guilty on both counts of conspiracy to commit murder."

Schwartz leaped to his feet, and before Traub could stop him, shouted at the jury.

"You lousy fuckers! You're dead meat! All of you! Dead meat, I say!"

"Order in the court!" shouted the judge as he rapped his gavel. "Order! Order! Will the bailiffs please again restrain the defendant?"

"Sit down and shut up!" Traub screamed at Schwartz.

Four good-sized court officers ran toward Bernie Schwartz in response to the judge's instructions. Before they got to him, he let fly again.

"And the same goes for you too, you dirty fucker!" he shouted at Bergen. "You're fucking dead! All of you! You hear me?"

The bailiffs reached Schwartz and slammed him down into his chair and held him there. He sat, his eyes wild with rage, his face red, and his body soaked with perspiration.

"Mr. Schwartz, you are in contempt! If you say or do anything further, I will ask the District Attorney to consider it as evidence of further criminal acts. Do I make myself clear?" Judge Benvinides stared at Schwartz. "In view of your outrageous behavior, I have decided to pass sentence now, rather than later."

Traub leaned over and in Schwartz's ear whispered, "Bernie, you're fucked."

"What the hell difference does it make at this point?"

"Mr. Schwartz, will you please rise?" asked the judge, as the courtroom quieted.

Schwartz and Traub both stood, and faced the judge, Bernie still seething with rage.

"Mr. Schwartz, it is not often that persons are brought before me who display the blatant disregard for human life that I have seen from you," Judge Benvinides said. "And furthermore, even after you were convicted of felonious crimes, you thought nothing of engaging in further criminal activity to attempt to take more lives, in an egregious spectacle of misdirected culpability for your actions."

His rage was barely controlled as Schwartz turned red and his lip curled.

"Your actions have blatantly demonstrated that you are incapable of remorse, and are a despicable threat to our society. I therefore sentence you to a term of imprisonment of twenty-five years to life in the death of Mary Lee Wen, and twenty-five years to life in the death of Christina Marino, to be served consecutively."

Realizing he had been sentenced to another fifty years, Schwartz felt his knees give for a second, but his anger kept him upright.

"And you will serve these sentences at a prison selected by the New York State Department of Corrections, only after such time as you have completed your federal prison sentence. You are hereby remanded to the custody of the federal government to commence your prison sentences. Court adjourned." Judge Benvinides rapped his gavel.

Noise burst out in the courtroom as reporters scrambled out to file their last story in the tragic saga. Schwartz stood as handcuffs were placed on his wrists, and leg irons on his ankles. He looked at Dan and LeBeau, and Casey, and just before he was led out, made the throat slashing gesture.

Fifty-Nine

7:15 PM
March 24th
Manhattan, New York

The gentle breeze blew off the Hudson River and chilled the night air, as the lights of Manhattan and the Jersey shore twinkled against the black sky. Only an occasional distant wailing siren or the sound of a honking horn disturbed the peaceful moment.

Dan puffed on his cigar, and enjoyed the view. He leaned against the fender of the FBI sedan parked on the mostly-deserted west side rooftop parking lot.

His private moment was interrupted by a taxicab as it pulled onto the lot, illuminating him in its headlights. The cab came to a stop, and someone stepped out and walked toward him. The person was backlighted by the headlights, and Dan shielded his eyes with his hand in an effort to see who it was. Remembering Schwartz's courtroom threats to kill everyone who had anything to do with his conviction, Dan tensed, his hand instinctively reaching for his pistol. The mystery was solved when he saw the fedora, silhouetted by the headlights.

"Thought I might find you here," LeBeau said, as the taxi turned around and drove down the ramp.

"How'd you know?"

"This is where it happened. I figured you might come and try to let go of it."

"Yeah. Want a cigar?"

"Sure. I don't usually, but tonight's different."

Dan pulled out his cigar case, and gave one to LeBeau. He struck a match, and lit LeBeau's cigar.

"Not bad," said LeBeau, who closely examined the cigar band. "Wait a minute. This is a Havana cigar. Where the hell did you get this?"

"I've got a friend who's a Customs Agent. They confiscate them all the time. Because of the Cuban embargo, the law says they have to be destroyed. I'm sure he appreciates our helping him with the destruction." Dan smiled.

For a few minutes the two of them stood, saying nothing. LeBeau broke the silence and said, "It's over, but it's hard to let go."

"Yeah, but it helped when O'Reilly and Schwartz got convicted. It also helped to learn that the leak that got all of those people killed didn't come out of the FBI."

The two men stood in silence, looking at the lights, both drawing on their cigars.

"Why do you do it, Richie?"

"Do what?"

"Work Homicide. You have enough seniority to work anything you want. Why Homicide?"

"It's a long story."

"I've got a few years."

"It won't take that long."

"I'm glad to hear that," said Dan. "So tell me."

"When I first joined the department, I walked a beat in Brooklyn. On my beat, there was a deli owned by a really nice man named Isaiah Gross. One evening as he was closing up, some punk came in and robbed him. Isaiah wasn't stupid. He knew how to survive on the street. He gave the kid all the money, but then the little shit put a bullet in his head. The detectives came, did their thing, you know, made all the right noises of doing an investigation. But that was it. They never came back. Never solved it. Mary Gross had to sell the business. She had no skills, and couldn't find anybody who'd give her a job. She went broke, and rather than going on welfare, she put a gun to her head. All of that, because one little punk had to show how tough he was. I swore if I ever became a Detective, I'd do a better job."

"They ever find the guy?"

"I'm not sure. The kid that I thought did it, tried to hold up another deli the next month. That time I was on the sidewalk, and saw him go in. I followed him through the door, and when he turned around to see who was behind him, I saw the gun in his hand. I blew him away. He was sixteen years old. I'll never know for sure if he was the one who killed Isaiah, but we never had anymore deli holdups in my precinct. I sent a message."

"I hope that's what we were able to do on this case ... send a message."

"You never know. But you have to believe that you do make a difference. You're ready to retire the day that you no longer believe that."

"Are you ready to retire, Richie?"

"Not for a long time. How about you?"

"No, not yet," Dan said as he took a long draw on his cigar. "Richie, I don't know if I'll get another chance. I want to tell you how fortunate I was to work with a detective as good as you."

"I knew that," LeBeau said before breaking into a smile. "And in spite of what all the other detectives say about you, I still think you're okay," said LeBeau.

"That's probably the nearest thing to a compliment I'll ever hear from you."

"Probably."

The two men quietly smoked their cigars in silence as they stared at the lights.

"Tell me, Dan. Why are you still carrying a badge and a gun. You're a smart guy. You could get a much better paying job in the private sector. Why stay in the FBI?"

"When I first joined, it was because of some gung-ho idea. It didn't take too long before I realized how little difference I could actually make."

"What made you stay then?"

"The faces of the victims of crimes. The father whose son was kidnapped; the businessman that got defrauded by some slick, fast-talking con man; the old widow who lost her life savings to a telephone boiler room scam. Who was going to make it right for them? If I didn't do something, the bad guys would win. I know what they feel. It happened to me. You know, my wife was murdered and the killer never found. It became personal."

"I heard about your wife. And so maybe you've taken all of these deaths personally."

"You're right. But Christy didn't have to die. I should have seen it coming."

"She chose her path long before you met her. It was her life, and her death. You got the guy that killed her, and the guy who paid him to do it. Feel good about that. Sometimes that's all you ever get out of it. And you sent a message. A loud one. It's gonna make the next guy stop and think before he tries it."

"I know. Too many murders of people close to me. I'll get past it."

"Yeah, Dan, it's time to get on with your life."

"What do you mean?"

"I'd have to be blind not to see that Casey wants to help you. And don't go stupid on me. She's a great lady. You could do a hell of a lot worse. You wait too long, and she's not going to be there."

"I know. Maybe now that this is finally over, I can begin to put all that behind me. Tell me Richie, were you ever married?"

"Twice. The first one divorced me after she discovered that she no longer loved me. I lost the second one to cancer. I don't think I'm up to a third try."

"I'm sorry. So you know how it still hurts, don't you?"

"Oh, yeah."

The quiet conversation was interrupted by the noise of the FBI radio in Dan's car.

"Base to 9959. Do you read?" said the dispatcher.

Dan opened the car door, picked up the mike, and said, "This is 9959, go ahead Base."

"Is NYPD Detective 723 with you?"

Dan handed the mike to LeBeau. "It's for you."

"Base, this is NYPD Detective 723. Go ahead."

"Detective 723, your dispatcher asked me to relay a message to you. Be advised that there is one dead in an alley off Forty-ninth, between Tenth and Eleventh. Uniforms at the scene request you respond as soon as possible."

"Ten-four. Tell them I'm on my way."

"How are you going to get there, Richie?"

"Would you mind dropping me off? It's on your way."

"No it's not, but come on, get in," Dan said as the two of them got into the car. He started the engine, Dan looked over at LeBeau, and said, "You know you're developing this non-driving thing of yours into a real art form."

LeBeau smiled. "Hey, works for me!"

About the Author

Donald Scott Richards was born and raised in New Mexico. He received a Bachelor's of Business Administration from the University of New Mexico and an MBA from the University of San Francisco. During his 22 year career with the FBI, he investigated numerous high-profile cases including: Patty Hearst kidnapping, Jonestown People's Temple mass suicide, New World Liberation Front bombings, Lufthansa kidnapping, Genovese Organized Crime investigations, Marc Rich case, Ferdinand and Imelda Marcos and Saudi businessman Adan Khashoggi, and The CBS Murders. As a Vice President for Bankers Trust Co., he directed worldwide financial and securities investigations. Through his own firm, he investigated numerous multi-million dollar financial cases throughout the world including the Bank of Credit & Commerce International (BCCI). Currently he is the Director of Investigations for a Securities Class-Action law firm in New York City. Presently, he is working on a novel of the next investigation involving Dan Robertson and Richie LeBeau.

For more information go to www.cbsmurders.com

You may email the author at:
donaldscottrichards@hotmail.com

Printed in the United States
1182300001B/136-201